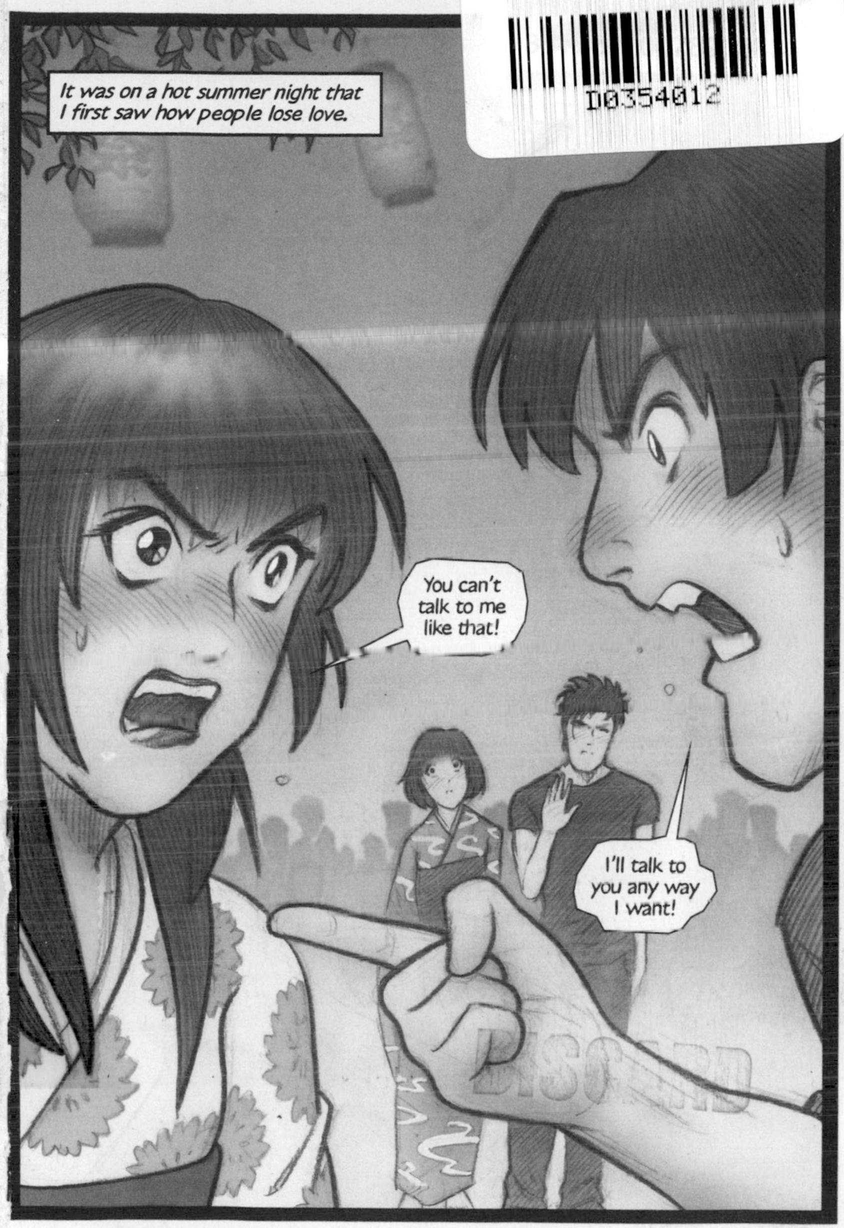
It was on a hot summer night that I first saw how people lose love.
You can't talk to me like that!
I'll talk to you any way I want!

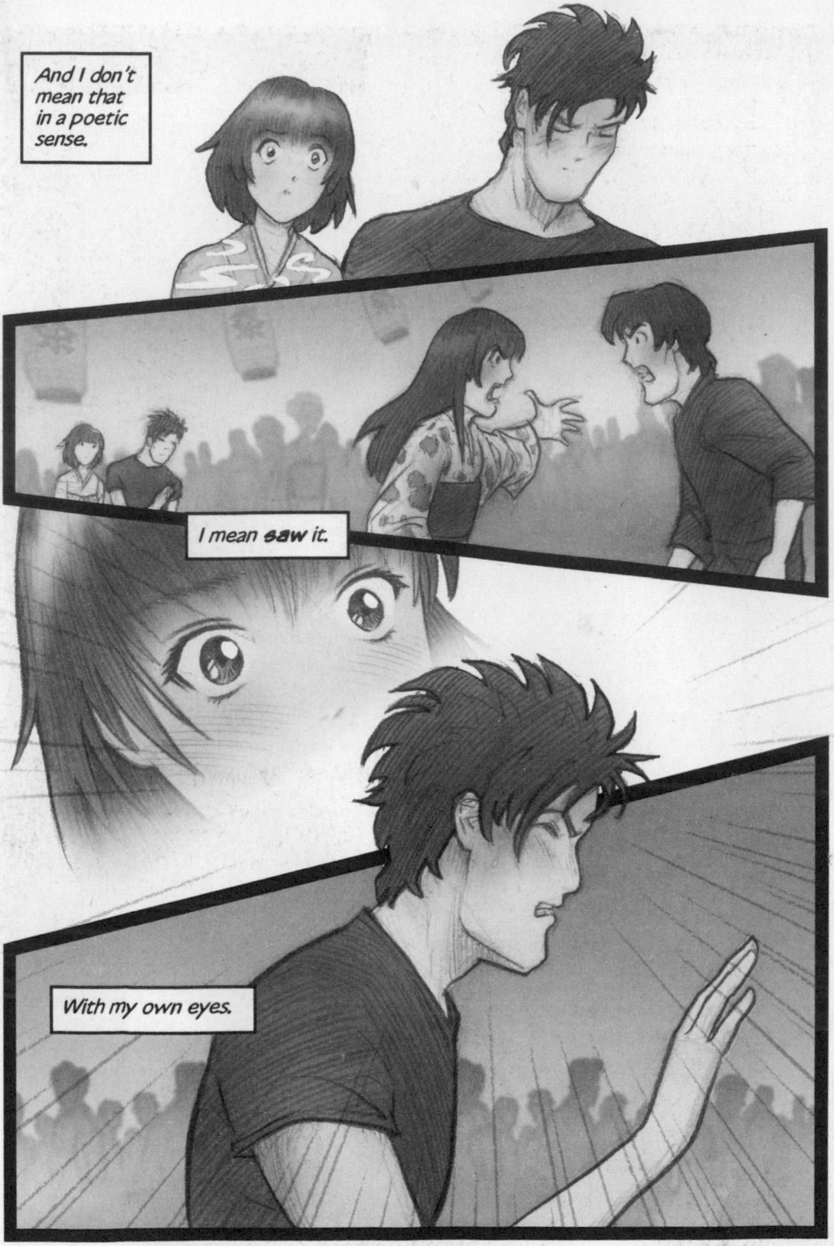
And I don't mean that in a poetic sense.
I mean **saw** it.
With my own eyes.

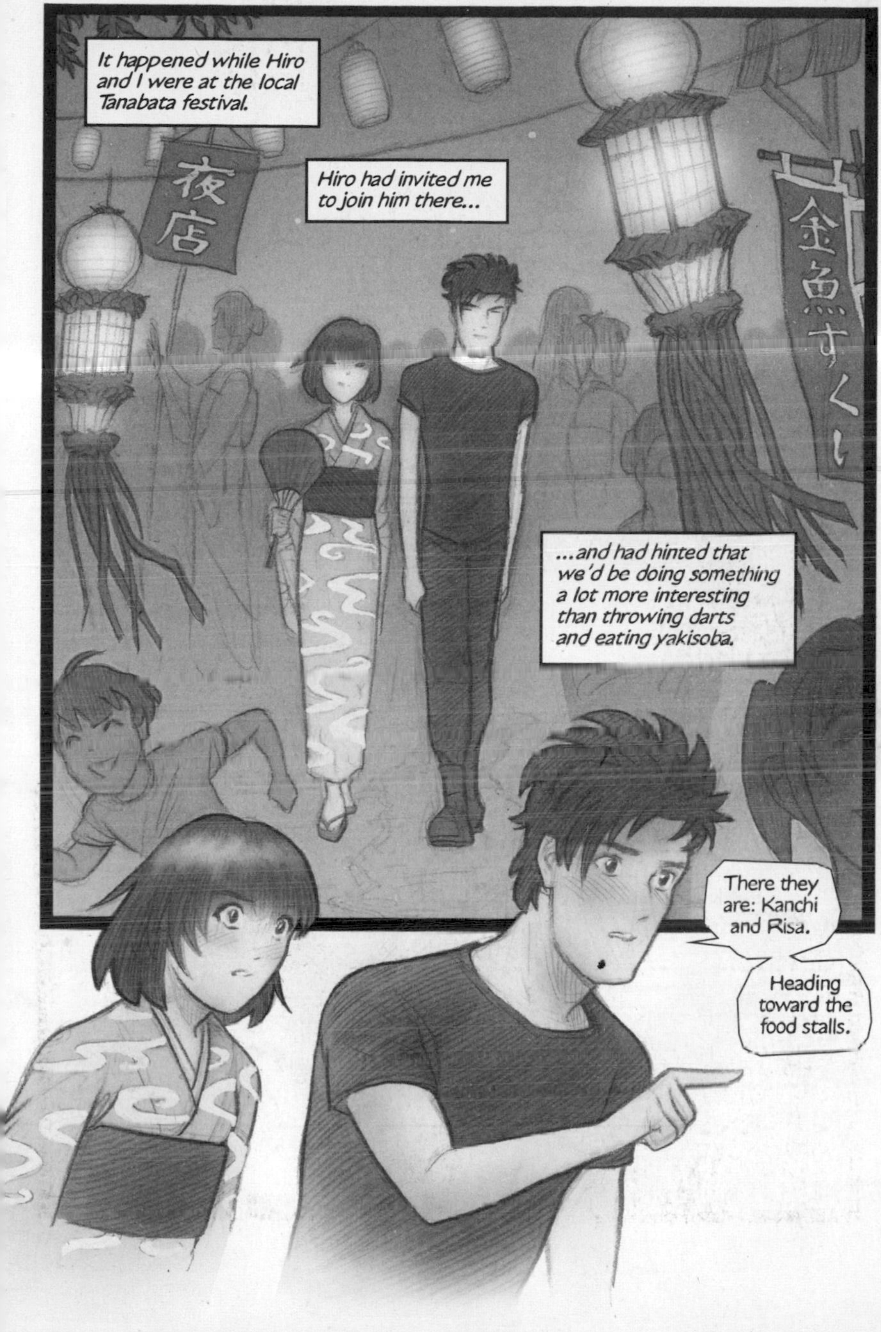
It happened while Hiro and I were at the local Tanabata festival.
夜店
Hiro had invited me to join him there...
金魚すくい
...and had hinted that we'd be doing something a lot more interesting than throwing darts and eating yakisoba.
There they are: Kanchi and Risa.
Heading toward the food stalls.

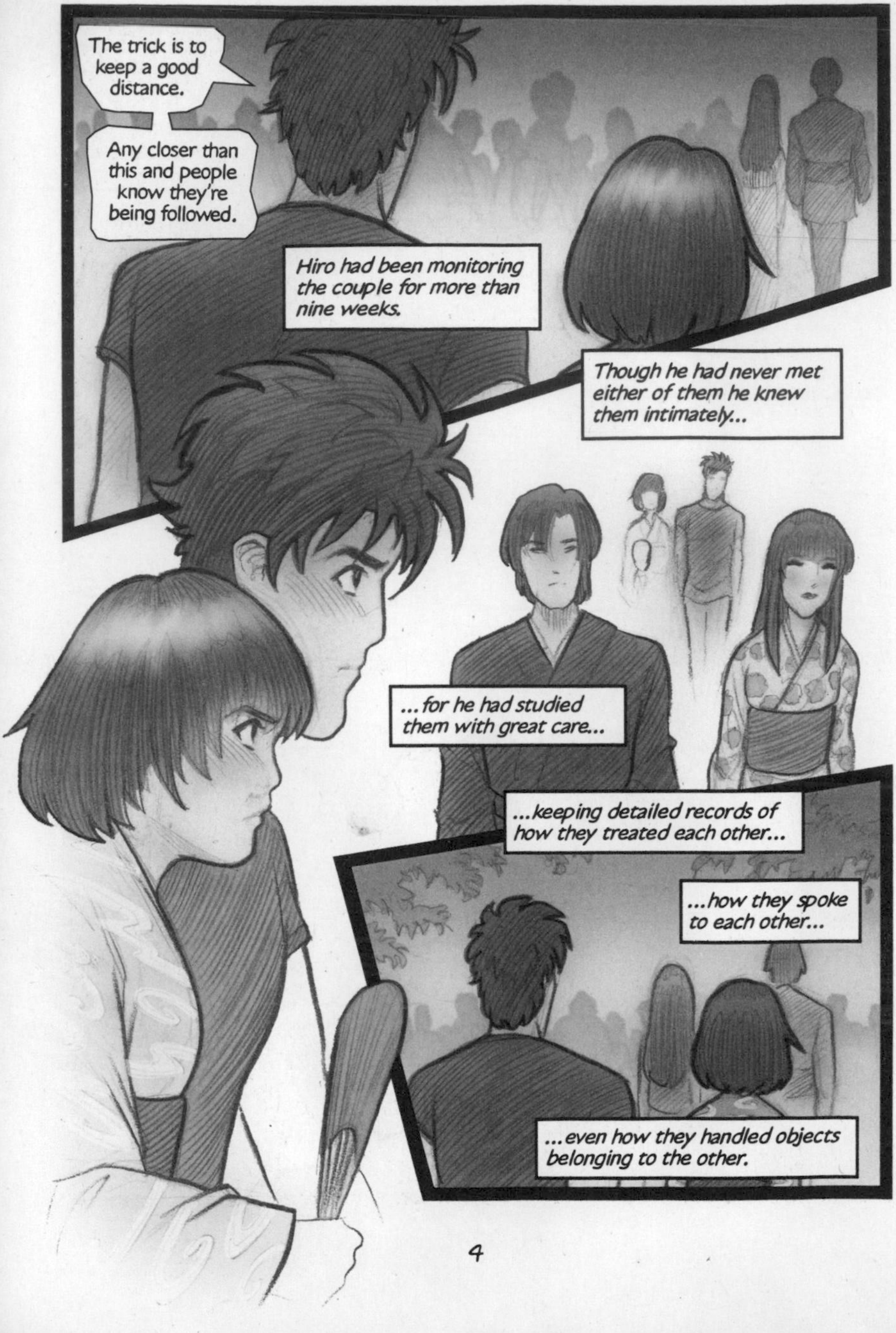
The trick is to keep a good distance.
Any closer than this and people know they're being followed.
Hiro had been monitoring the couple for more than nine weeks.
Though he had never met either of them he knew them intimately...
...for he had studied them with great care...
...keeping detailed records of how they treated each other...
...how they spoke to each other...
...even how they handled objects belonging to the other.

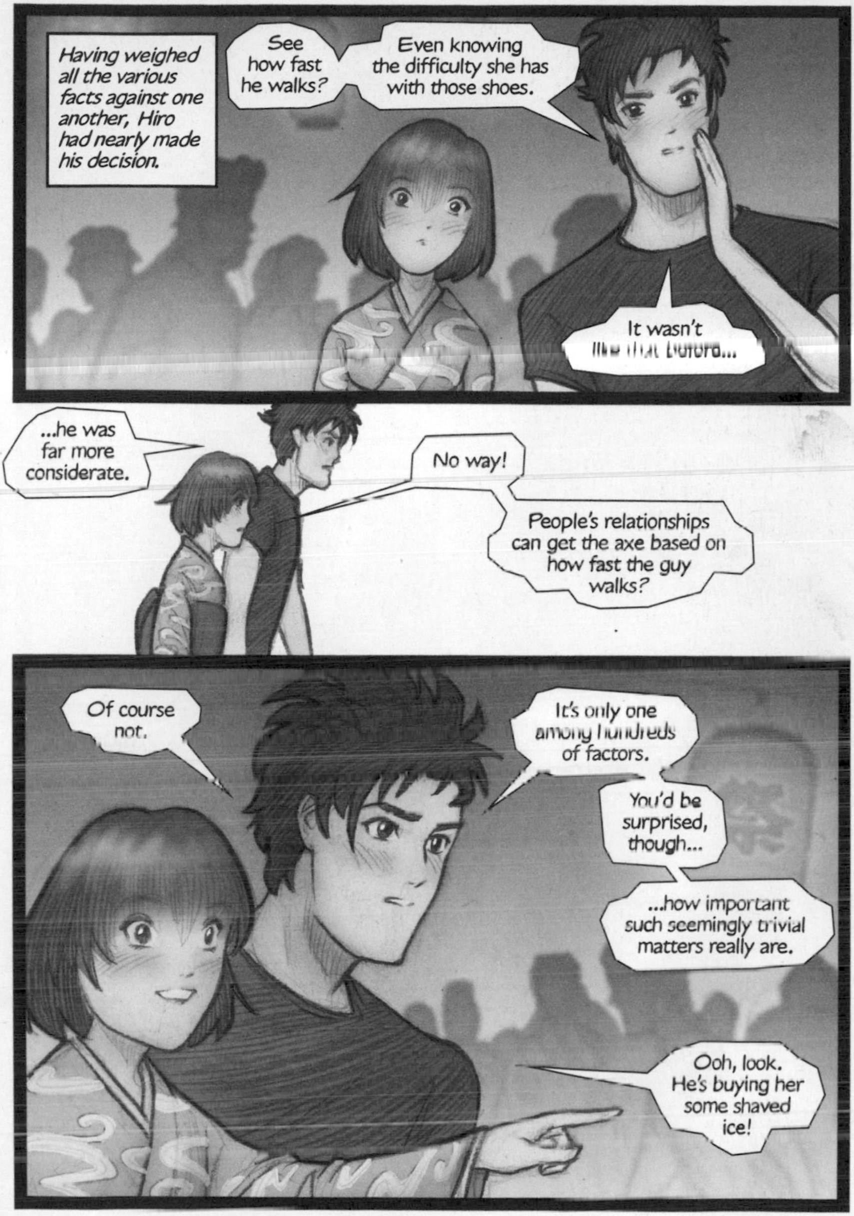
Having weighed all the various facts against one another, Hiro had nearly made his decision.
See how fast he walks?
Even knowing the difficulty she has with those shoes.
It wasn't like that before...
...he was far more considerate.
No way!
People's relationships can get the axe based on how fast the guy walks?
Of course not.
It's only one among hundreds of factors.
You'd be surprised, though...
...how important such seemingly trivial matters really are.
Ooh, look. He's buying her some shaved ice!

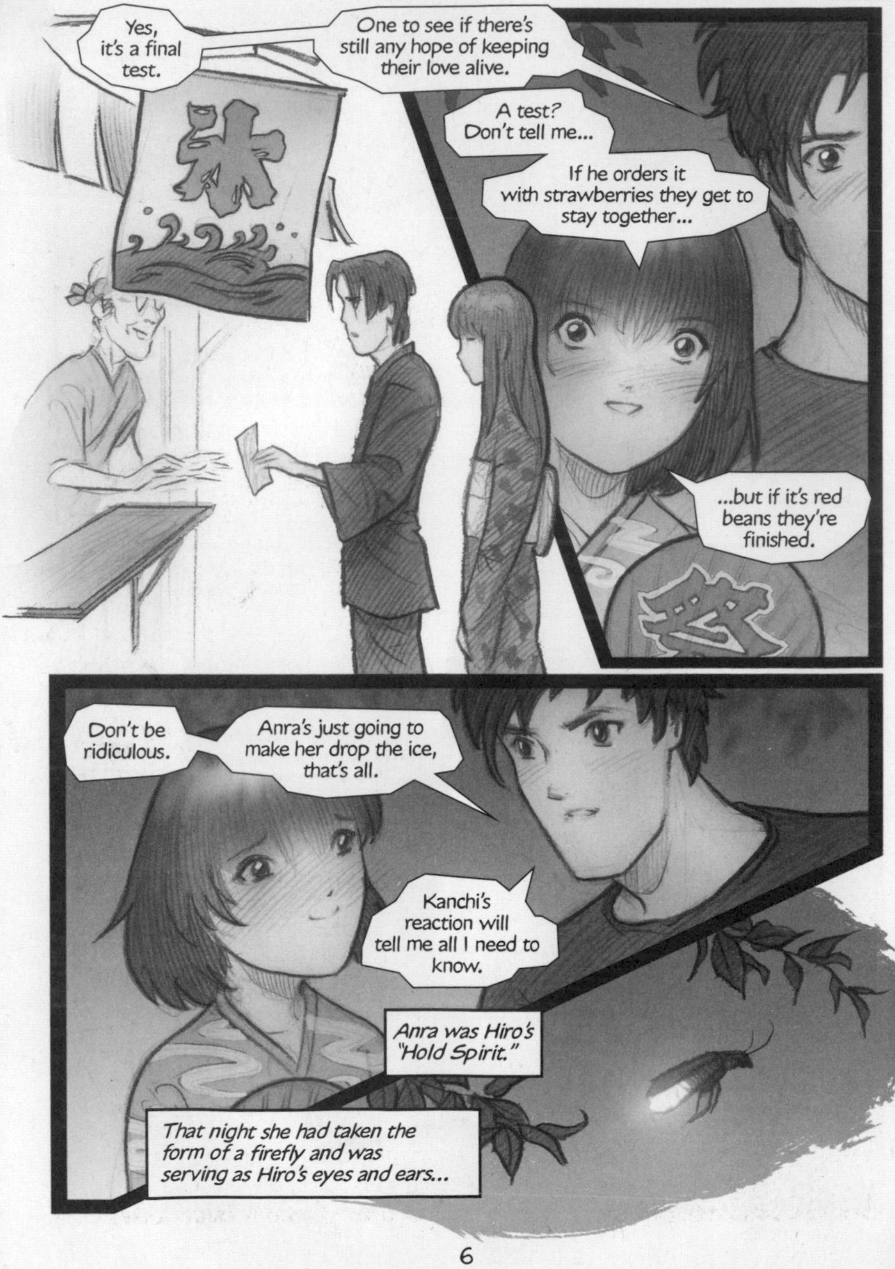
Yes, it's a final test.
One to see if there's still any hope of keeping their love alive.
A test? Don't tell me...
If he orders it with strawberries they get to stay together...
...but if it's red beans they're finished.
Don't be ridiculous.
Anra's just going to make her drop the ice, that's all.
Kanchi's reaction will tell me all I need to know.
Anra was Hiro's "Hold Spirit."
That night she had taken the form of a firefly and was serving as Hiro's eyes and ears...

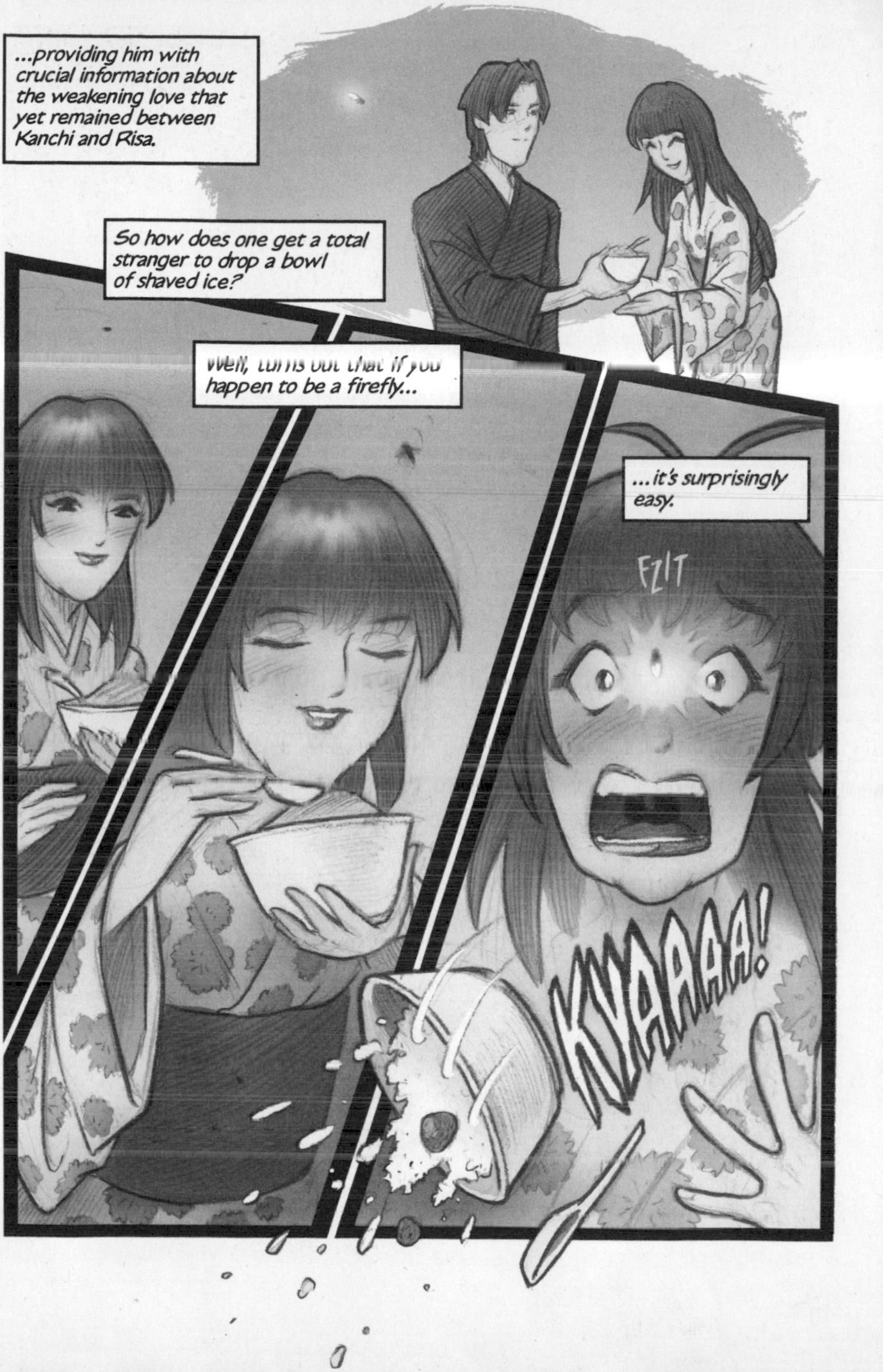
...providing him with crucial information about the weakening love that yet remained between Kanchi and Risa.
So how does one get a total stranger to drop a bowl of shaved ice?
Well, turns out that if you happen to be a firefly...
...it's surprisingly easy.
FZIT
KYAAAA!

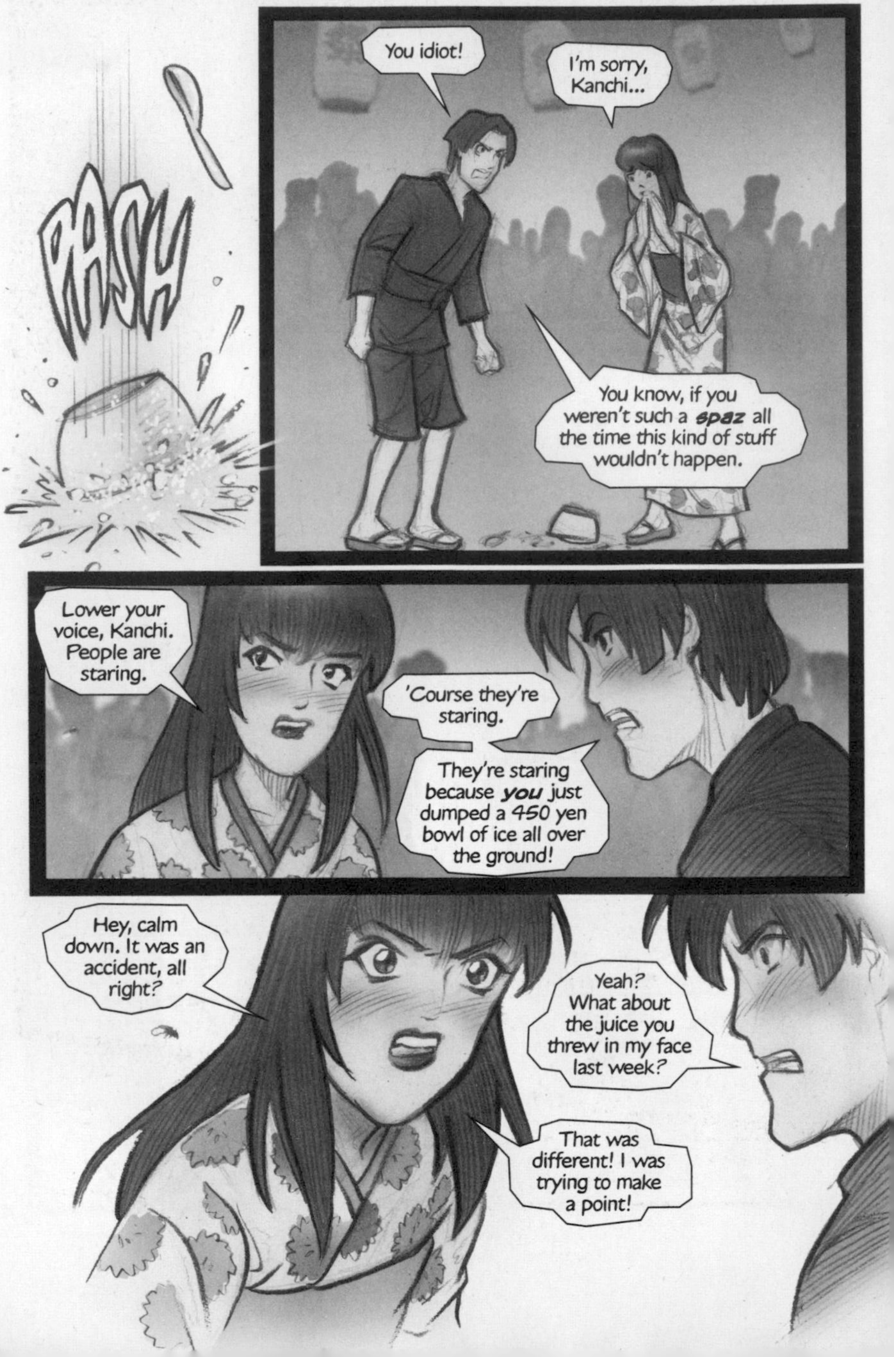
PASH
You idiot!
I'm sorry, Kanchi...
You know, if you weren't such a **spaz** all the time this kind of stuff wouldn't happen.
Lower your voice, Kanchi. People are staring.
'Course they're staring.
They're staring because **you** just dumped a 450 yen bowl of ice all over the ground!
Hey, calm down. It was an accident, all right?
Yeah? What about the juice you threw in my face last week?
That was different! I was trying to make a point!

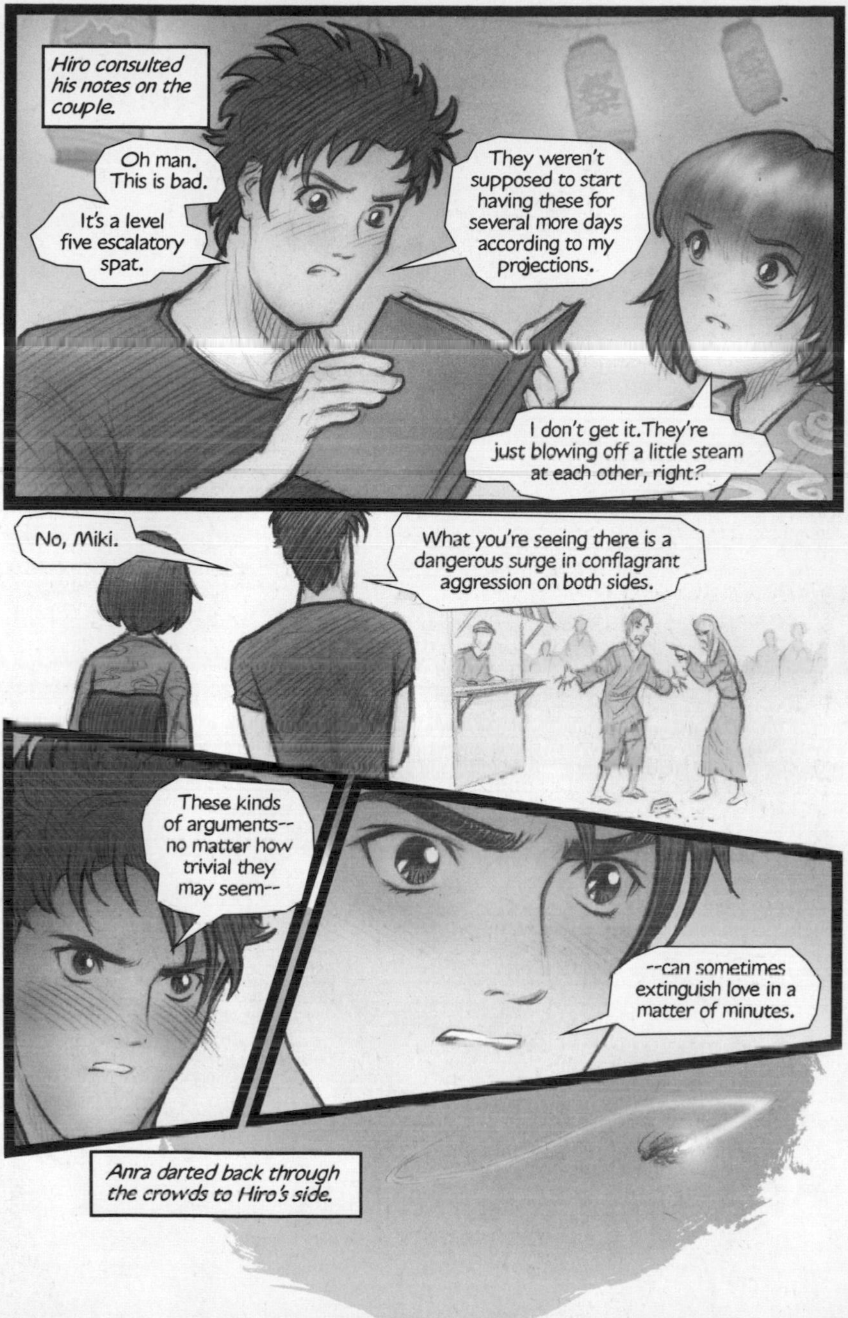
Hiro consulted his notes on the couple.
Oh man. This is bad.
It's a level five escalatory spat.
They weren't supposed to start having these for several more days according to my projections.
I don't get it. They're just blowing off a little steam at each other, right?
No, Miki.
What you're seeing there is a dangerous surge in conflagrant aggression on both sides.
These kinds of arguments-- no matter how trivial they may seem--
--can sometimes extinguish love in a matter of minutes.
Anra darted back through the crowds to Hiro's side.

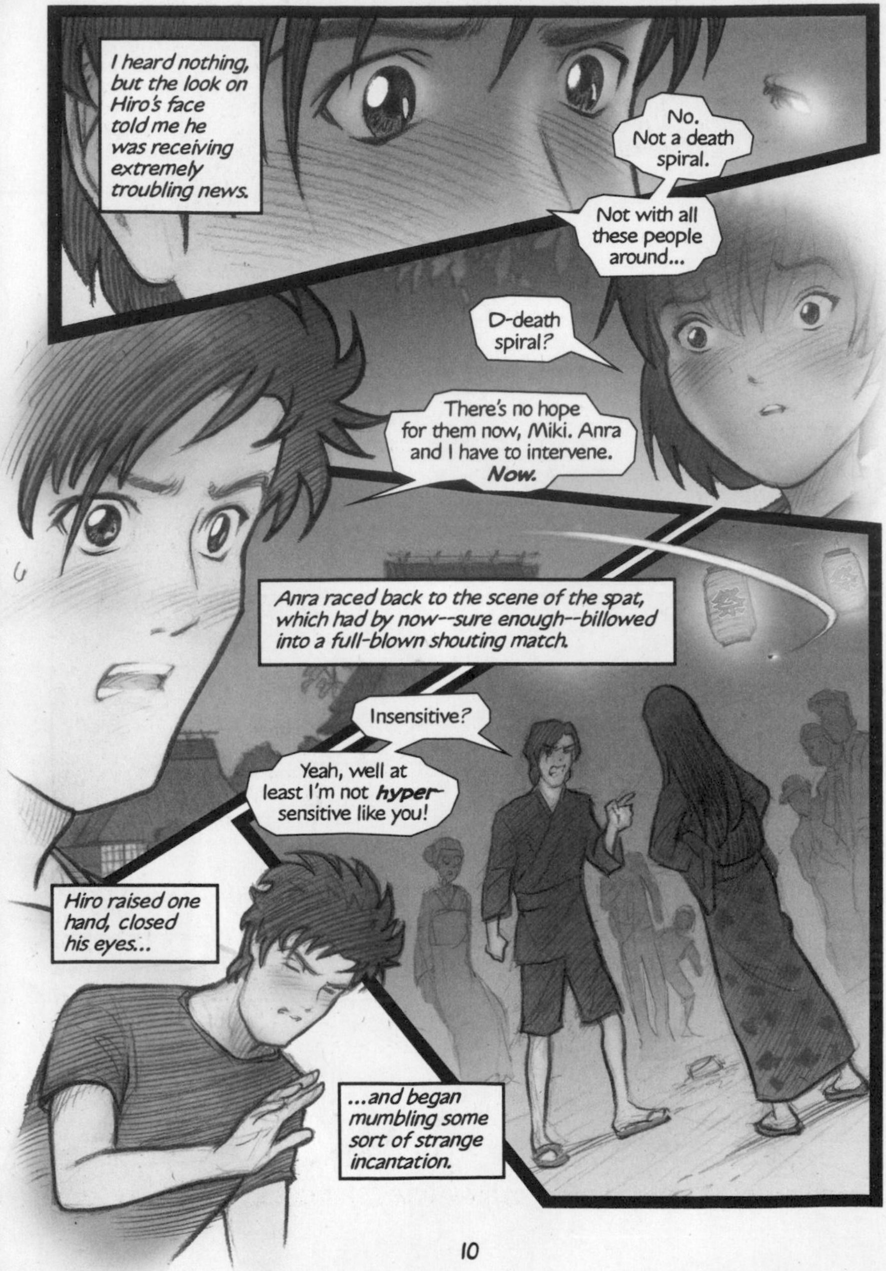
I heard nothing, but the look on Hiro's face told me he was receiving extremely troubling news.
No. Not a death spiral.
Not with all these people around...
D-death spiral?
There's no hope for them now, Miki. Anra and I have to intervene. *Now.*
Anra raced back to the scene of the spat, which had by now--sure enough--billowed into a full-blown shouting match.
Insensitive?
Yeah, well at least I'm not *hyper*-sensitive like you!
Hiro raised one hand, closed his eyes...
...and began mumbling some sort of strange incantation.

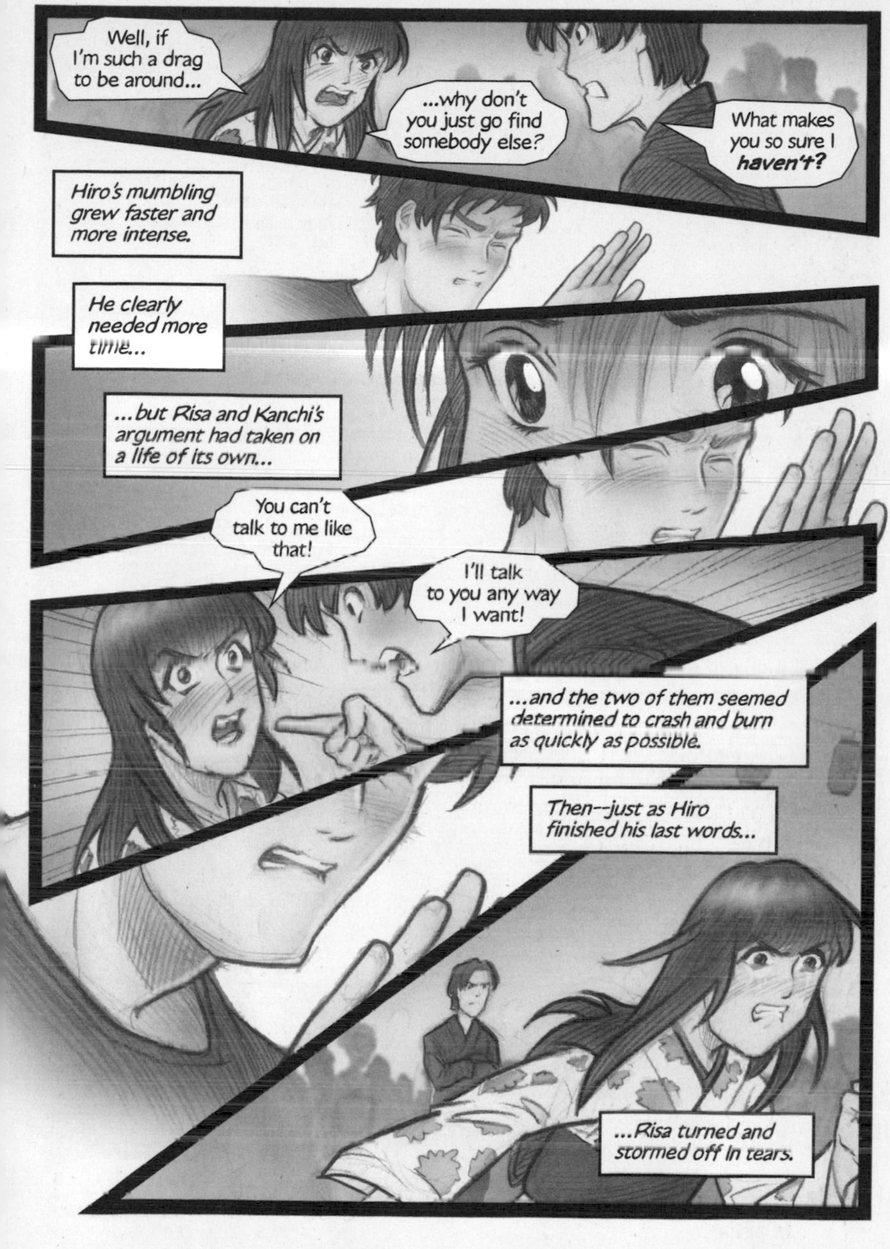
Well, if I'm such a drag to be around...
...why don't you just go find somebody else?
What makes you so sure I ***haven't?***
Hiro's mumbling grew faster and more intense.
He clearly needed more time...
...but Risa and Kanchi's argument had taken on a life of its own...
You can't talk to me like that!
I'll talk to you any way I want!
...and the two of them seemed determined to crash and burn as quickly as possible.
Then--just as Hiro finished his last words...
...Risa turned and stormed off in tears.

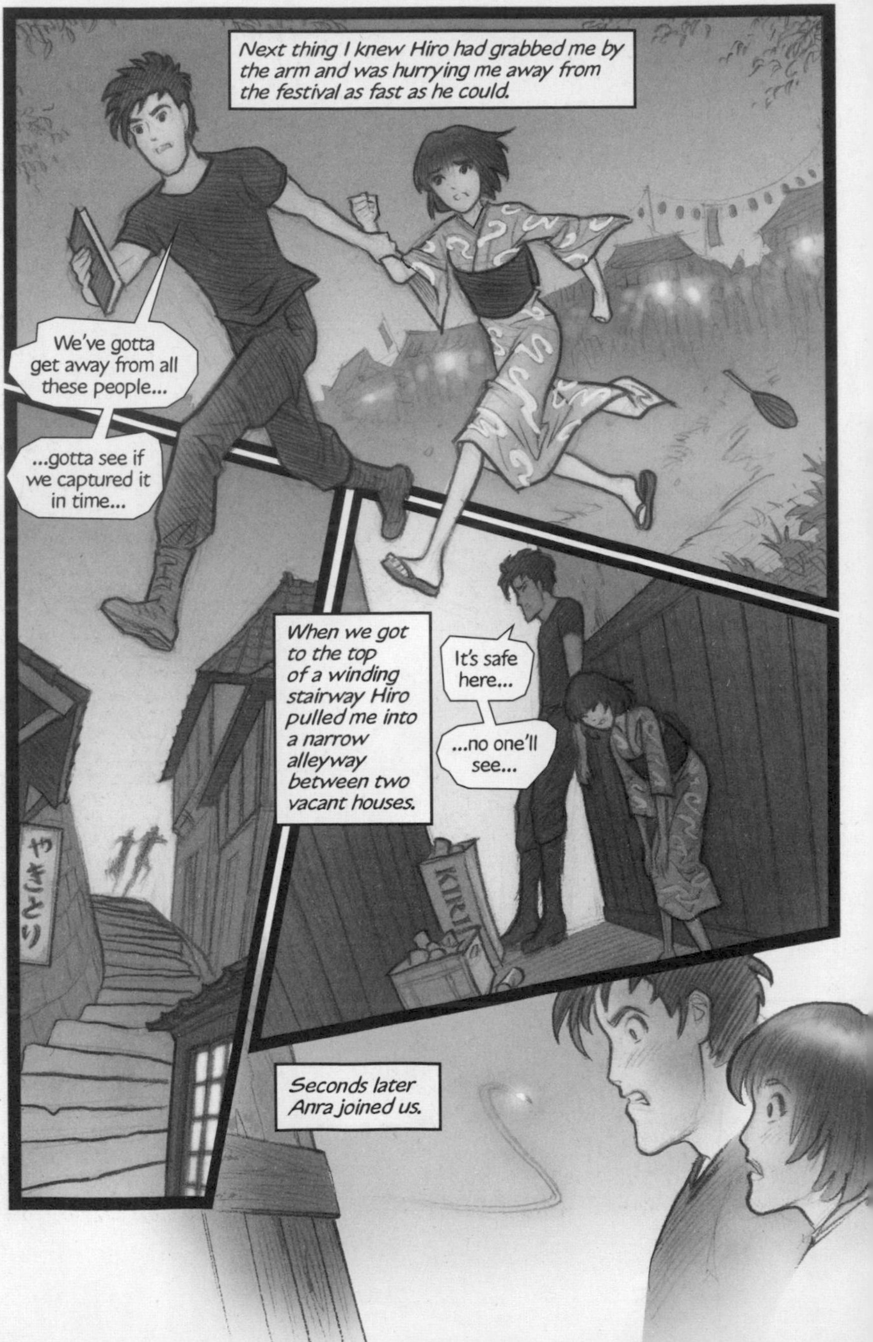
Next thing I knew Hiro had grabbed me by the arm and was hurrying me away from the festival as fast as he could.
We've gotta get away from all these people...
...gotta see if we captured it in time...
やきとり
When we got to the top of a winding stairway Hiro pulled me into a narrow alleyway between two vacant houses.
It's safe here...
...no one'll see...
Seconds later Anra joined us.

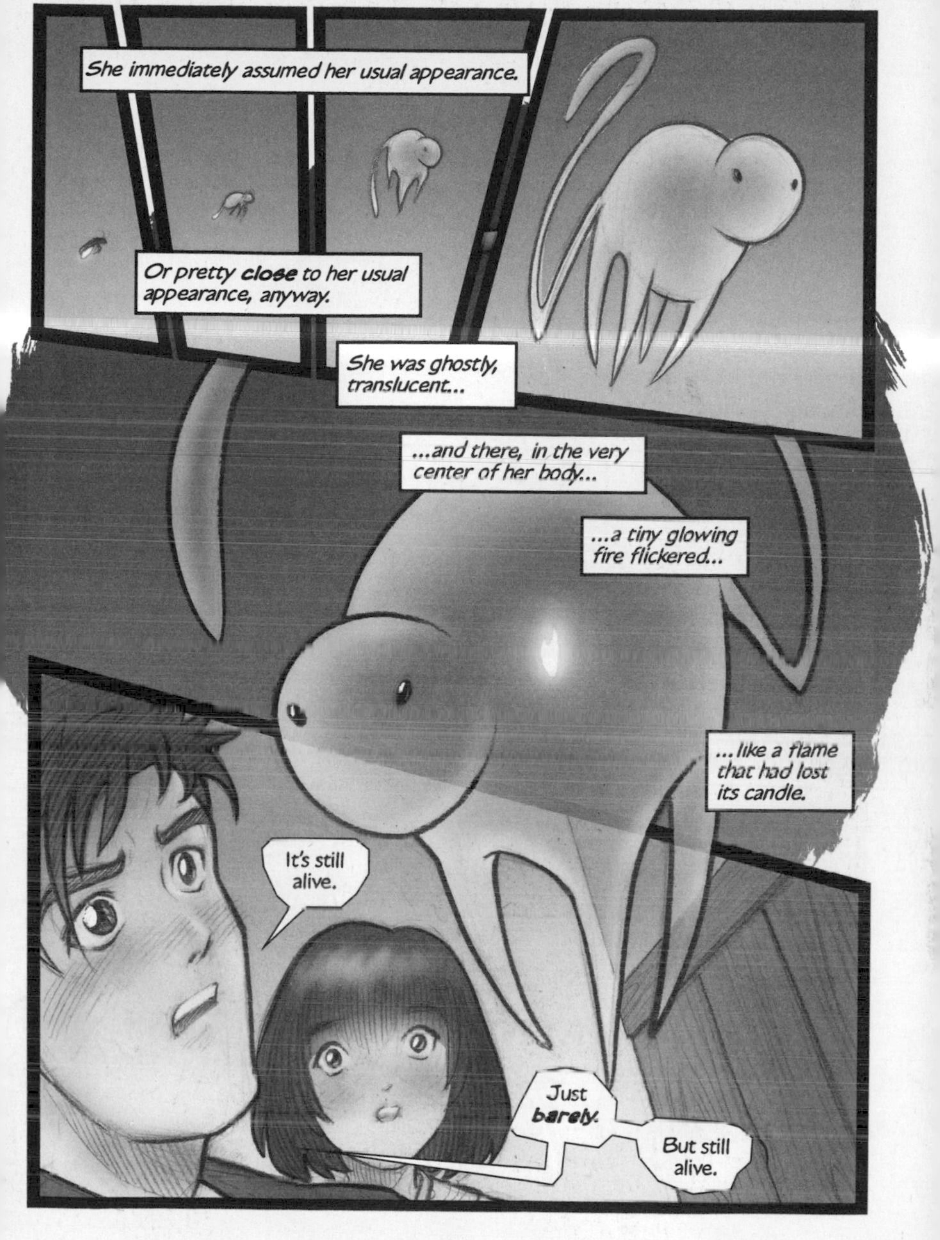
She immediately assumed her usual appearance.
Or pretty **close** to her usual appearance, anyway.
She was ghostly, translucent...
...and there, in the very center of her body...
...a tiny glowing fire flickered...
...like a flame that had lost its candle.
It's still alive.
Just **barely**.
But still alive.

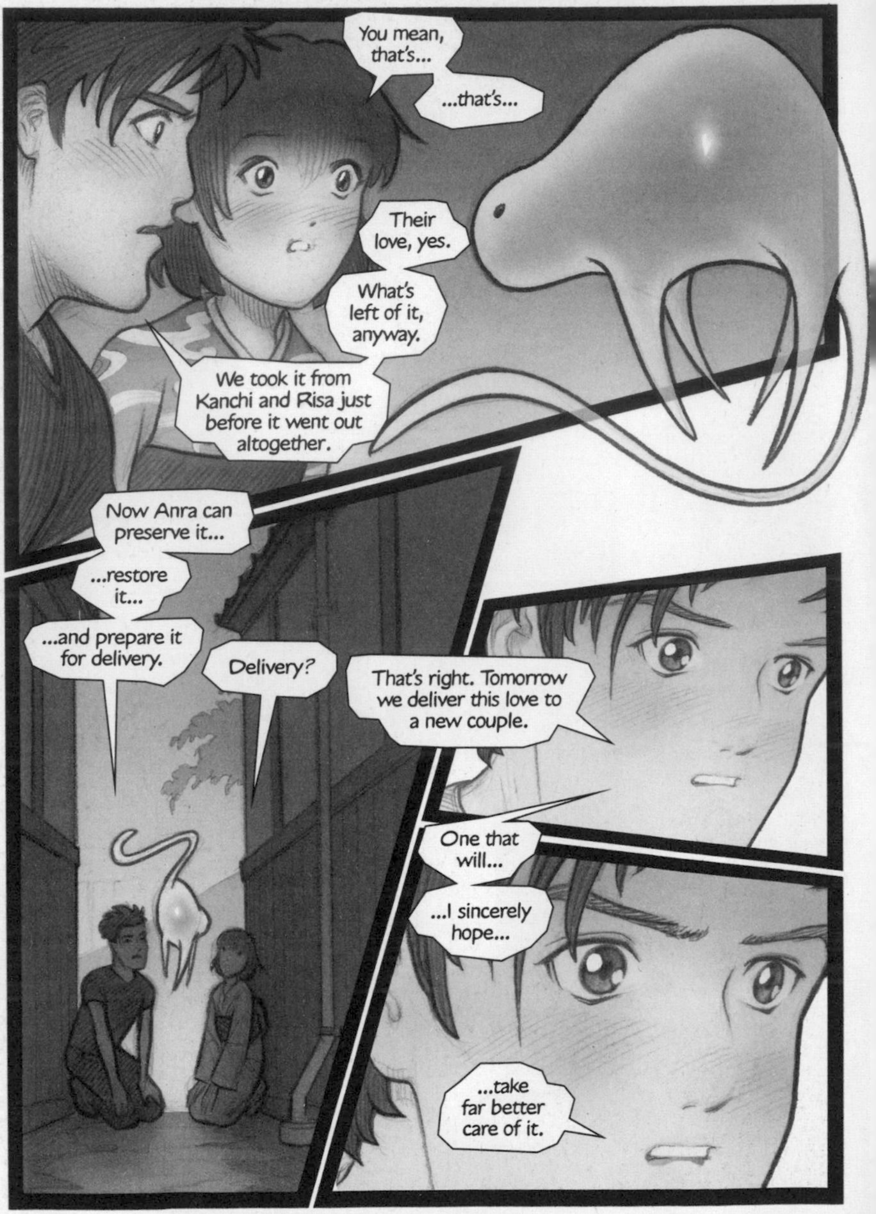
You mean, that's...
...that's...
Their love, yes.
What's left of it, anyway.
We took it from Kanchi and Risa just before it went out altogether.
Now Anra can preserve it...
...restore it...
...and prepare it for delivery.
Delivery?
That's right. Tomorrow we deliver this love to a new couple.
One that will...
...I sincerely hope...
...take far better care of it.

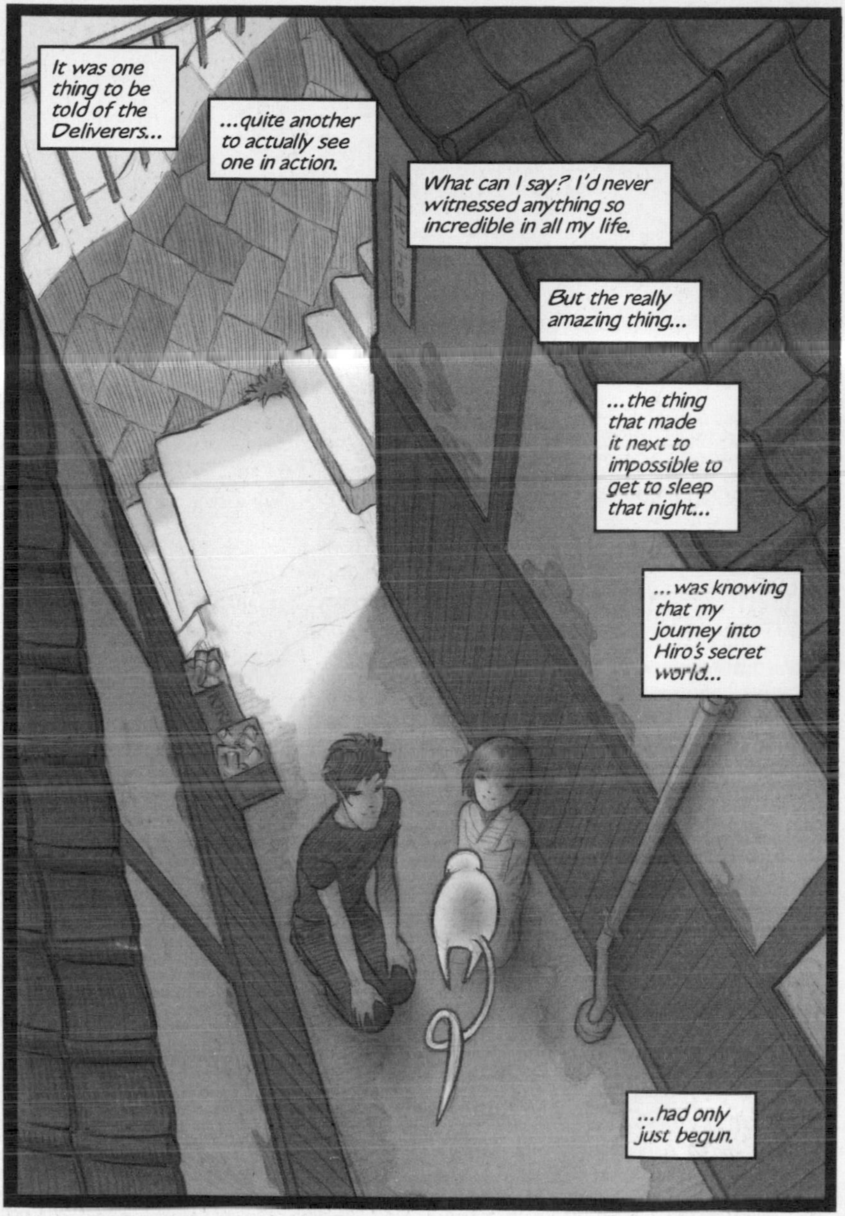
It was one thing to be told of the Deliverers...
...quite another to actually see one in action.
What can I say? I'd never witnessed anything so incredible in all my life.
But the really amazing thing...
...the thing that made it next to impossible to get to sleep that night...
...was knowing that my journey into Hiro's secret world...
...had only just begun.

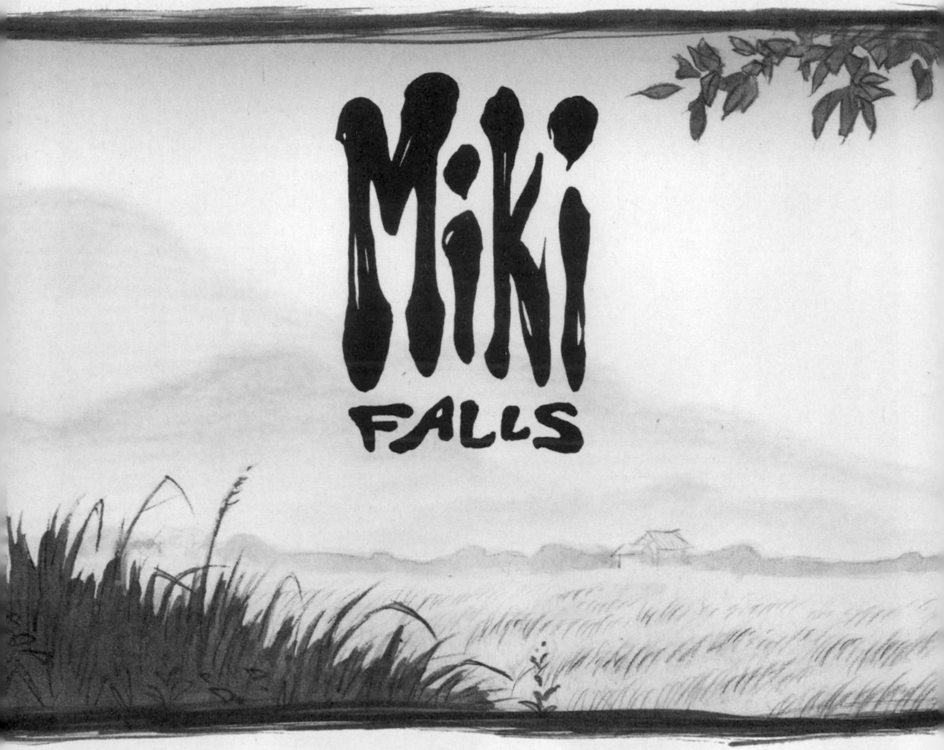
MIKI
FALLS

MARK CRILLEY

HARPER TEEN
An Imprint of HarperCollins*Publishers*

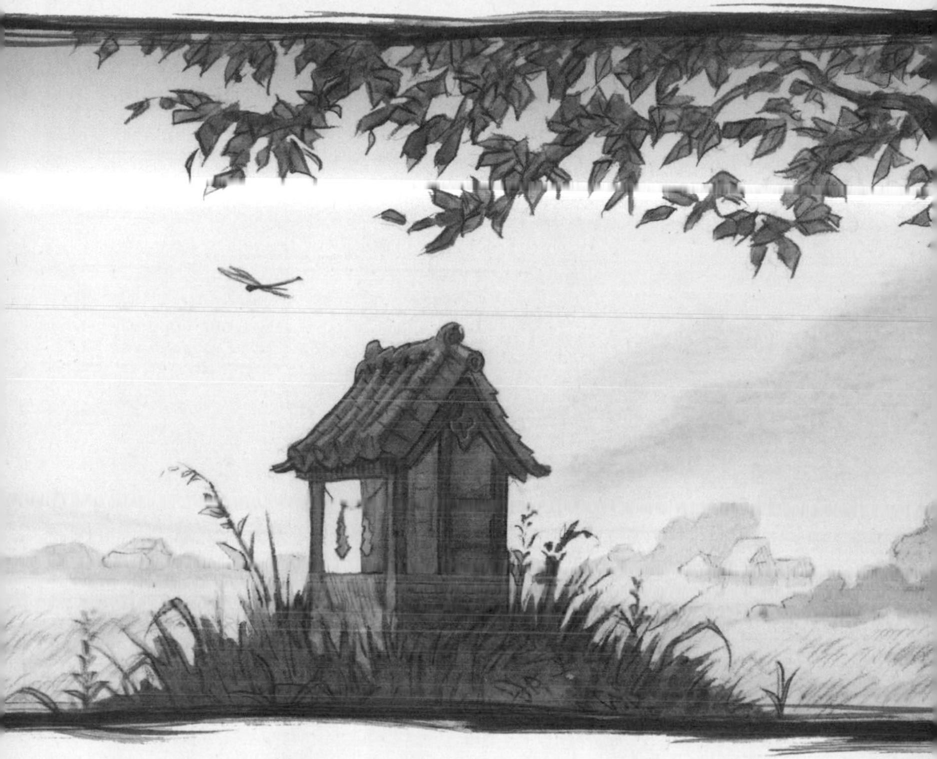

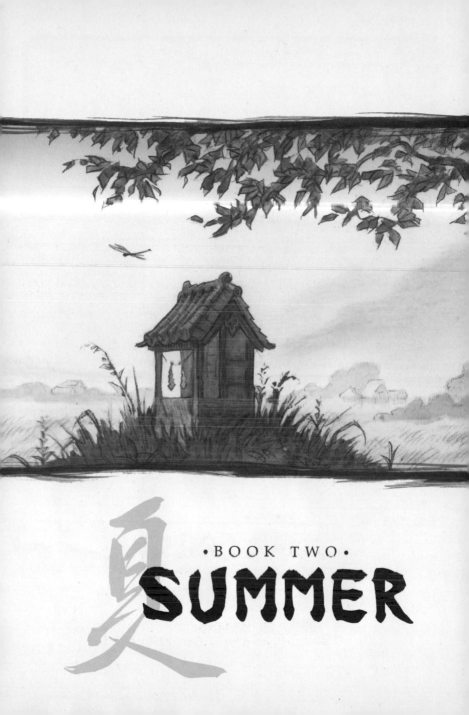

夏

•BOOK TWO•

SUMMER

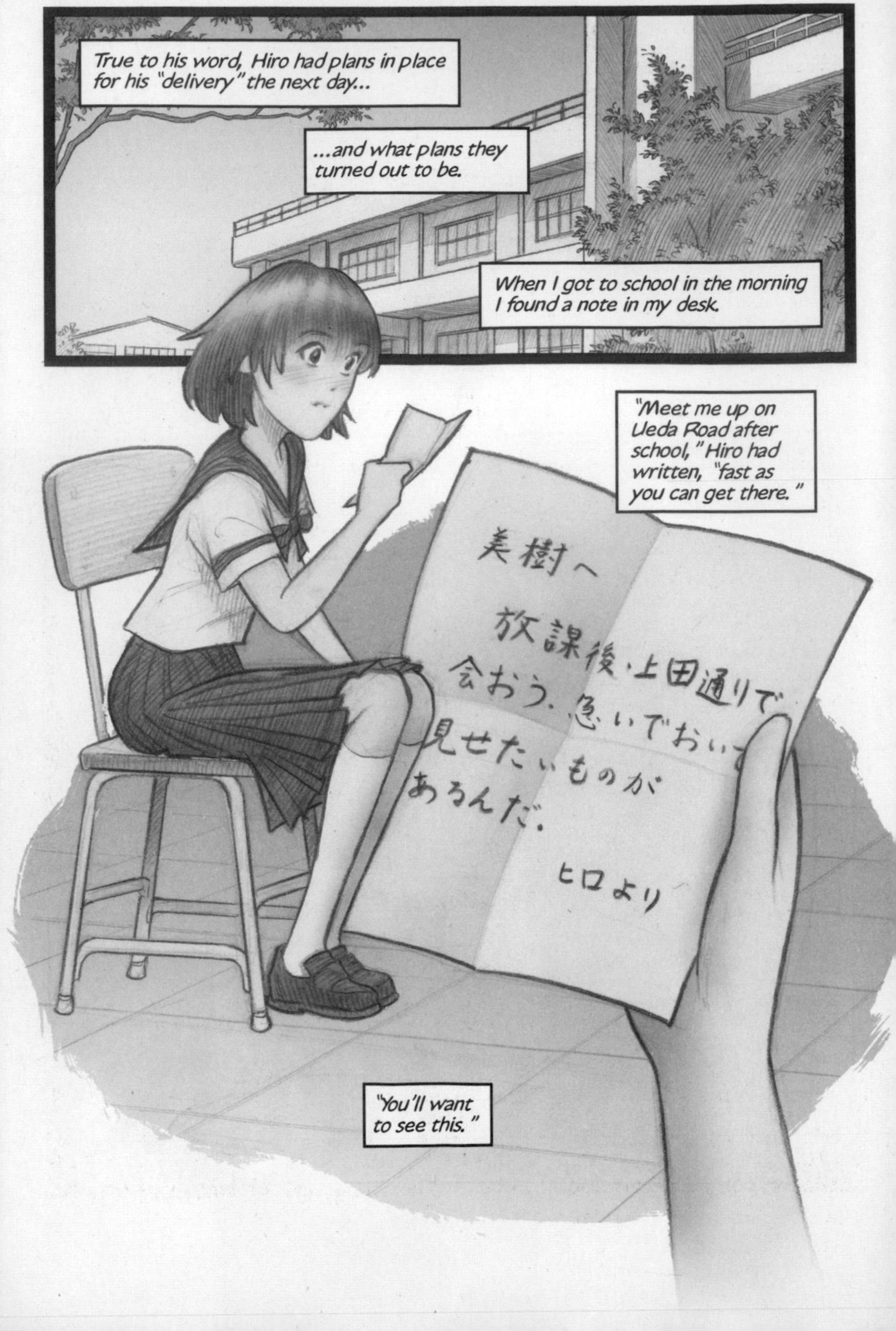
True to his word, Hiro had plans in place for his "delivery" the next day...
...and what plans they turned out to be.
When I got to school in the morning I found a note in my desk.
"Meet me up on Ueda Road after school," Hiro had written, "fast as you can get there."
美樹へ
放課後・上田通りで
会おう. 急いでおい
見せたいものが
あるんだ.
ヒロより
"You'll want to see this."

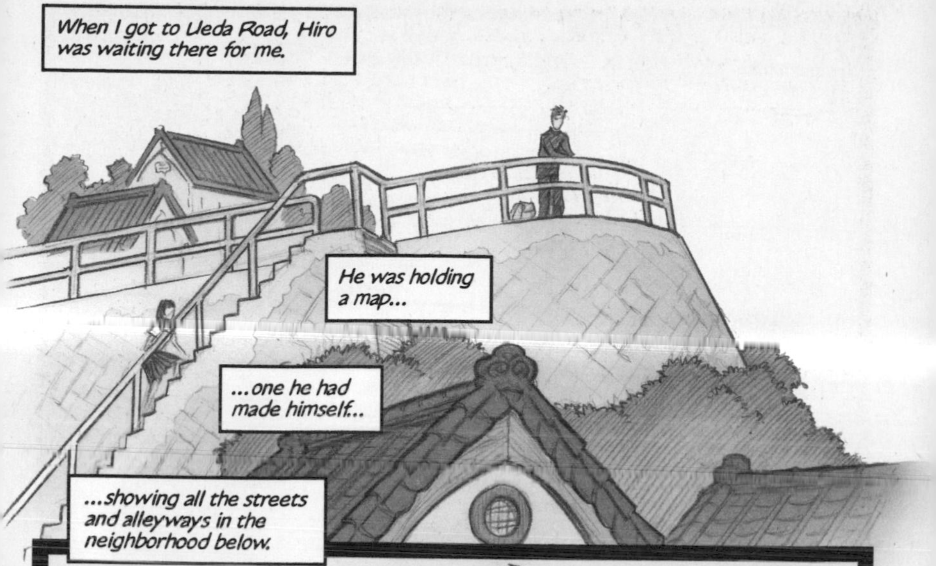
When I got to Ueda Road, Hiro was waiting there for me.
He was holding a map...
...one he had made himself...
...showing all the streets and alleyways in the neighborhood below.
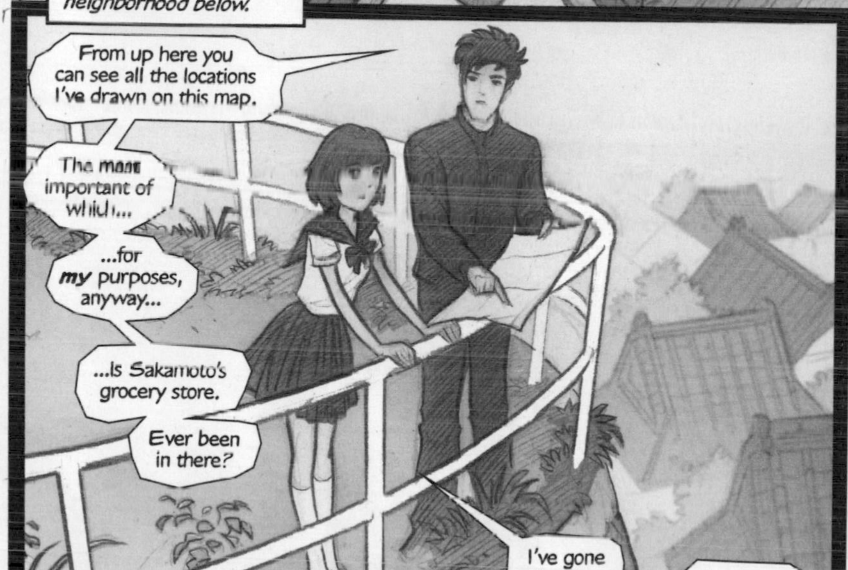
From up here you can see all the locations I've drawn on this map.
The most important of which...
...for *my* purposes, anyway...
...Is Sakamoto's grocery store.
Ever been in there?
I've gone *by* it...
...but never stepped inside, no.

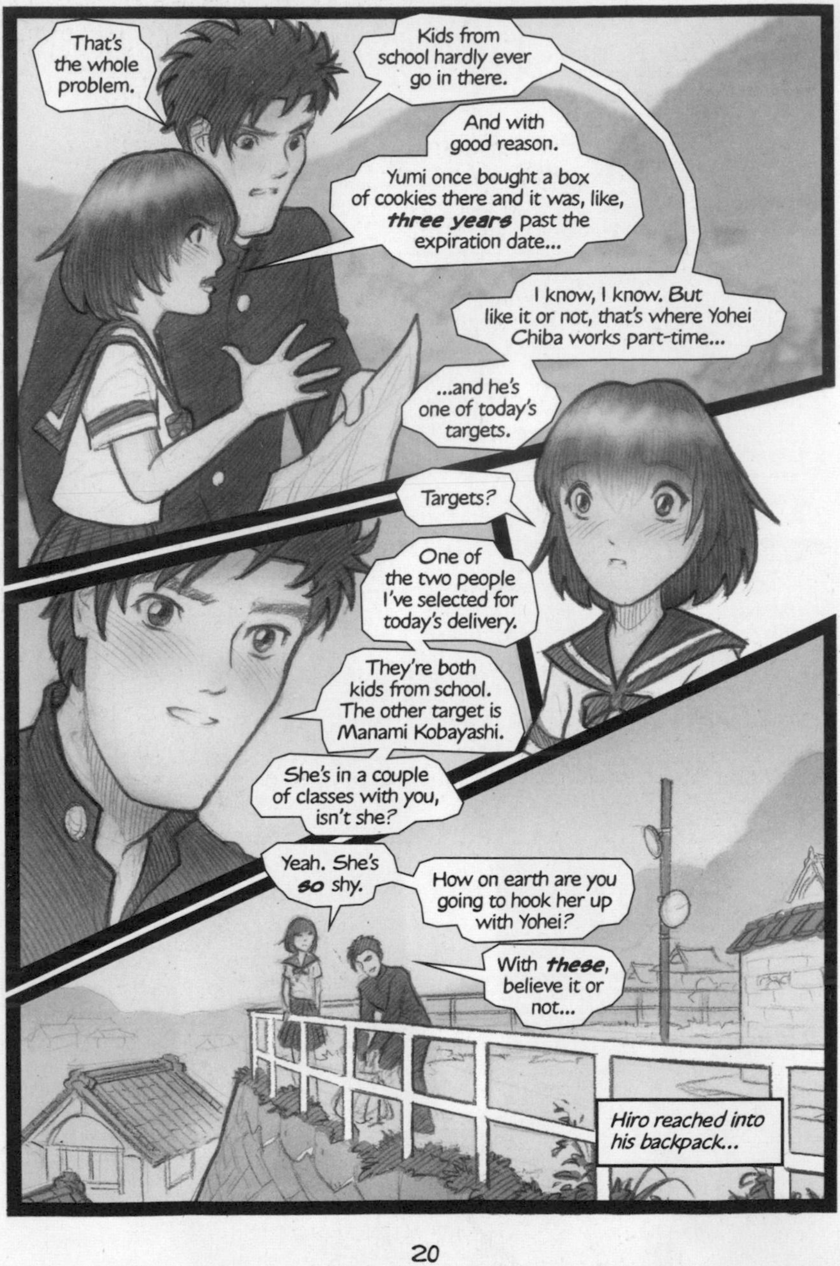
That's the whole problem.
Kids from school hardly ever go in there.
And with good reason.
Yumi once bought a box of cookies there and it was, like, **three years** past the expiration date...
I know, I know. But like it or not, that's where Yohei Chiba works part-time...
...and he's one of today's targets.
Targets?
One of the two people I've selected for today's delivery.
They're both kids from school. The other target is Manami Kobayashi.
She's in a couple of classes with you, isn't she?
Yeah. She's **so** shy.
How on earth are you going to hook her up with Yohei?
With **these**, believe it or not...
Hiro reached into his backpack...

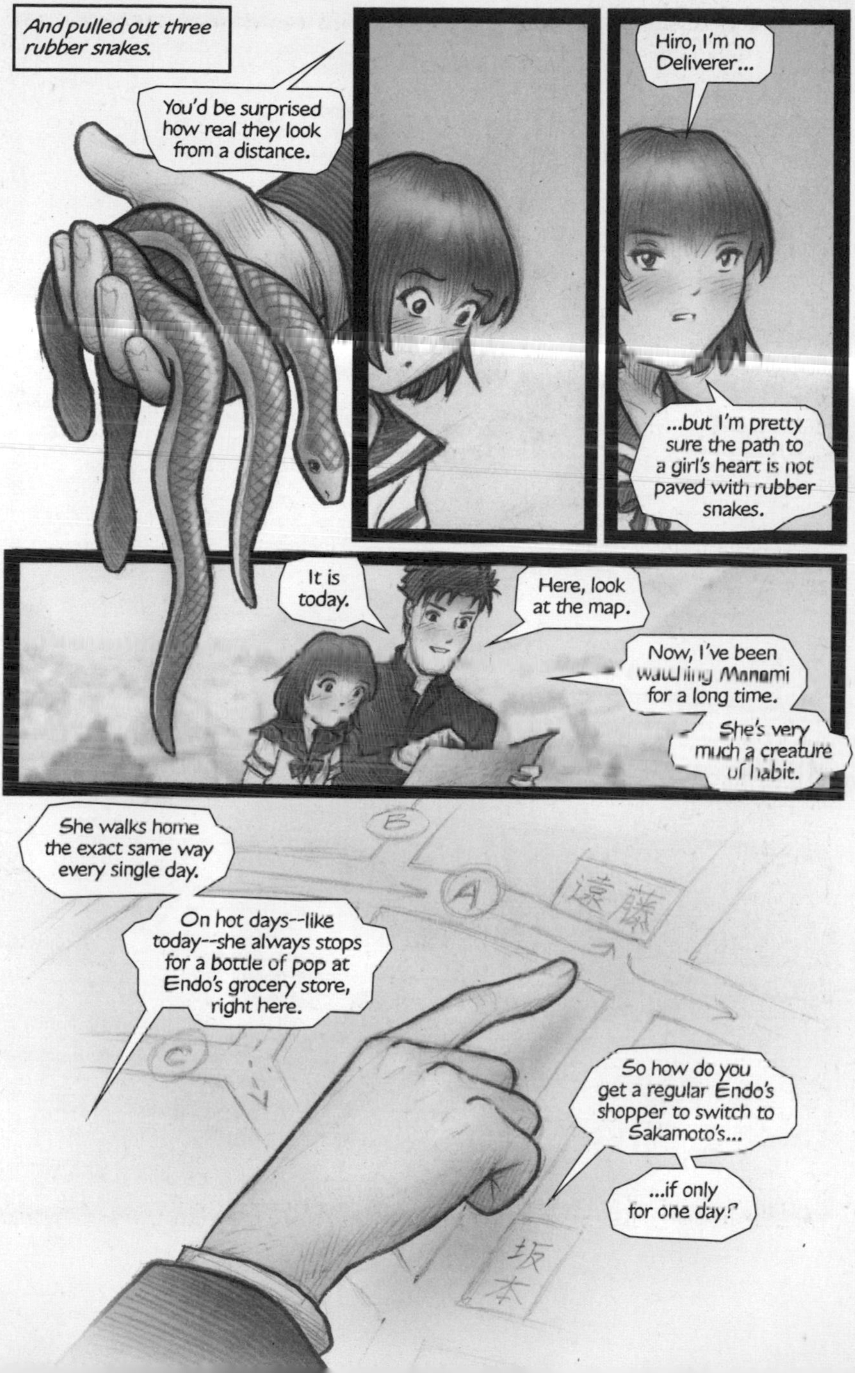
And pulled out three rubber snakes.
You'd be surprised how real they look from a distance.
Hiro, I'm no Deliverer...
...but I'm pretty sure the path to a girl's heart is not paved with rubber snakes.
It is today.
Here, look at the map.
Now, I've been watching Manami for a long time.
She's very much a creature of habit.
She walks home the exact same way every single day.
B
A
遠藤
On hot days--like today--she always stops for a bottle of pop at Endo's grocery store, right here.
C
So how do you get a regular Endo's shopper to switch to Sakamoto's...
...if only for one day?
坂本

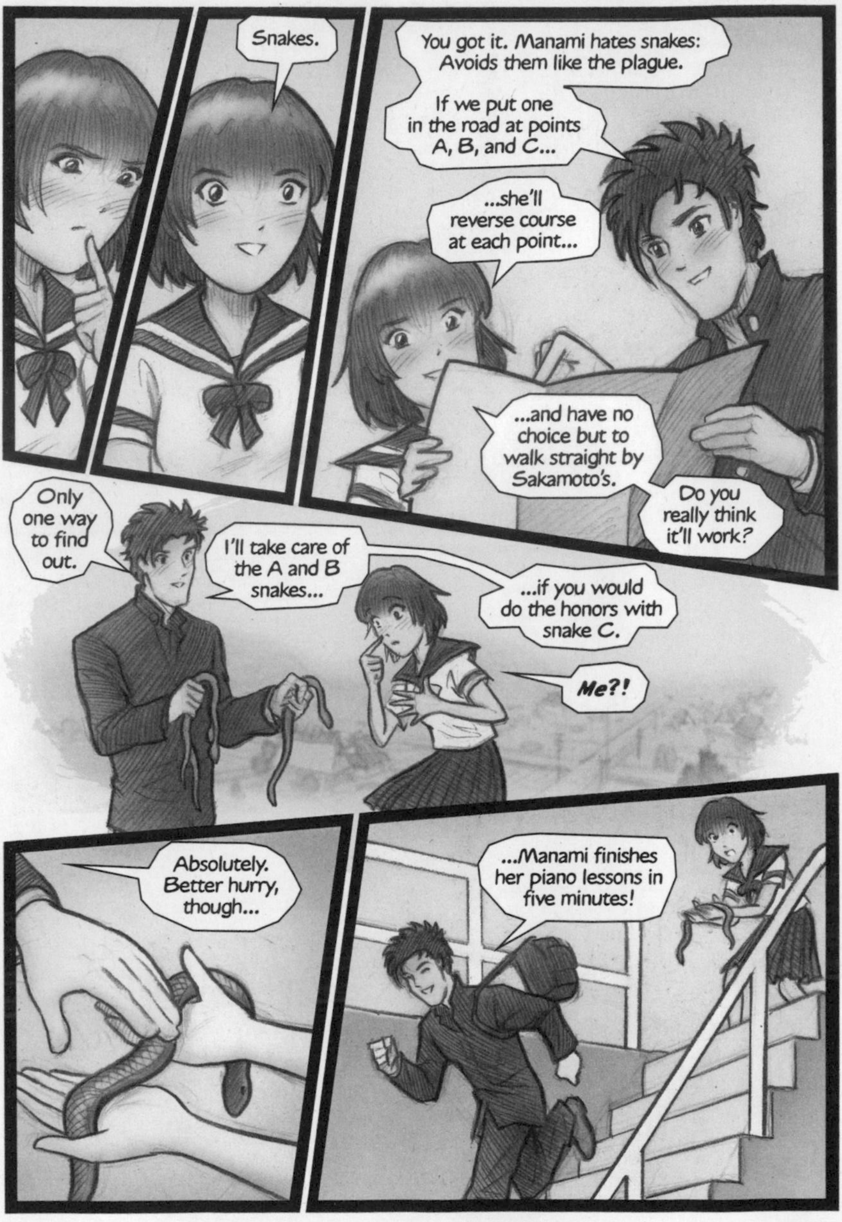
Snakes.
You got it. Manami hates snakes: Avoids them like the plague.
If we put one in the road at points A, B, and C...
...she'll reverse course at each point...
...and have no choice but to walk straight by Sakamoto's.
Do you really think it'll work?
Only one way to find out.
I'll take care of the A and B snakes...
...if you would do the honors with snake C.
Me?!
Absolutely. Better hurry, though...
...Manami finishes her piano lessons in five minutes!

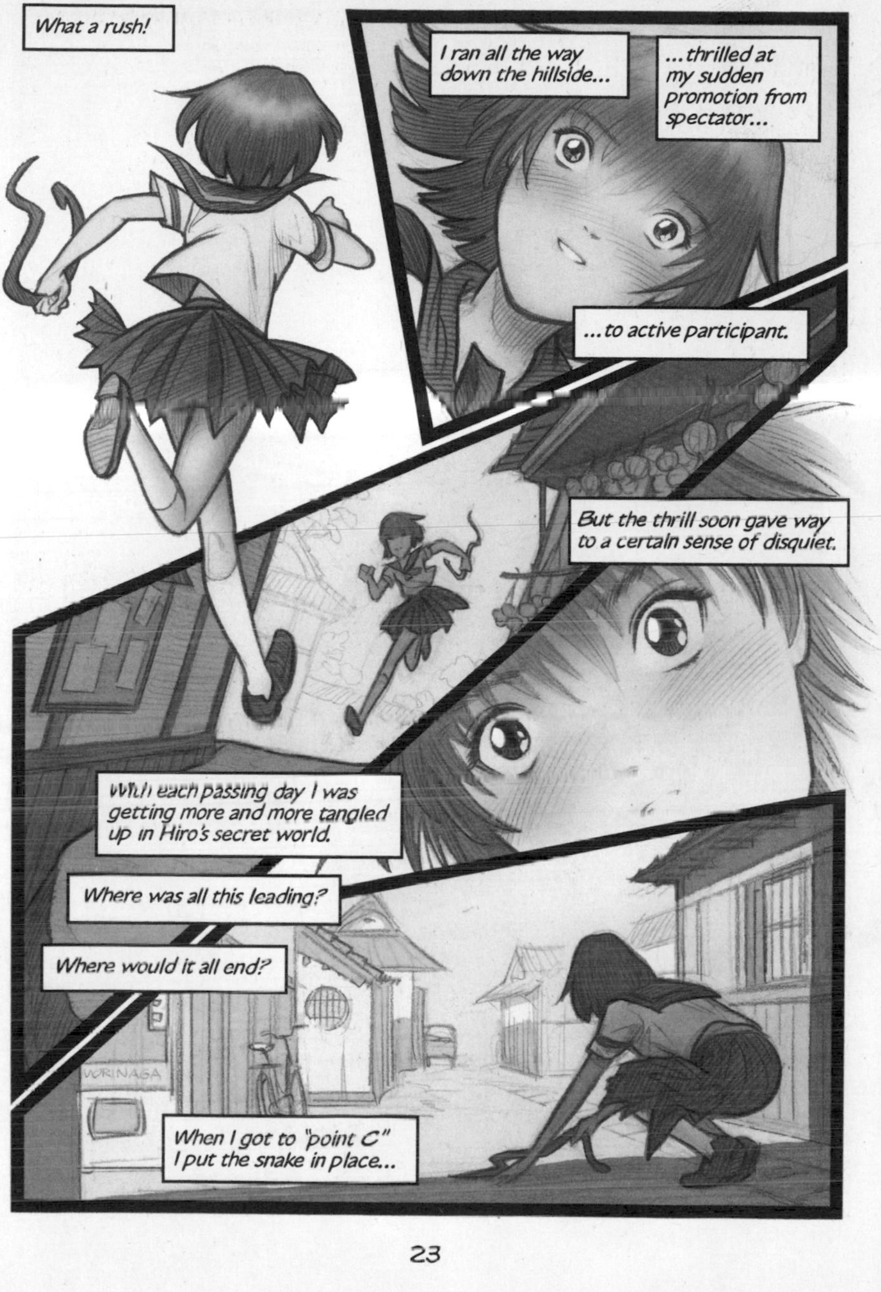

What a rush!
I ran all the way down the hillside...
...thrilled at my sudden promotion from spectator...
...to active participant.
But the thrill soon gave way to a certain sense of disquiet.
With each passing day I was getting more and more tangled up in Hiro's secret world.
Where was all this leading?
Where would it all end?
When I got to "point C" I put the snake in place...

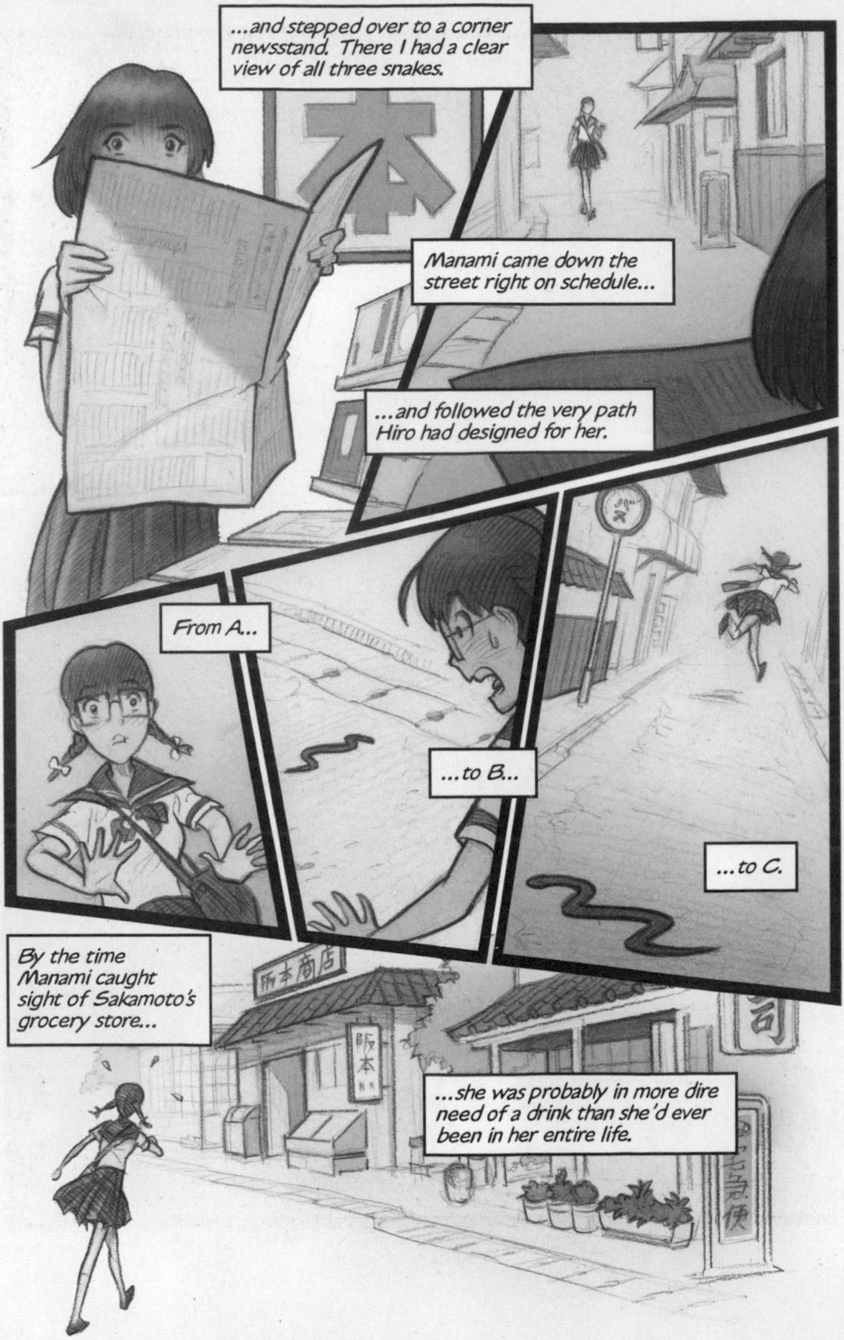
...and stepped over to a corner newsstand. There I had a clear view of all three snakes.
本
Manami came down the street right on schedule...
...and followed the very path Hiro had designed for her.
From A...
...to B...
...to C.
By the time Manami caught sight of Sakamoto's grocery store...
...she was probably in more dire need of a drink than she'd ever been in her entire life.

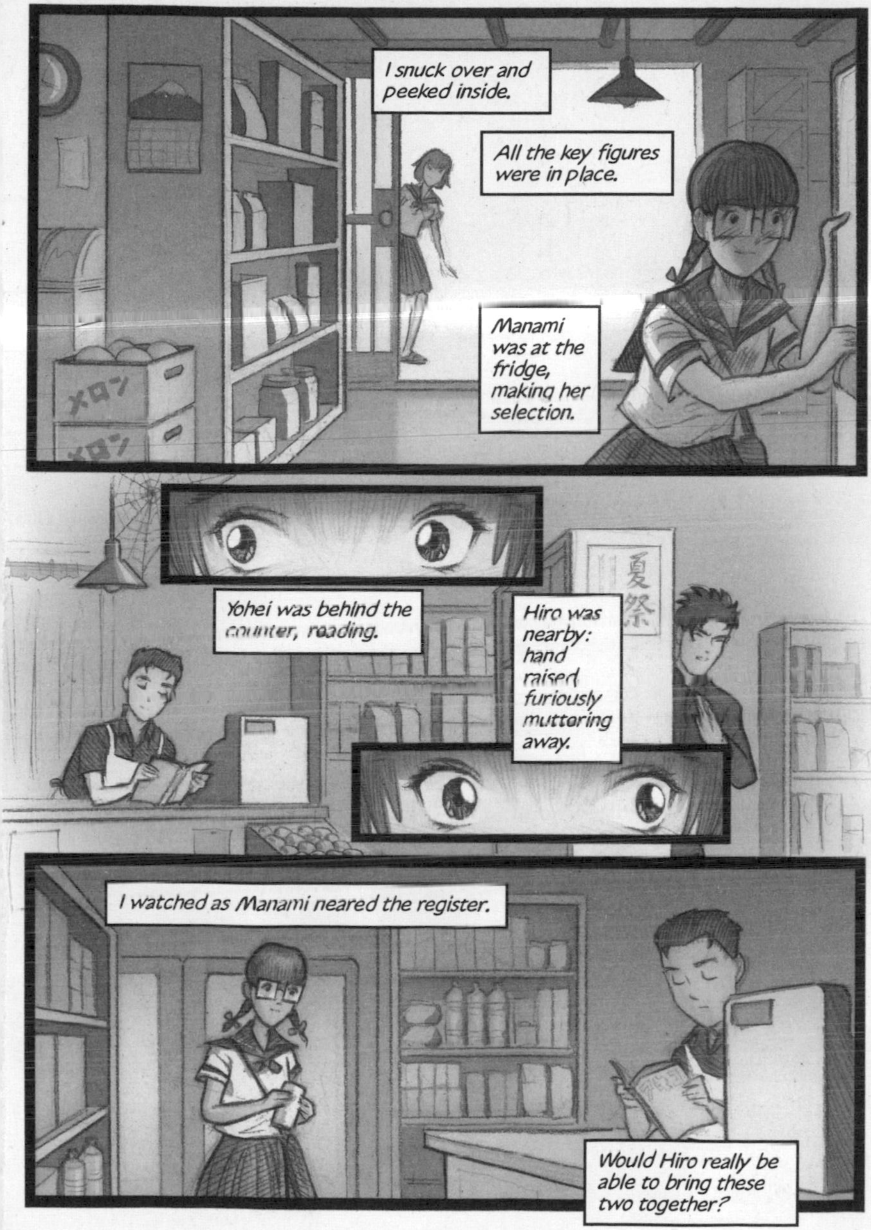
I snuck over and peeked inside.
All the key figures were in place.
メロン
メロン
Manami was at the fridge, making her selection.
Yohei was behind the counter, reading.
夏祭
Hiro was nearby: hand raised furiously muttering away.
I watched as Manami neared the register.
Would Hiro really be able to bring these two together?

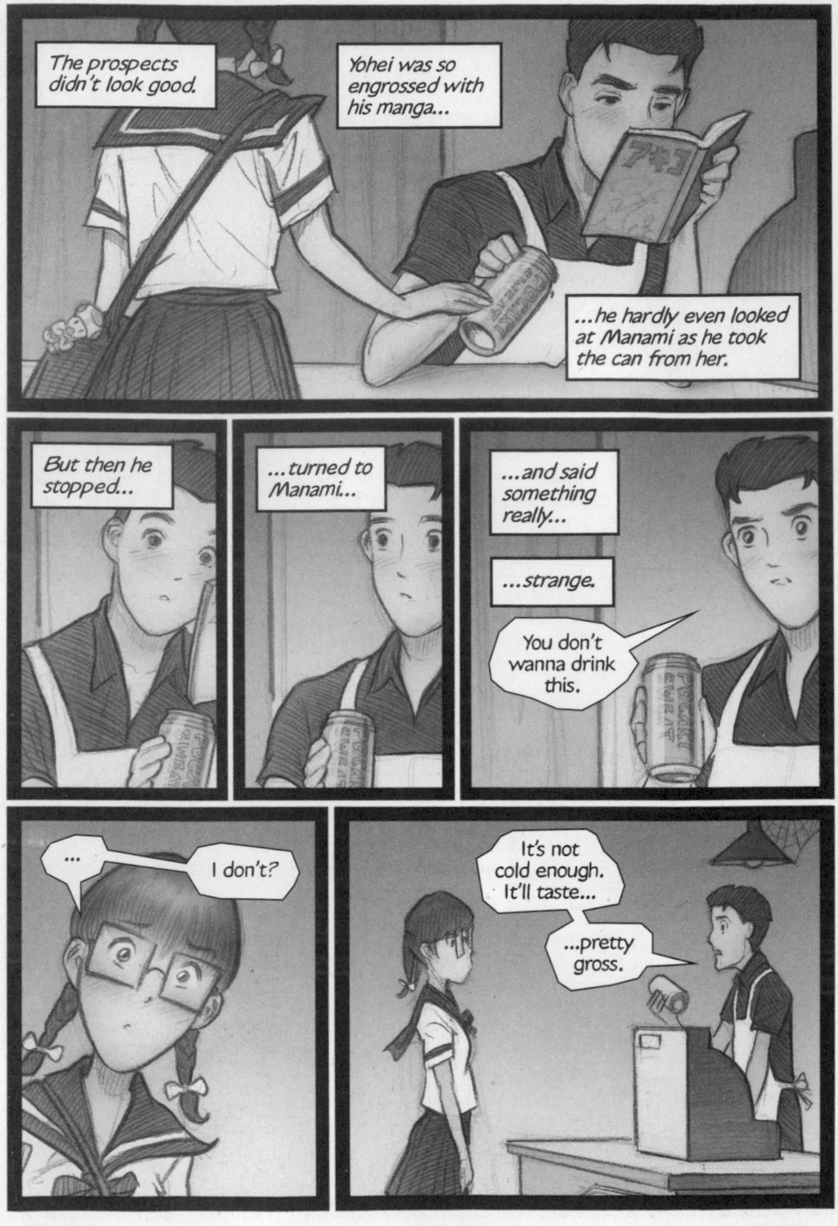
The prospects didn't look good.
Yohei was so engrossed with his manga...
...he hardly even looked at Manami as he took the can from her.
But then he stopped...
...turned to Manami...
...and said something really...
...strange.
You don't wanna drink this.
...
I don't?
It's not cold enough. It'll taste...
...pretty gross.

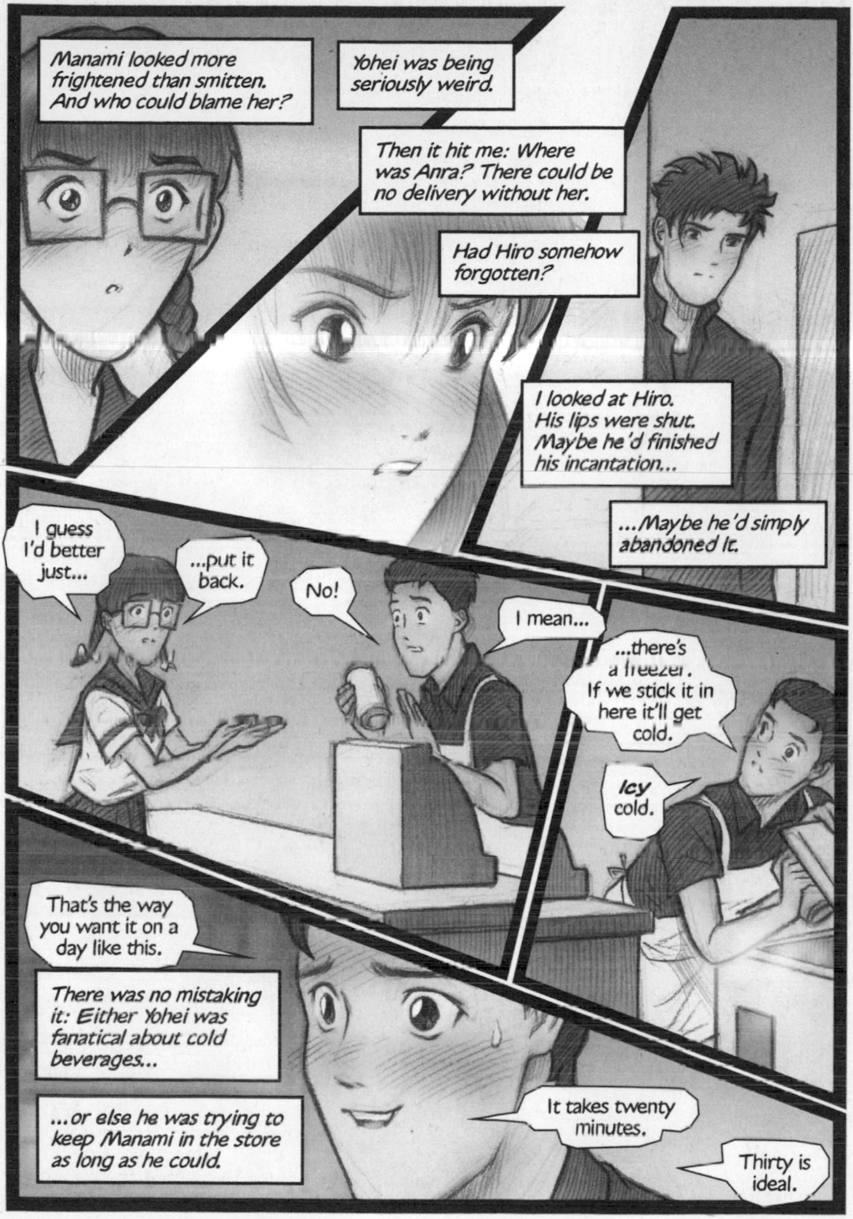
Manami looked more frightened than smitten. And who could blame her?
Yohei was being seriously weird.
Then it hit me: Where was Anra? There could be no delivery without her.
Had Hiro somehow forgotten?
I looked at Hiro. His lips were shut. Maybe he'd finished his incantation...
...Maybe he'd simply abandoned it.
I guess I'd better just...
...put it back.
No!
I mean...
...there's a freezer. If we stick it in here it'll get cold.
Icy cold.
That's the way you want it on a day like this.
There was no mistaking it: Either Yohei was fanatical about cold beverages...
...or else he was trying to keep Manami in the store as long as he could.
It takes twenty minutes.
Thirty is ideal.

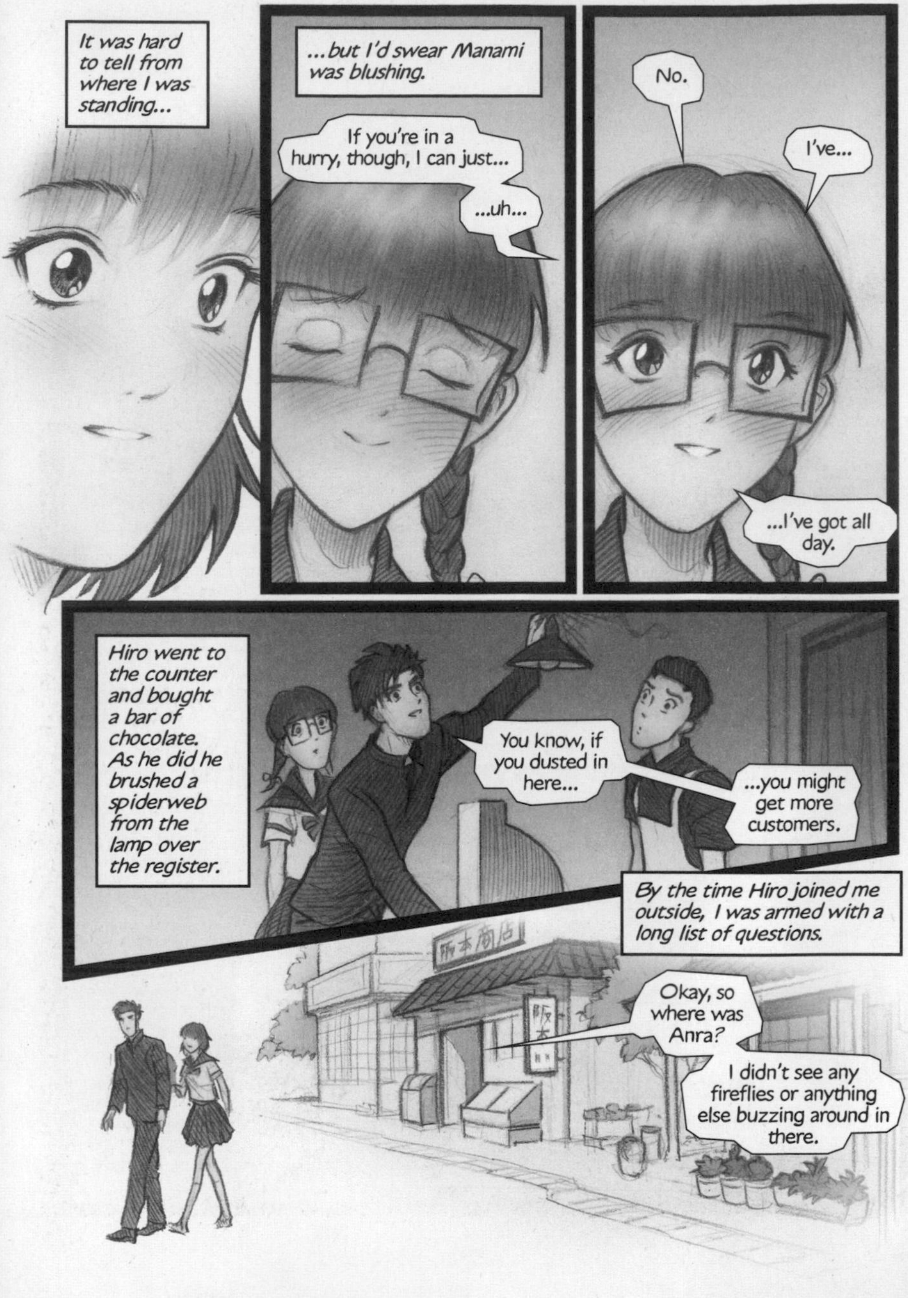
It was hard to tell from where I was standing...
...but I'd swear Manami was blushing.
If you're in a hurry, though, I can just...
...uh...
No.
I've...
...I've got all day.
Hiro went to the counter and bought a bar of chocolate. As he did he brushed a spiderweb from the lamp over the register.
You know, if you dusted in here...
...you might get more customers.
By the time Hiro joined me outside, I was armed with a long list of questions.
阪本商店
Okay, so where was Anra?
I didn't see any fireflies or anything else buzzing around in there.

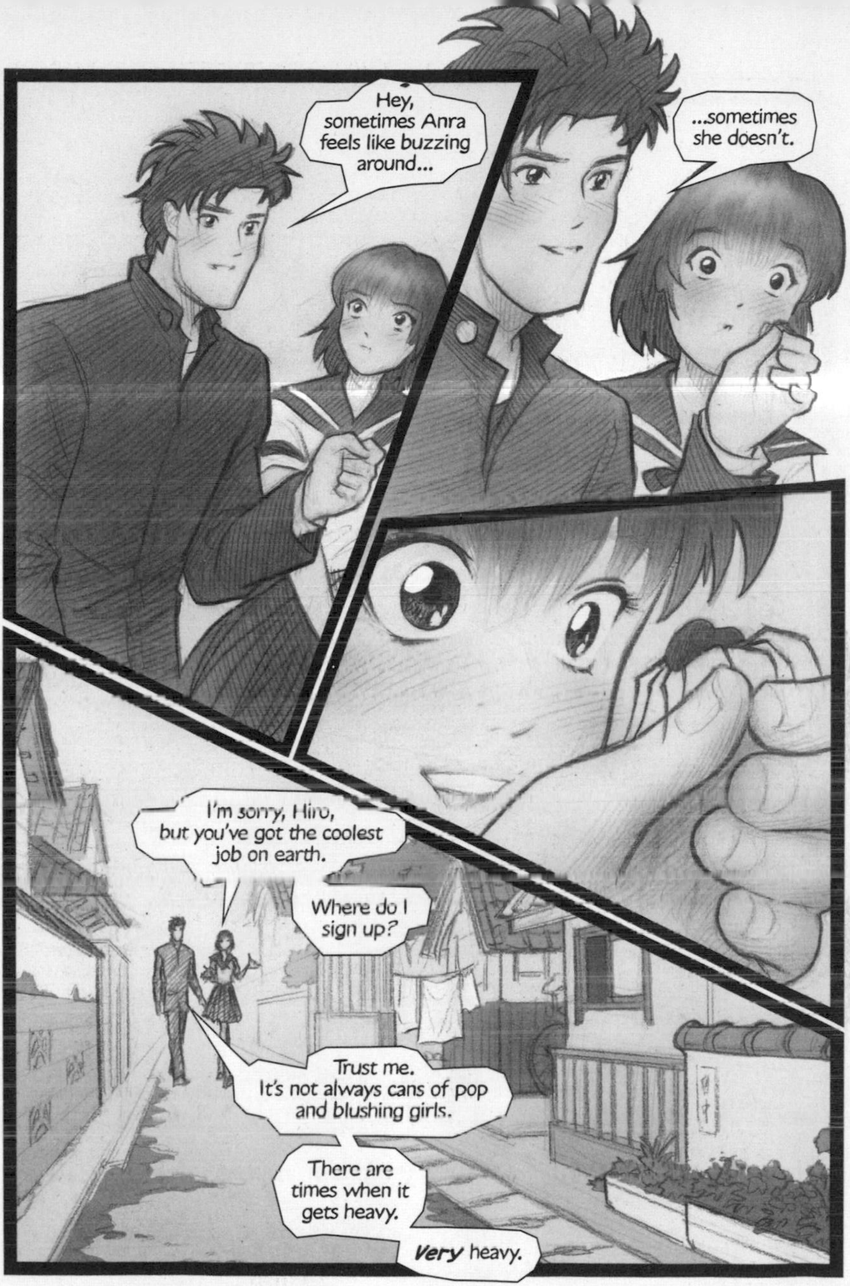
Hey, sometimes Anra feels like buzzing around...
...sometimes she doesn't.
I'm sorry, Hiro, but you've got the coolest job on earth.
Where do I sign up?
Trust me. It's not always cans of pop and blushing girls.
There are times when it gets heavy.
Very heavy.

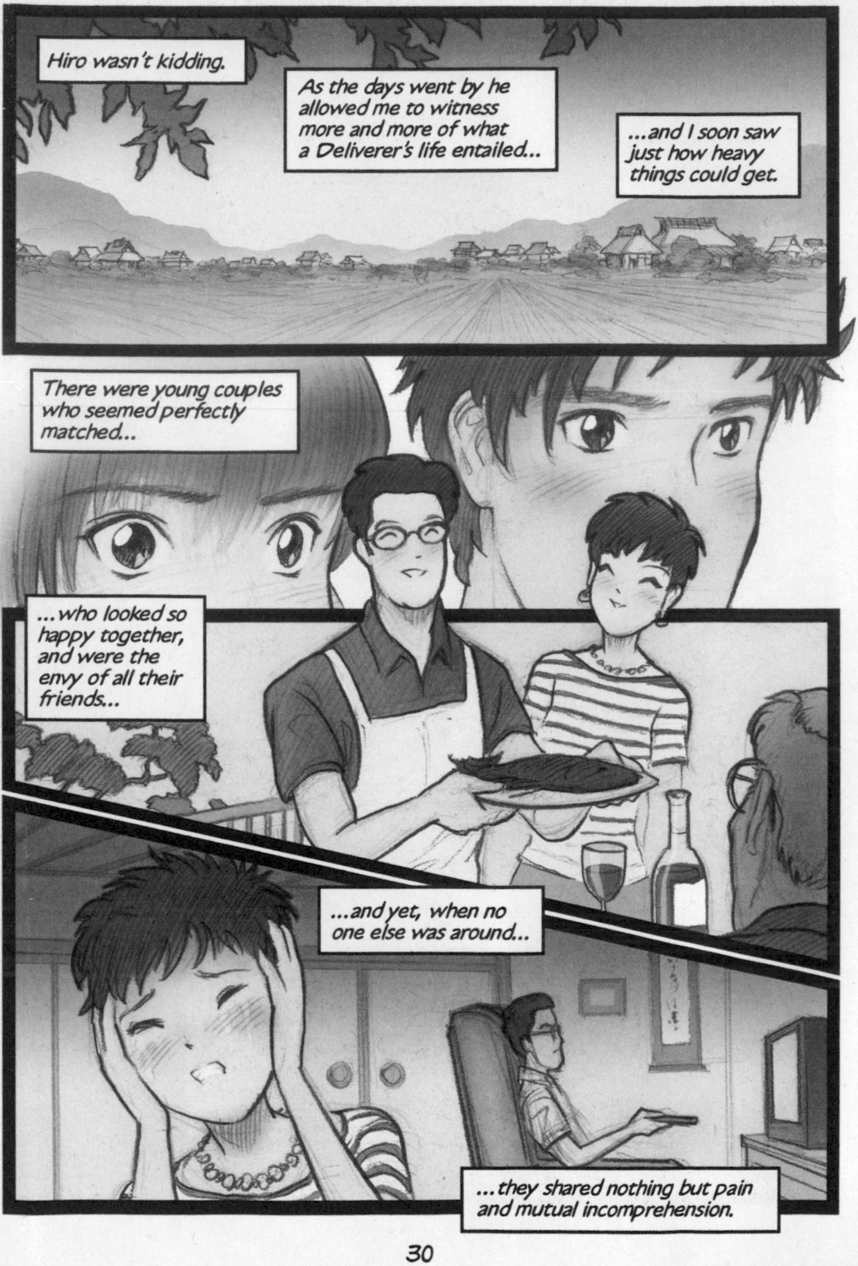
Hiro wasn't kidding.
As the days went by he allowed me to witness more and more of what a Deliverer's life entailed...
...and I soon saw just how heavy things could get.
There were young couples who seemed perfectly matched...
...who looked so happy together, and were the envy of all their friends...
...and yet, when no one else was around...
...they shared nothing but pain and mutual incomprehension.

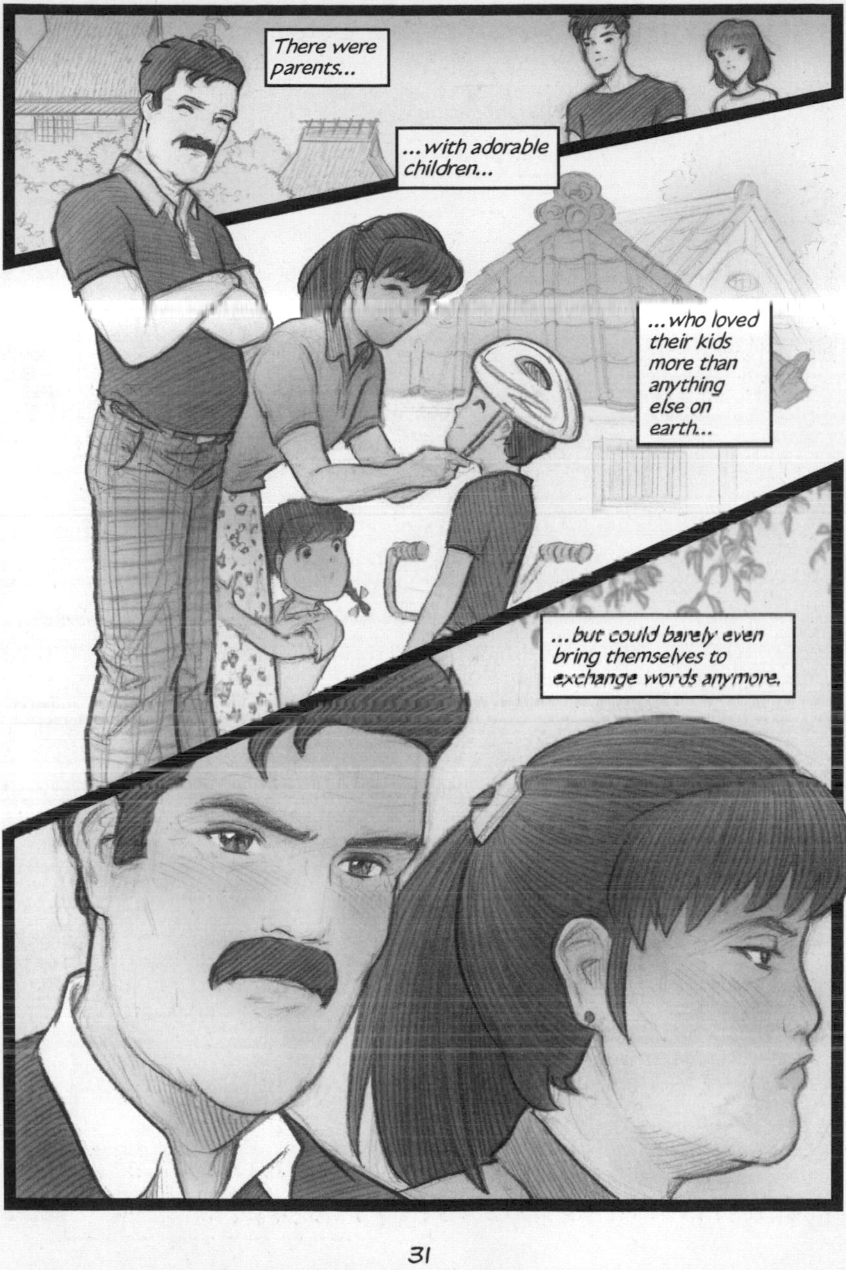

There were parents...
...with adorable children...
...who loved their kids more than anything else on earth...
...but could barely even bring themselves to exchange words anymore.

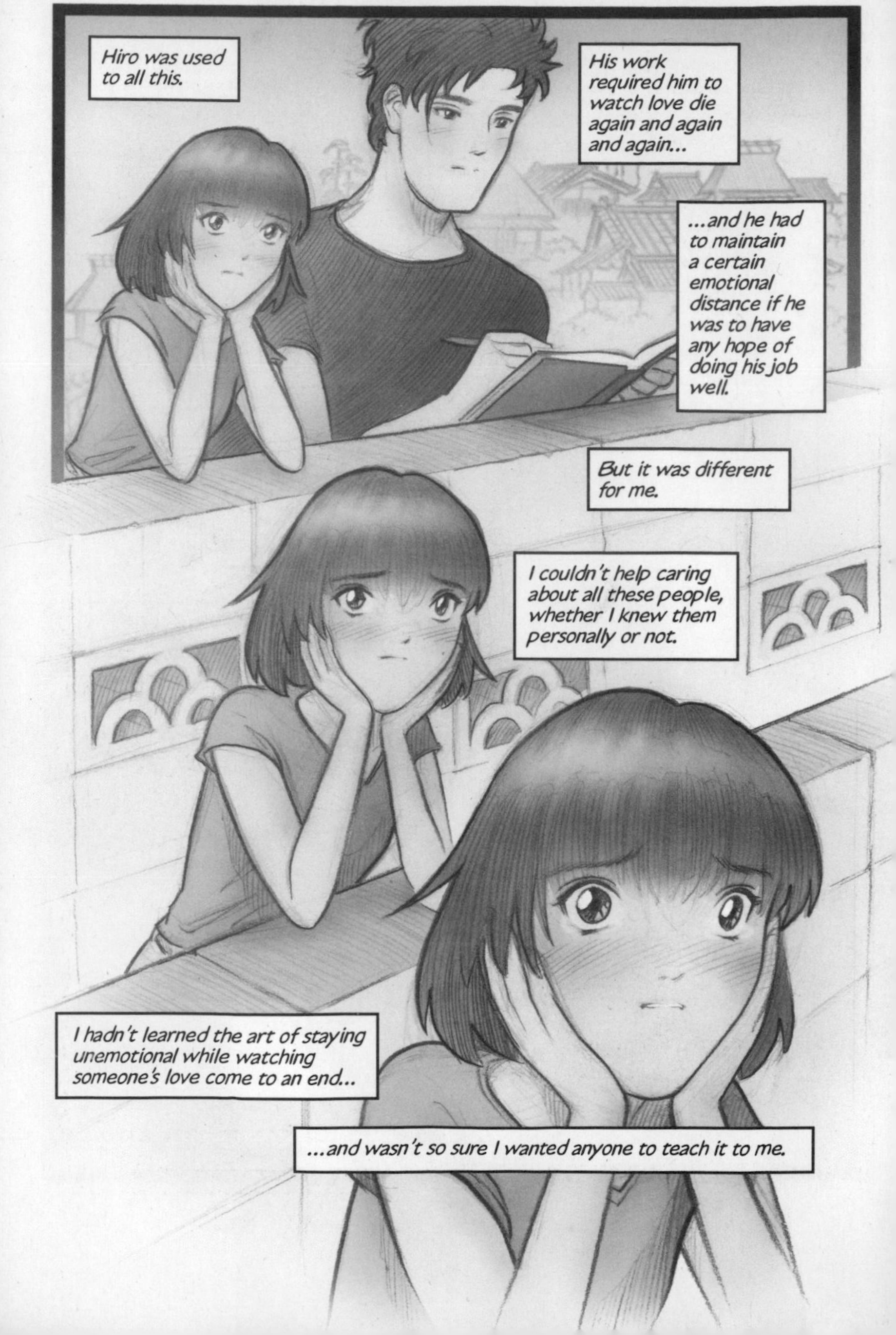
Hiro was used to all this.
His work required him to watch love die again and again and again...
...and he had to maintain a certain emotional distance if he was to have any hope of doing his job well.
But it was different for me.
I couldn't help caring about all these people, whether I knew them personally or not.
I hadn't learned the art of staying unemotional while watching someone's love come to an end...
...and wasn't so sure I wanted anyone to teach it to me.

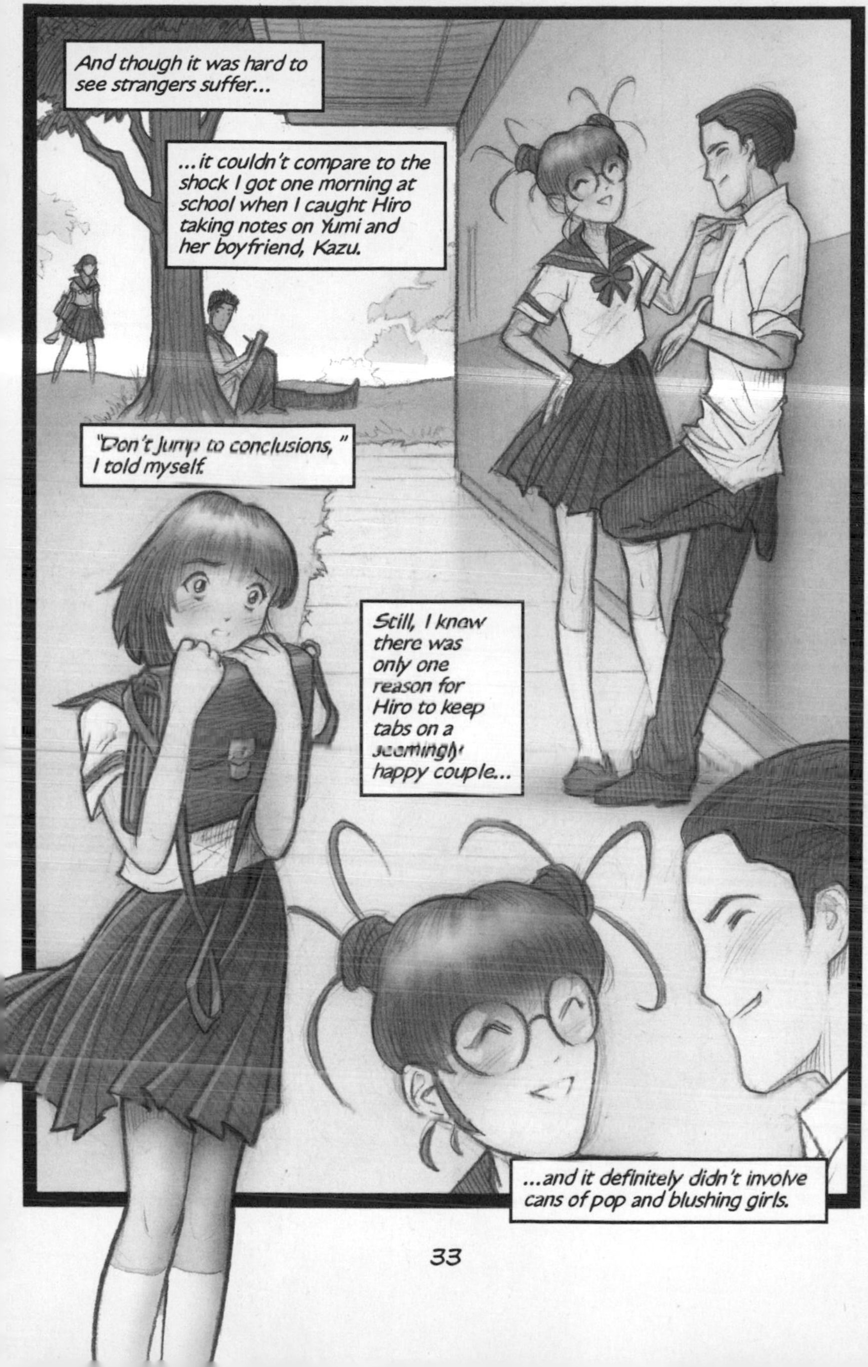
And though it was hard to see strangers suffer...
...it couldn't compare to the shock I got one morning at school when I caught Hiro taking notes on Yumi and her boyfriend, Kazu.
"Don't jump to conclusions," I told myself.
Still, I knew there was only one reason for Hiro to keep tabs on a seemingly happy couple...
...and it definitely didn't involve cans of pop and blushing girls.

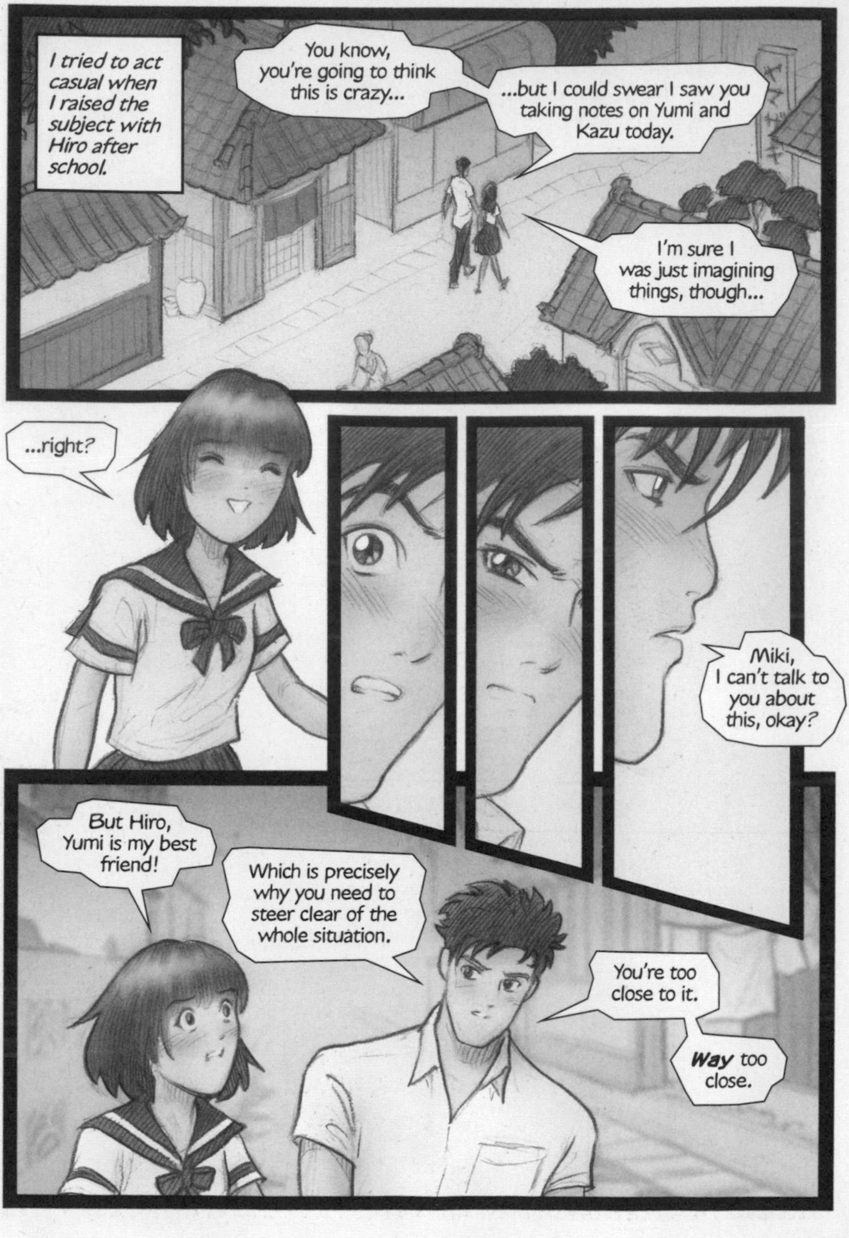
I tried to act casual when I raised the subject with Hiro after school.
You know, you're going to think this is crazy...
...but I could swear I saw you taking notes on Yumi and Kazu today.
I'm sure I was just imagining things, though...
...right?
Miki, I can't talk to you about this, okay?
But Hiro, Yumi is my best friend!
Which is precisely why you need to steer clear of the whole situation.
You're too close to it.
Way too close.

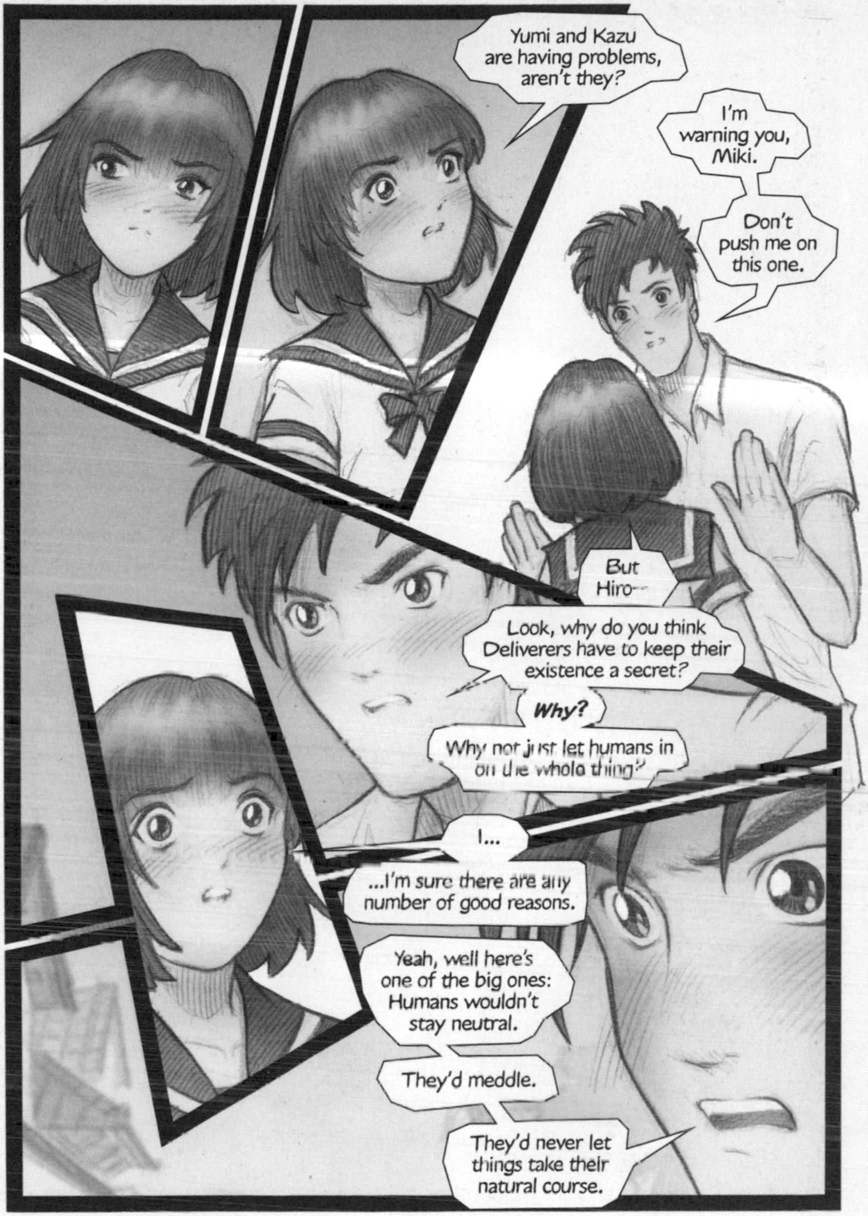
Yumi and Kazu are having problems, aren't they?
I'm warning you, Miki.
Don't push me on this one.
But Hiro--
Look, why do you think Deliverers have to keep their existence a secret?
Why?
Why not just let humans in on the whole thing?
I...
...I'm sure there are any number of good reasons.
Yeah, well here's one of the big ones: Humans wouldn't stay neutral.
They'd meddle.
They'd never let things take their natural course.

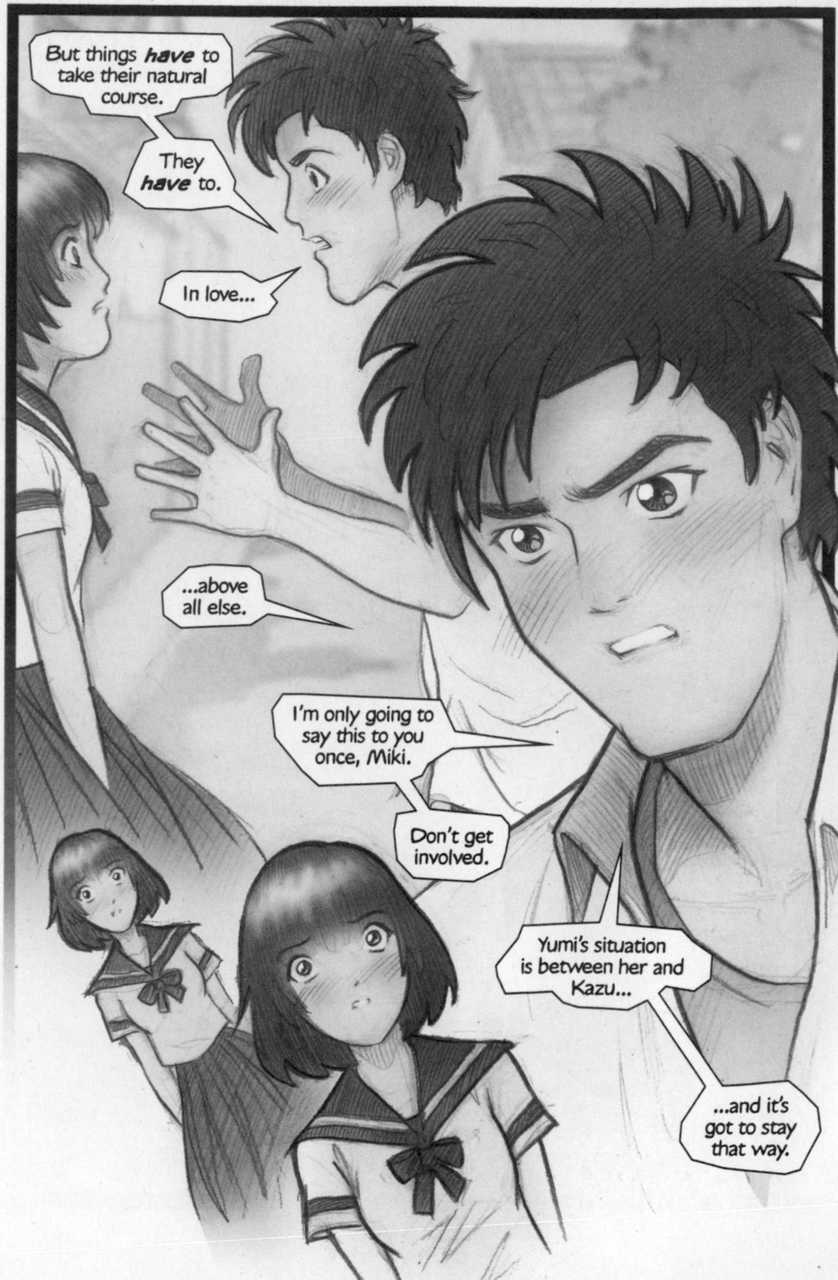
But things **have** to take their natural course.
They **have** to.
In love...
...above all else.
I'm only going to say this to you once, Miki.
Don't get involved.
Yumi's situation is between her and Kazu...
...and it's got to stay that way.

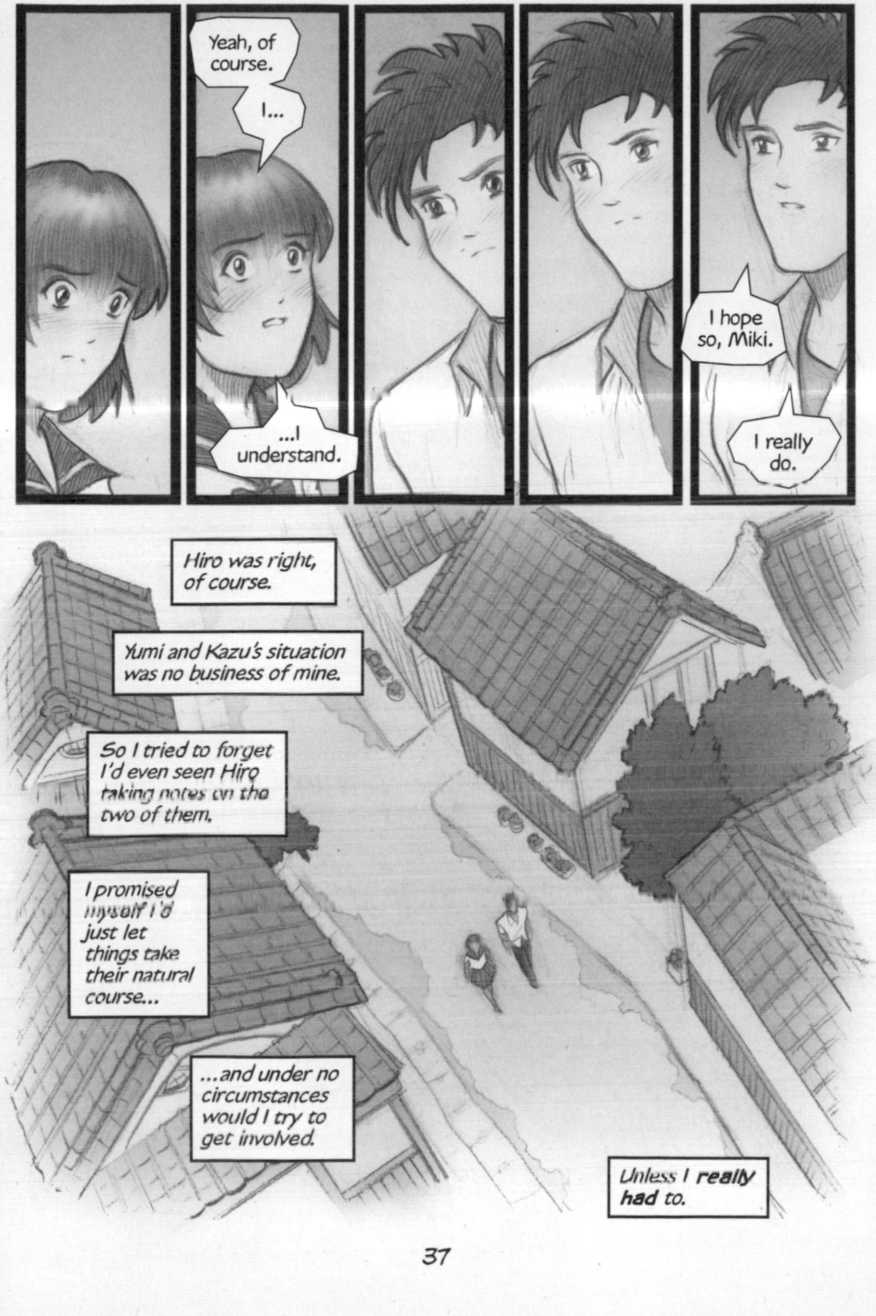
Yeah, of course.
I...
...I understand.
I hope so, Miki.
I really do.
Hiro was right, of course.
Yumi and Kazu's situation was no business of mine.
So I tried to forget I'd even seen Hiro taking notes on the two of them.
I promised myself I'd just let things take their natural course...
...and under no circumstances would I try to get involved.
Unless I ***really had*** to.

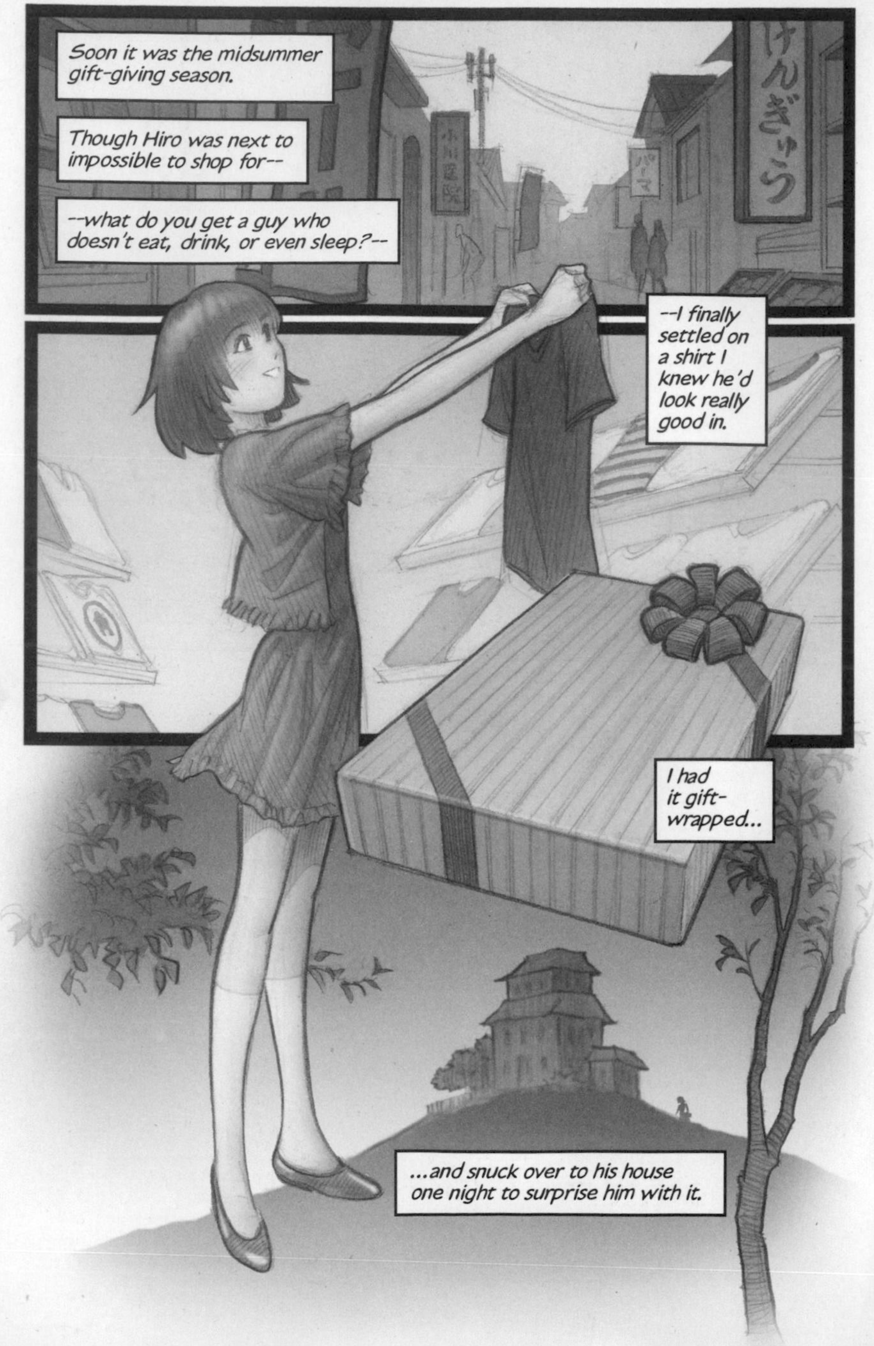
Soon it was the midsummer gift-giving season.
Though Hiro was next to impossible to shop for--
--what do you get a guy who doesn't eat, drink, or even sleep?--
けんぎゅう
パーマ
--I finally settled on a shirt I knew he'd look really good in.
I had it gift-wrapped...
...and snuck over to his house one night to surprise him with it.

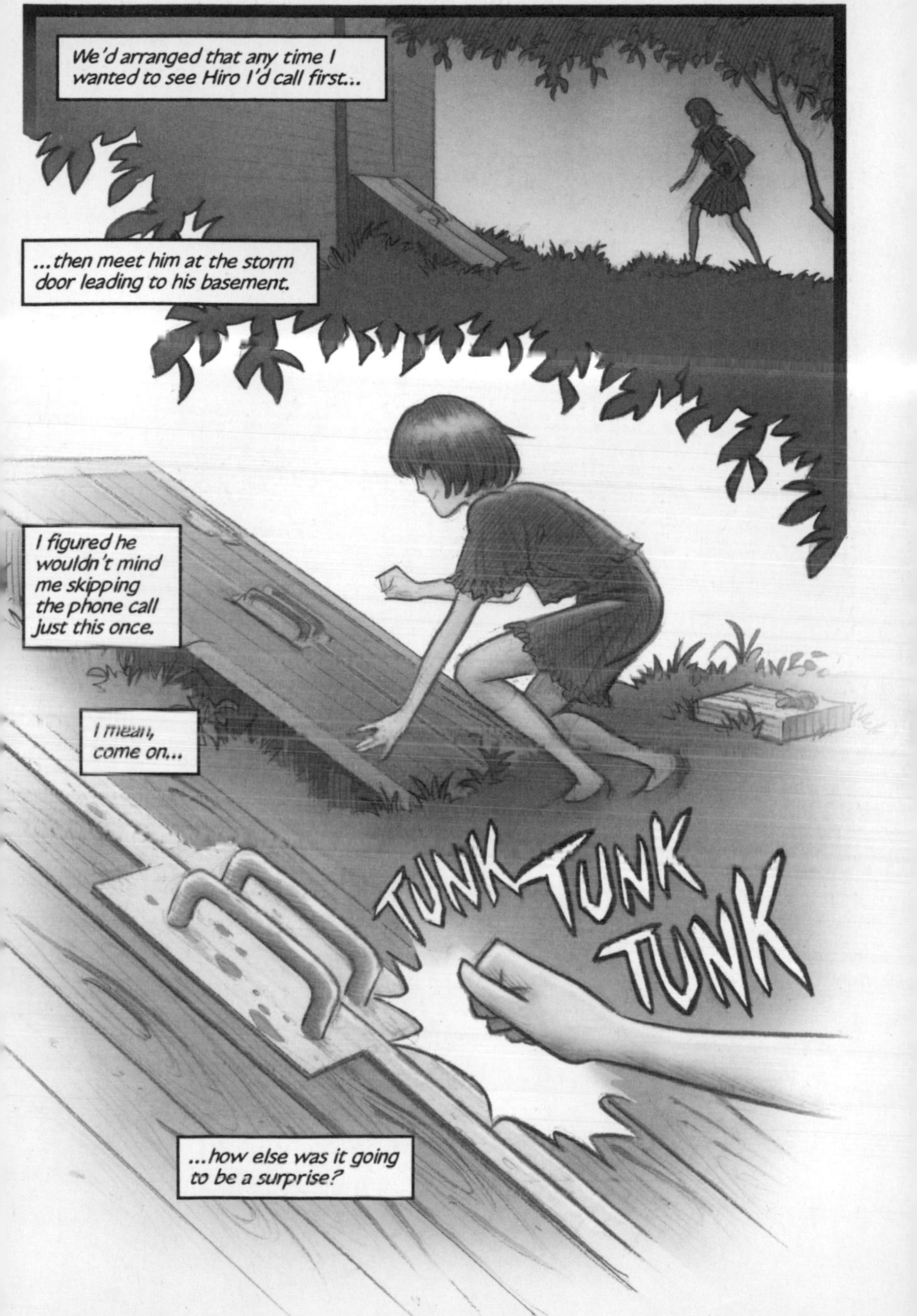
We'd arranged that any time I wanted to see Hiro I'd call first...
...then meet him at the storm door leading to his basement.
I figured he wouldn't mind me skipping the phone call just this once.
I mean, come on...
TUNK TUNK TUNK
...how else was it going to be a surprise?

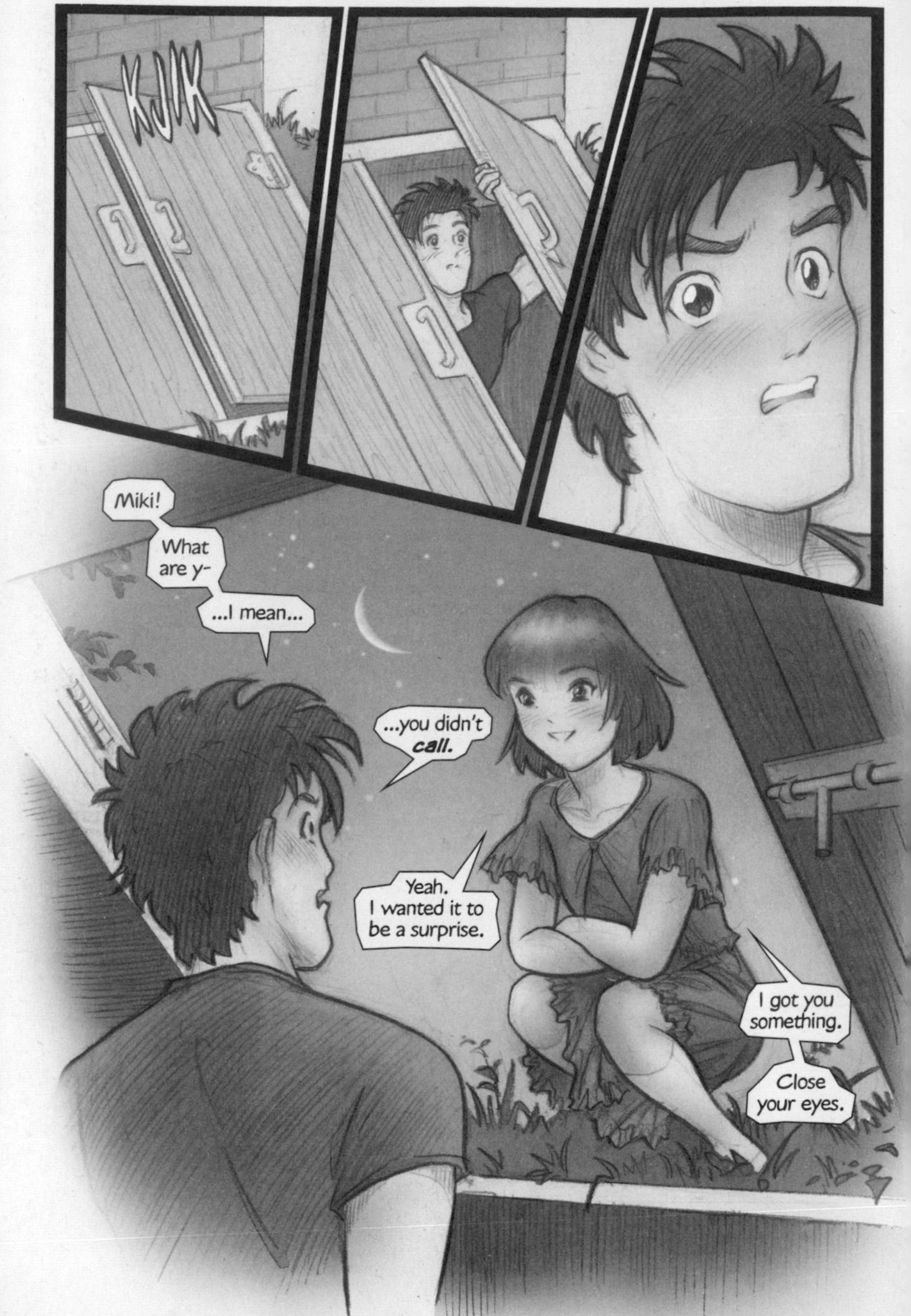
KJIK
Miki!
What are y-
...I mean...
...you didn't *call.*
Yeah. I wanted it to be a surprise.
I got you something.
Close your eyes.

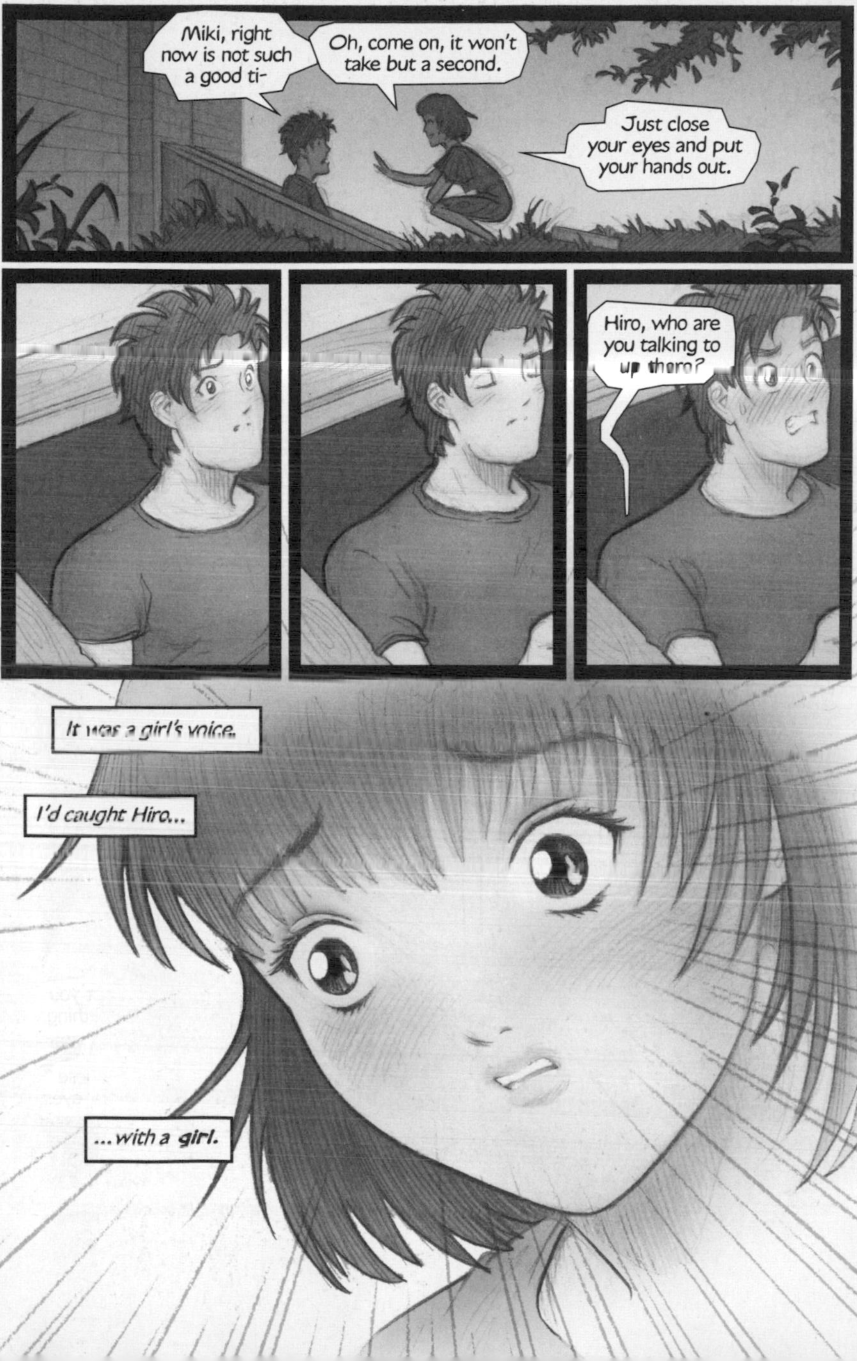
Miki, right now is not such a good ti-
Oh, come on, it won't take but a second.
Just close your eyes and put your hands out.
Hiro, who are you talking to up there?
It was a girl's voice.
I'd caught Hiro...
...with a girl.

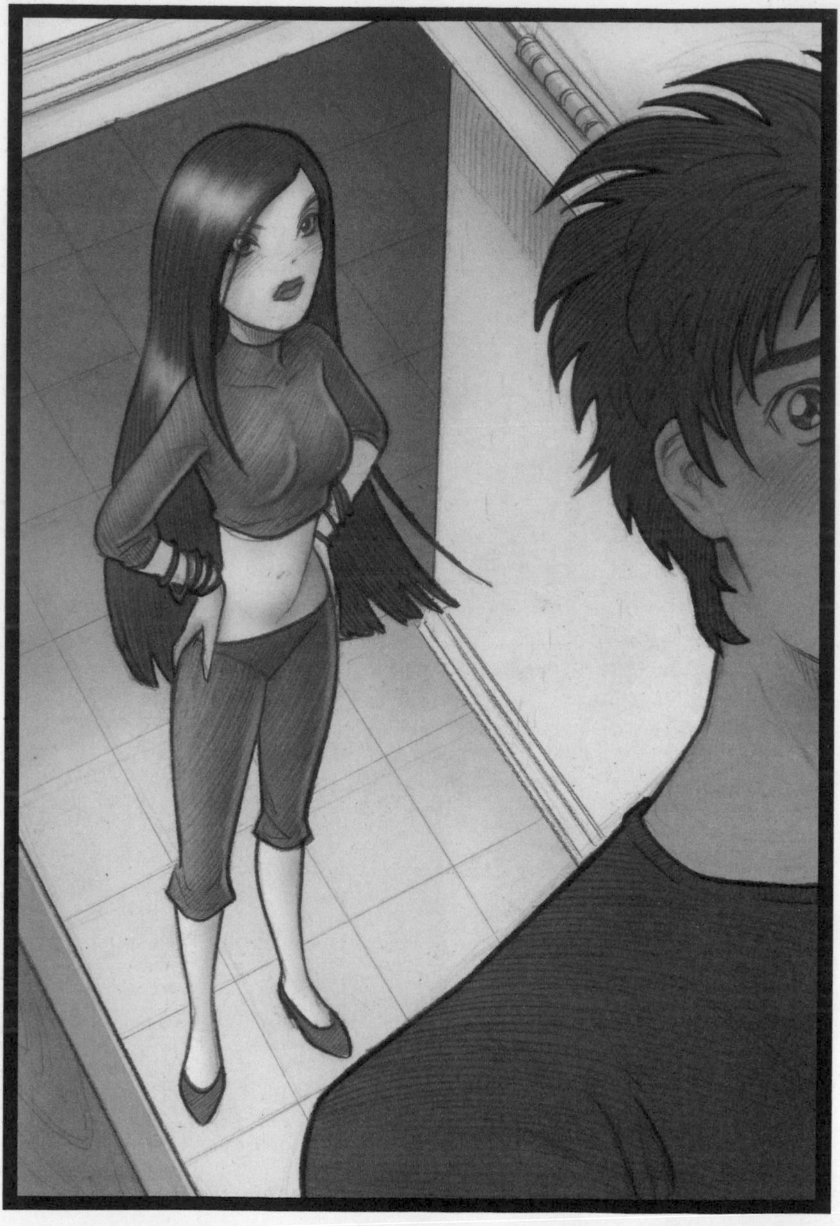

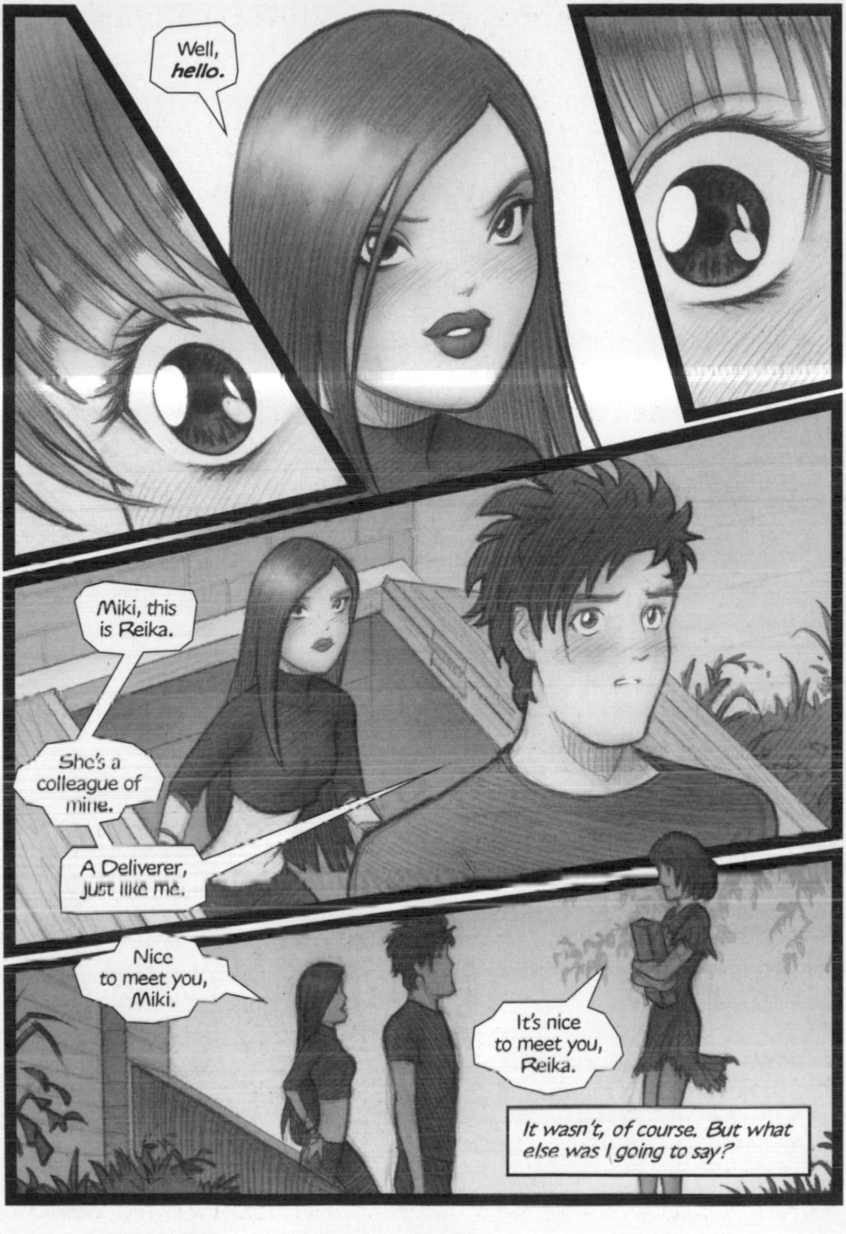

Well, **hello.**
Miki, this is Reika.
She's a colleague of mine.
A Deliverer, just like me.
Nice to meet you, Miki.
It's nice to meet you, Reika.
It wasn't, of course. But what else was I going to say?

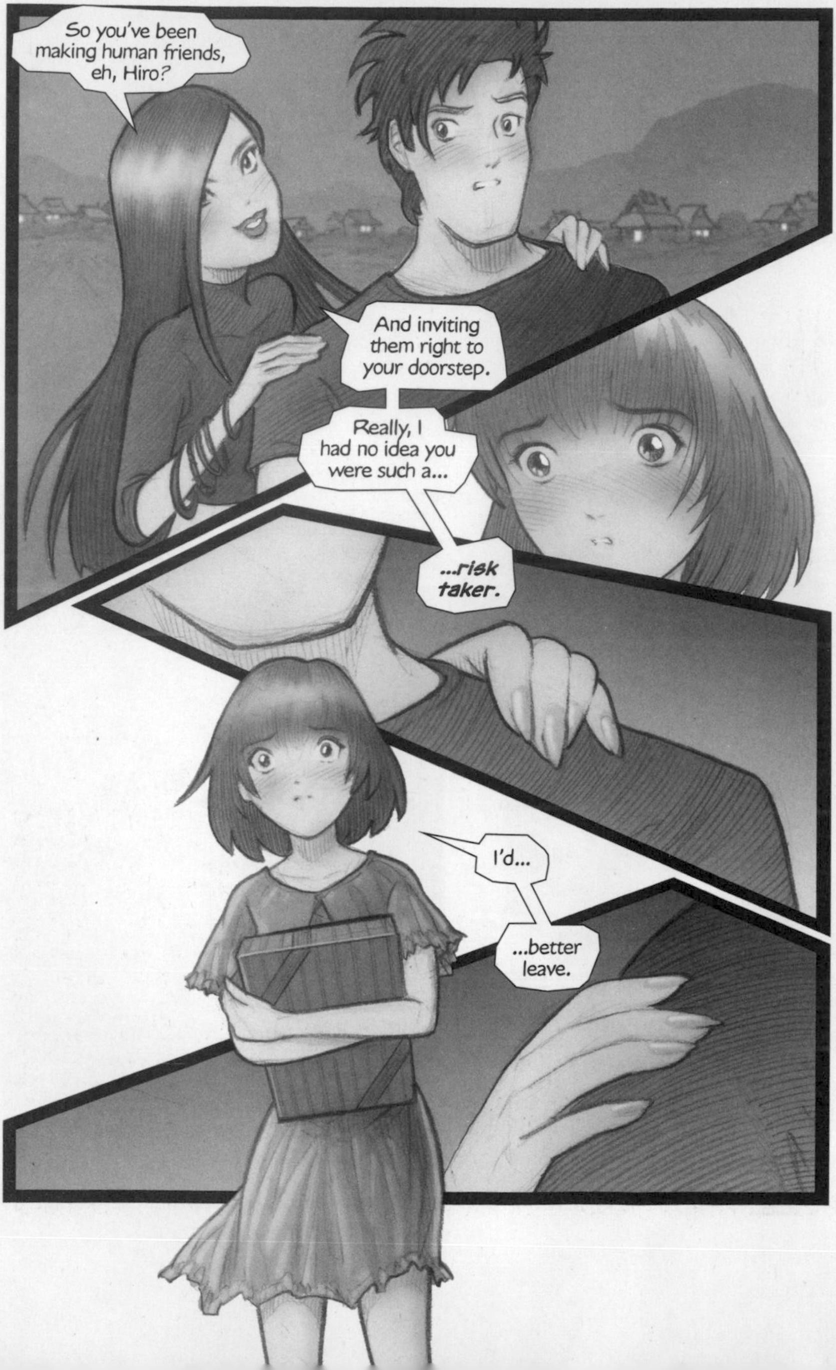
So you've been making human friends, eh, Hiro?
And inviting them right to your doorstep.
Really, I had no idea you were such a...
...risk taker.
I'd...
...better leave.

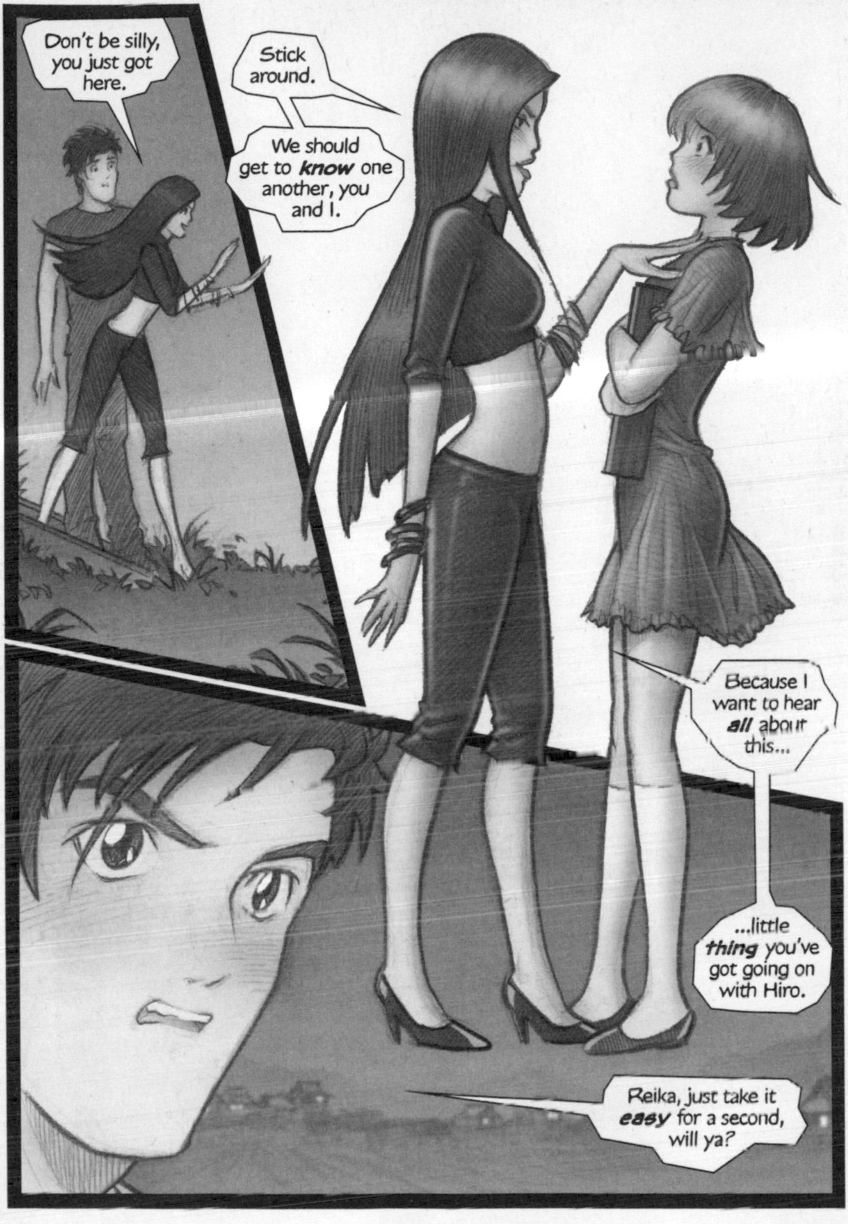

Don't be silly, you just got here.
Stick around.
We should get to **know** one another, you and I.
Because I want to hear **all** about this...
...little **thing** you've got going on with Hiro.
Reika, just take it **easy** for a second, will ya?

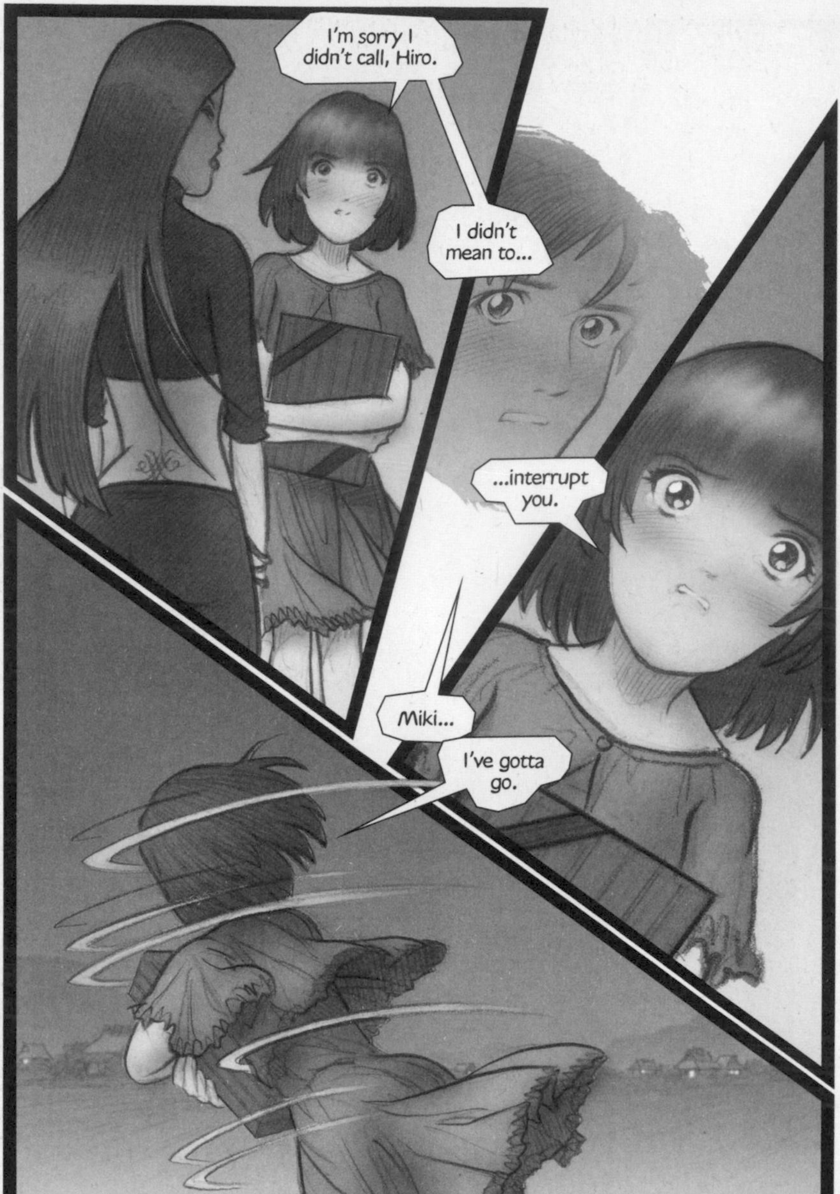
I'm sorry I didn't call, Hiro.
I didn't mean to...
...interrupt you.
Miki...
I've gotta go.

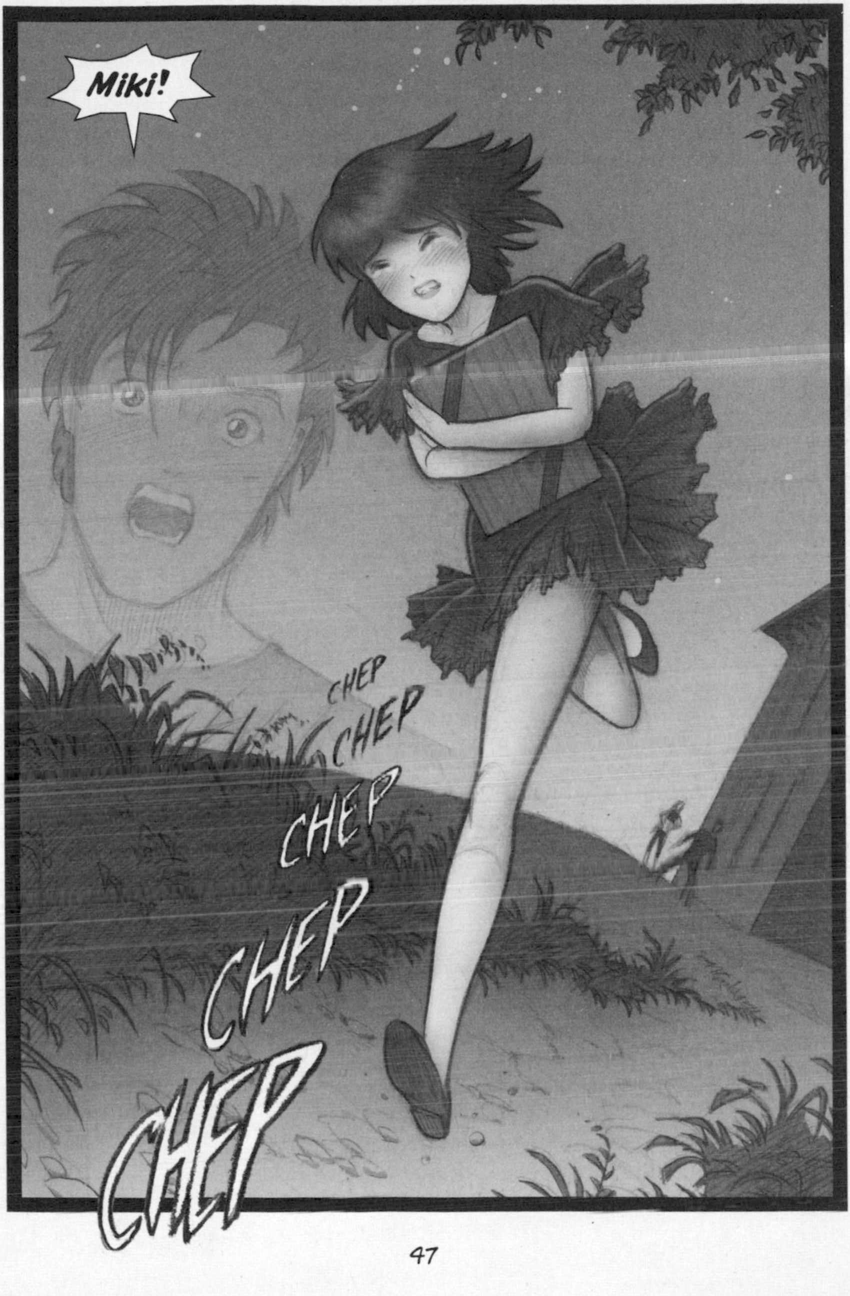
Miki!
CHEP
CHEP
CHEP
CHEP
CHEP

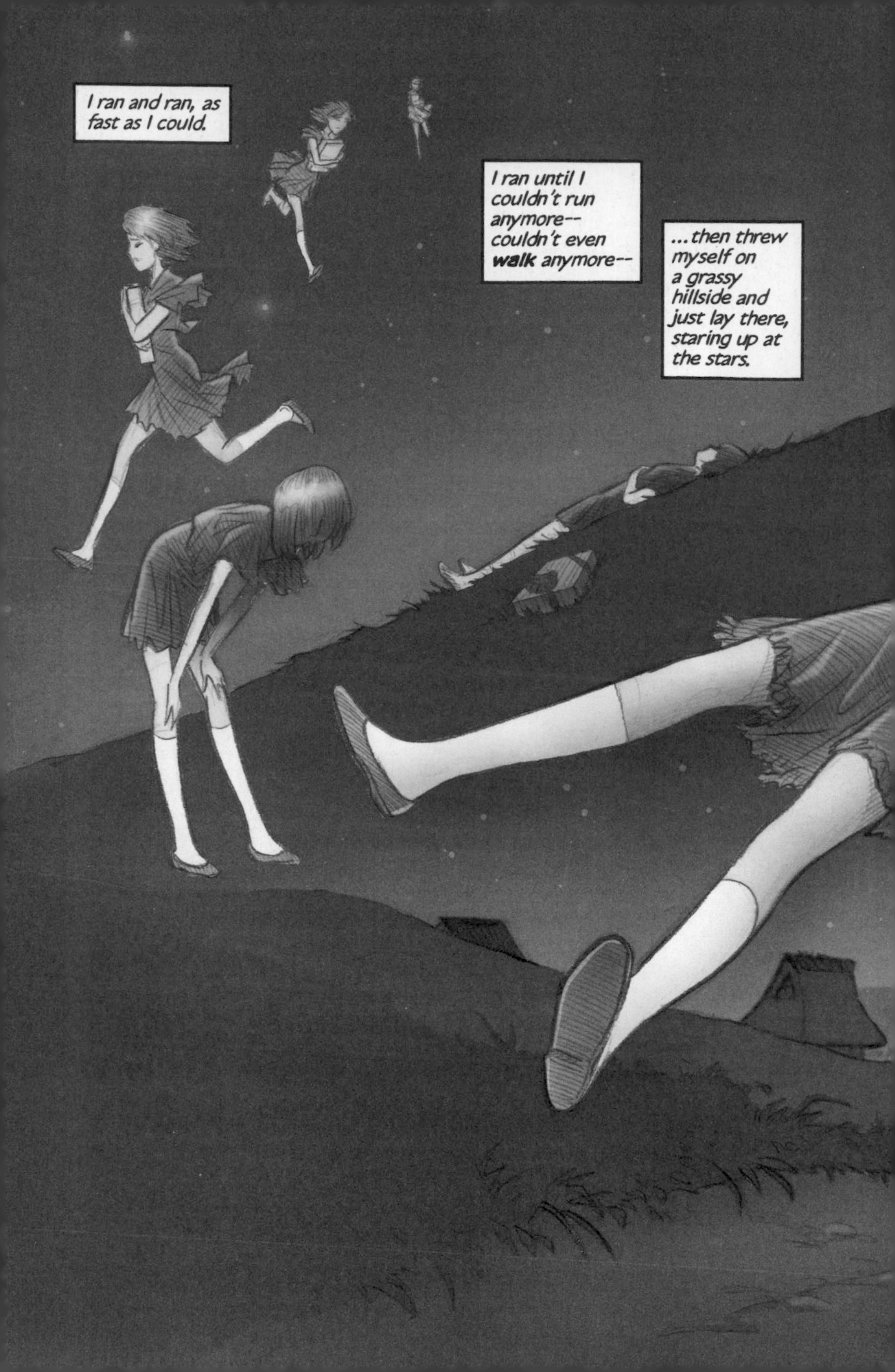
I ran and ran, as fast as I could.
I ran until I couldn't run anymore-- couldn't even **walk** anymore--
...then threw myself on a grassy hillside and just lay there, staring up at the stars.

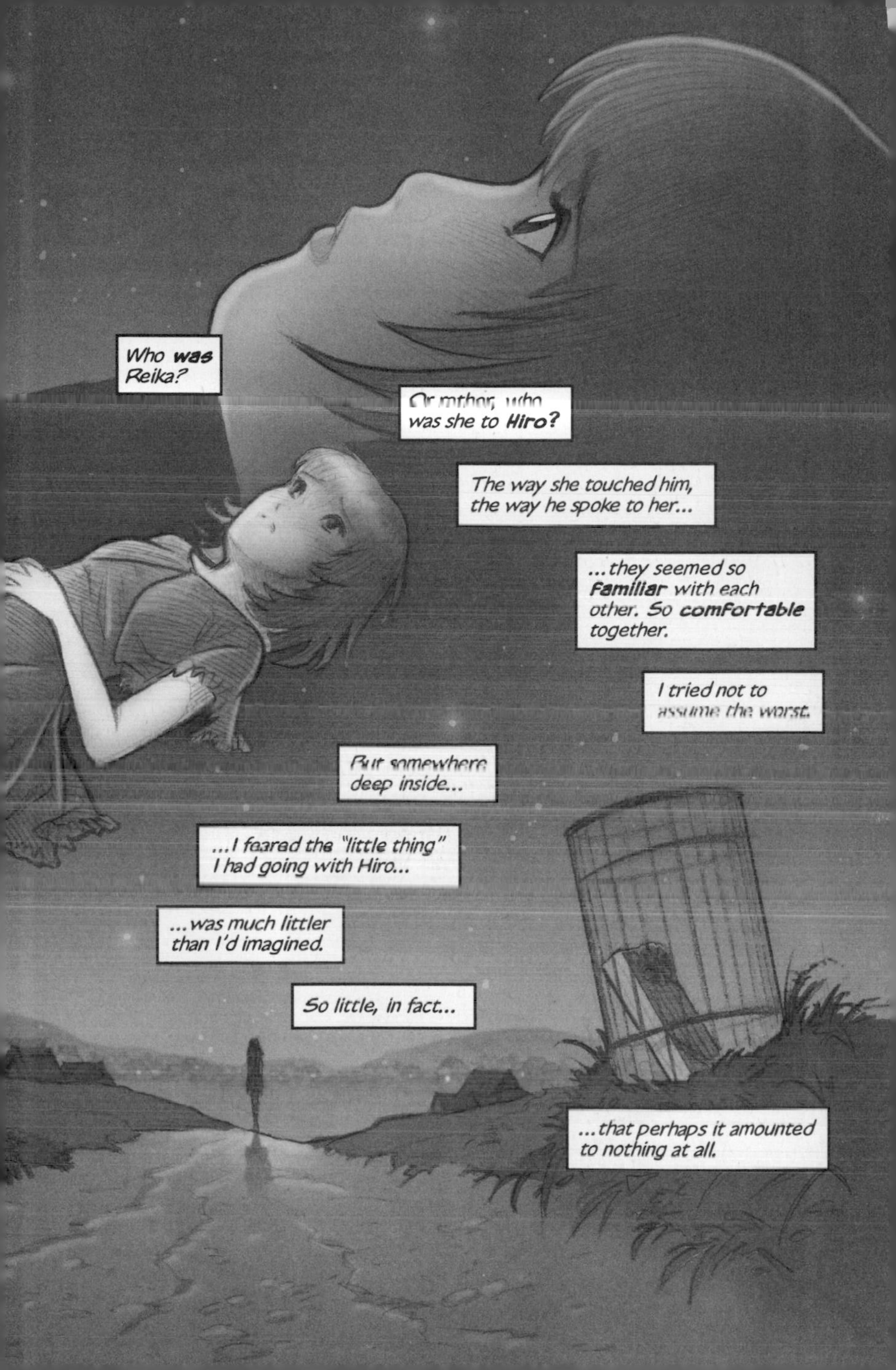
Who was Reika?
Or rather, who was she to Hiro?
The way she touched him, the way he spoke to her...
...they seemed so familiar with each other. So comfortable together.
I tried not to assume the worst.
But somewhere deep inside...
...I feared the "little thing" I had going with Hiro...
...was much littler than I'd imagined.
So little, in fact...
...that perhaps it amounted to nothing at all.

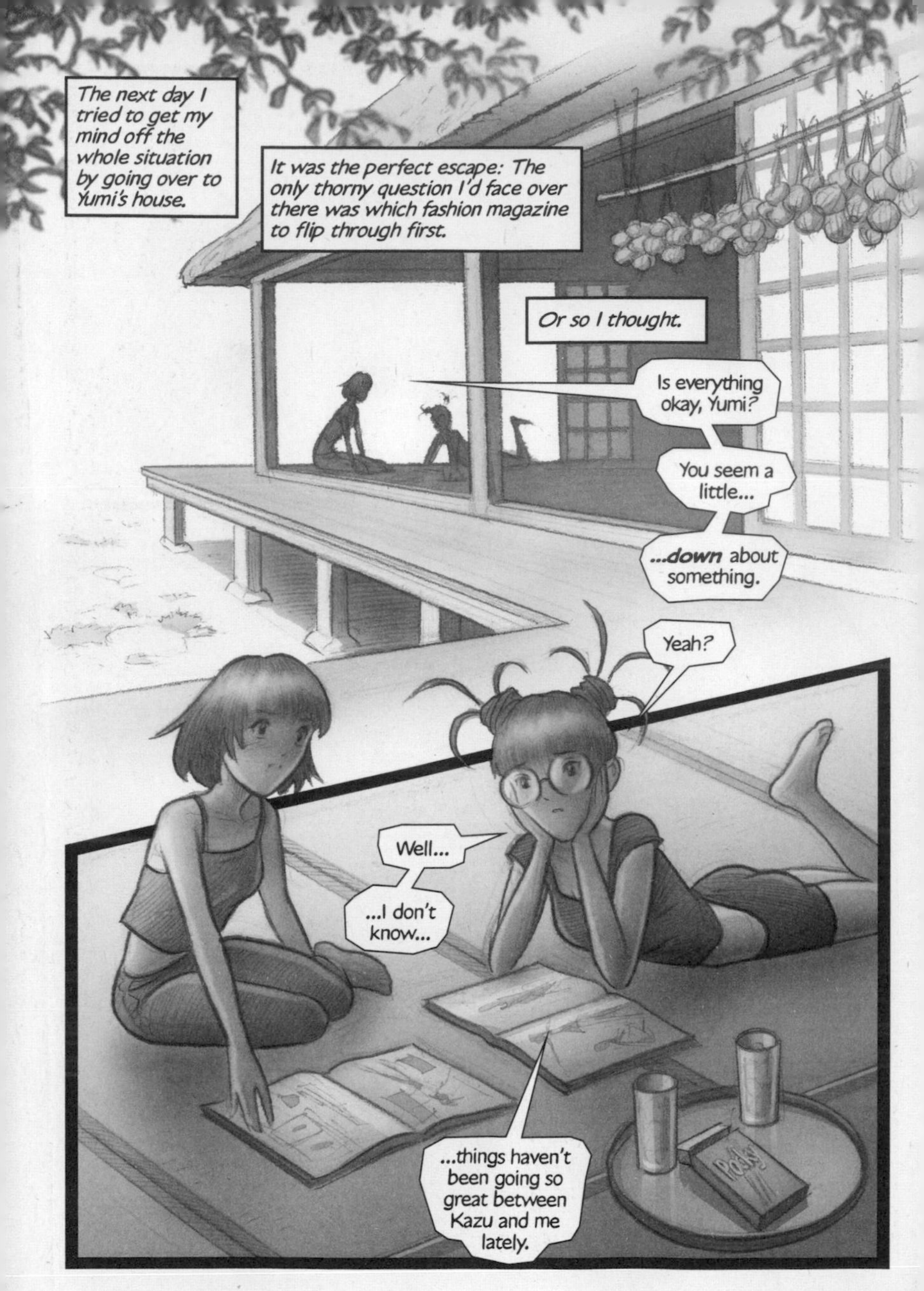
The next day I tried to get my mind off the whole situation by going over to Yumi's house.
It was the perfect escape: The only thorny question I'd face over there was which fashion magazine to flip through first.
Or so I thought.
Is everything okay, Yumi?
You seem a little...
...**down** about something.
Yeah?
Well...
...I don't know...
...things haven't been going so great between Kazu and me lately.
Pocky

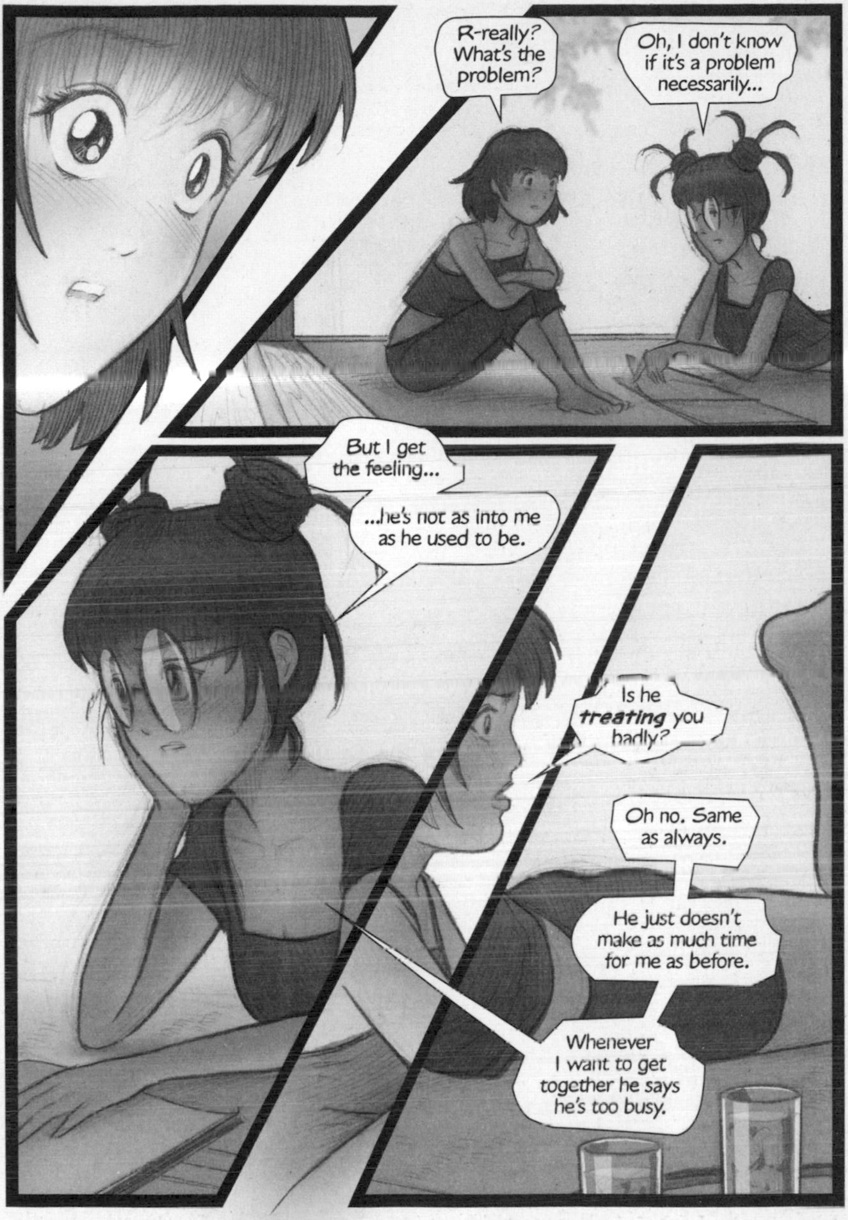
R-really? What's the problem?
Oh, I don't know if it's a problem necessarily...
But I get the feeling...
...he's not as into me as he used to be.
Is he ***treating*** you badly?
Oh no. Same as always.
He just doesn't make as much time for me as before.
Whenever I want to get together he says he's too busy.

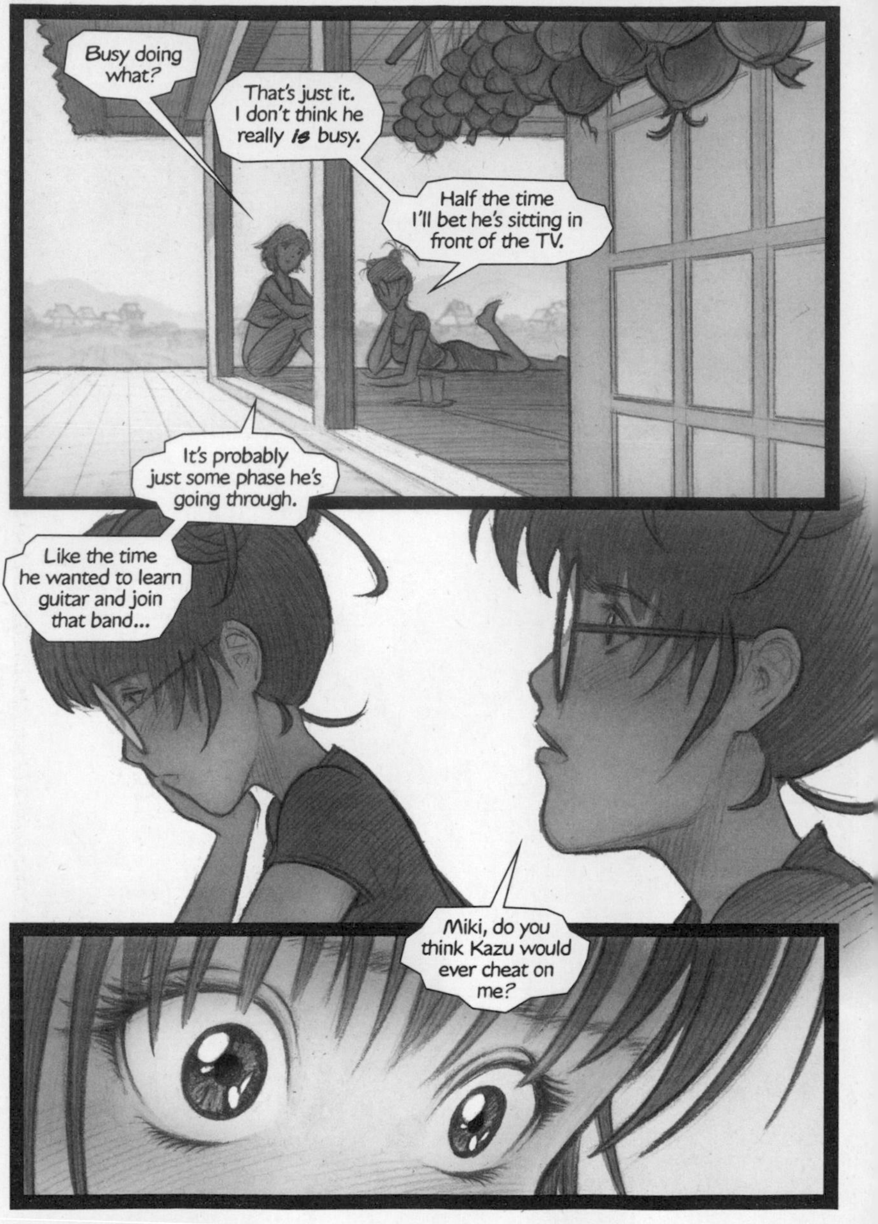
Busy doing what?
That's just it. I don't think he really is busy.
Half the time I'll bet he's sitting in front of the TV.
It's probably just some phase he's going through.
Like the time he wanted to learn guitar and join that band...
Miki, do you think Kazu would ever cheat on me?

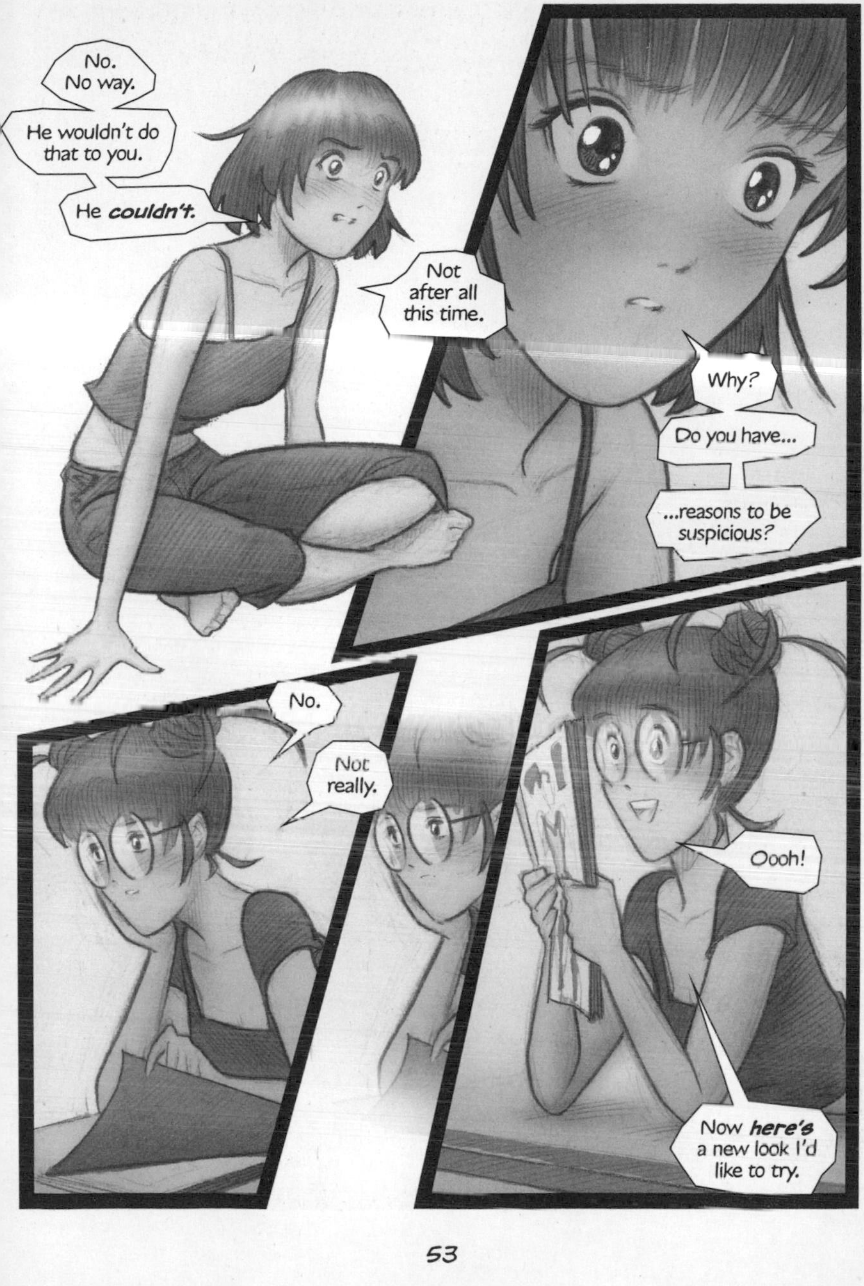

No. No way.
He wouldn't do that to you.
He **couldn't.**
Not after all this time.
Why?
Do you have...
...reasons to be suspicious?
No.
Not really.
Oooh!
Now **here's** a new look I'd like to try.

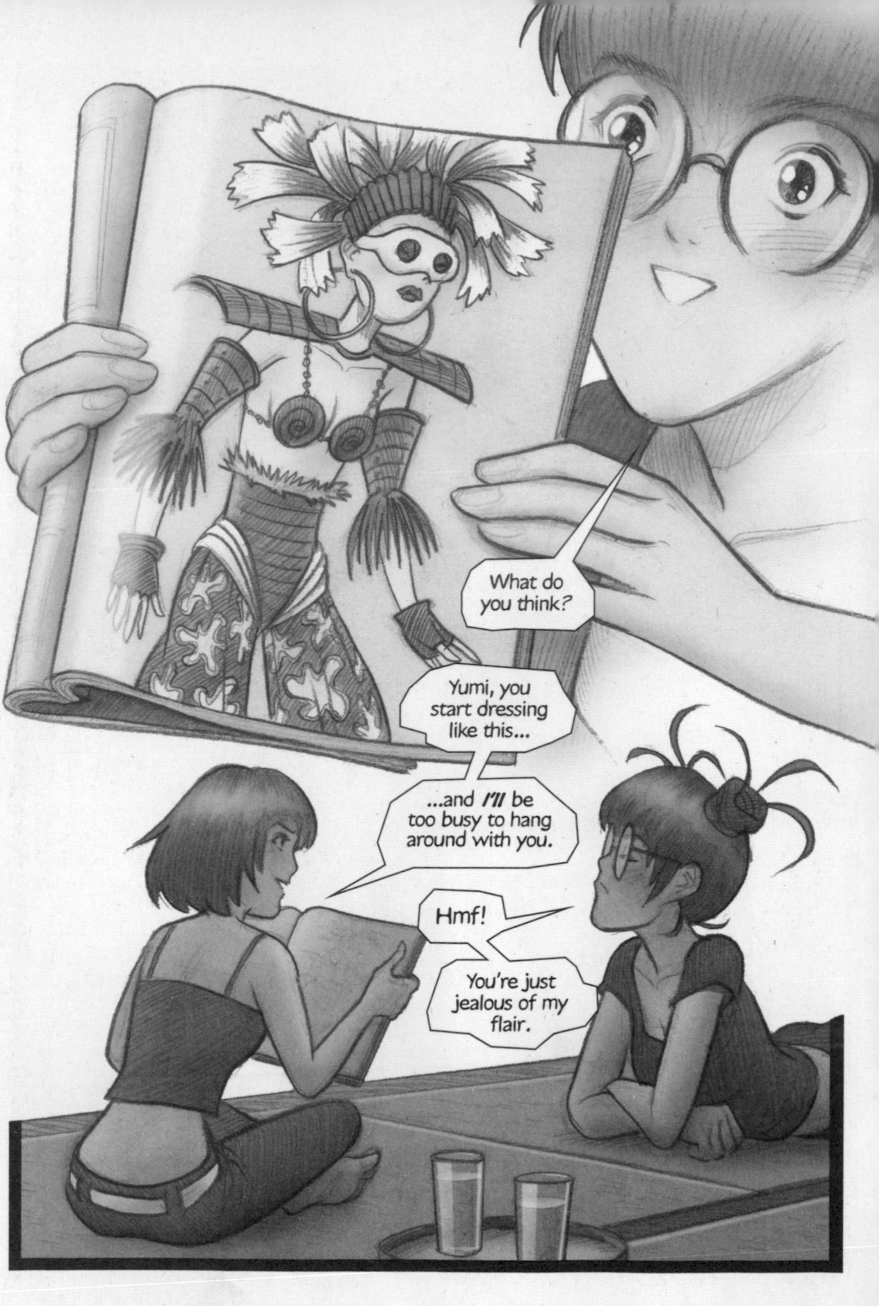
What do you think?
Yumi, you start dressing like this...
...and *I'll* be too busy to hang around with you.
Hmf!
You're just jealous of my flair.

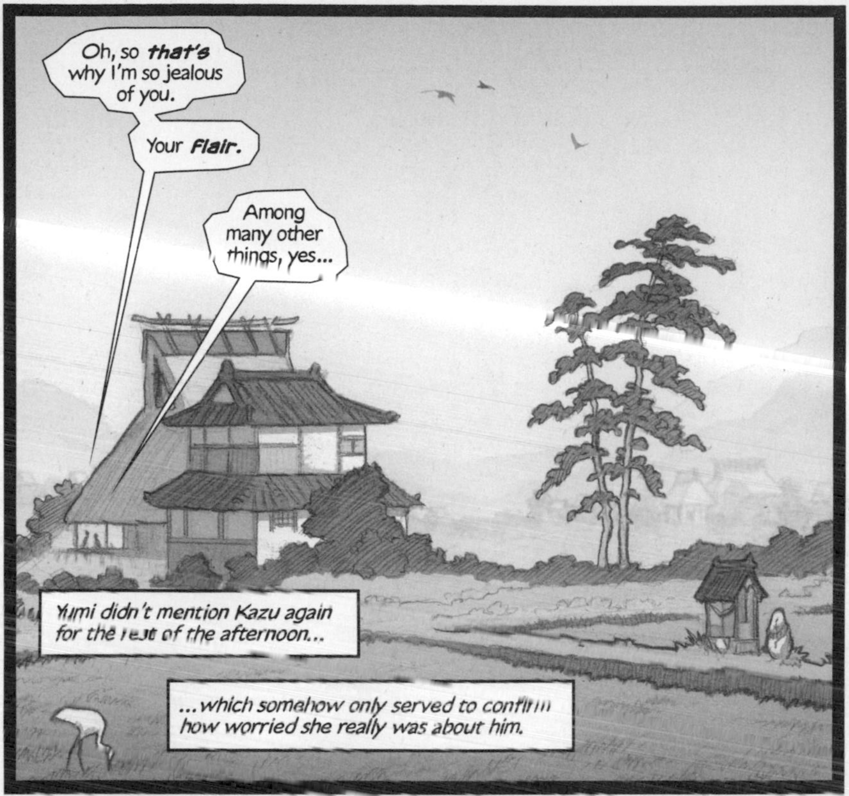
Oh, so that's why I'm so jealous of you.
Your flair.
Among many other things, yes...
Yumi didn't mention Kazu again for the rest of the afternoon...
...which somehow only served to confirm how worried she really was about him.

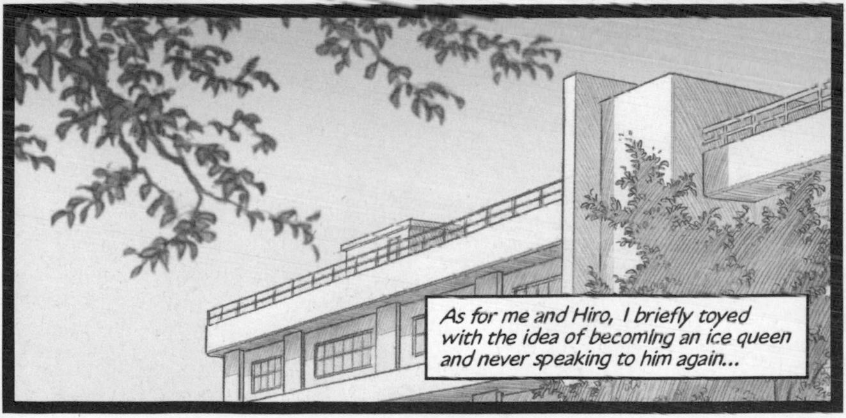
As for me and Hiro, I briefly toyed with the idea of becoming an ice queen and never speaking to him again...

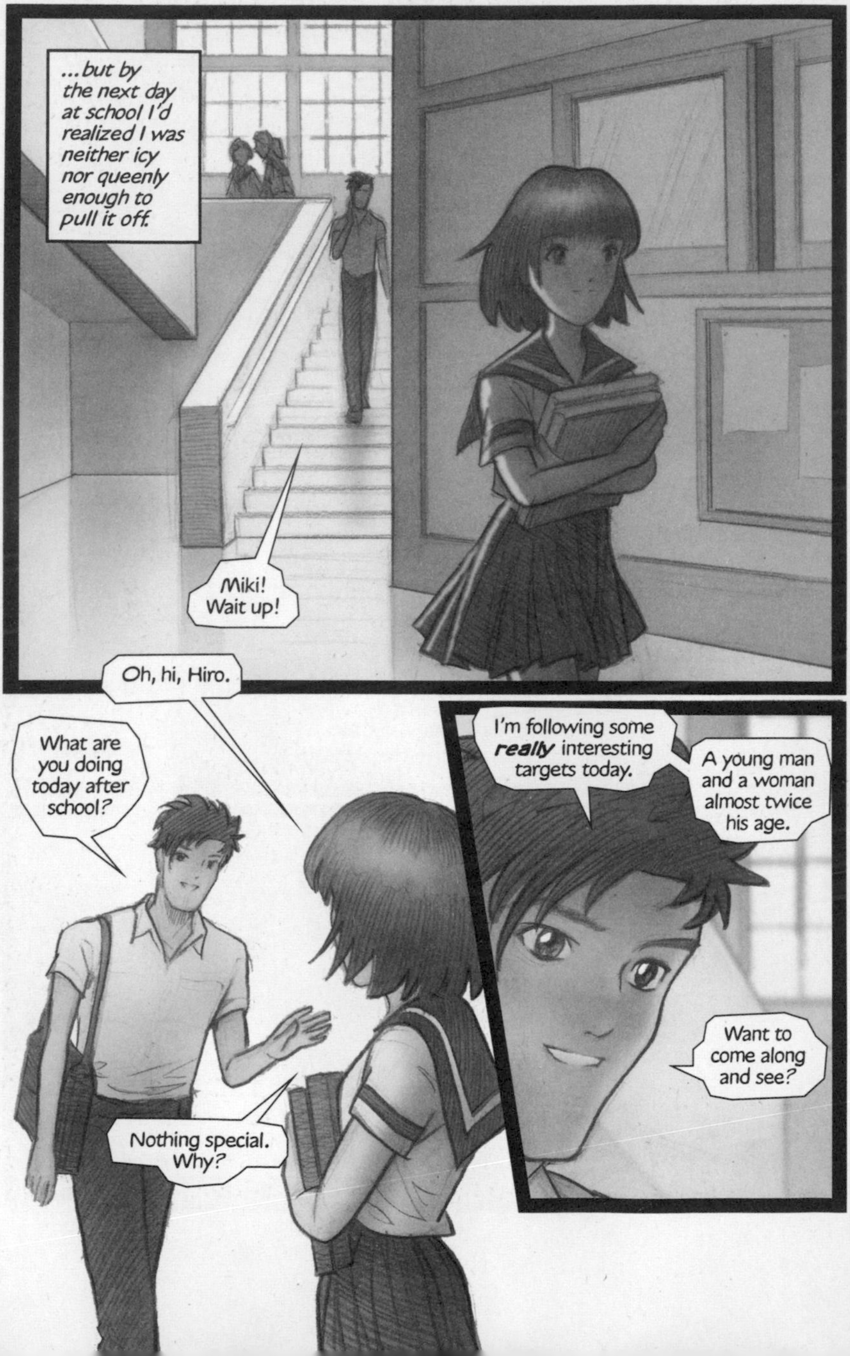
...but by the next day at school I'd realized I was neither icy nor queenly enough to pull it off.
Miki! Wait up!
Oh, hi, Hiro.
What are you doing today after school?
Nothing special. Why?
I'm following some **really** interesting targets today.
A young man and a woman almost twice his age.
Want to come along and see?

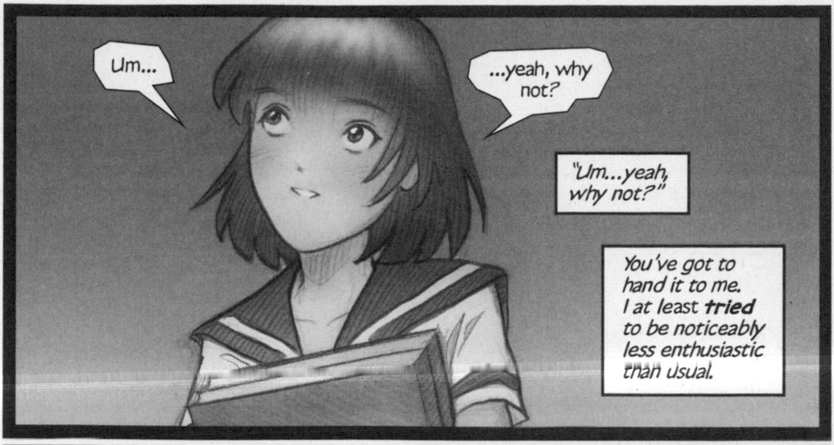

Um...
...yeah, why not?
"Um...yeah, why not?"
You've got to hand it to me. I at least **tried** to be noticeably less enthusiastic than usual.

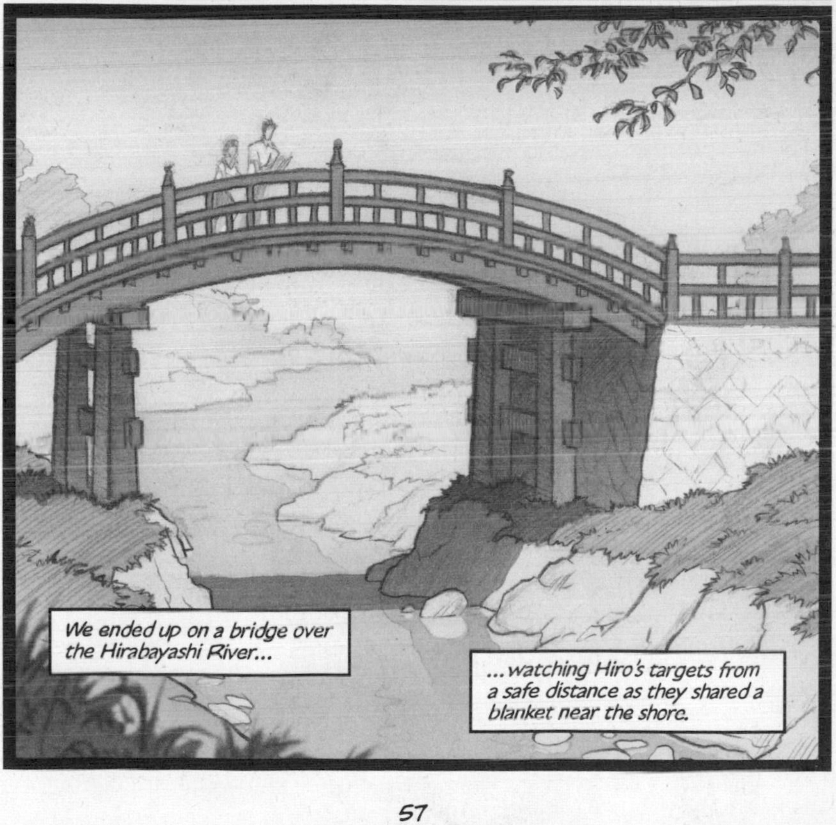

We ended up on a bridge over the Hirabayashi River...
...watching Hiro's targets from a safe distance as they shared a blanket near the shore.

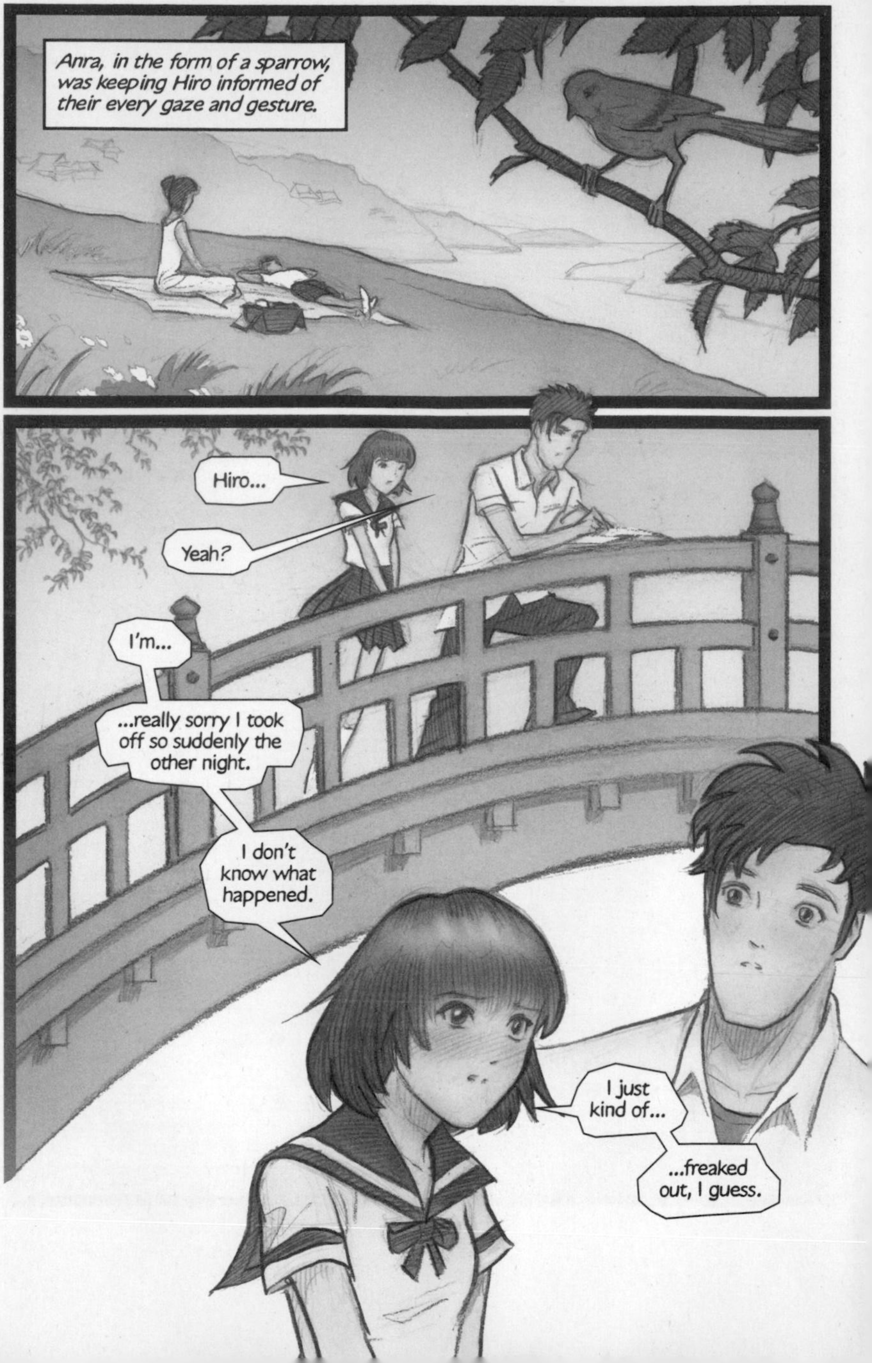
Anra, in the form of a sparrow, was keeping Hiro informed of their every gaze and gesture.
Hiro...
Yeah?
I'm...
...really sorry I took off so suddenly the other night.
I don't know what happened.
I just kind of...
...freaked out, I guess.

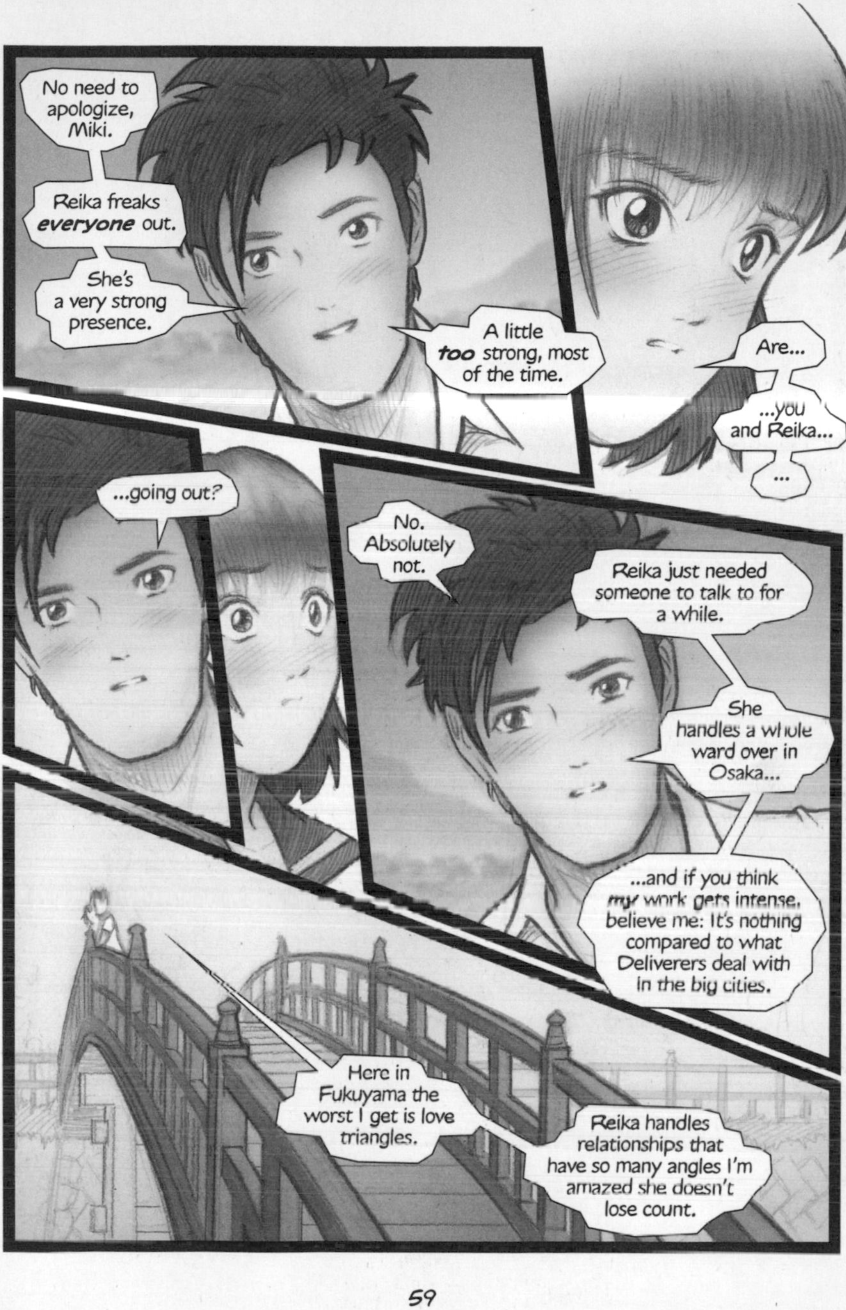
No need to apologize, Miki.
Reika freaks **everyone** out.
She's a very strong presence.
A little **too** strong, most of the time.
Are...
...you and Reika...
...
...going out?
No. Absolutely not.
Reika just needed someone to talk to for a while.
She handles a whole ward over in Osaka...
...and if you think *my* work gets intense, believe me: It's nothing compared to what Deliverers deal with in the big cities.
Here in Fukuyama the worst I get is love triangles.
Reika handles relationships that have so many angles I'm amazed she doesn't lose count.

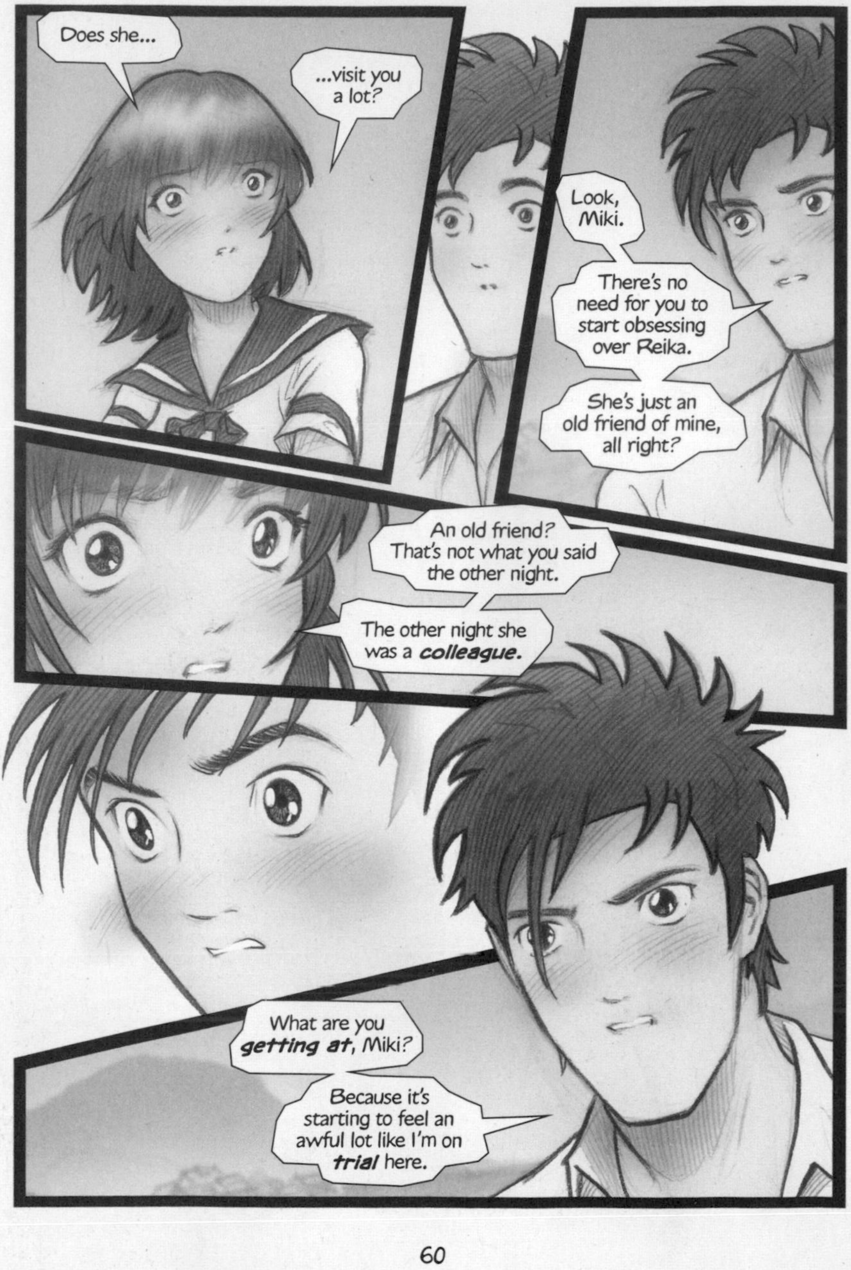
Does she...
...visit you a lot?
Look, Miki.
There's no need for you to start obsessing over Reika.
She's just an old friend of mine, all right?
An old friend? That's not what you said the other night.
The other night she was a **colleague.**
What are you **getting at**, Miki?
Because it's starting to feel an awful lot like I'm on **trial** here.

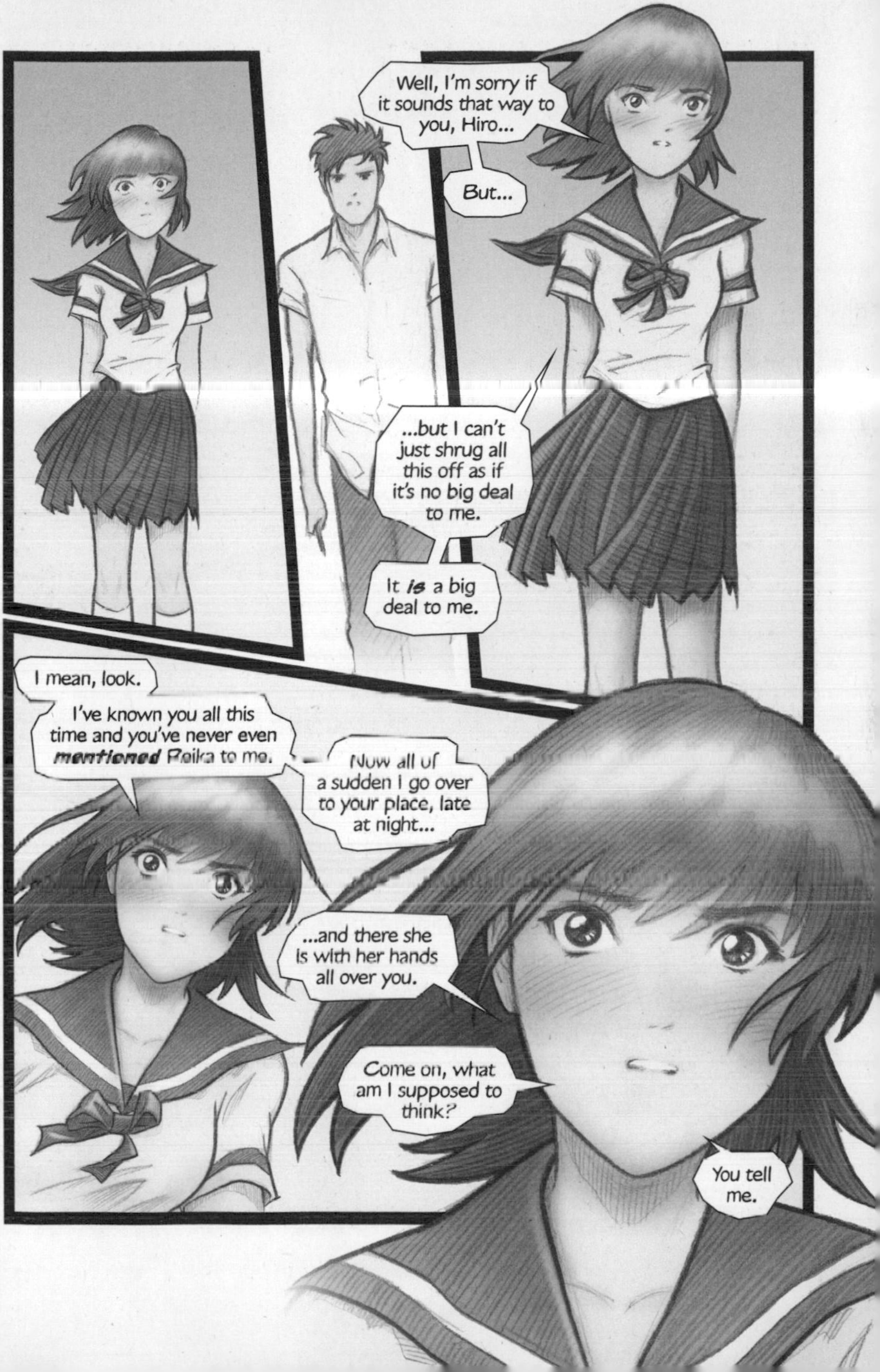

Well, I'm sorry if it sounds that way to you, Hiro...
But...
...but I can't just shrug all this off as if it's no big deal to me.
It *is* a big deal to me.
I mean, look.
I've known you all this time and you've never even *mentioned* Reika to me.
Now all of a sudden I go over to your place, late at night...
...and there she is with her hands all over you.
Come on, what am I supposed to think?
You tell me.

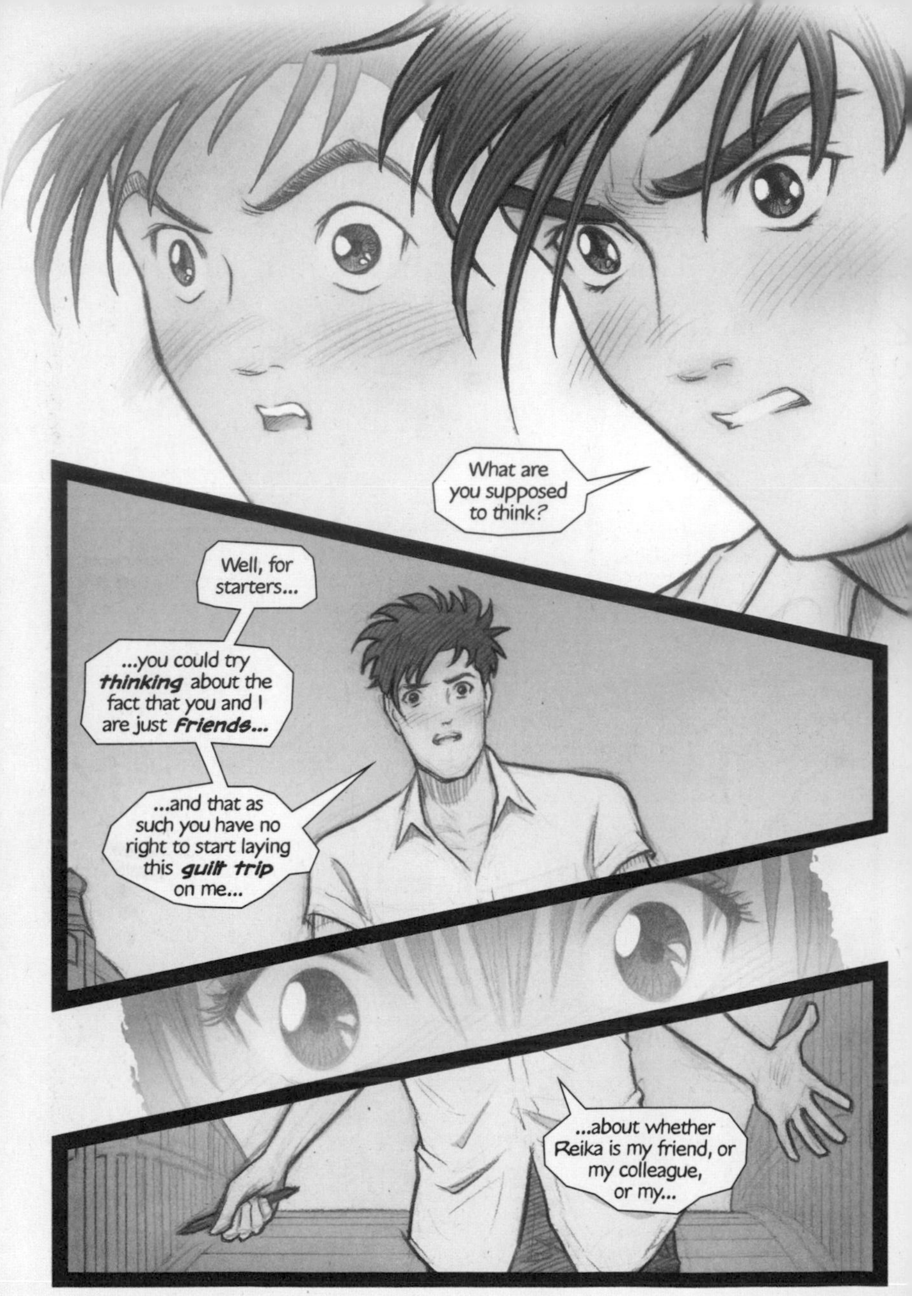
What are you supposed to think?
Well, for starters...
...you could try **thinking** about the fact that you and I are just **friends...**
...and that as such you have no right to start laying this **guilt trip** on me...
...about whether Reika is my friend, or my colleague, or my...

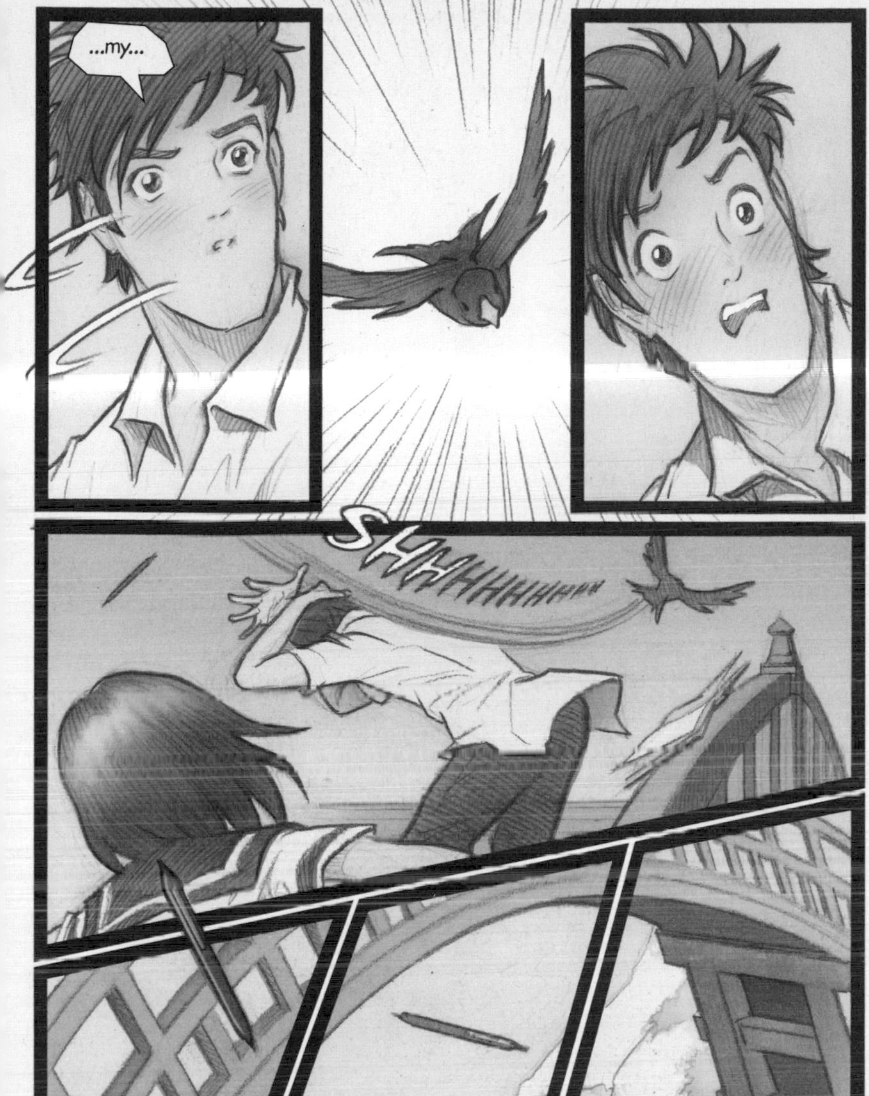
...my...
SHHHHHHHHHHH

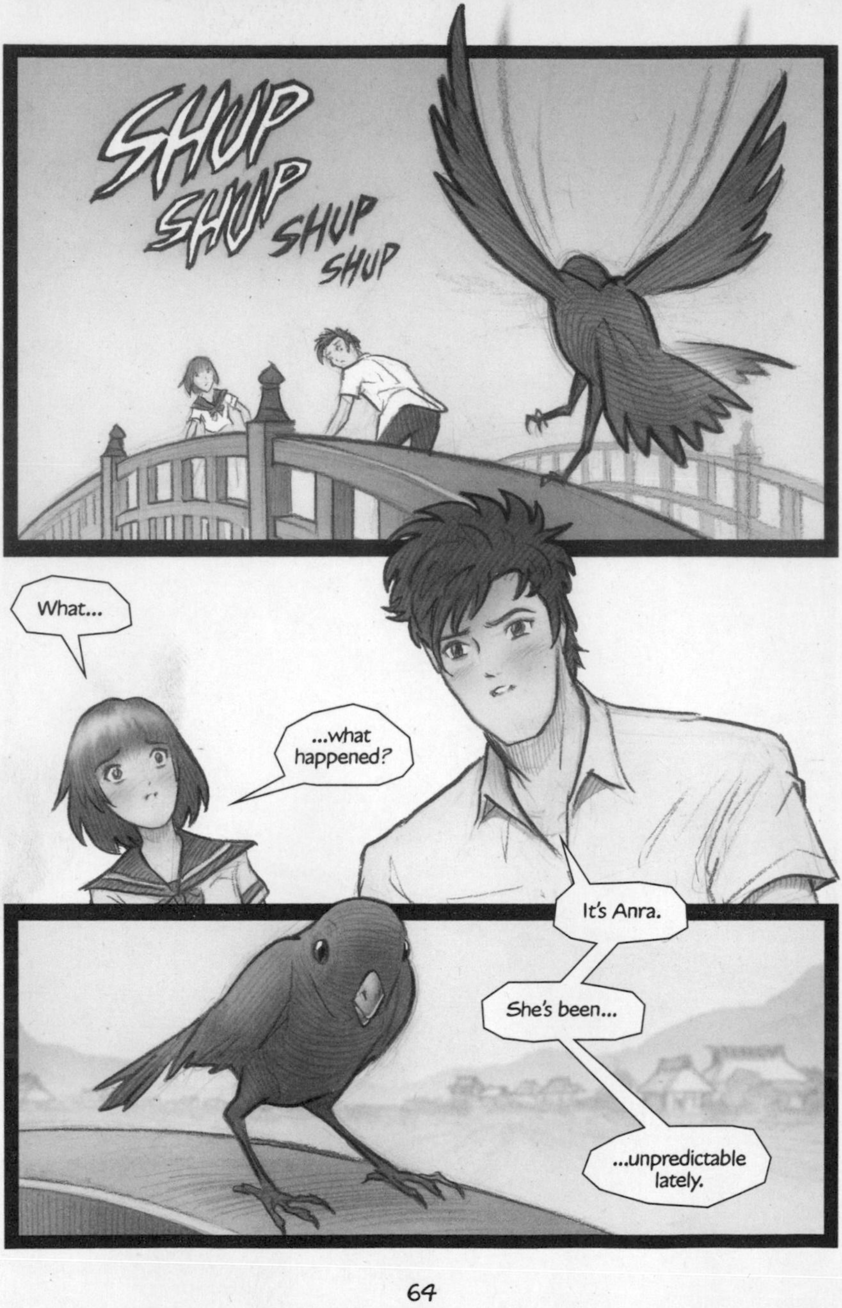
SHUP
SHUP
SHUP
SHUP
What...
...what happened?
It's Anra.
She's been...
...unpredictable lately.

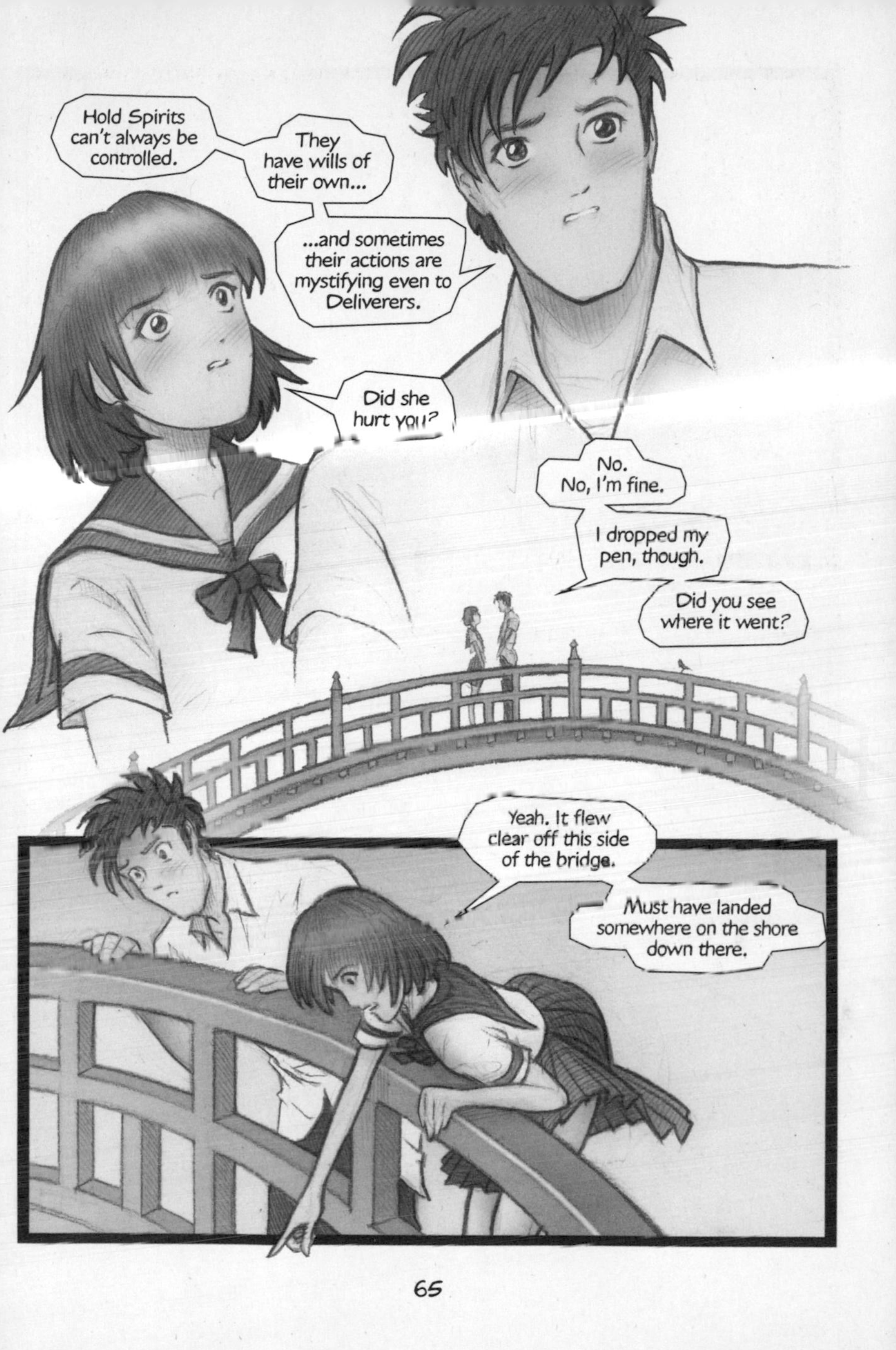
Hold Spirits can't always be controlled.
They have wills of their own...
...and sometimes their actions are mystifying even to Deliverers.
Did she hurt you?
No. No, I'm fine.
I dropped my pen, though.
Did you see where it went?
Yeah. It flew clear off this side of the bridge.
Must have landed somewhere on the shore down there.

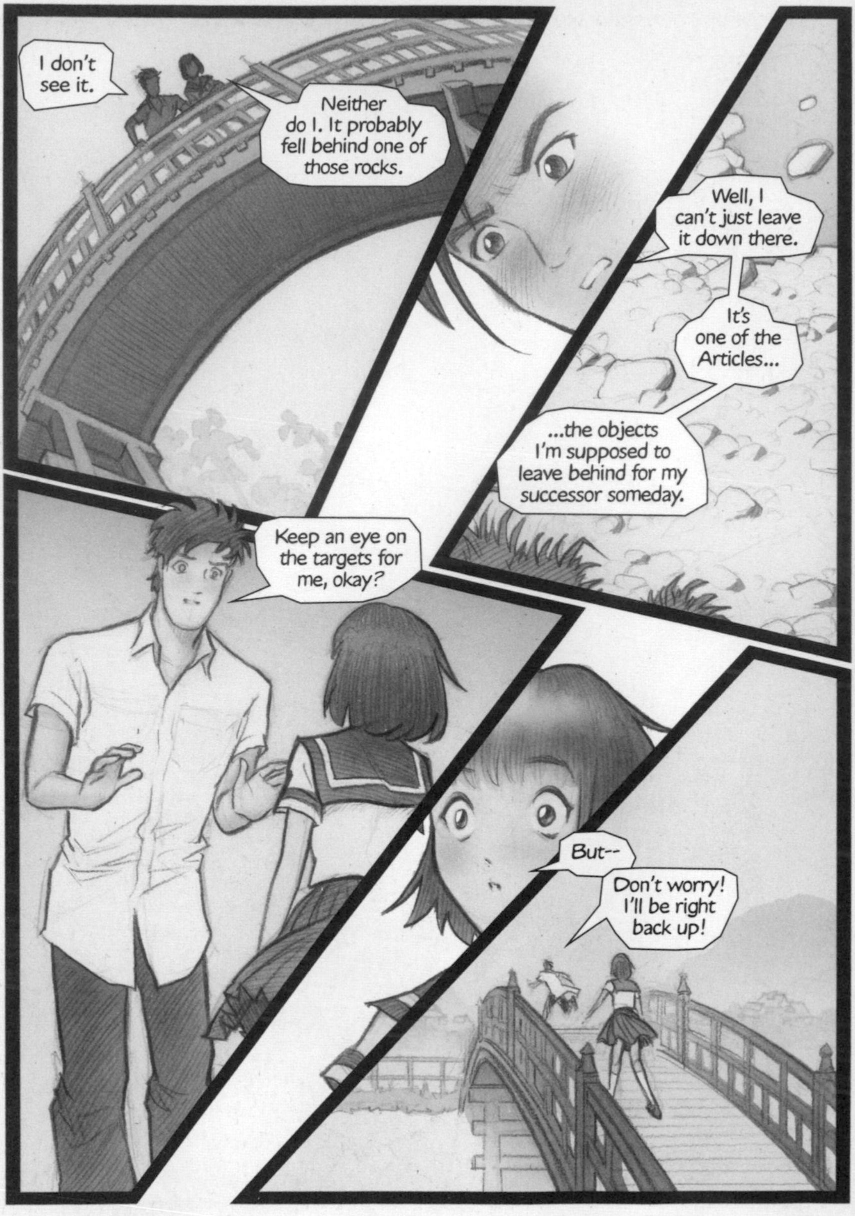
I don't see it.
Neither do I. It probably fell behind one of those rocks.
Well, I can't just leave it down there.
It's one of the Articles...
...the objects I'm supposed to leave behind for my successor someday.
Keep an eye on the targets for me, okay?
But--
Don't worry! I'll be right back up!

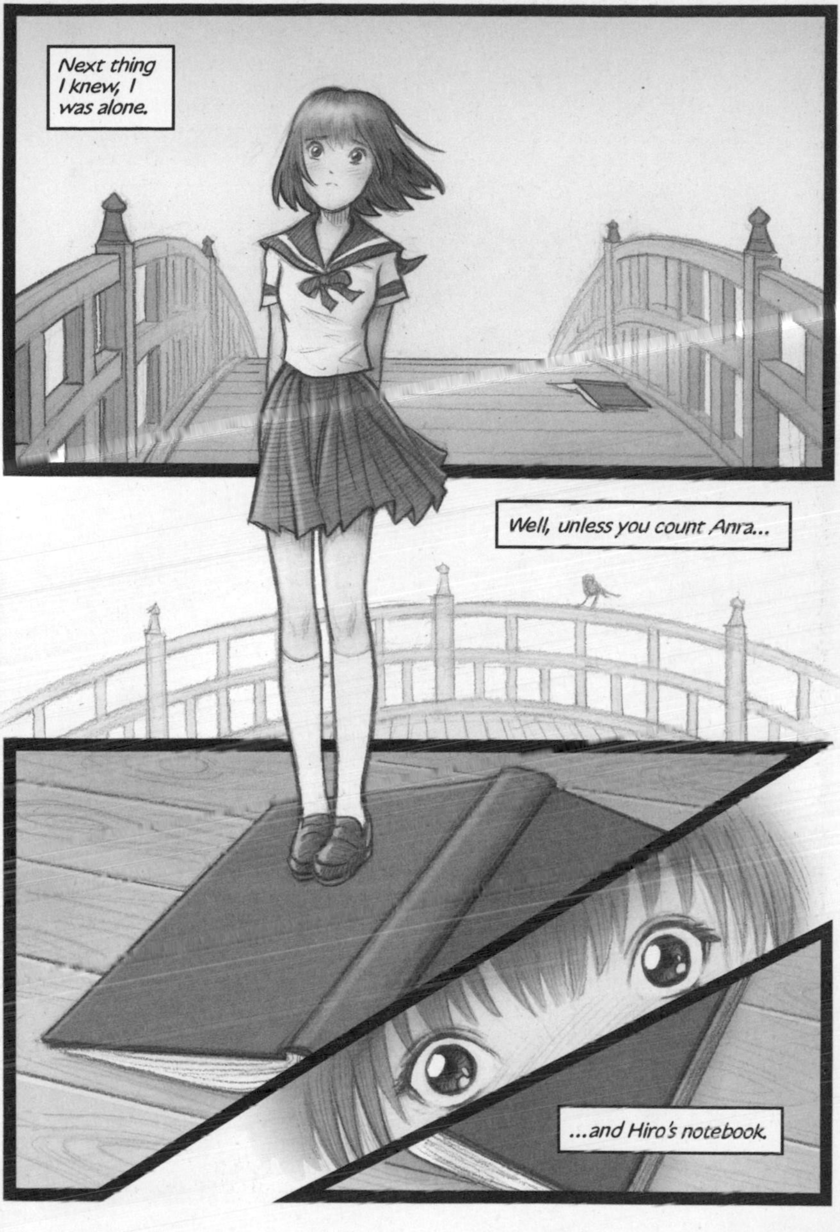
Next thing
I knew, I
was alone.
Well, unless you count Anra...
...and Hiro's notebook.

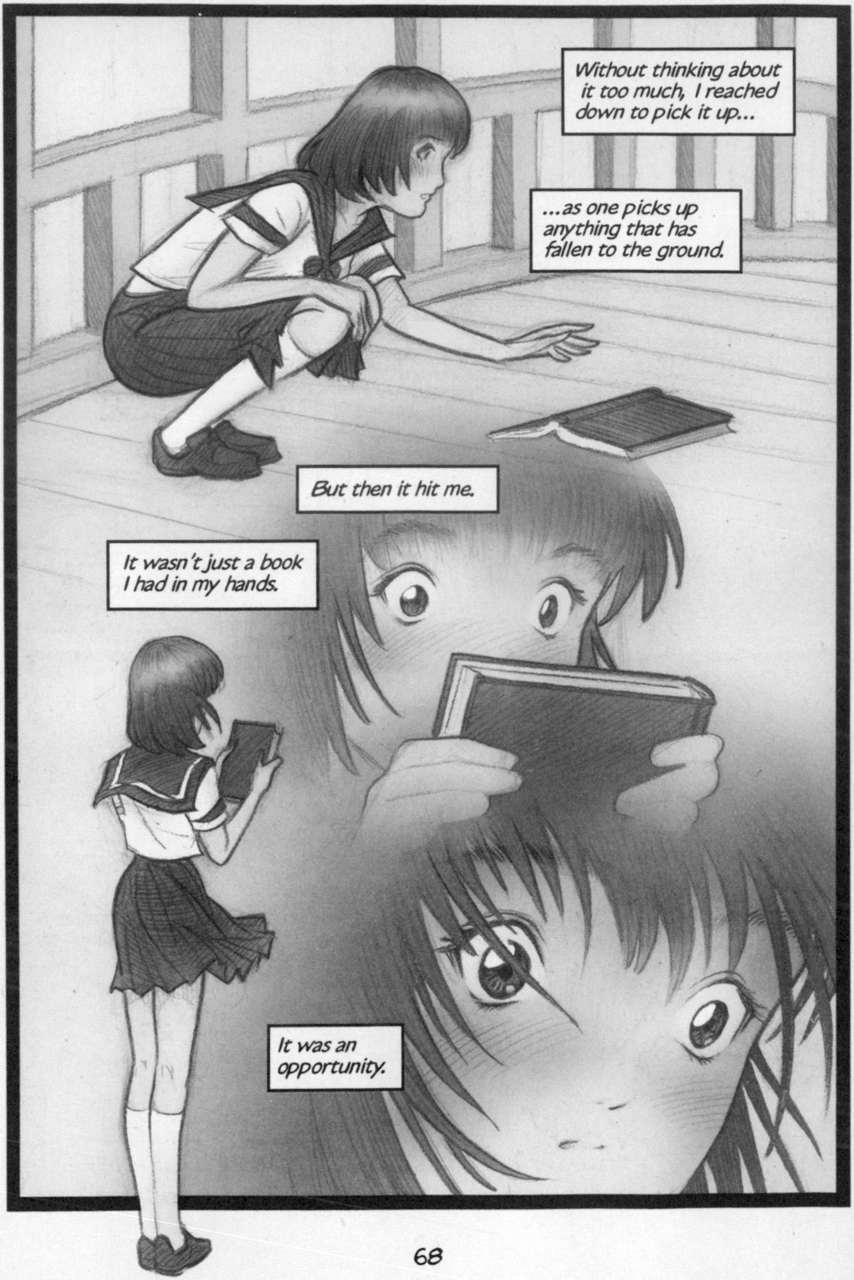

Without thinking about it too much, I reached down to pick it up...
...as one picks up anything that has fallen to the ground.
But then it hit me.
It wasn't just a book I had in my hands.
It was an opportunity.

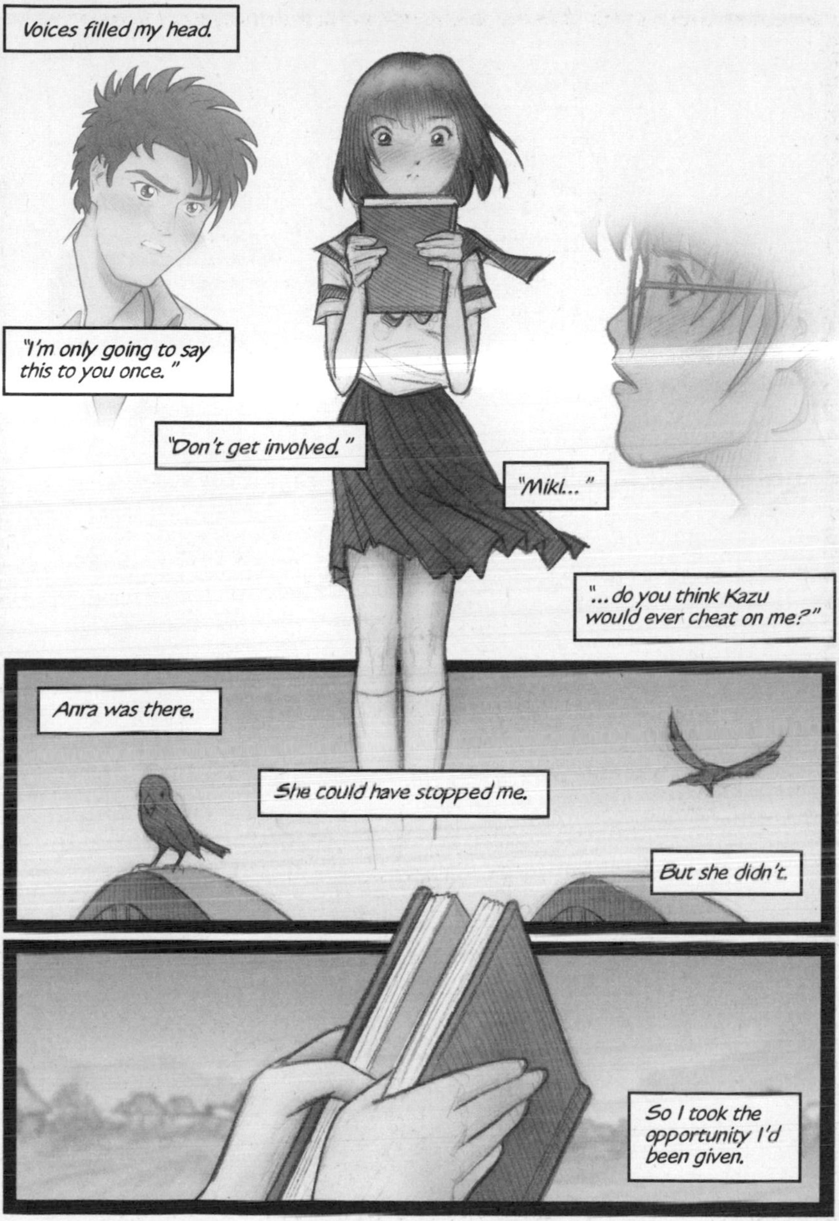
Voices filled my head.
"I'm only going to say this to you once."
"Don't get involved."
"Miki..."
"...do you think Kazu would ever cheat on me?"
Anra was there.
She could have stopped me.
But she didn't.
So I took the opportunity I'd been given.

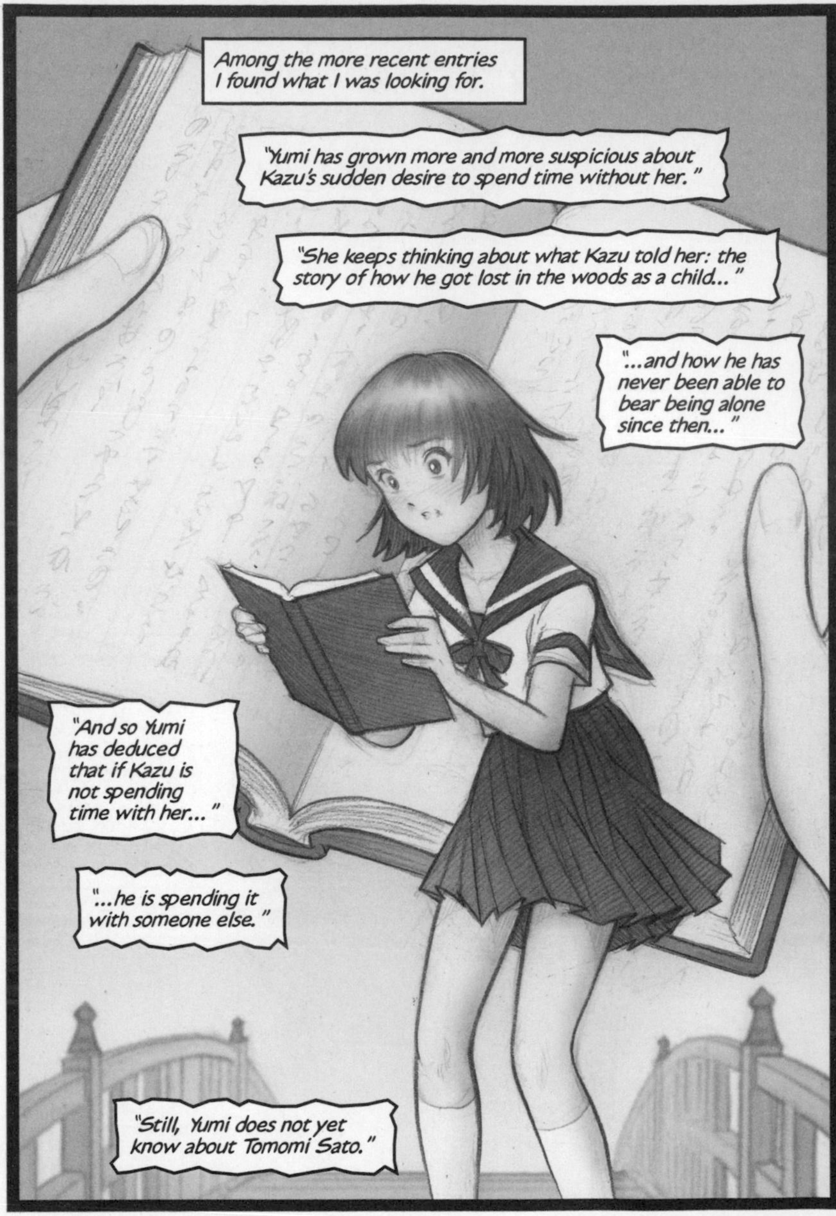
Among the more recent entries I found what I was looking for.
"Yumi has grown more and more suspicious about Kazu's sudden desire to spend time without her."
"She keeps thinking about what Kazu told her: the story of how he got lost in the woods as a child..."
"...and how he has never been able to bear being alone since then..."
"And so Yumi has deduced that if Kazu is not spending time with her..."
"...he is spending it with someone else."
"Still, Yumi does not yet know about Tomomi Sato."

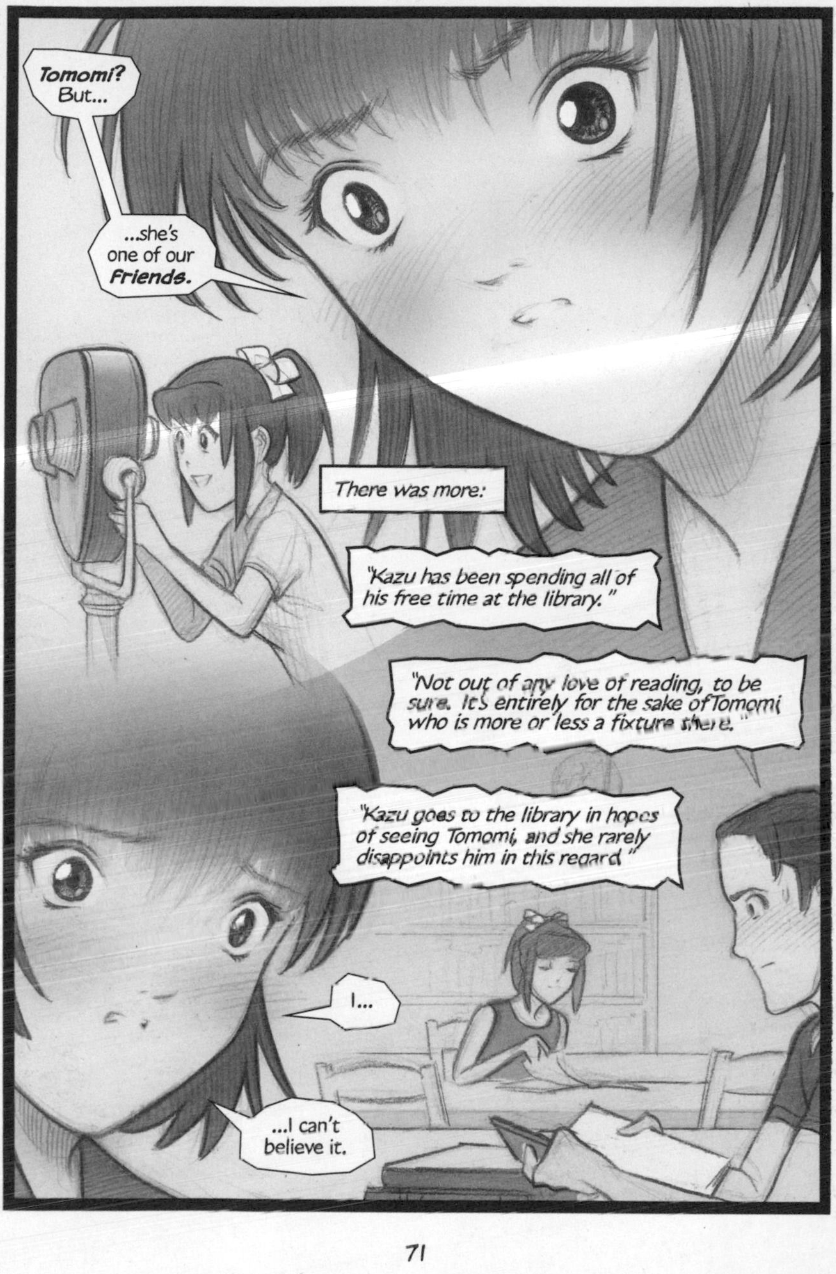
Tomomi? But...
...she's one of our Friends.
There was more:
"Kazu has been spending all of his free time at the library."
"Not out of any love of reading, to be sure. It's entirely for the sake of Tomomi who is more or less a fixture there."
"Kazu goes to the library in hopes of seeing Tomomi, and she rarely disappoints him in this regard."
I...
...I can't believe it.

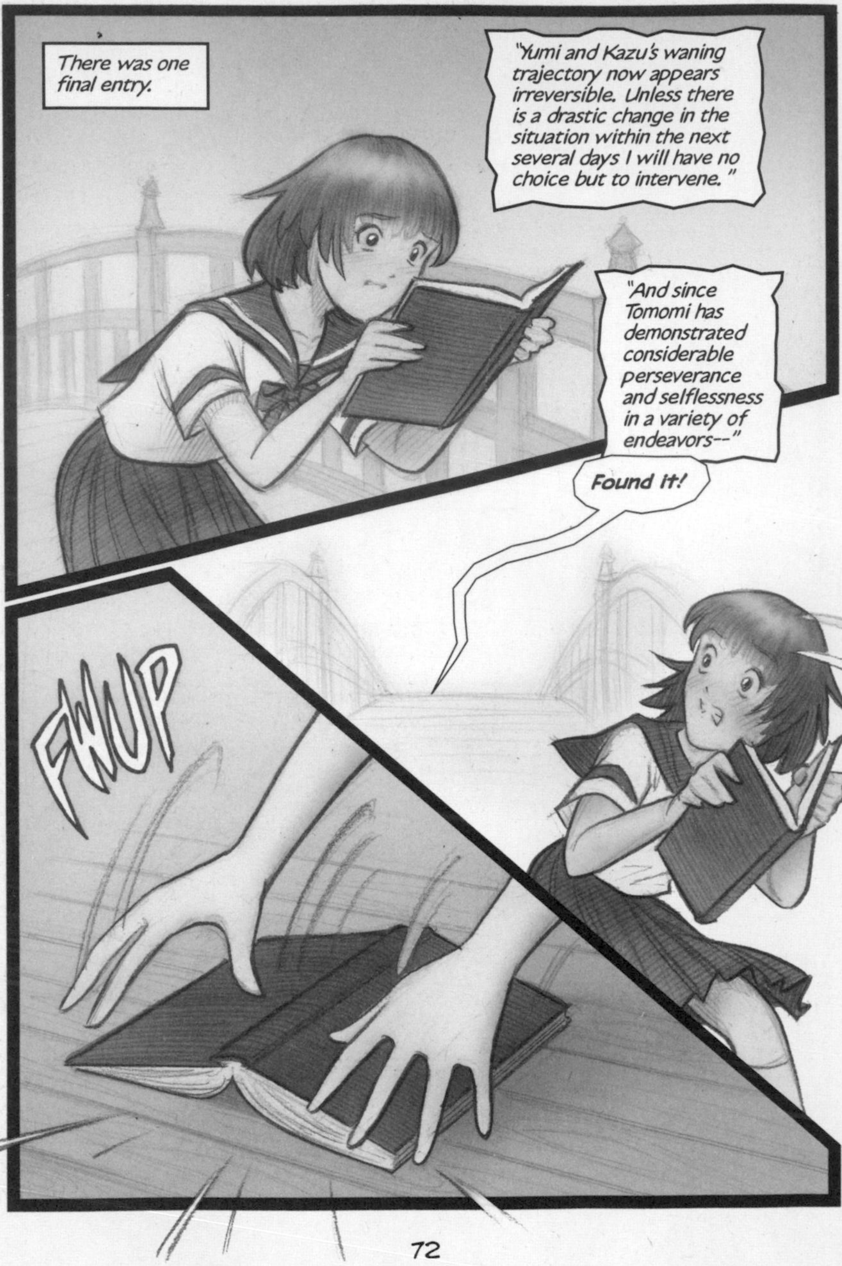

There was one final entry.
"Yumi and Kazu's waning trajectory now appears irreversible. Unless there is a drastic change in the situation within the next several days I will have no choice but to intervene."
"And since Tomomi has demonstrated considerable perseverance and selflessness in a variety of endeavors--"
Found it!
FWUP

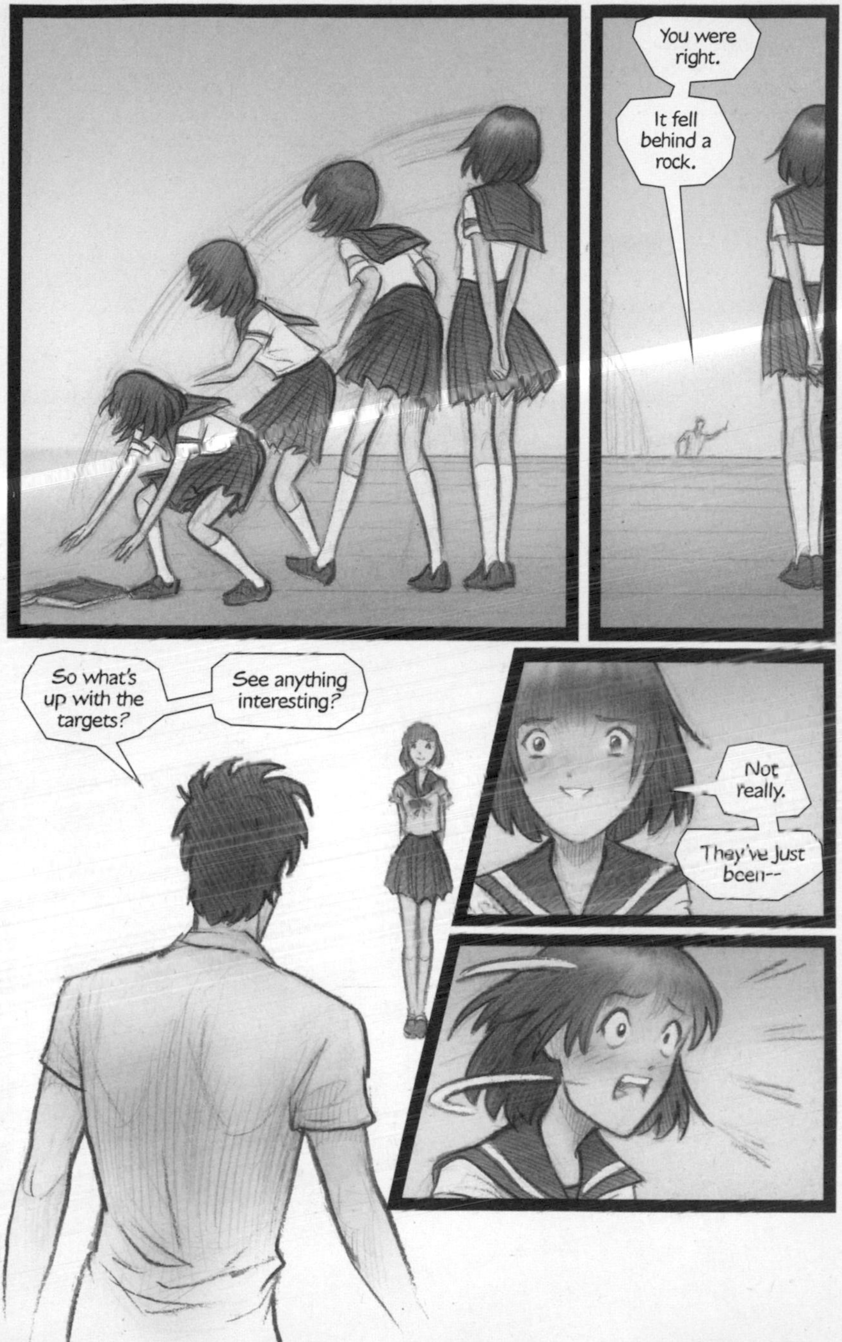

You were right.
It fell behind a rock.
So what's up with the targets?
See anything interesting?
Not really.
They've just been--

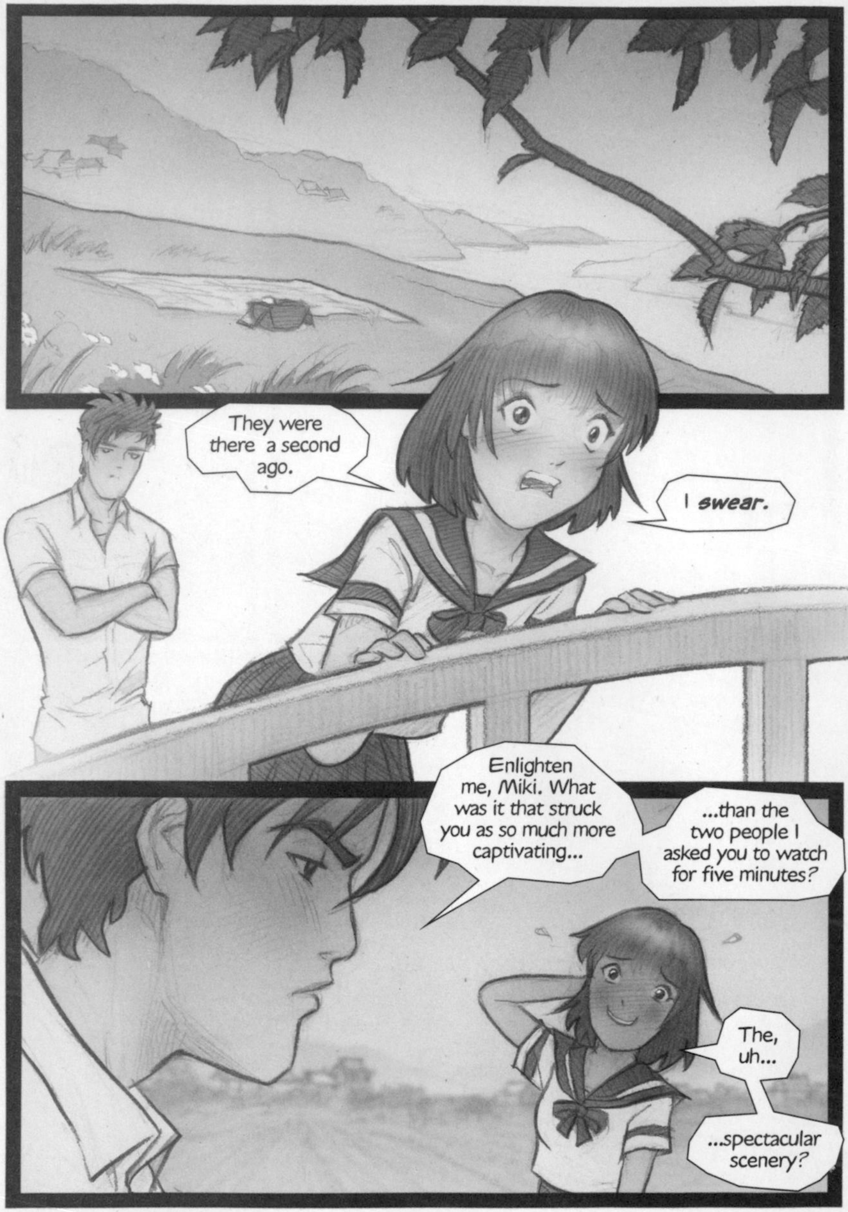
They were there a second ago.
I swear.
Enlighten me, Miki. What was it that struck you as so much more captivating...
...than the two people I asked you to watch for five minutes?
The, uh...
...spectacular scenery?

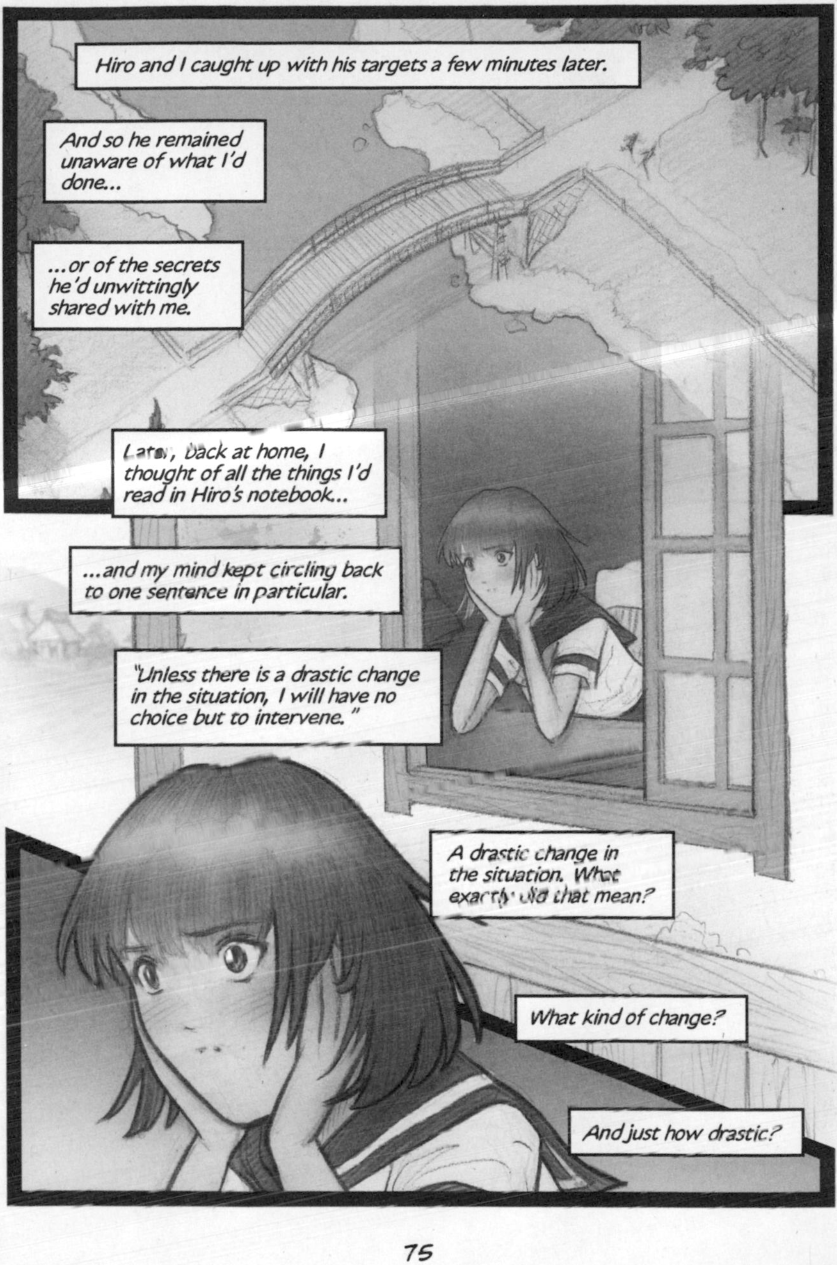
Hiro and I caught up with his targets a few minutes later.
And so he remained unaware of what I'd done...
...or of the secrets he'd unwittingly shared with me.
Later, back at home, I thought of all the things I'd read in Hiro's notebook...
...and my mind kept circling back to one sentence in particular.
"Unless there is a drastic change in the situation, I will have no choice but to intervene."
A drastic change in the situation. What exactly did that mean?
What kind of change?
And just how drastic?

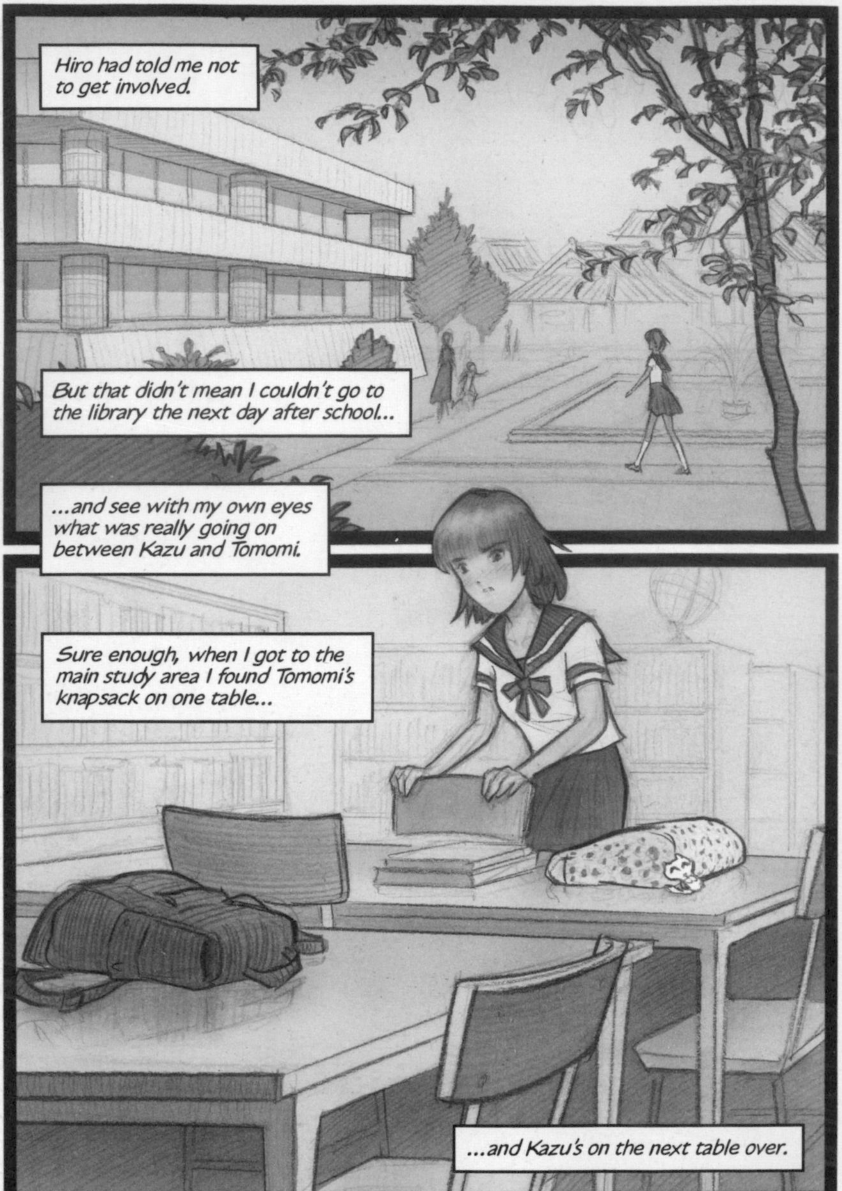
Hiro had told me not to get involved.
But that didn't mean I couldn't go to the library the next day after school...
...and see with my own eyes what was really going on between Kazu and Tomomi.
Sure enough, when I got to the main study area I found Tomomi's knapsack on one table...
...and Kazu's on the next table over.

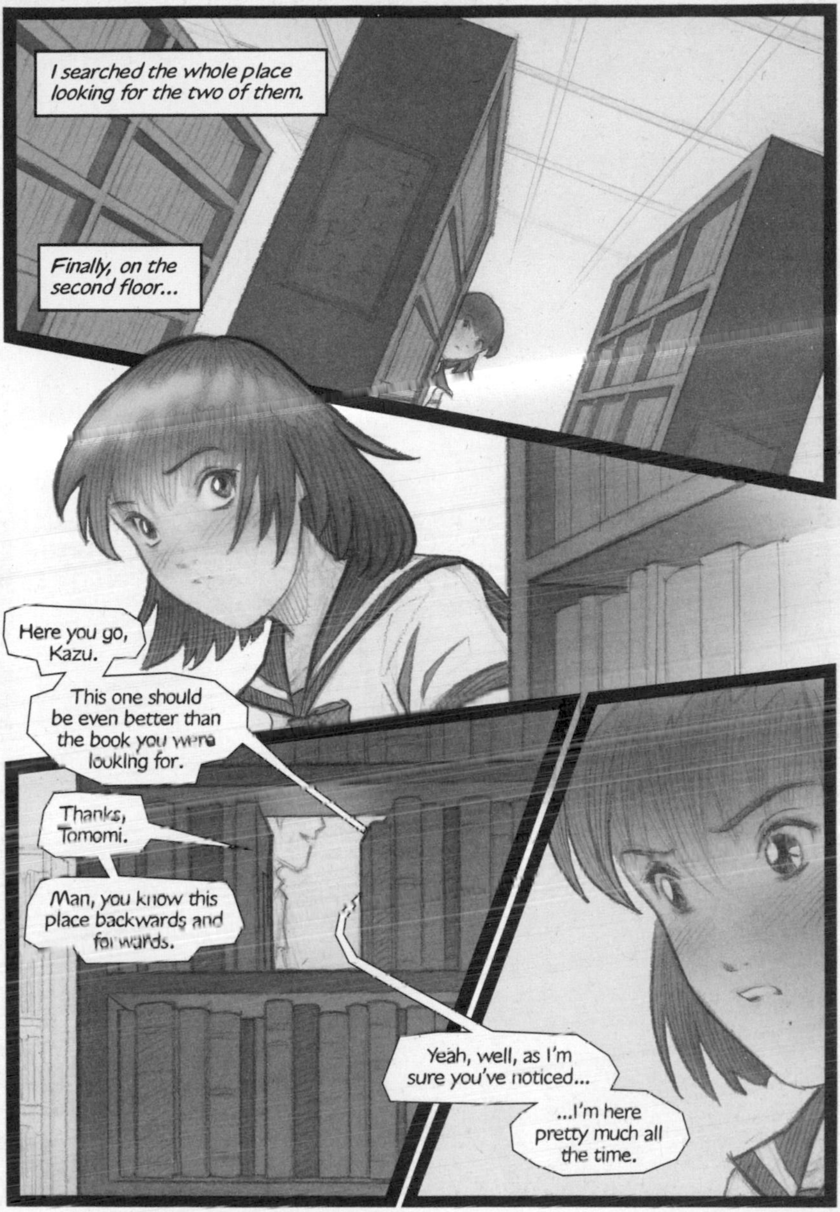

I searched the whole place looking for the two of them.
Finally, on the second floor...
Here you go, Kazu.
This one should be even better than the book you were looking for.
Thanks, Tomomi.
Man, you know this place backwards and forwards.
Yeah, well, as I'm sure you've noticed...
...I'm here pretty much all the time.

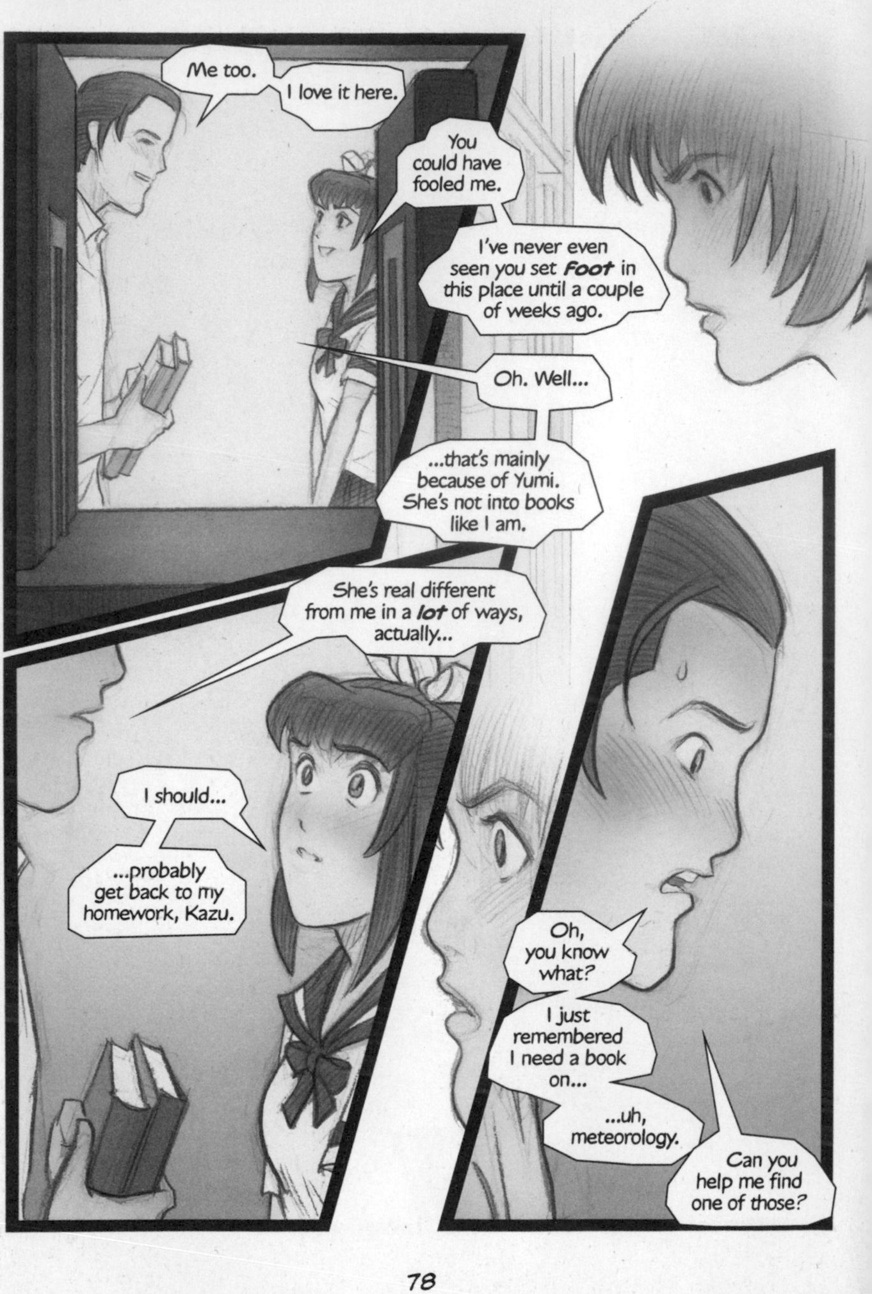
Me too.
I love it here.
You could have fooled me.
I've never even seen you set *foot* in this place until a couple of weeks ago.
Oh. Well...
...that's mainly because of Yumi. She's not into books like I am.
She's real different from me in a *lot* of ways, actually...
I should...
...probably get back to my homework, Kazu.
Oh, you know what?
I just remembered I need a book on...
...uh, meteorology.
Can you help me find one of those?

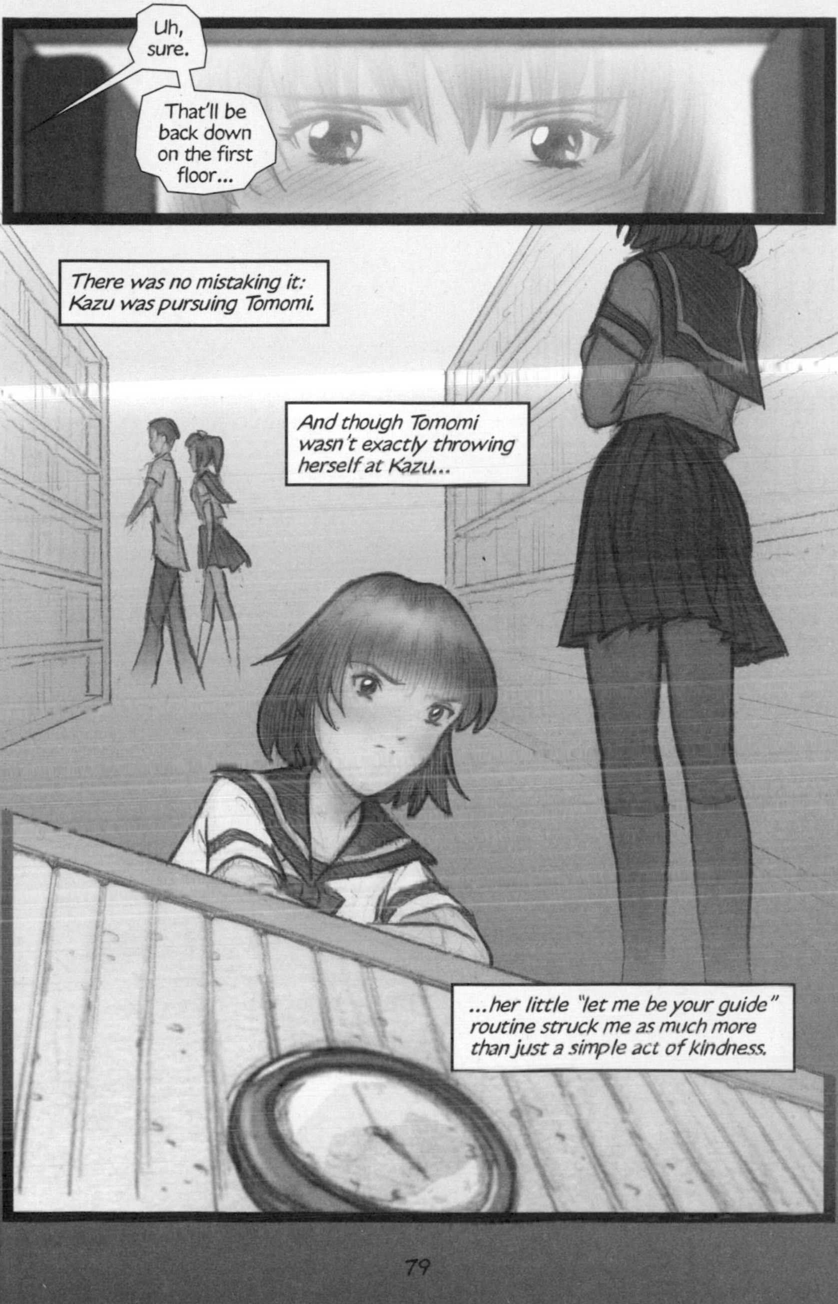
Uh, sure.
That'll be back down on the first floor...
There was no mistaking it: Kazu was pursuing Tomomi.
And though Tomomi wasn't exactly throwing herself at Kazu...
...her little "let me be your guide" routine struck me as much more than just a simple act of kindness.

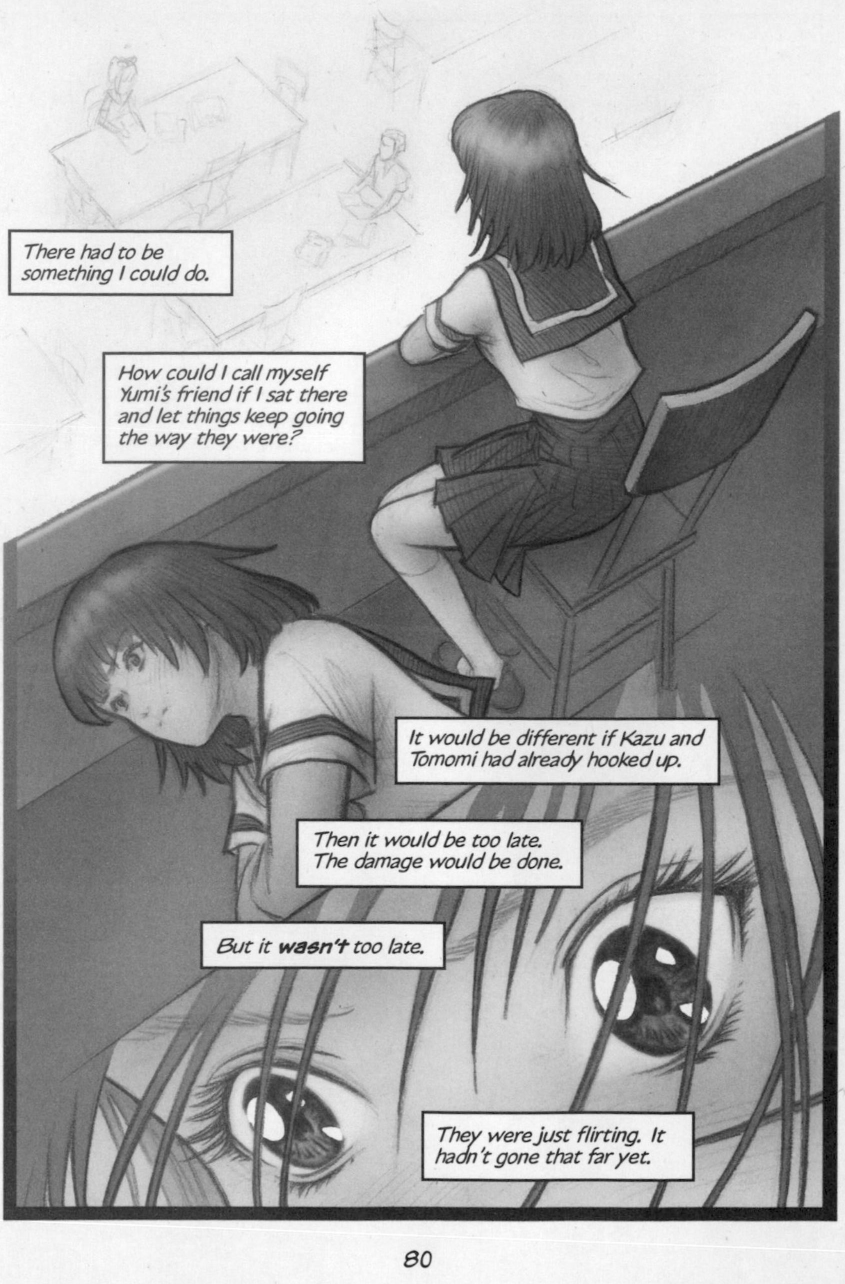
There had to be something I could do.
How could I call myself Yumi's friend if I sat there and let things keep going the way they were?
It would be different if Kazu and Tomomi had already hooked up.
Then it would be too late. The damage would be done.
But it **wasn't** too late.
They were just flirting. It hadn't gone that far yet.

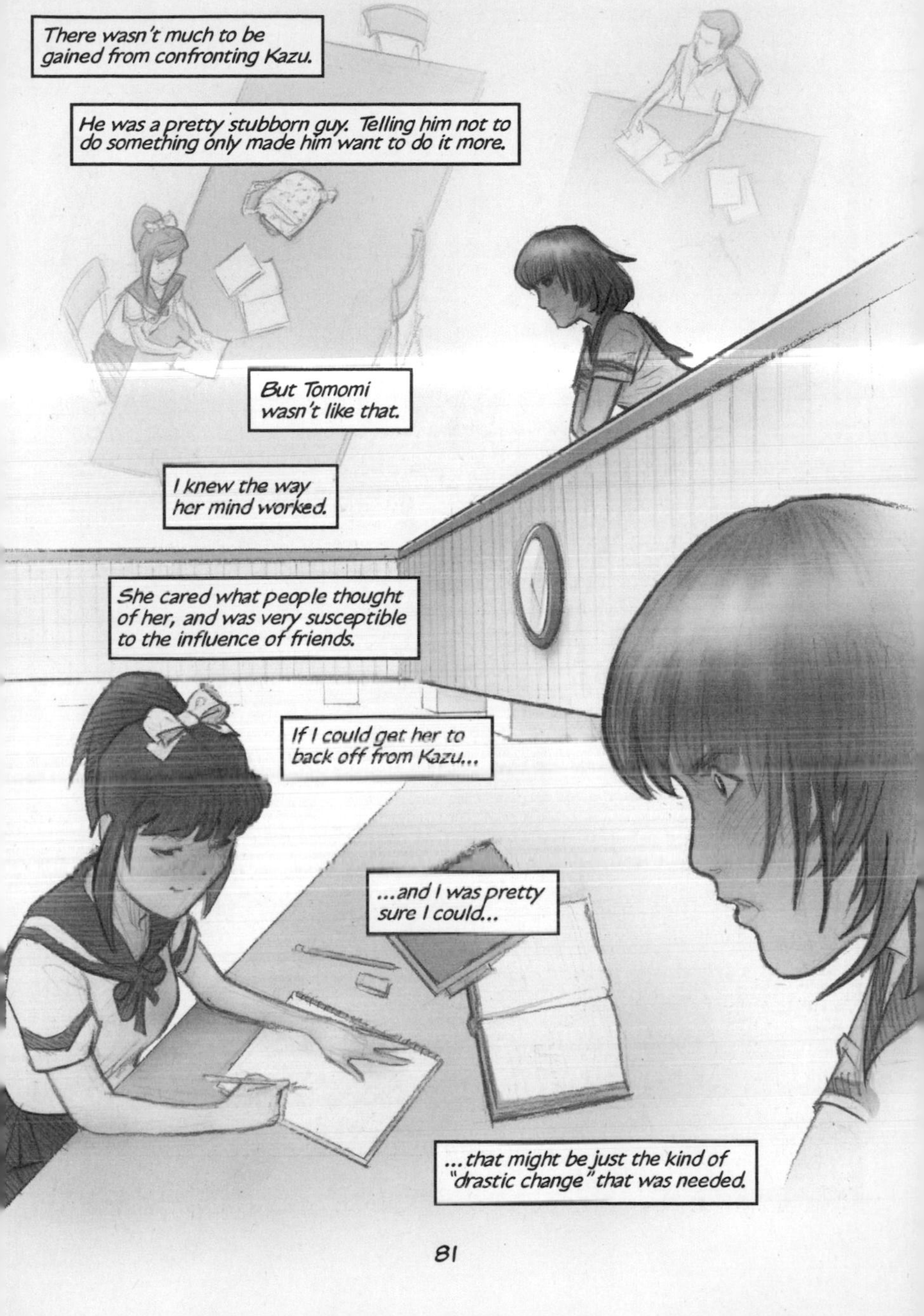
There wasn't much to be gained from confronting Kazu.
He was a pretty stubborn guy. Telling him not to do something only made him want to do it more.
But Tomomi wasn't like that.
I knew the way her mind worked.
She cared what people thought of her, and was very susceptible to the influence of friends.
If I could get her to back off from Kazu...
...and I was pretty sure I could...
...that might be just the kind of "drastic change" that was needed.

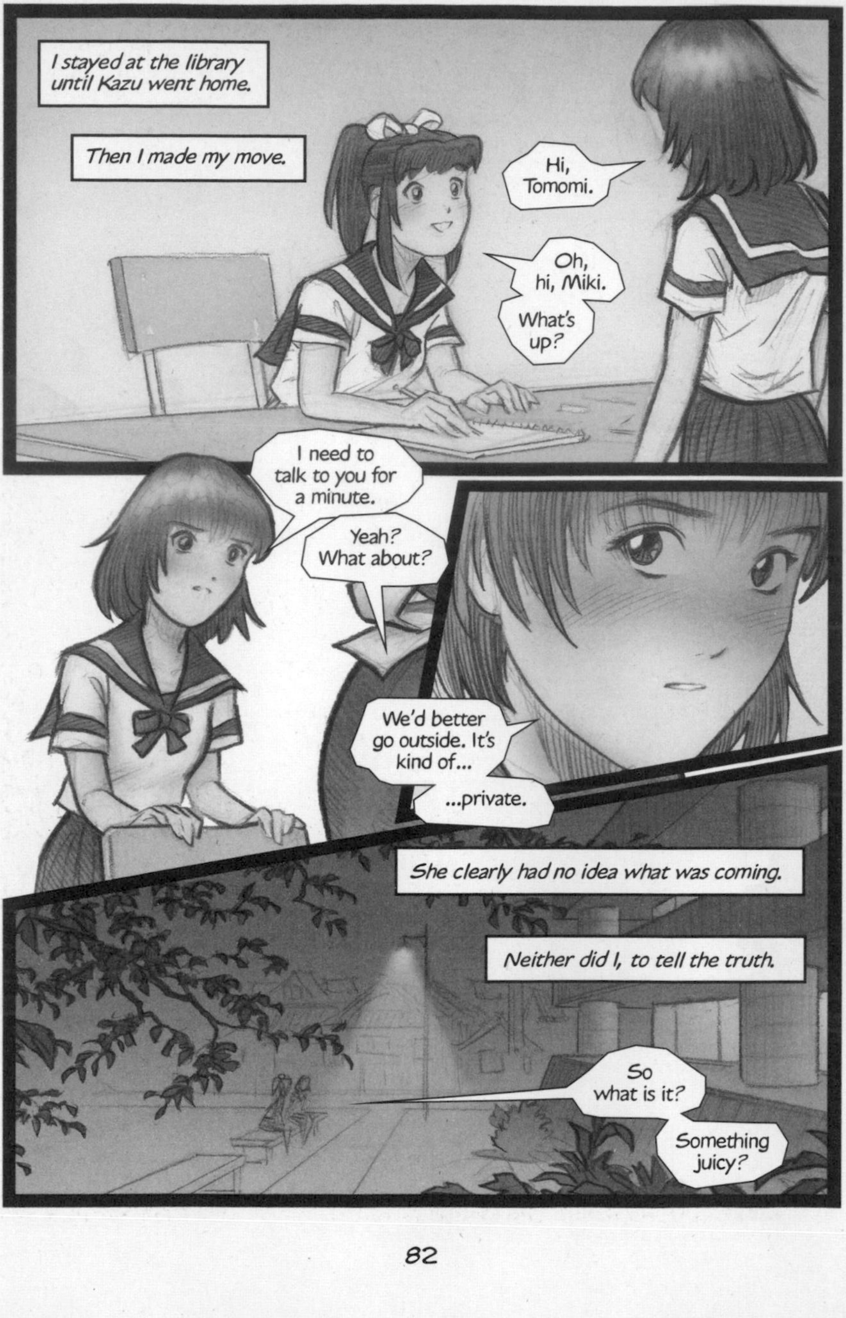
I stayed at the library until Kazu went home.
Then I made my move.
Hi, Tomomi.
Oh, hi, Miki.
What's up?
I need to talk to you for a minute.
Yeah? What about?
We'd better go outside. It's kind of...
...private.
She clearly had no idea what was coming.
Neither did I, to tell the truth.
So what is it?
Something juicy?

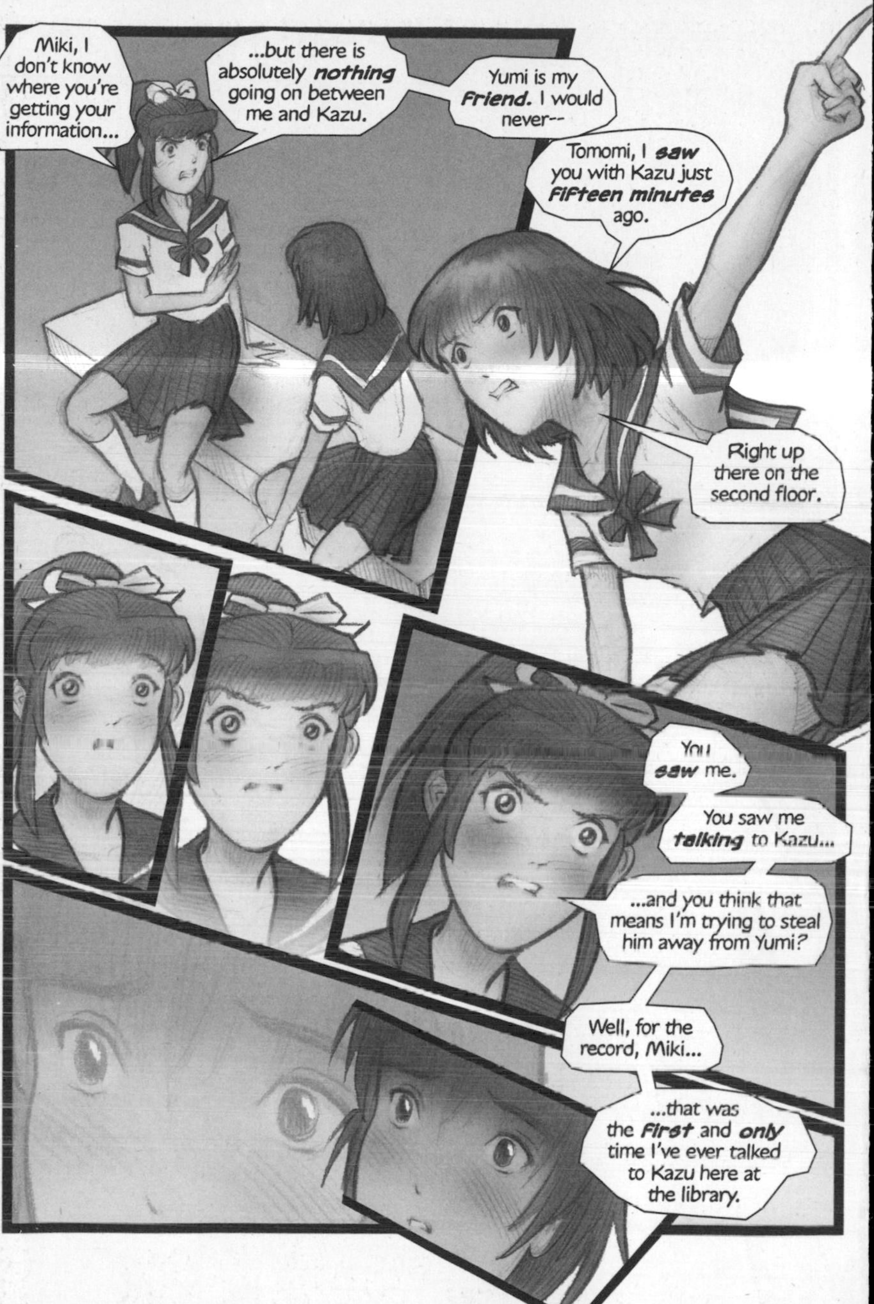

Miki, I don't know where you're getting your information...
...but there is absolutely *nothing* going on between me and Kazu.
Yumi is my *friend.* I would never--
Tomomi, I *saw* you with Kazu just *fifteen minutes* ago.
Right up there on the second floor.
You *saw* me.
You saw me *talking* to Kazu...
...and you think that means I'm trying to steal him away from Yumi?
Well, for the record, Miki...
...that was the *first* and *only* time I've ever talked to Kazu here at the library.

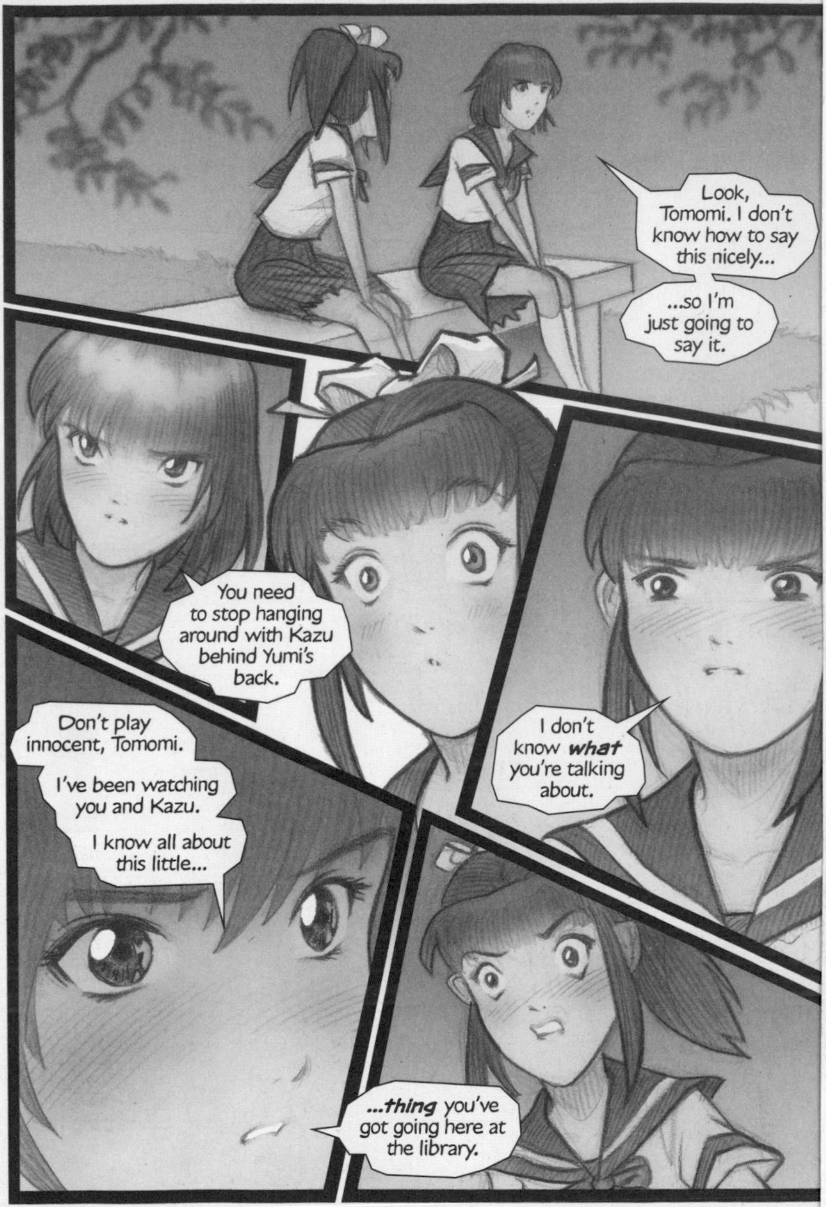
Look, Tomomi. I don't know how to say this nicely...
...so I'm just going to say it.
You need to stop hanging around with Kazu behind Yumi's back.
I don't know *what* you're talking about.
Don't play innocent, Tomomi.
I've been watching you and Kazu.
I know all about this little...
...thing you've got going here at the library.

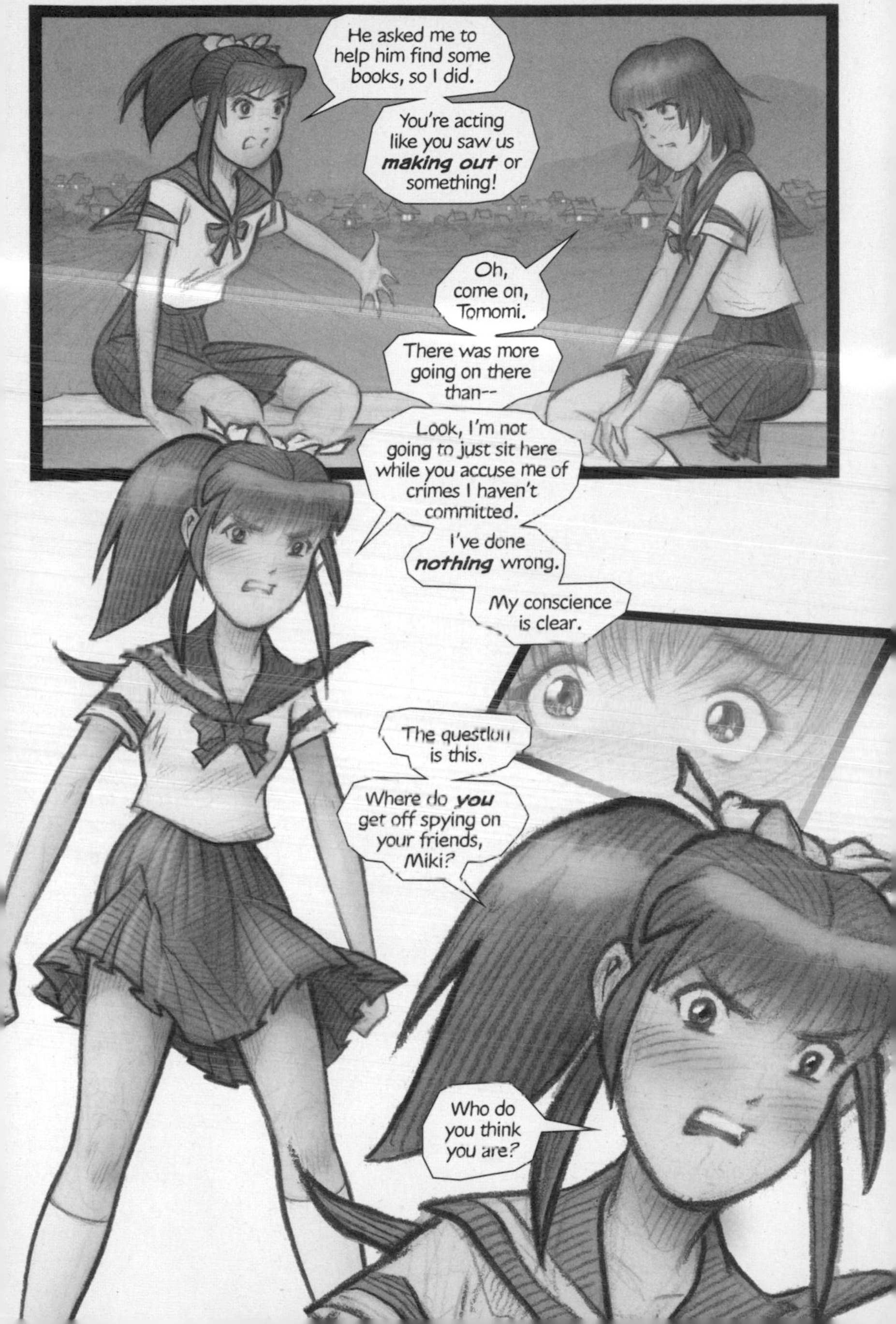
He asked me to help him find some books, so I did.
You're acting like you saw us **making out** or something!
Oh, come on, Tomomi.
There was more going on there than--
Look, I'm not going to just sit here while you accuse me of crimes I haven't committed.
I've done **nothing** wrong.
My conscience is clear.
The question is this.
Where do **you** get off spying on your friends, Miki?
Who do you think you are?

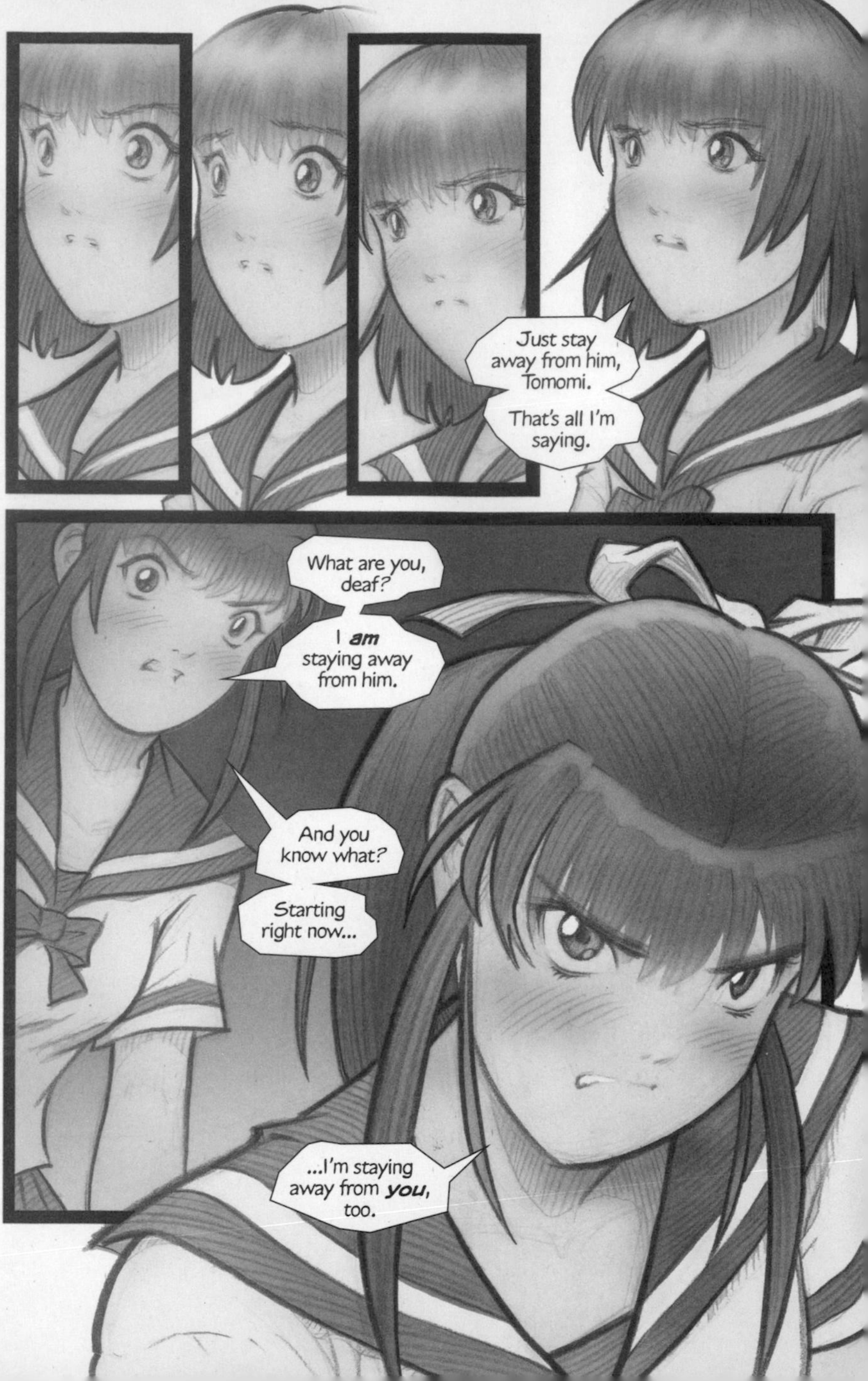
Just stay away from him, Tomomi.
That's all I'm saying.
What are you, deaf?
I **am** staying away from him.
And you know what?
Starting right now...
...I'm staying away from **you**, too.

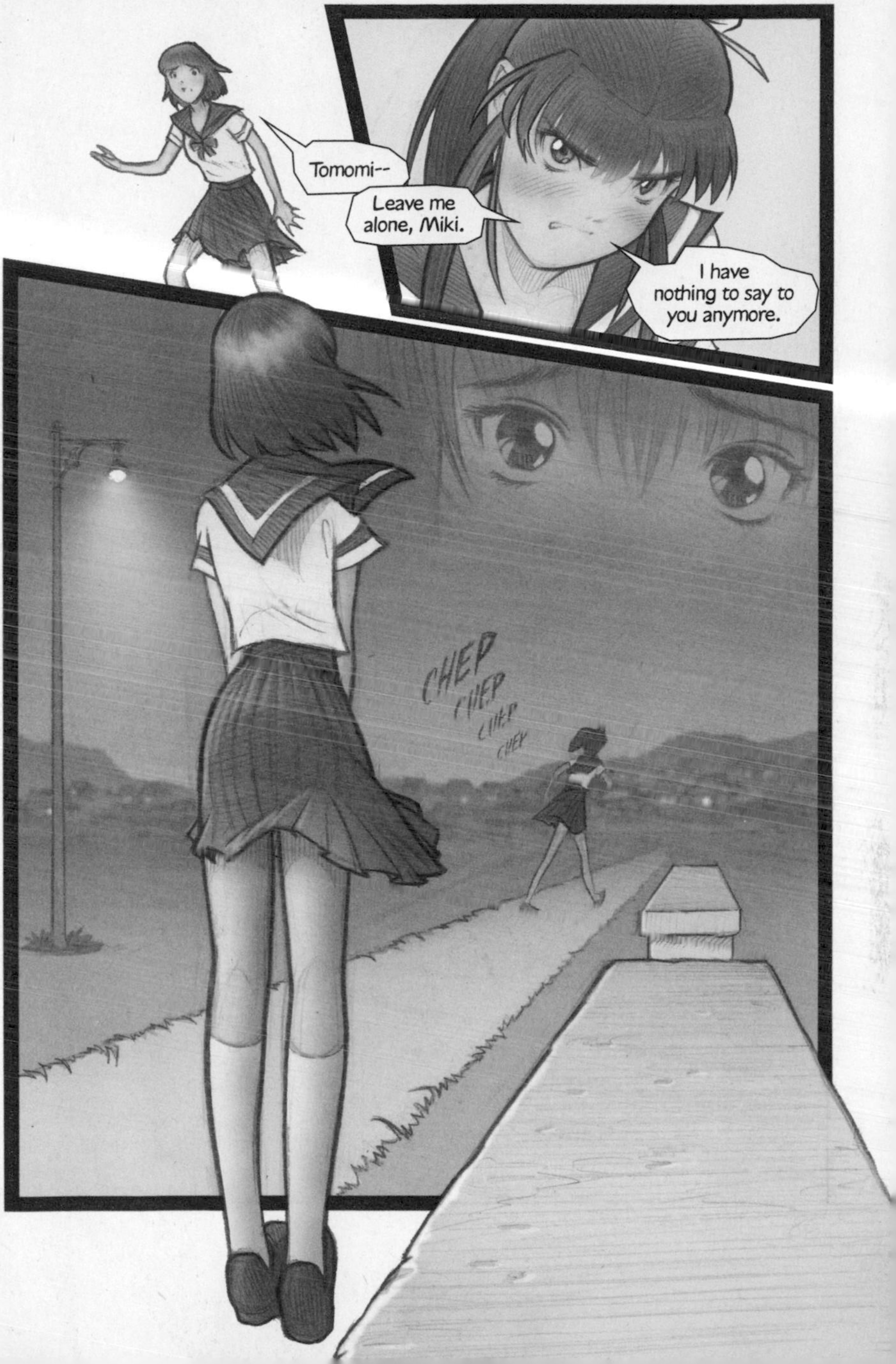
Tomomi--
Leave me alone, Miki.
I have nothing to say to you anymore.
CHEP
CHEP
CHEP
CHEP

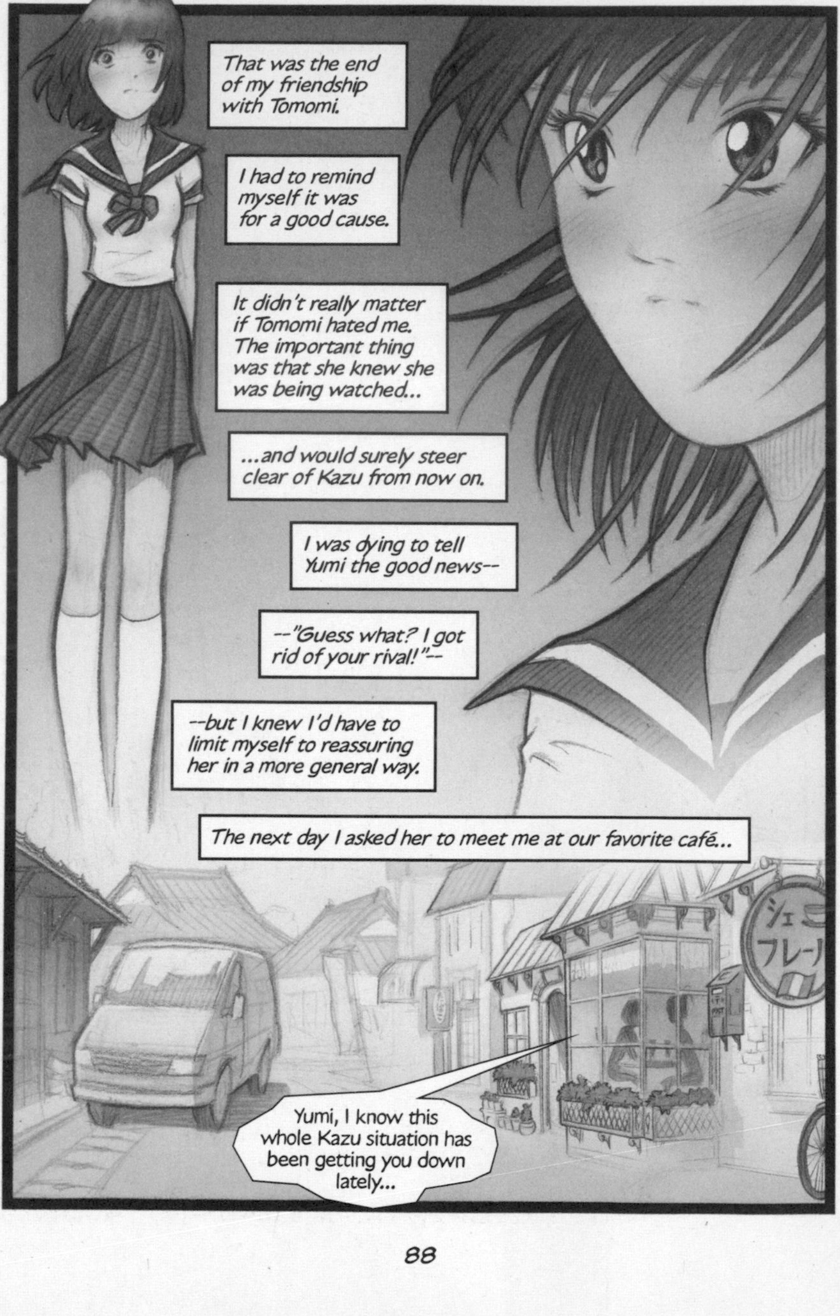
That was the end of my friendship with Tomomi.
I had to remind myself it was for a good cause.
It didn't really matter if Tomomi hated me. The important thing was that she knew she was being watched...
...and would surely steer clear of Kazu from now on.
I was dying to tell Yumi the good news--
--"Guess what? I got rid of your rival!"--
--but I knew I'd have to limit myself to reassuring her in a more general way.
The next day I asked her to meet me at our favorite café...
Yumi, I know this whole Kazu situation has been getting you down lately...

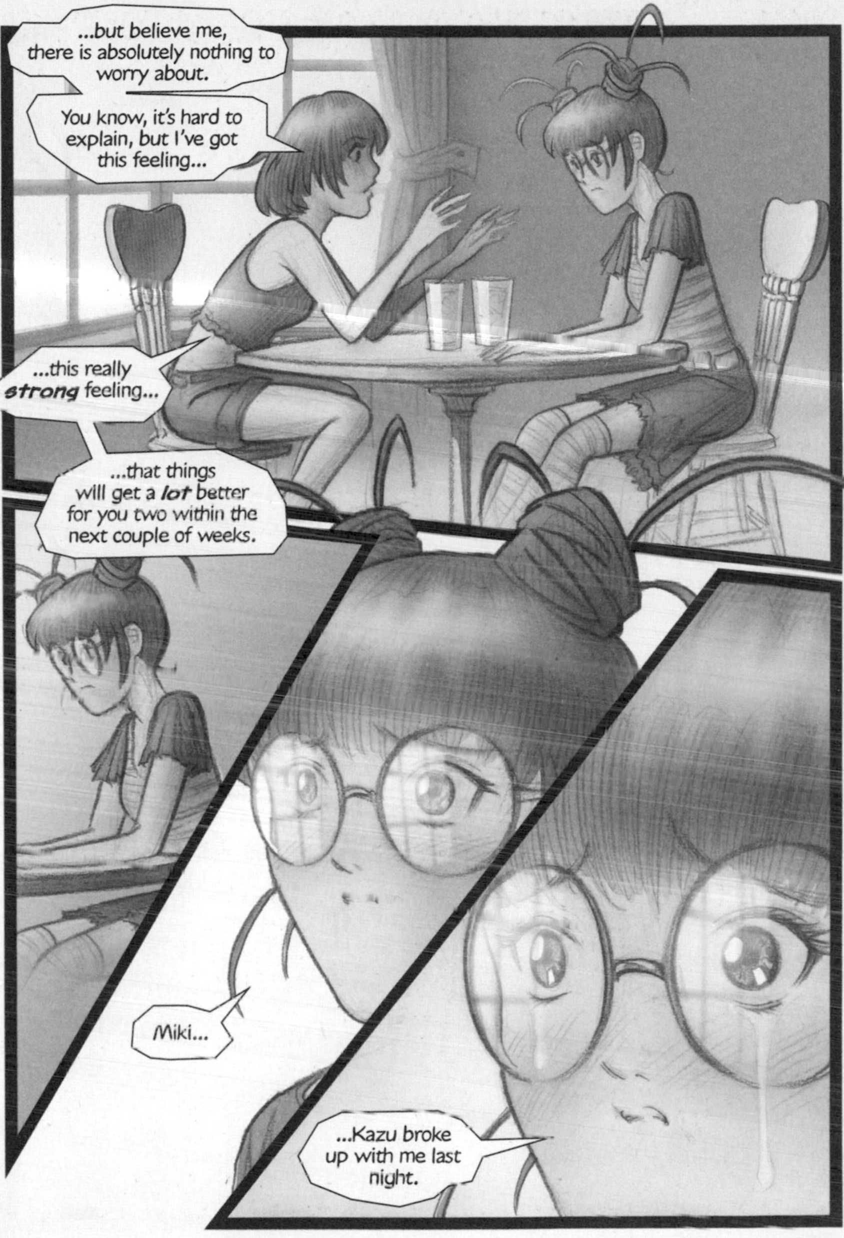
...but believe me, there is absolutely nothing to worry about.
You know, it's hard to explain, but I've got this feeling...
...this really *strong* feeling...
...that things will get a *lot* better for you two within the next couple of weeks.
Miki...
...Kazu broke up with me last night.

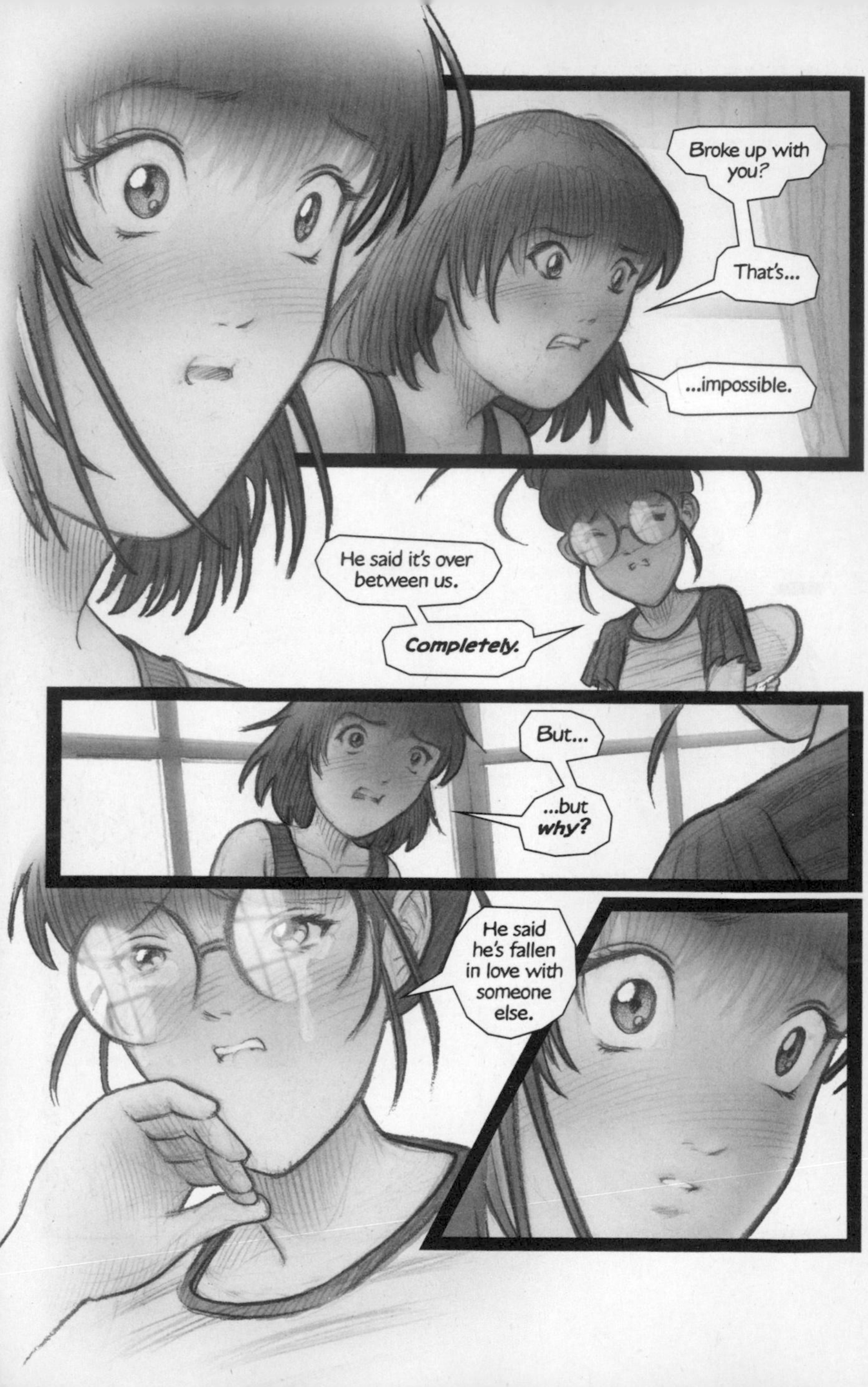
Broke up with you?
That's...
...impossible.
He said it's over between us.
Completely.
But...
...but *why?*
He said he's fallen in love with someone else.

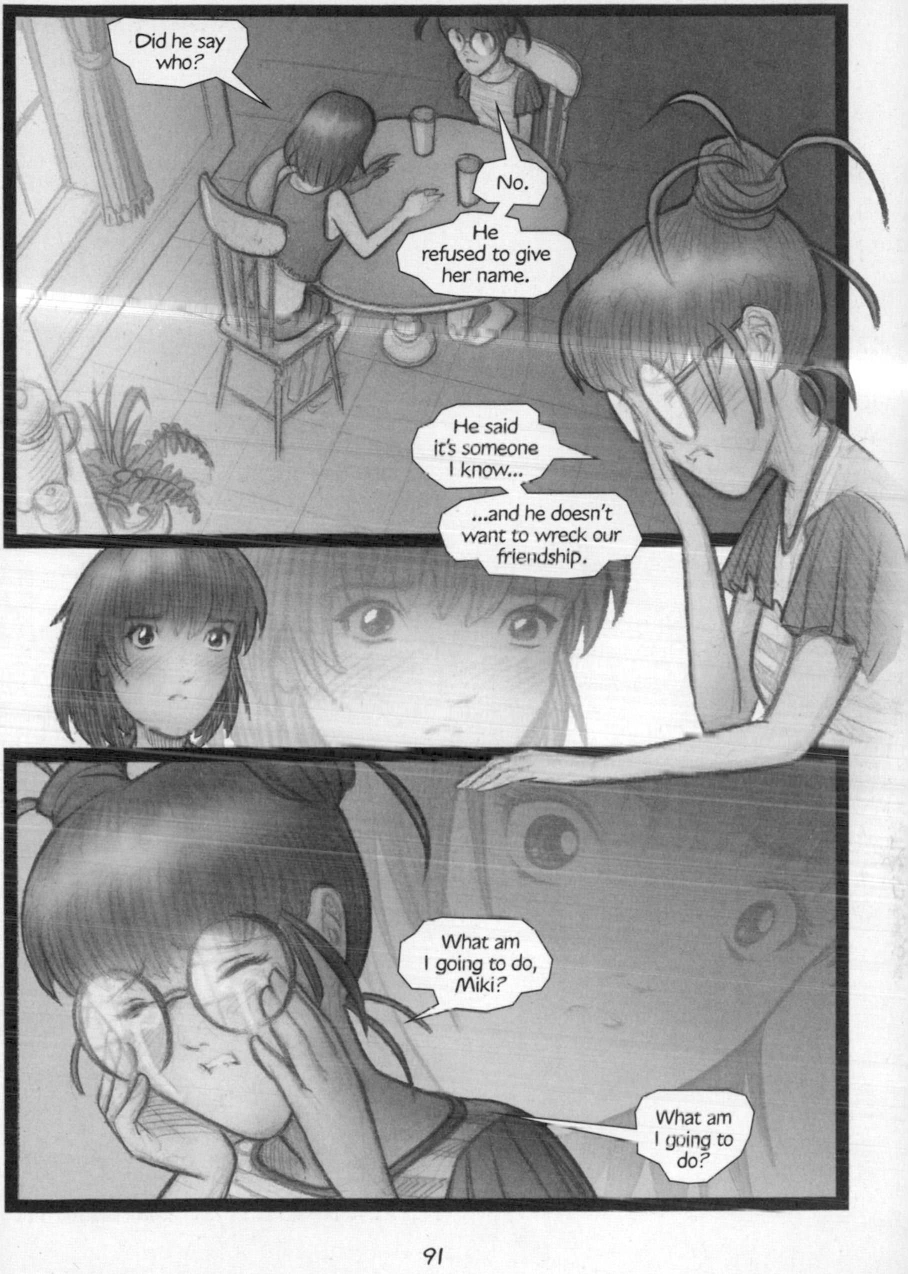
Did he say who?
No.
He refused to give her name.
He said it's someone I know...
...and he doesn't want to wreck our friendship.
What am I going to do, Miki?
What am I going to do?

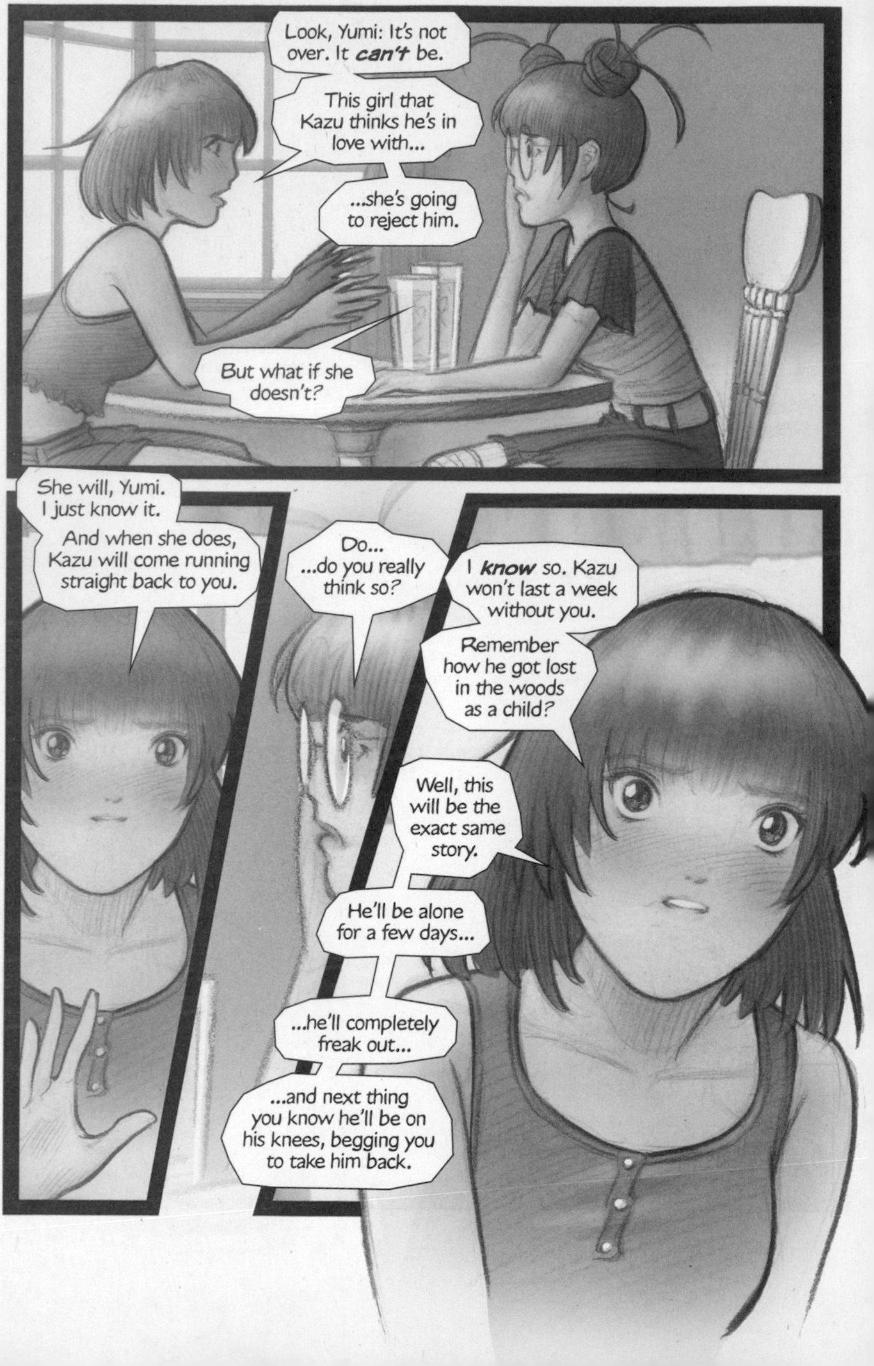
Look, Yumi: It's not over. It can't be.
This girl that Kazu thinks he's in love with...
...she's going to reject him.
But what if she doesn't?
She will, Yumi. I just know it.
And when she does, Kazu will come running straight back to you.
Do... ...do you really think so?
I know so. Kazu won't last a week without you.
Remember how he got lost in the woods as a child?
Well, this will be the exact same story.
He'll be alone for a few days...
...he'll completely freak out...
...and next thing you know he'll be on his knees, begging you to take him back.

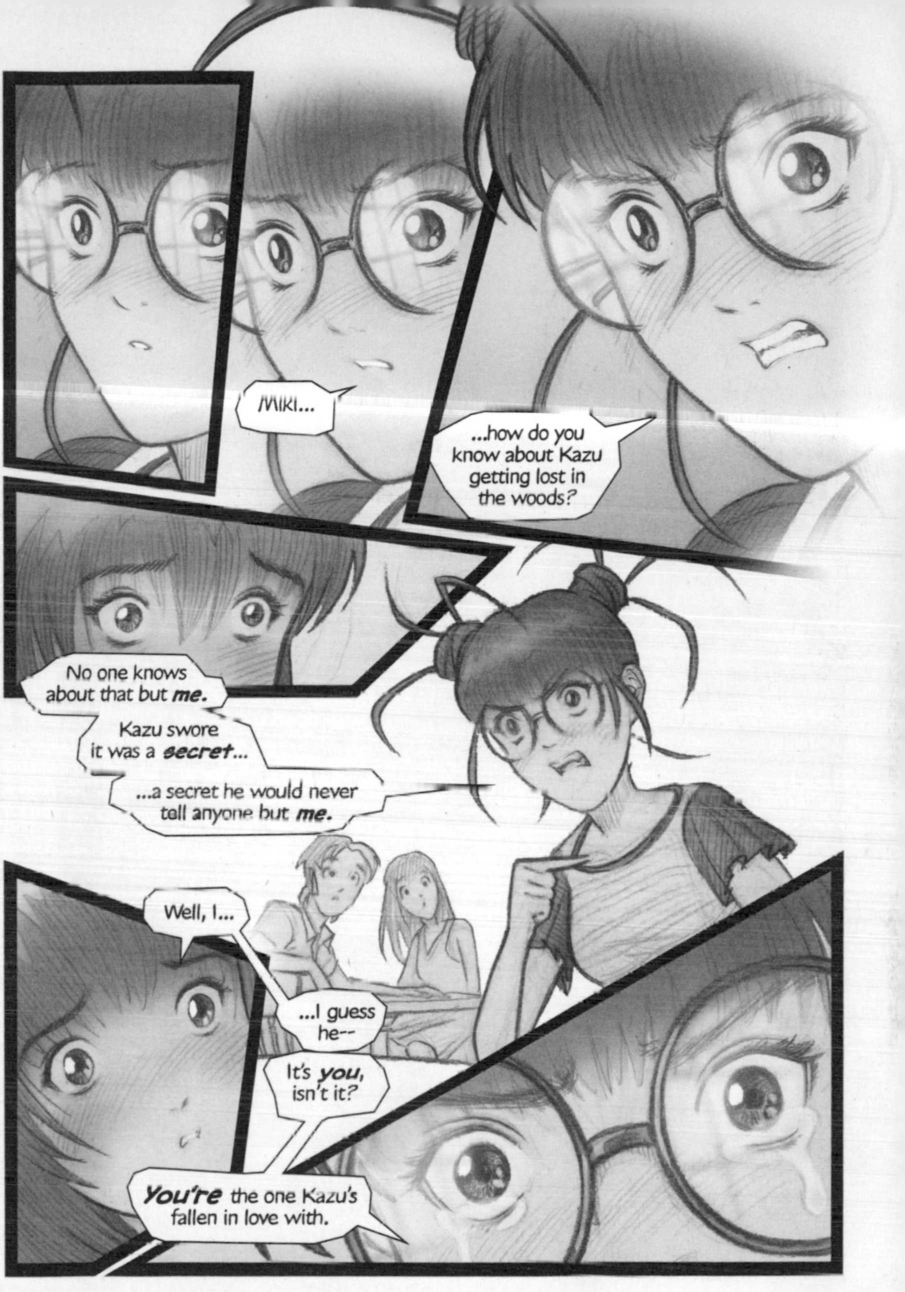
MIKI...
...how do you know about Kazu getting lost in the woods?
No one knows about that but ***me.***
Kazu swore it was a ***secret***...
...a secret he would never tell anyone but ***me.***
Well, I...
...I guess he--
It's ***you,*** isn't it?
You're the one Kazu's fallen in love with.

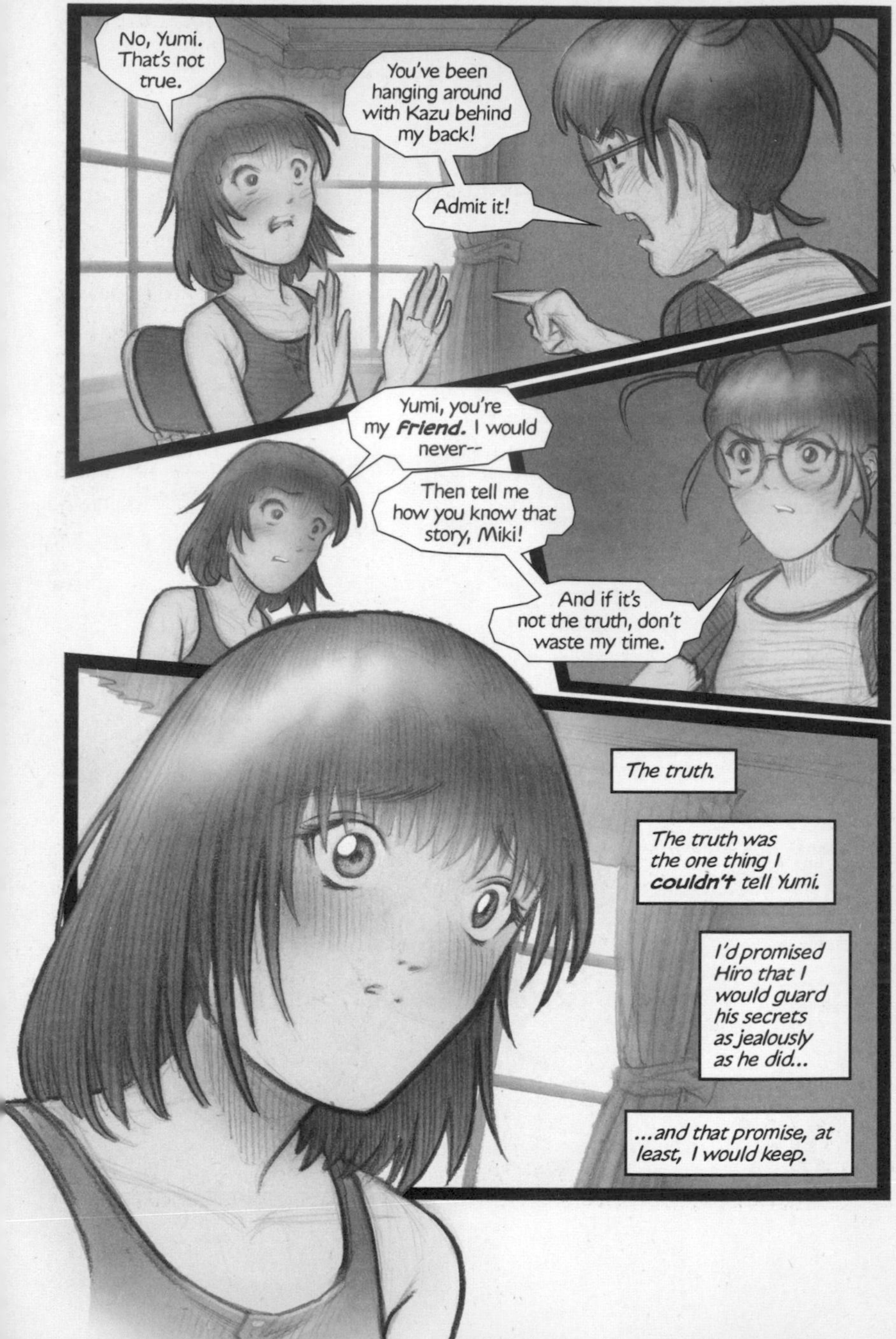
No, Yumi. That's not true.
You've been hanging around with Kazu behind my back!
Admit it!
Yumi, you're my **friend.** I would never--
Then tell me how you know that story, Miki!
And if it's not the truth, don't waste my time.
The truth.
The truth was the one thing I ***couldn't*** *tell Yumi.*
I'd promised Hiro that I would guard his secrets as jealously as he did...
...and that promise, at least, I would keep.

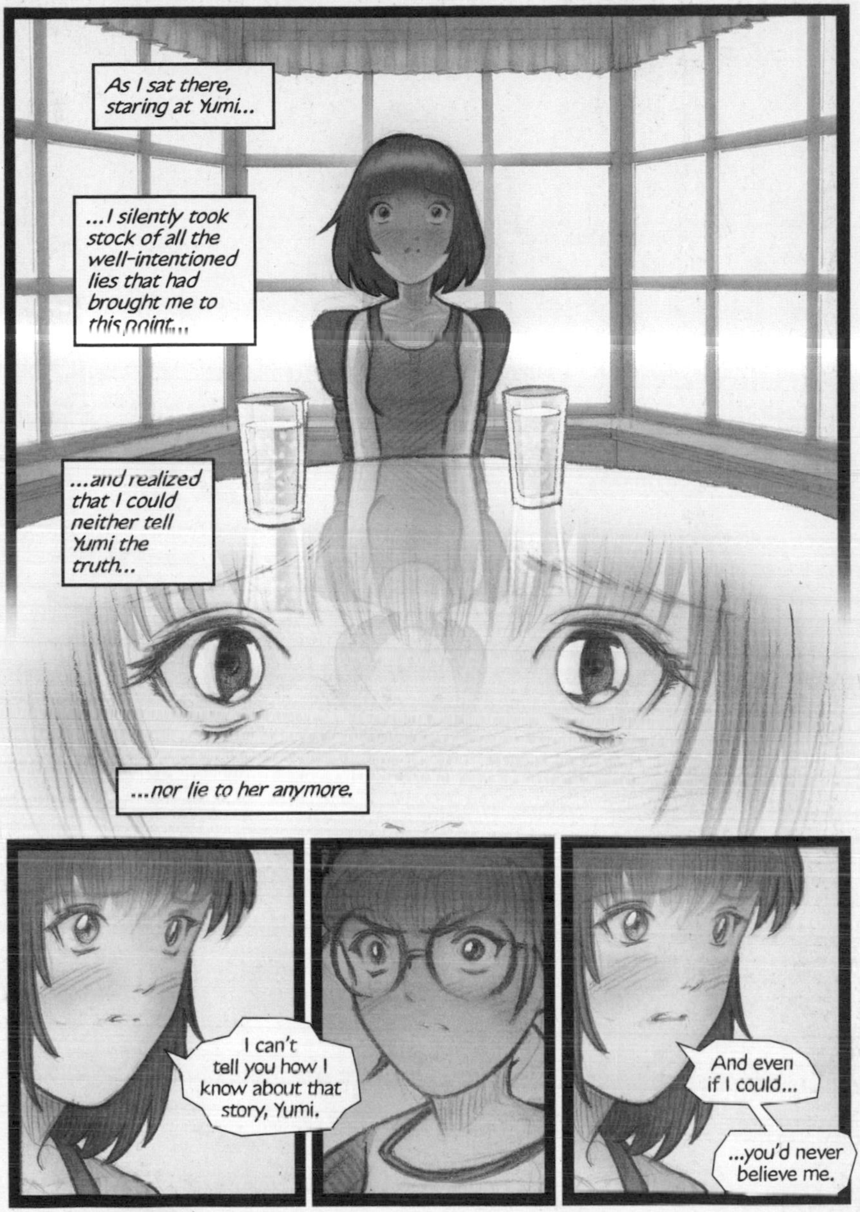
As I sat there, staring at Yumi...
...I silently took stock of all the well-intentioned lies that had brought me to this point...
...and realized that I could neither tell Yumi the truth...
...nor lie to her anymore.
I can't tell you how I know about that story, Yumi.
And even if I could...
...you'd never believe me.

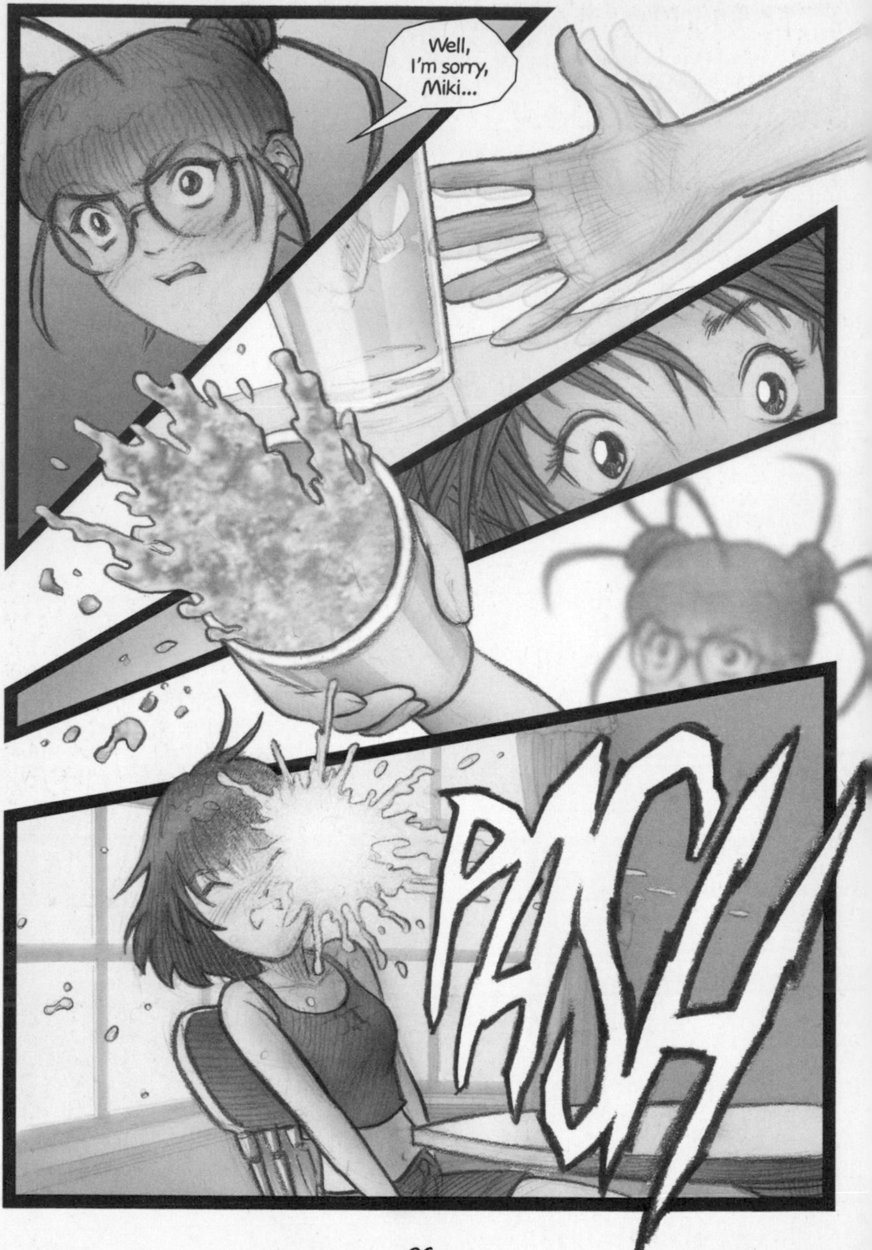
Well, I'm sorry, Miki...
PASH

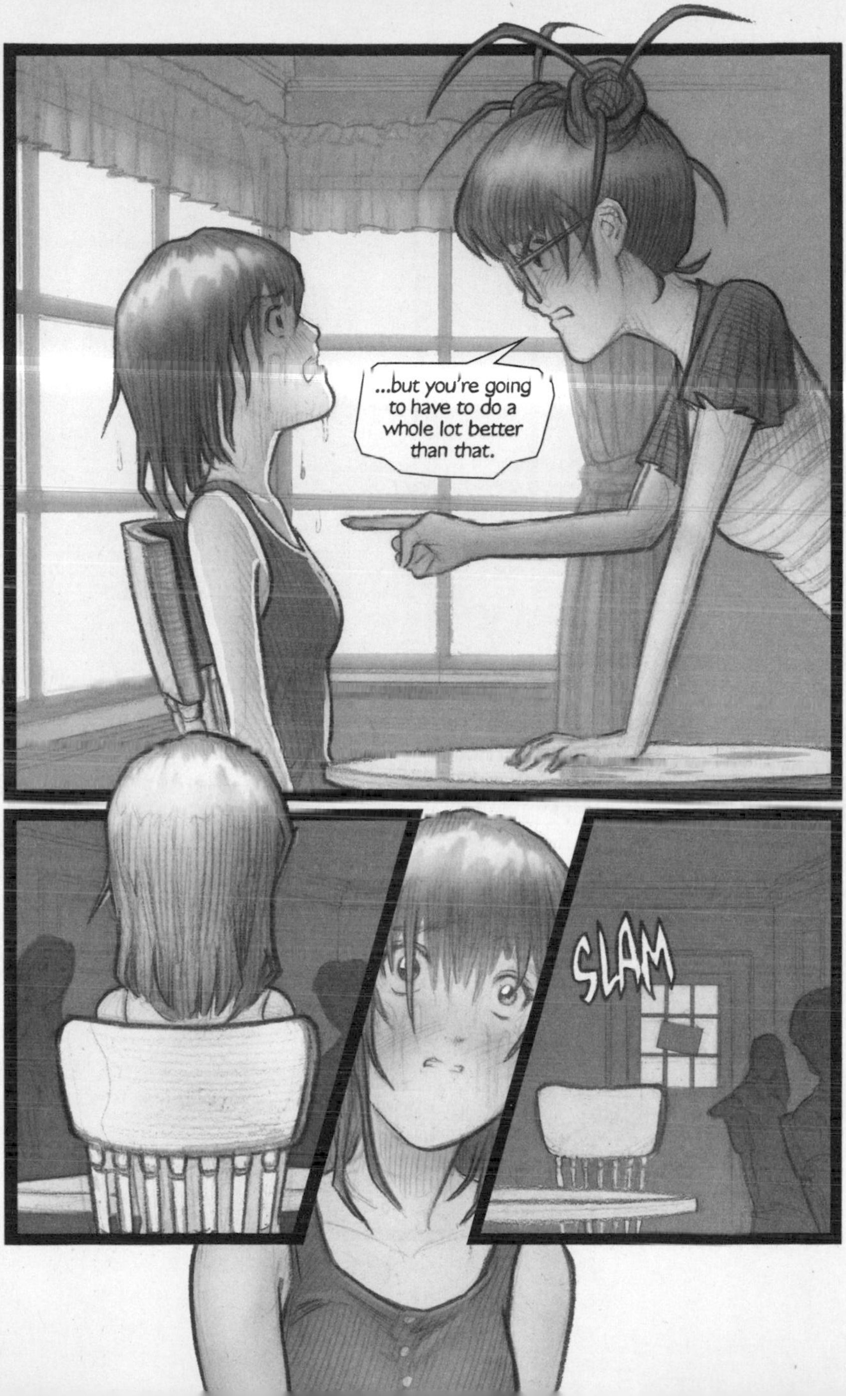
...but you're going to have to do a whole lot better than that.
SLAM

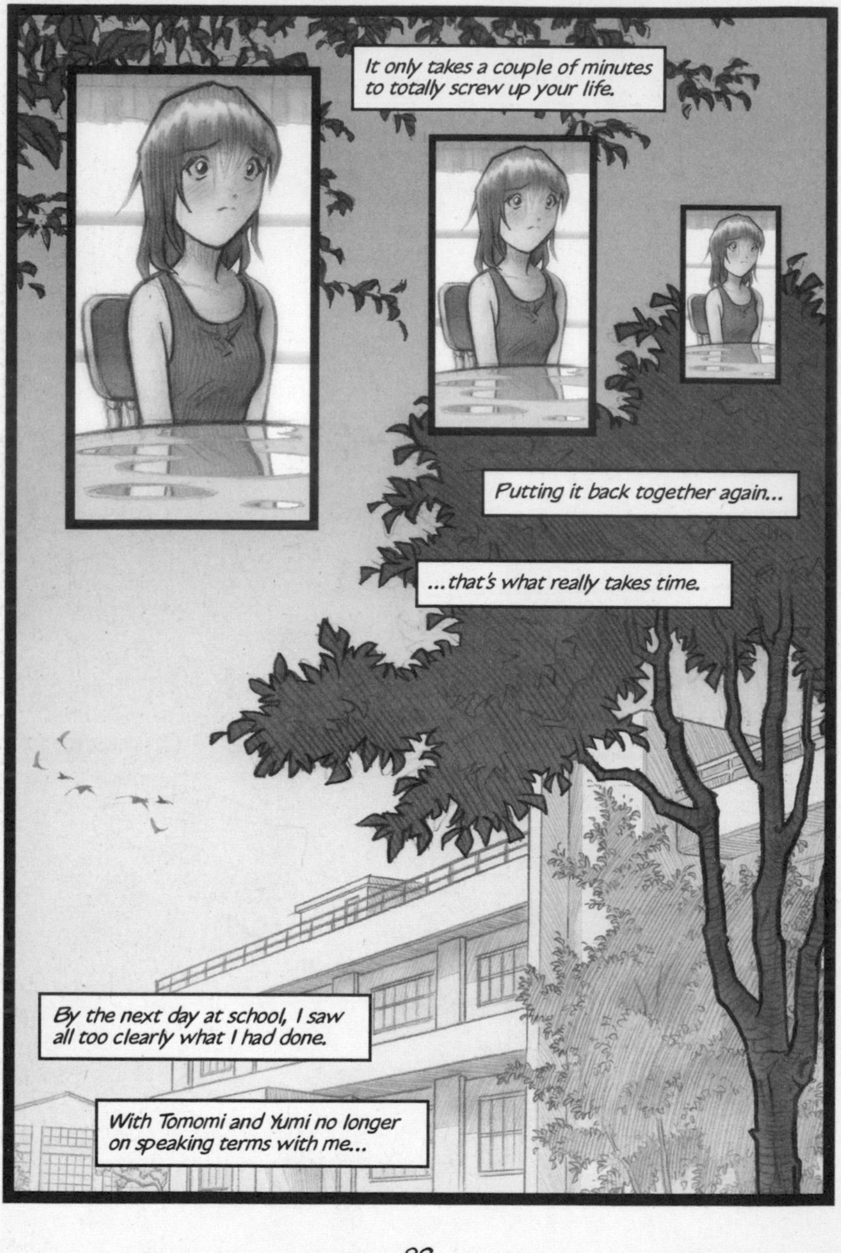

It only takes a couple of minutes to totally screw up your life.
Putting it back together again...
...that's what really takes time.
By the next day at school, I saw all too clearly what I had done.
With Tomomi and Yumi no longer on speaking terms with me...

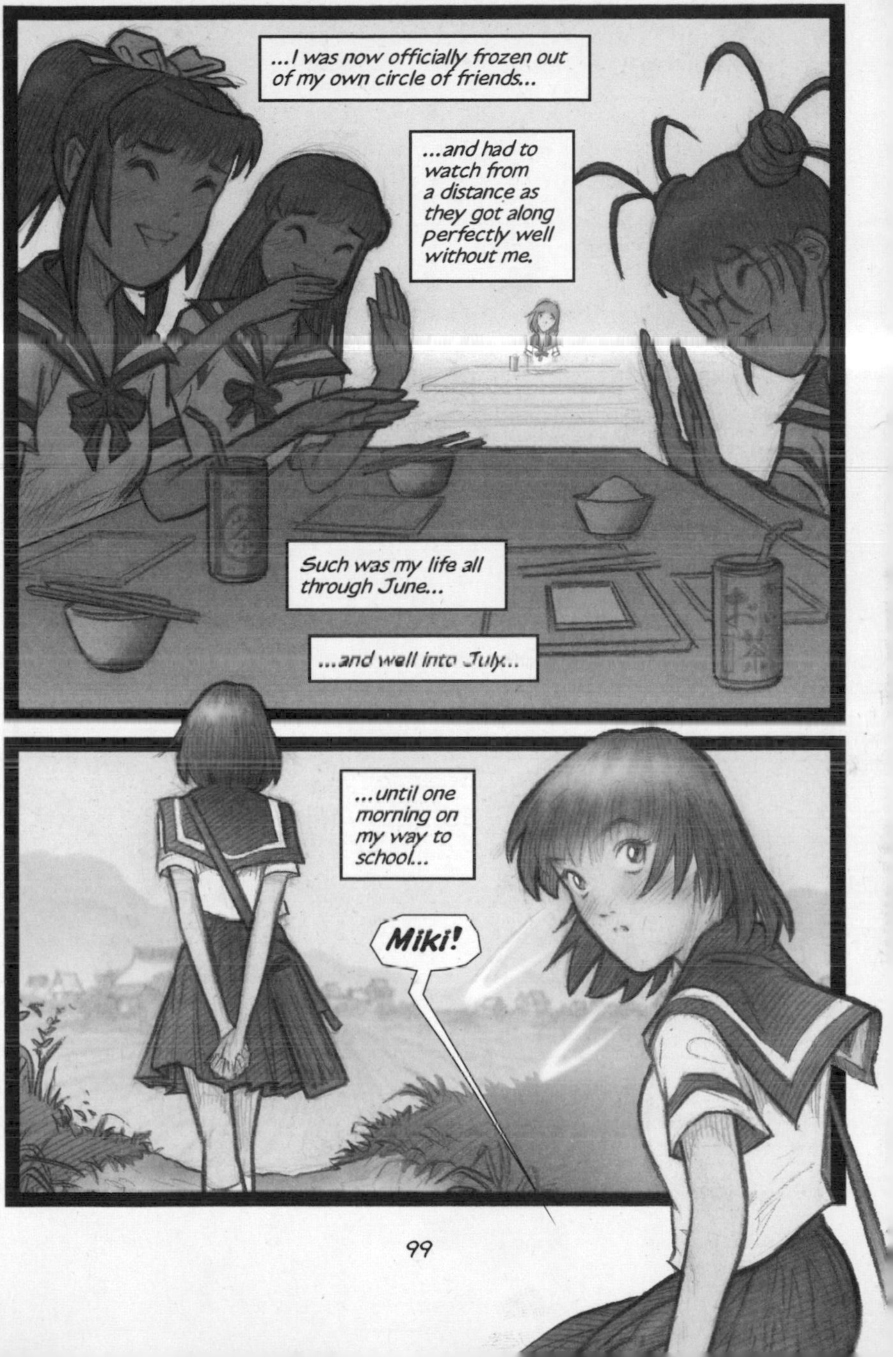
...I was now officially frozen out of my own circle of friends...
...and had to watch from a distance as they got along perfectly well without me.
Such was my life all through June...
...and well into July...
...until one morning on my way to school...
Miki!

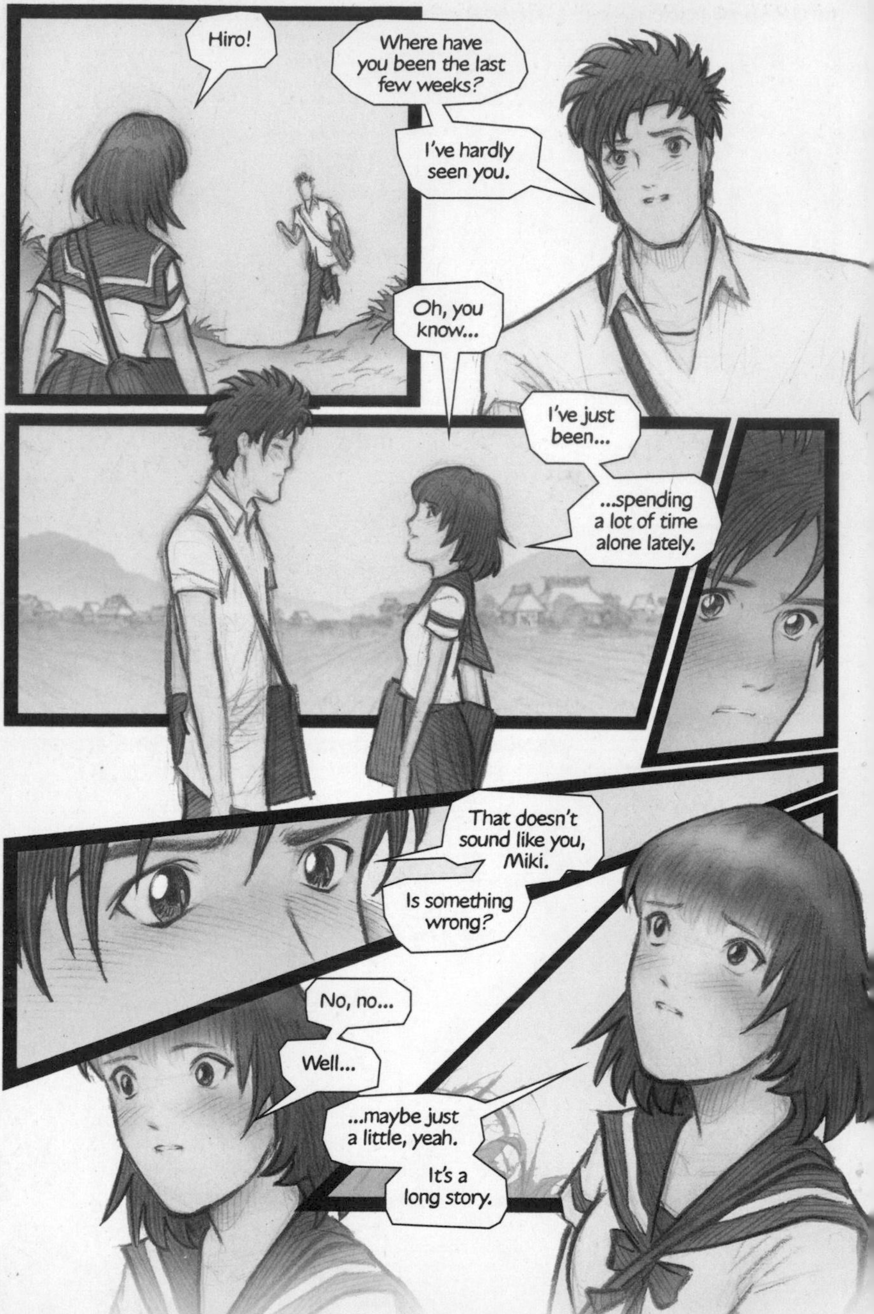
Hiro!
Where have you been the last few weeks?
I've hardly seen you.
Oh, you know...
I've just been...
...spending a lot of time alone lately.
That doesn't sound like you, Miki.
Is something wrong?
No, no...
Well...
...maybe just a little, yeah.
It's a long story.

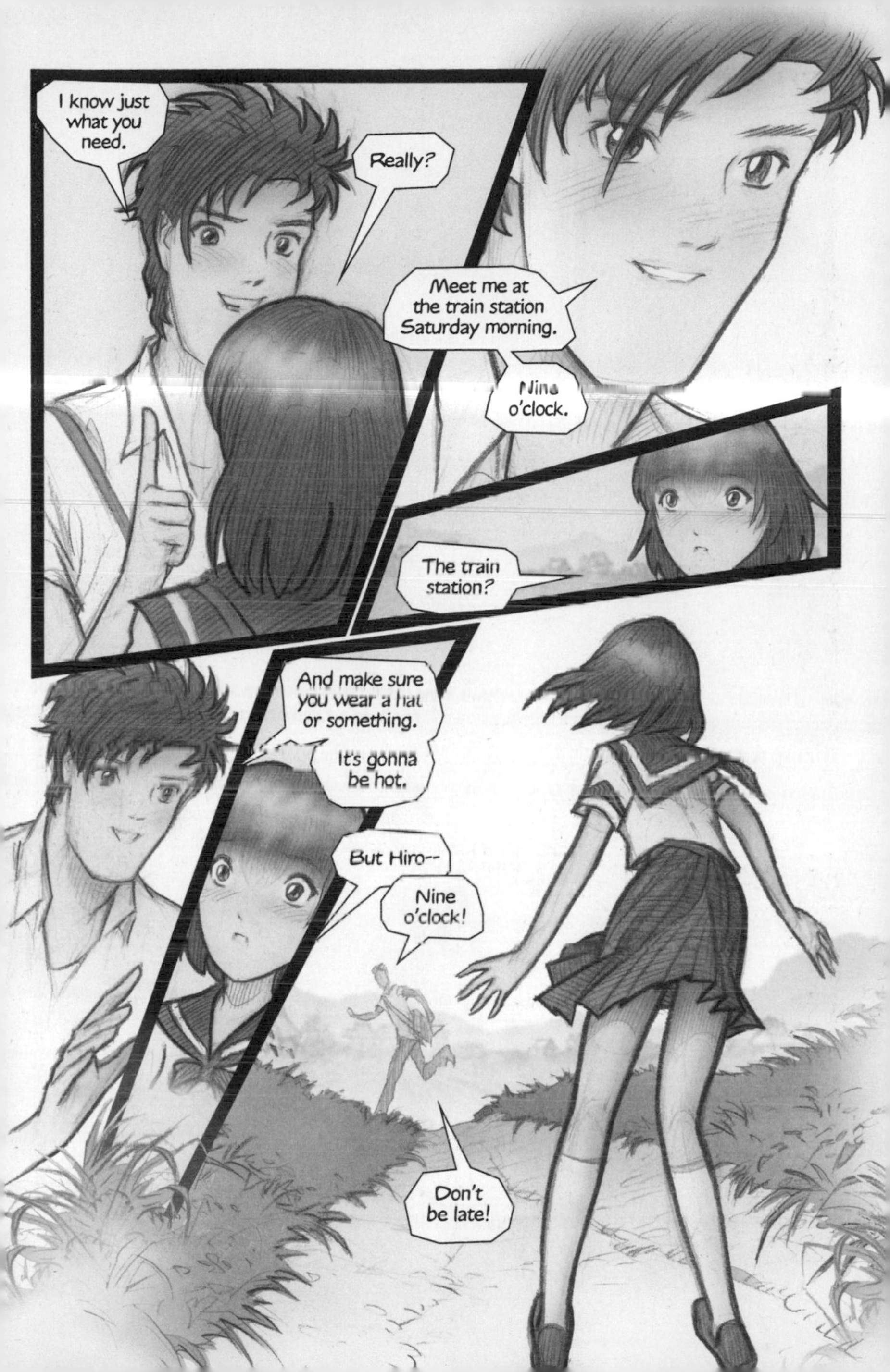
I know just what you need.
Really?
Meet me at the train station Saturday morning.
Nine o'clock.
The train station?
And make sure you wear a hat or something.
It's gonna be hot.
But Hiro--
Nine o'clock!
Don't be late!

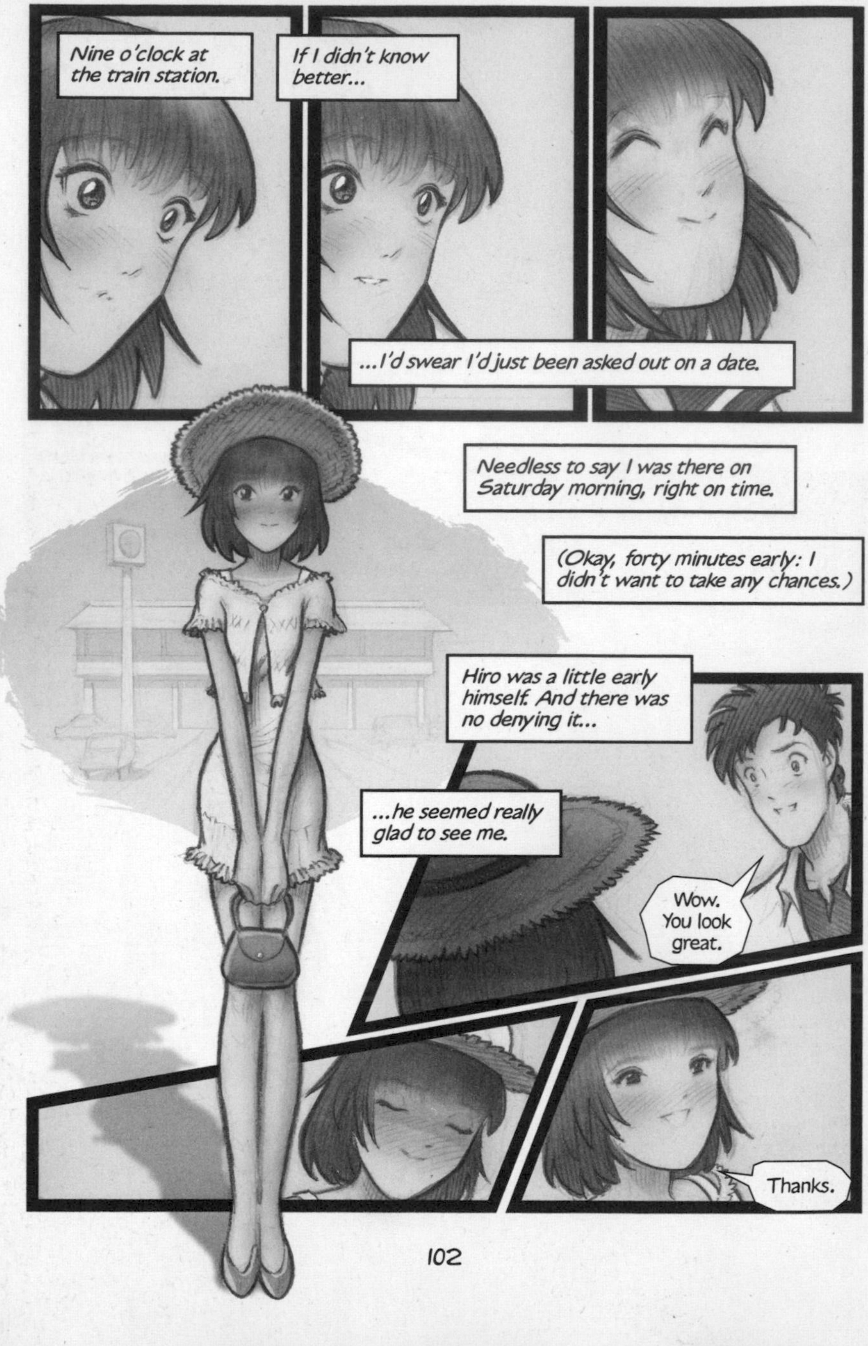
Nine o'clock at the train station.
If I didn't know better...
...I'd swear I'd just been asked out on a date.
Needless to say I was there on Saturday morning, right on time.
(Okay, forty minutes early: I didn't want to take any chances.)
Hiro was a little early himself. And there was no denying it...
...he seemed really glad to see me.
Wow. You look great.
Thanks.

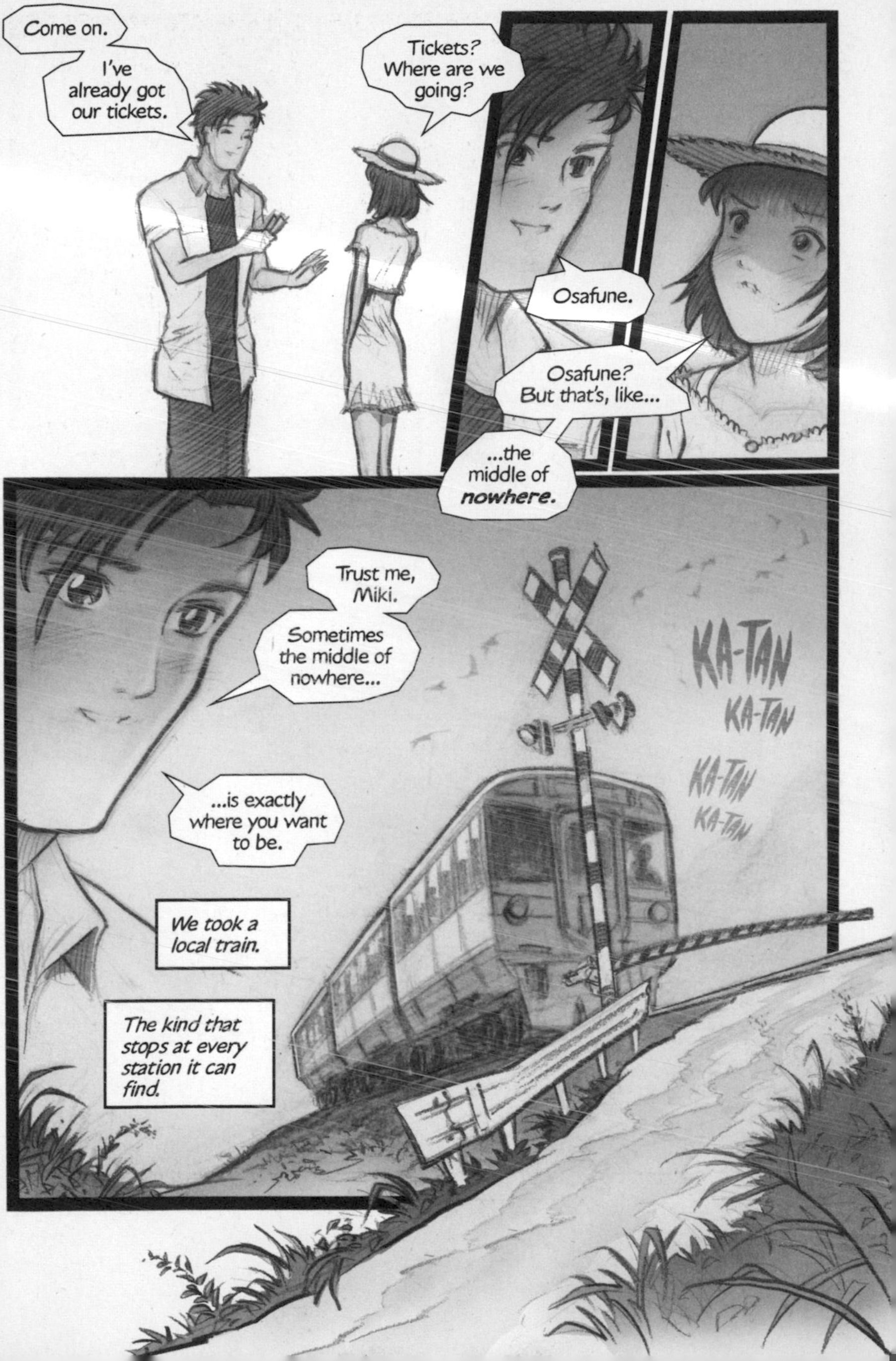
Come on.
I've already got our tickets.
Tickets? Where are we going?
Osafune.
Osafune? But that's, like...
...the middle of *nowhere.*
Trust me, Miki.
Sometimes the middle of nowhere...
...is exactly where you want to be.
KA-TAN
KA-TAN
KA-TAN
KA-TAN
We took a local train.
The kind that stops at every station it can find.

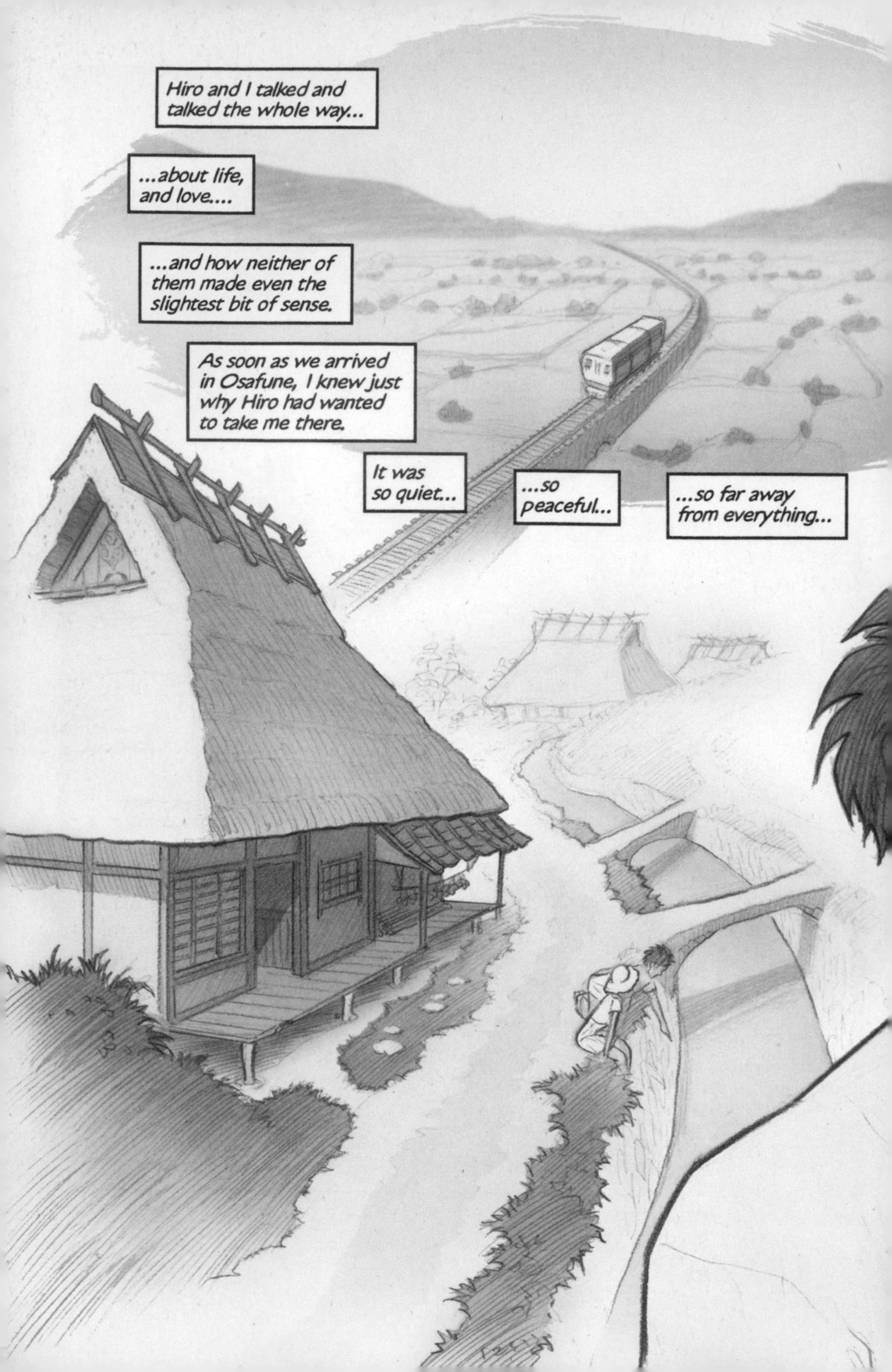
Hiro and I talked and talked the whole way...
...about life, and love....
...and how neither of them made even the slightest bit of sense.
As soon as we arrived in Osafune, I knew just why Hiro had wanted to take me there.
It was so quiet...
...so peaceful...
...so far away from everything...

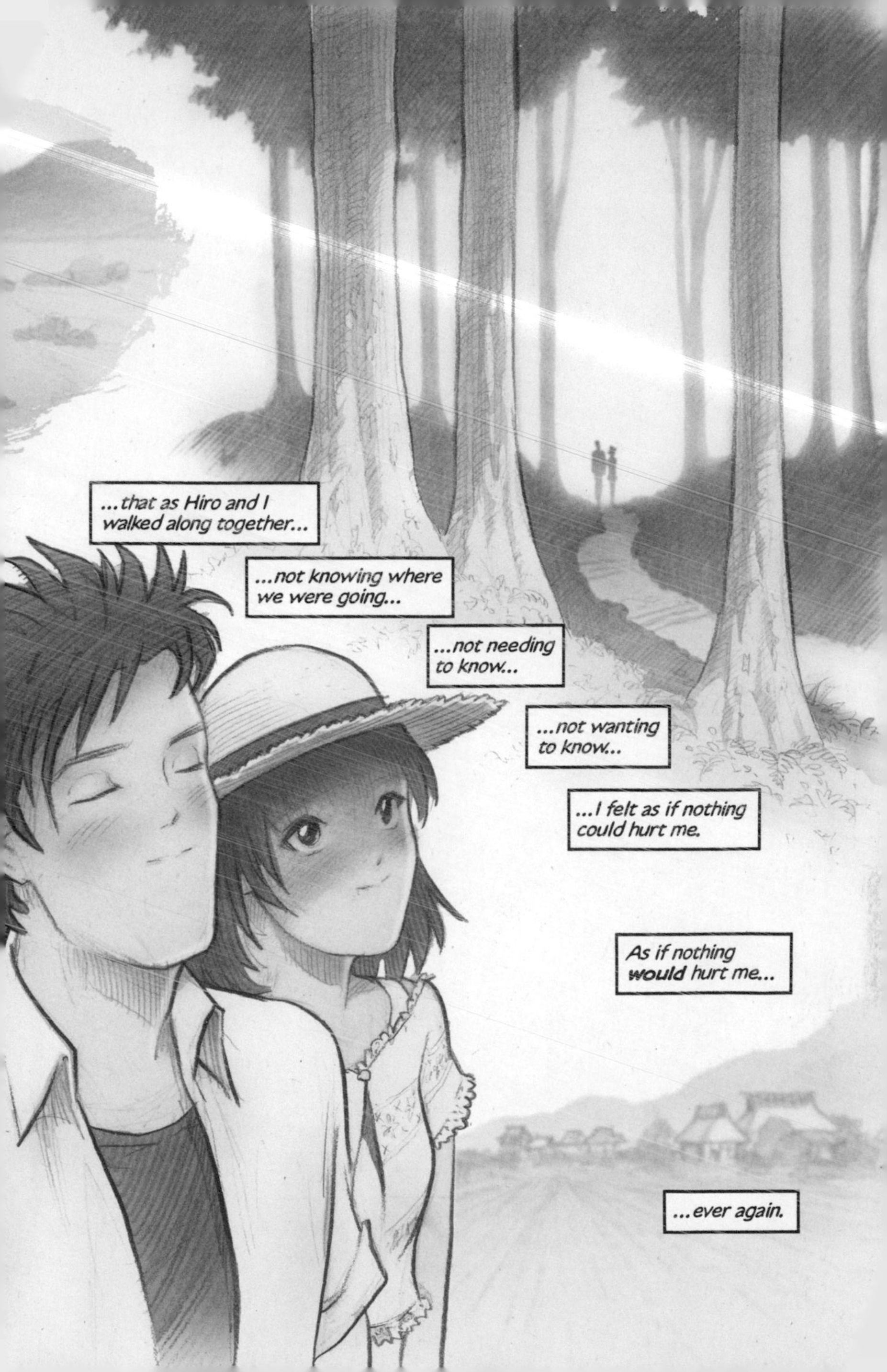
...that as Hiro and I walked along together...
...not knowing where we were going...
...not needing to know...
...not wanting to know...
...I felt as if nothing could hurt me.
As if nothing **would** hurt me...
...ever again.

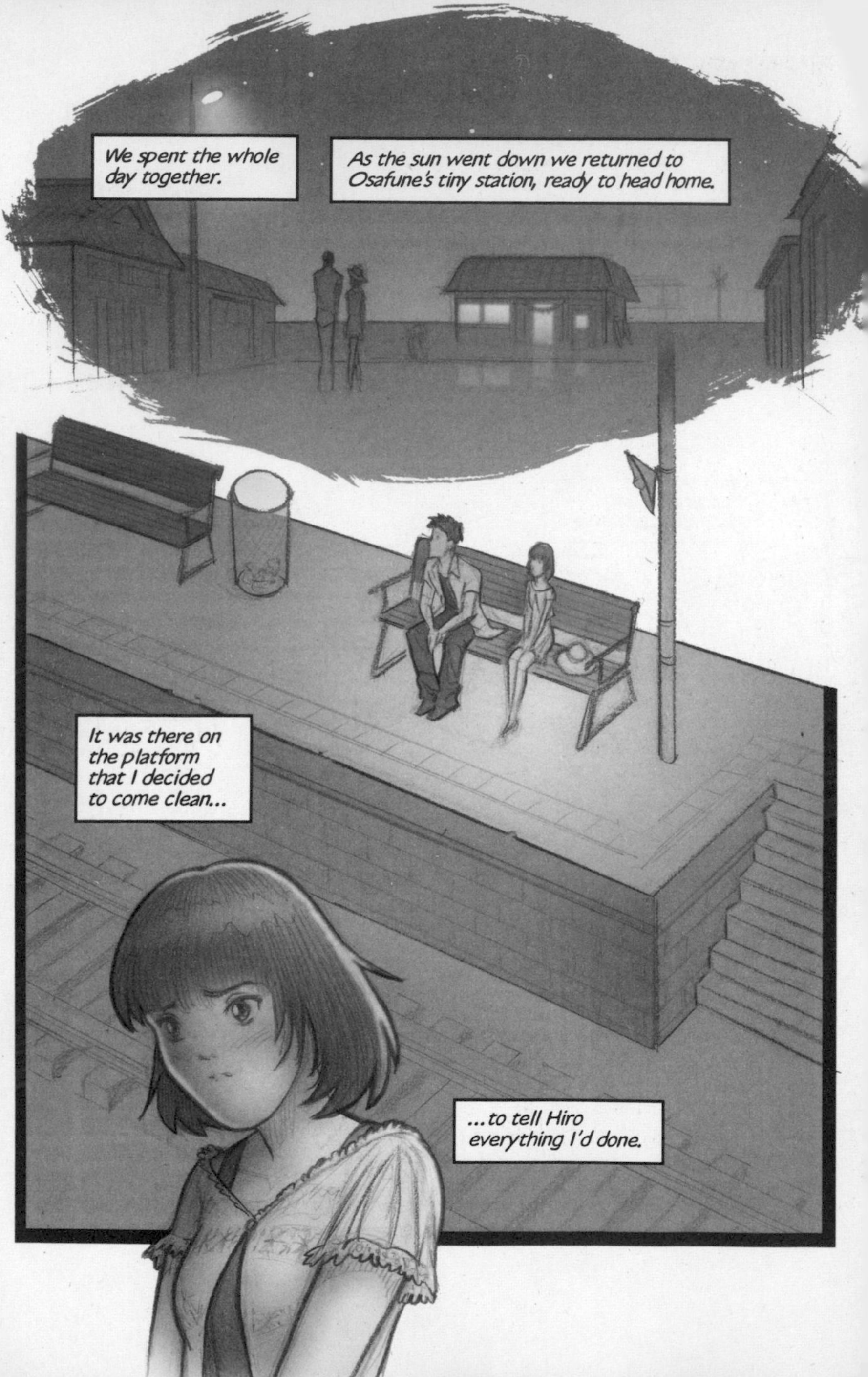
We spent the whole day together.
As the sun went down we returned to Osafune's tiny station, ready to head home.
It was there on the platform that I decided to come clean...
...to tell Hiro everything I'd done.

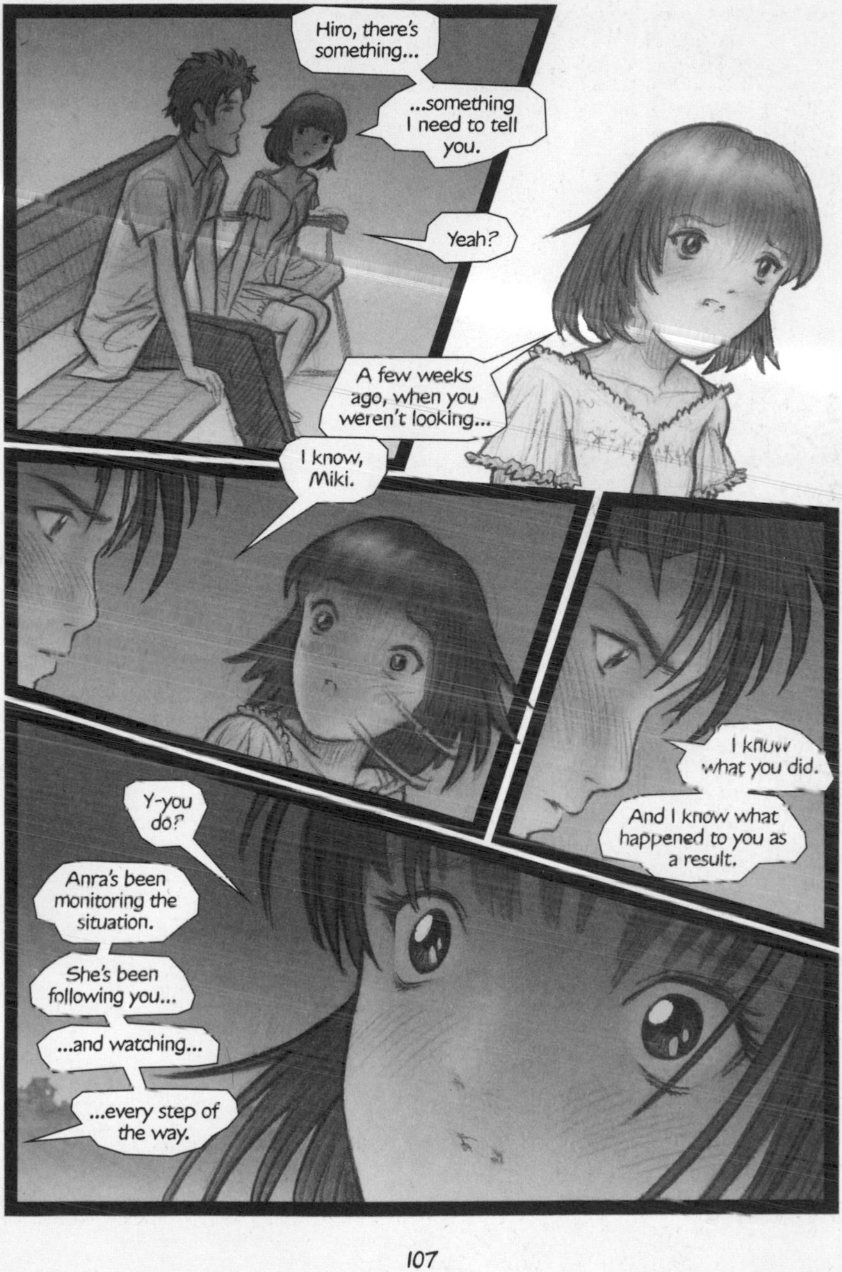
Hiro, there's something...
...something I need to tell you.
Yeah?
A few weeks ago, when you weren't looking...
I know, Miki.
I know what you did.
And I know what happened to you as a result.
Y-you do?
Anra's been monitoring the situation.
She's been following you...
...and watching...
...every step of the way.

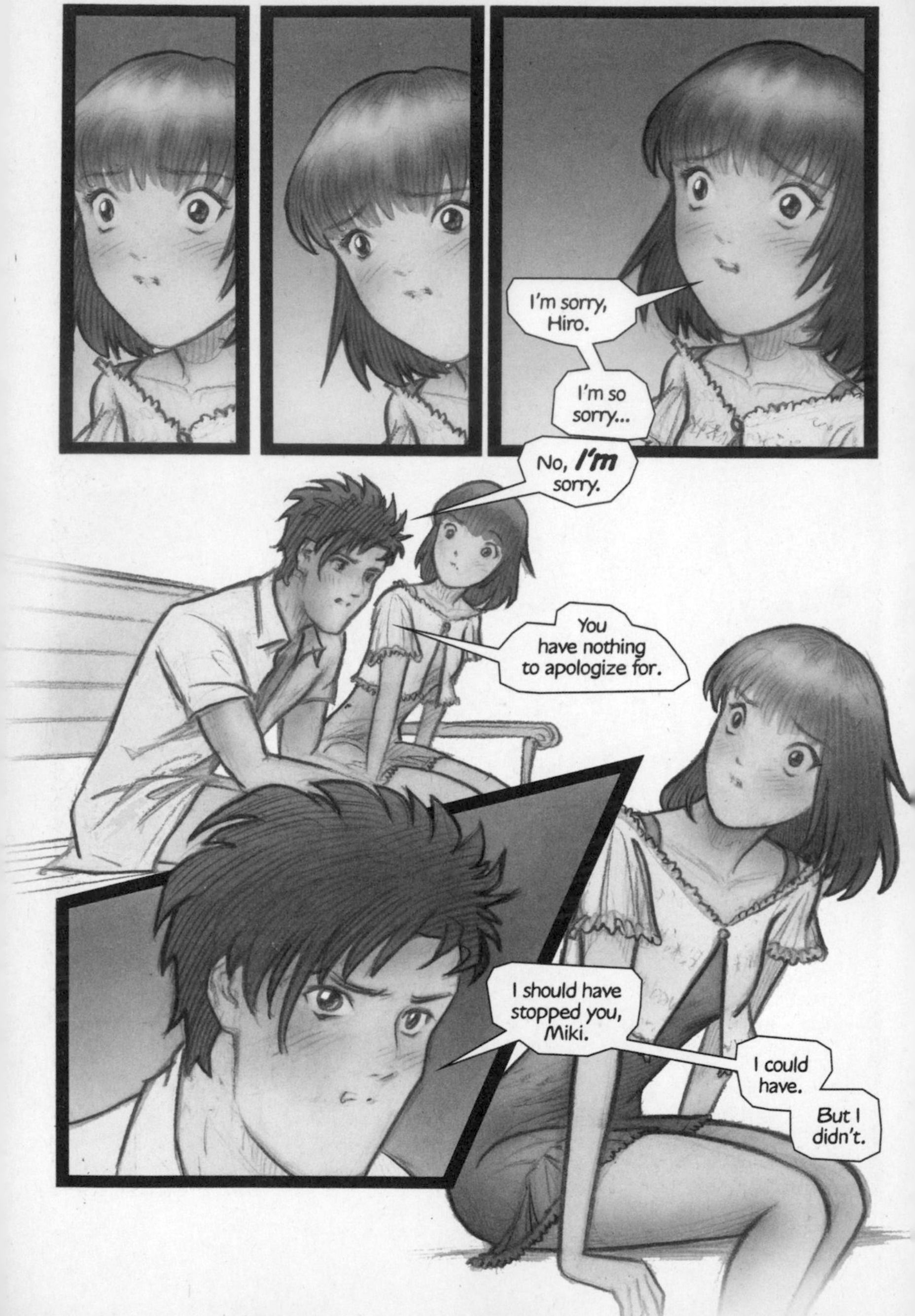
I'm sorry, Hiro.
I'm so sorry...
No, *I'm* sorry.
You have nothing to apologize for.
I should have stopped you, Miki.
I could have.
But I didn't.

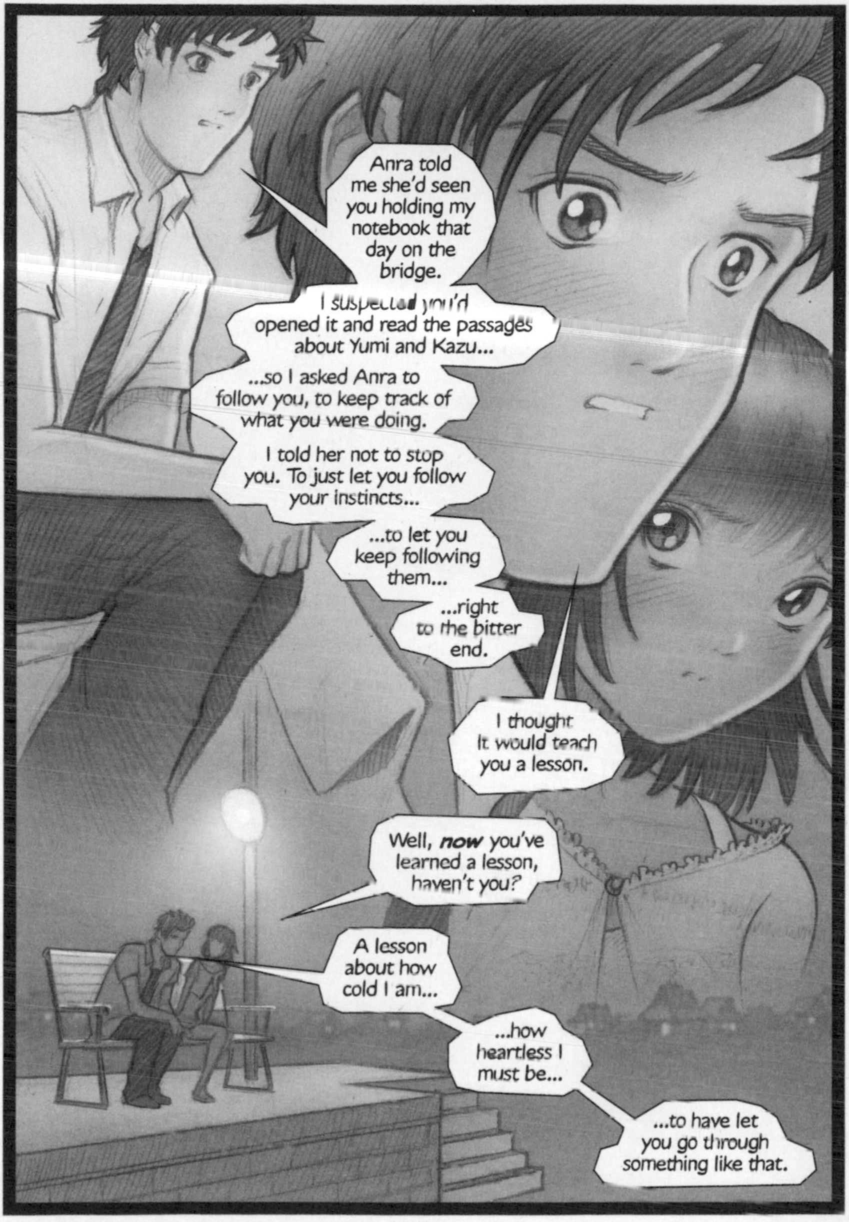
Anra told me she'd seen you holding my notebook that day on the bridge.
I suspected you'd opened it and read the passages about Yumi and Kazu...
...so I asked Anra to follow you, to keep track of what you were doing.
I told her not to stop you. To just let you follow your instincts...
...to let you keep following them...
...right to the bitter end.
I thought it would teach you a lesson.
Well, *now* you've learned a lesson, haven't you?
A lesson about how cold I am...
...how heartless I must be...
...to have let you go through something like that.

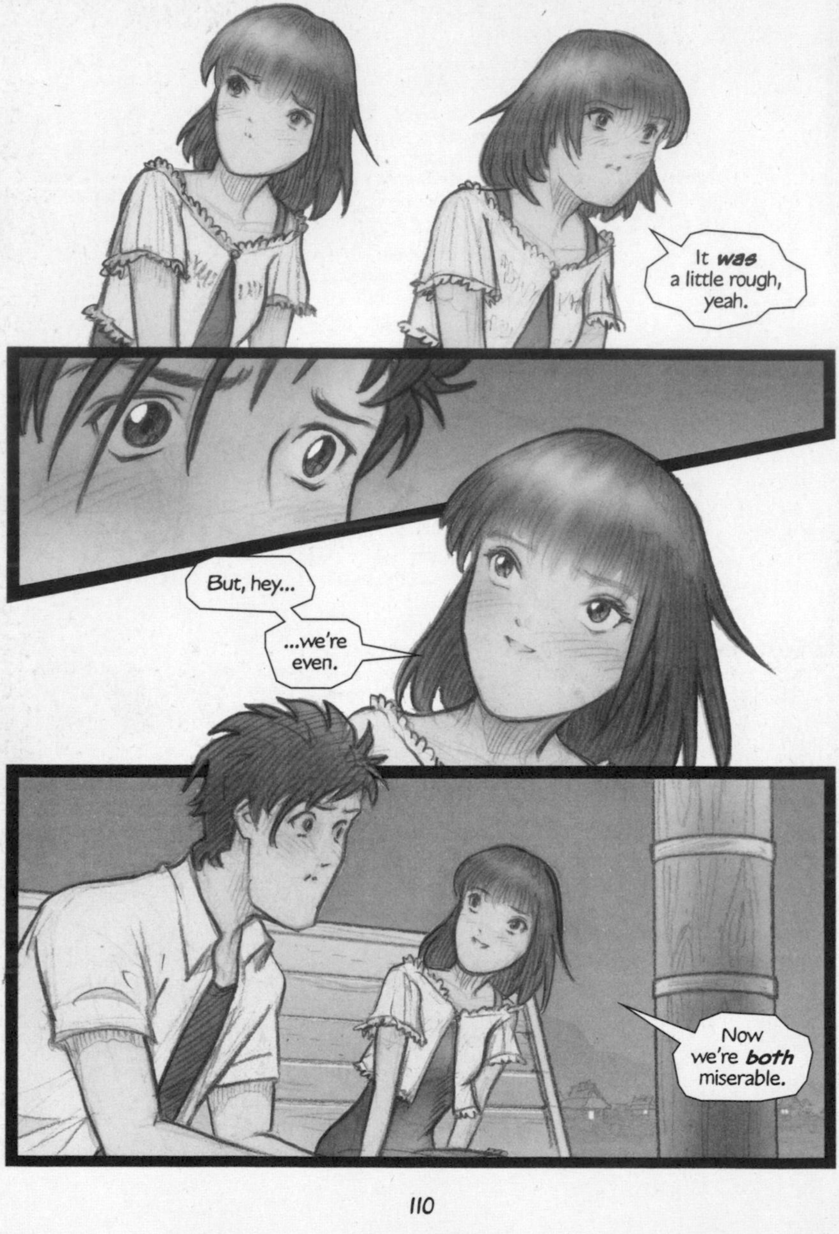
It **was** a little rough, yeah.
But, hey...
...we're even.
Now we're **both** miserable.

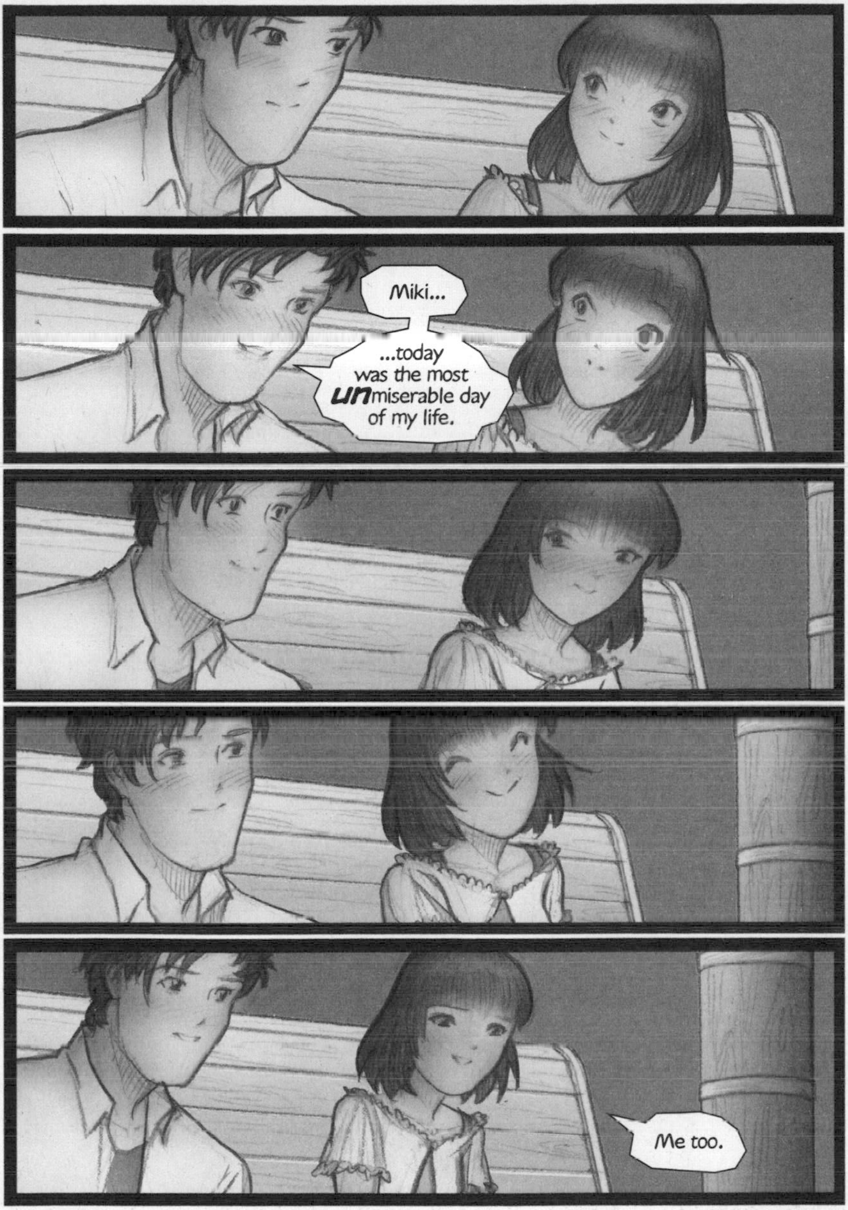
Miki...
...today was the most unmiserable day of my life.
Me too.

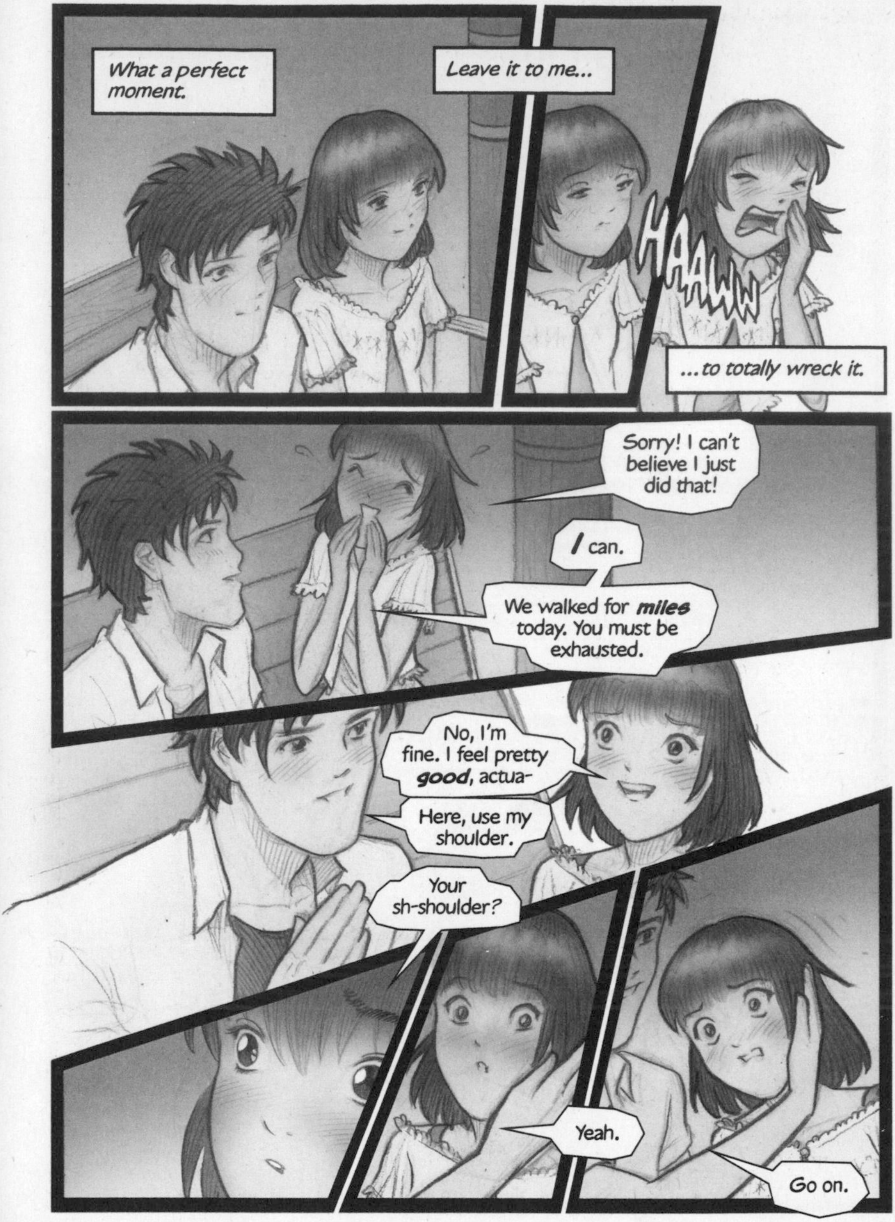
What a perfect moment.
Leave it to me...
HAAAWW
...to totally wreck it.
Sorry! I can't believe I just did that!
I can.
We walked for ***miles*** today. You must be exhausted.
No, I'm fine. I feel pretty ***good***, actua-
Here, use my shoulder.
Your sh-shoulder?
Yeah.
Go on.

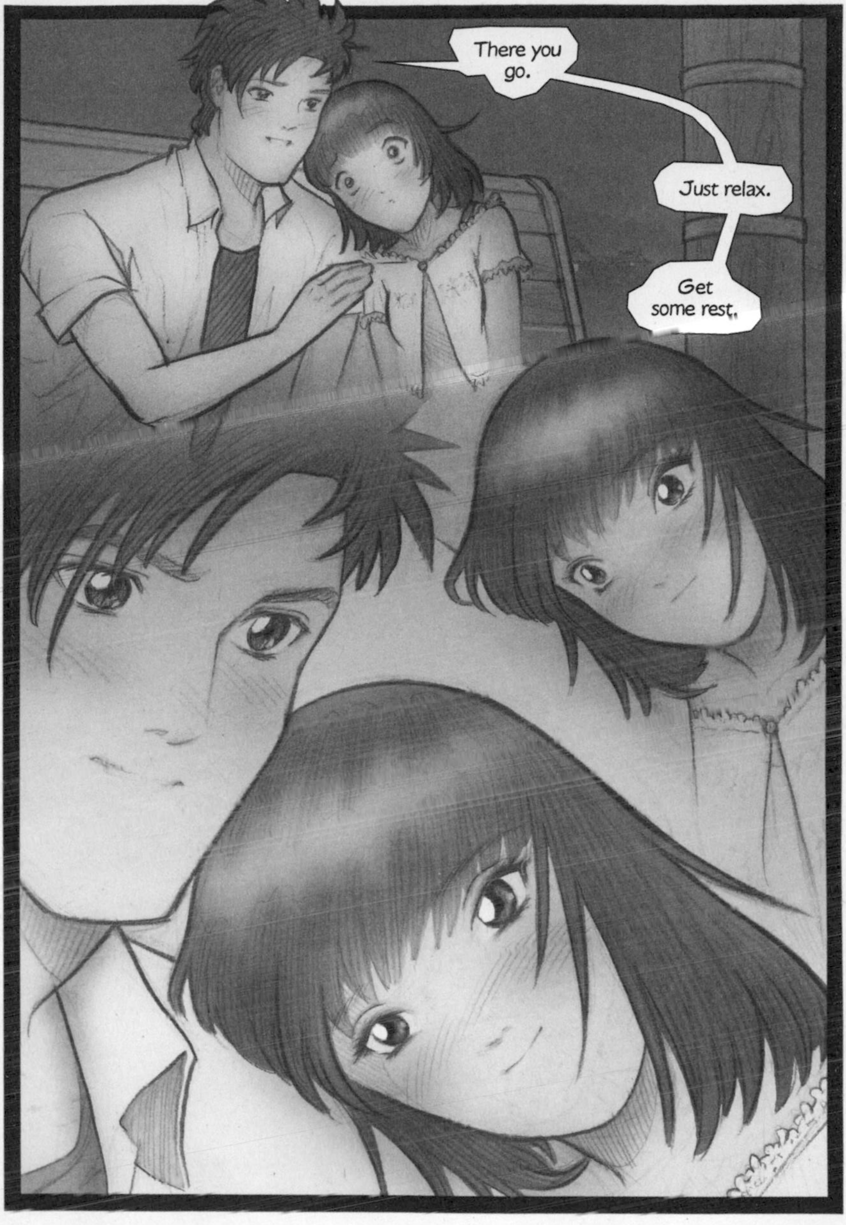
There you go.
Just relax.
Get some rest.

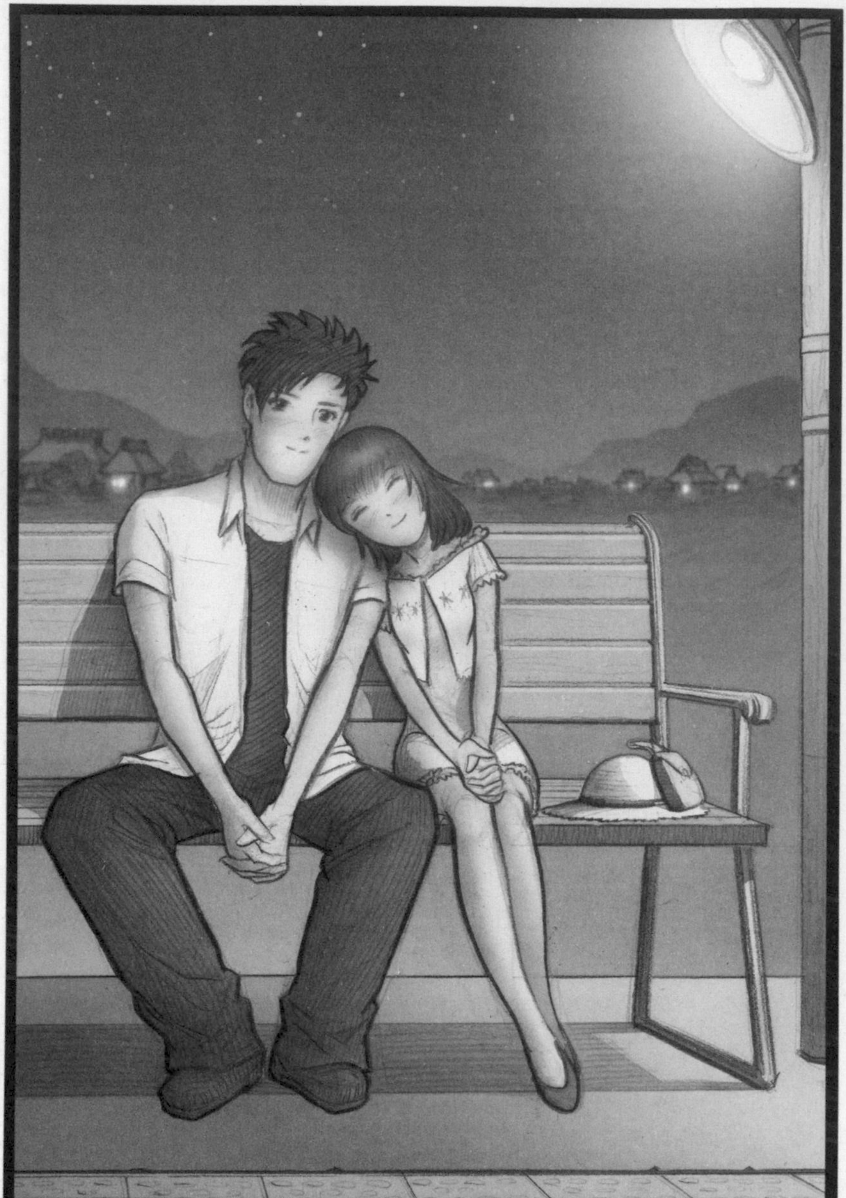

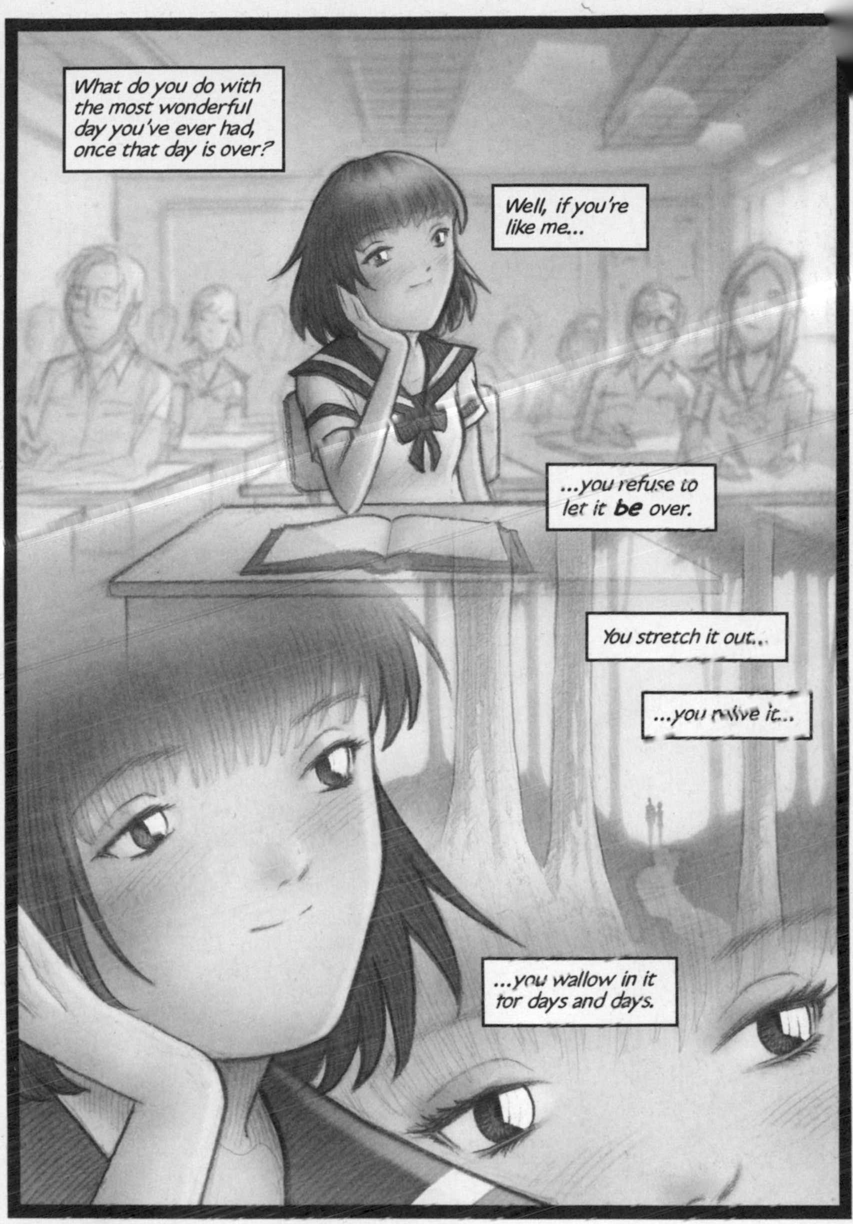
What do you do with the most wonderful day you've ever had, once that day is over?
Well, if you're like me...
...you refuse to let it **be** over.
You stretch it out...
...you relive it...
...you wallow in it for days and days.

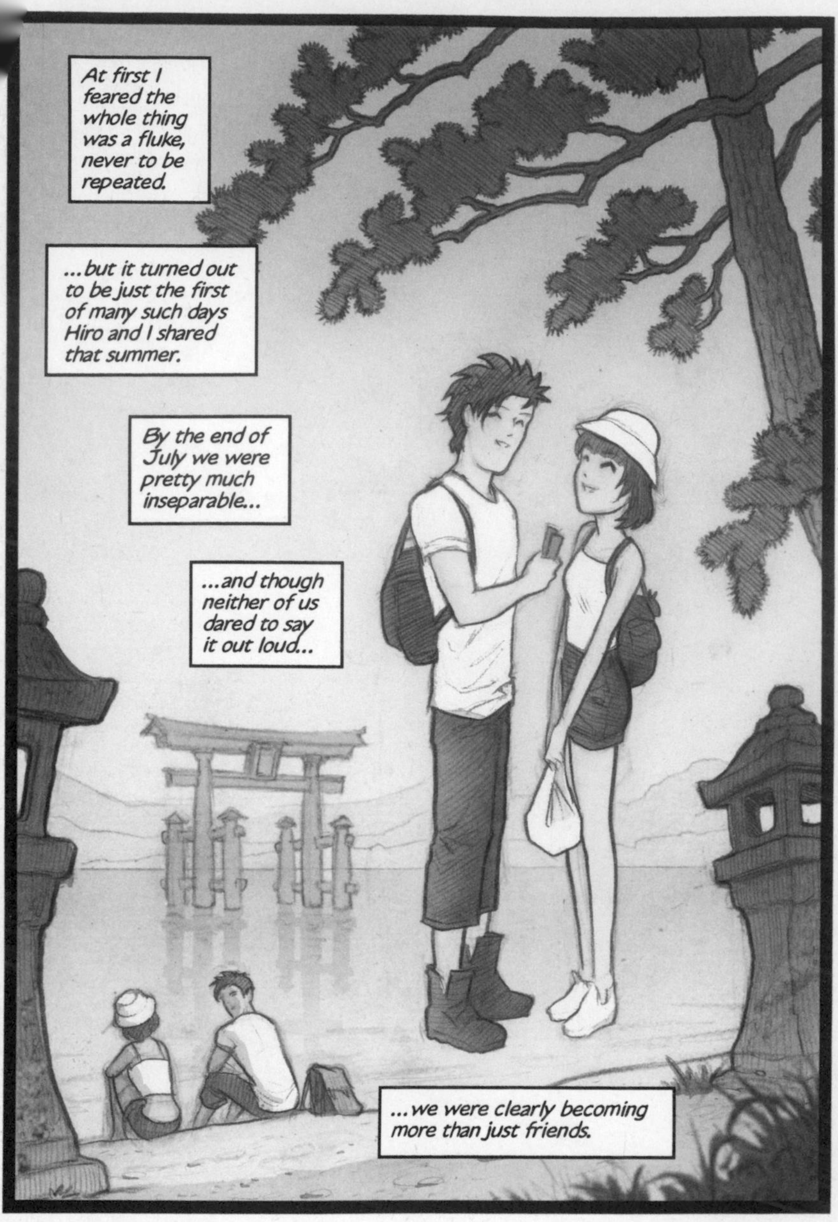
At first I feared the whole thing was a fluke, never to be repeated.
...but it turned out to be just the first of many such days Hiro and I shared that summer.
By the end of July we were pretty much inseparable...
...and though neither of us dared to say it out loud...
...we were clearly becoming more than just friends.

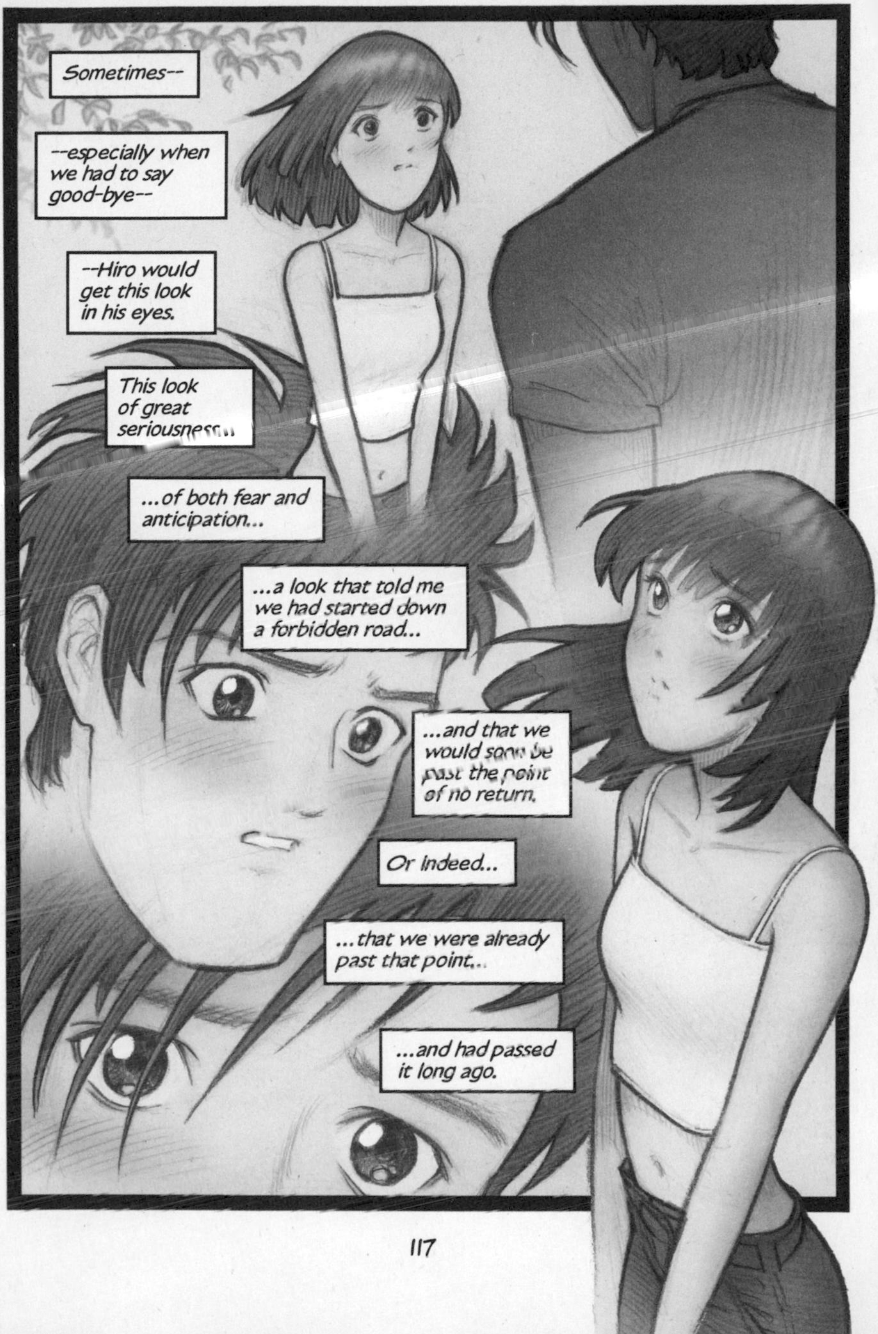

Sometimes--
--especially when we had to say good-bye--
--Hiro would get this look in his eyes.
This look of great seriousness...
...of both fear and anticipation...
...a look that told me we had started down a forbidden road...
...and that we would soon be past the point of no return.
Or indeed...
...that we were already past that point...
...and had passed it long ago.

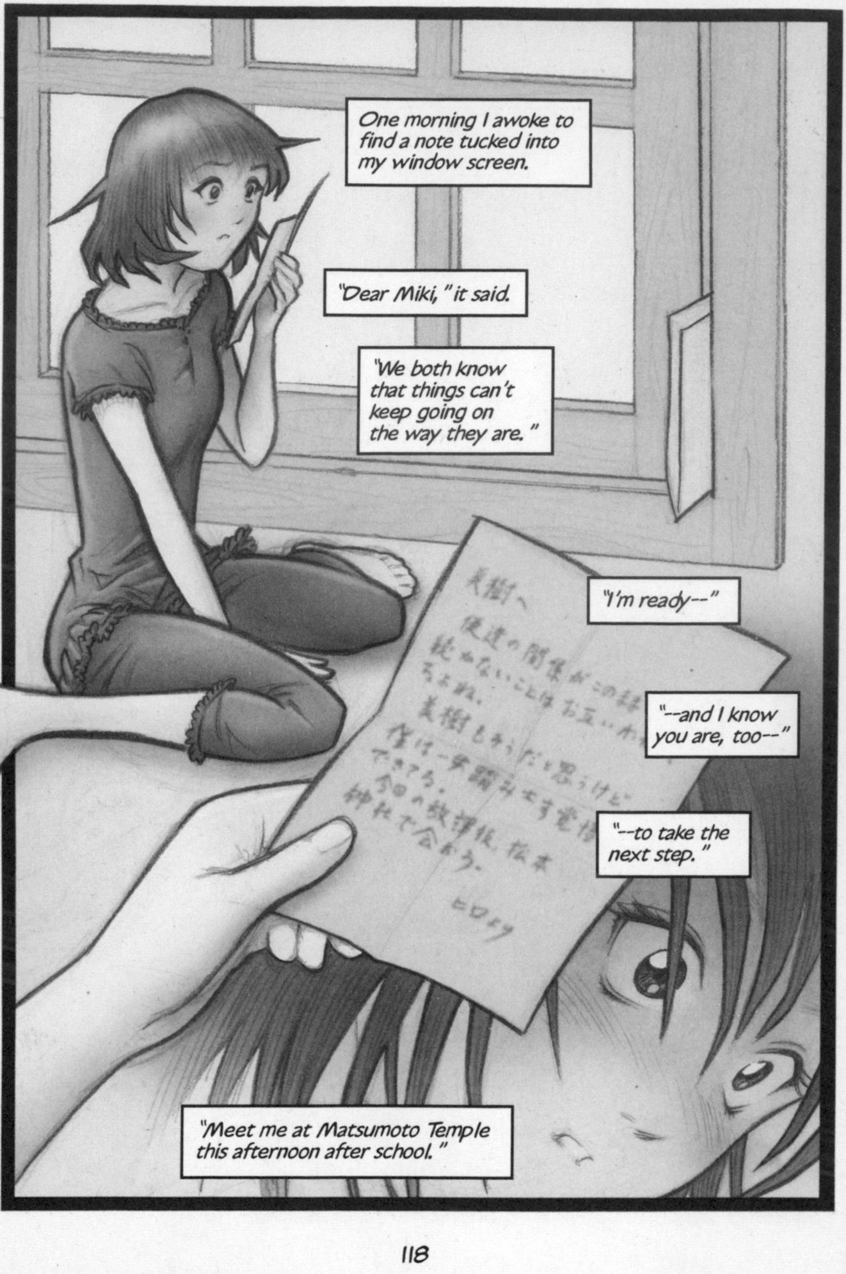
One morning I awoke to find a note tucked into my window screen.
"Dear Miki," it said.
"We both know that things can't keep going on the way they are."
"I'm ready--"
"--and I know you are, too--"
"--to take the next step."
"Meet me at Matsumoto Temple this afternoon after school."

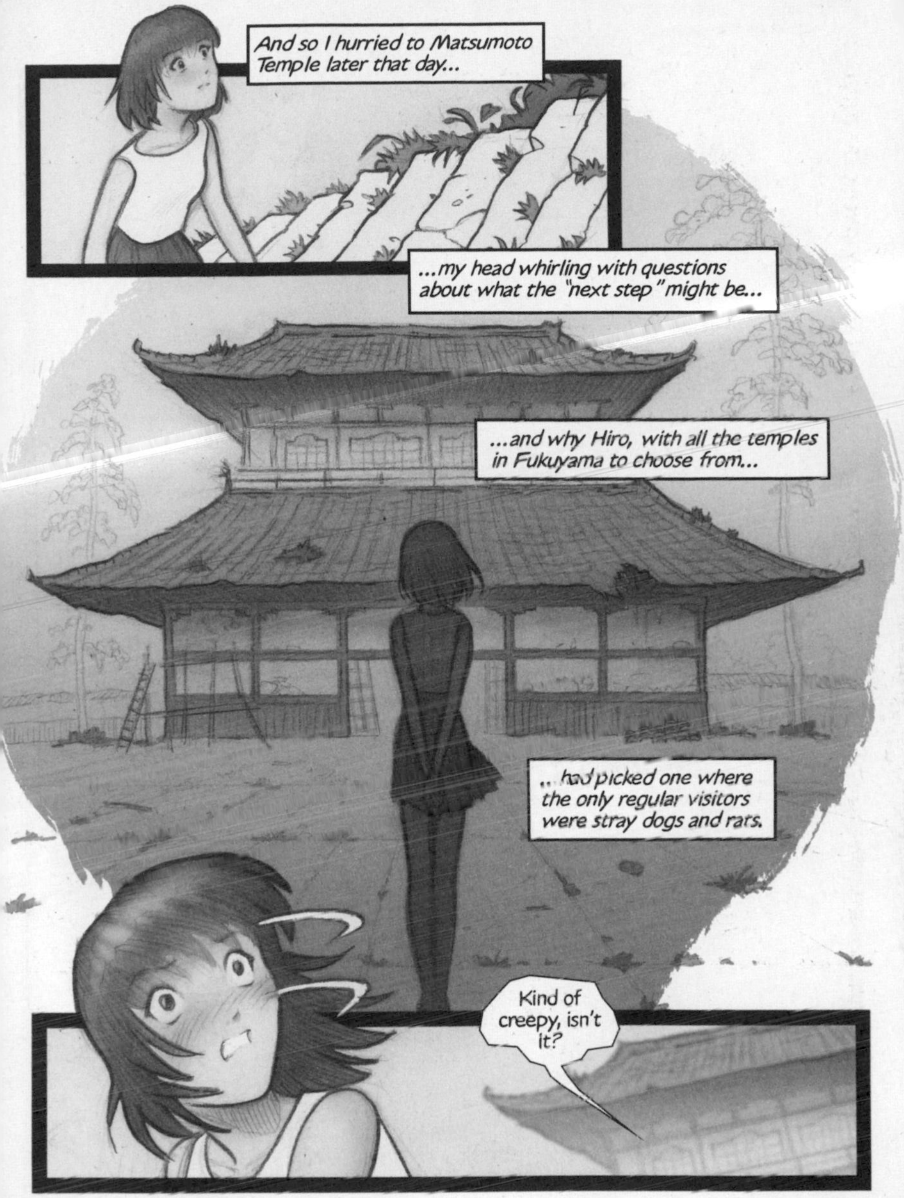
And so I hurried to Matsumoto Temple later that day...
...my head whirling with questions about what the "next step" might be...
...and why Hiro, with all the temples in Fukuyama to choose from...
...had picked one where the only regular visitors were stray dogs and rats.
Kind of creepy, isn't it?

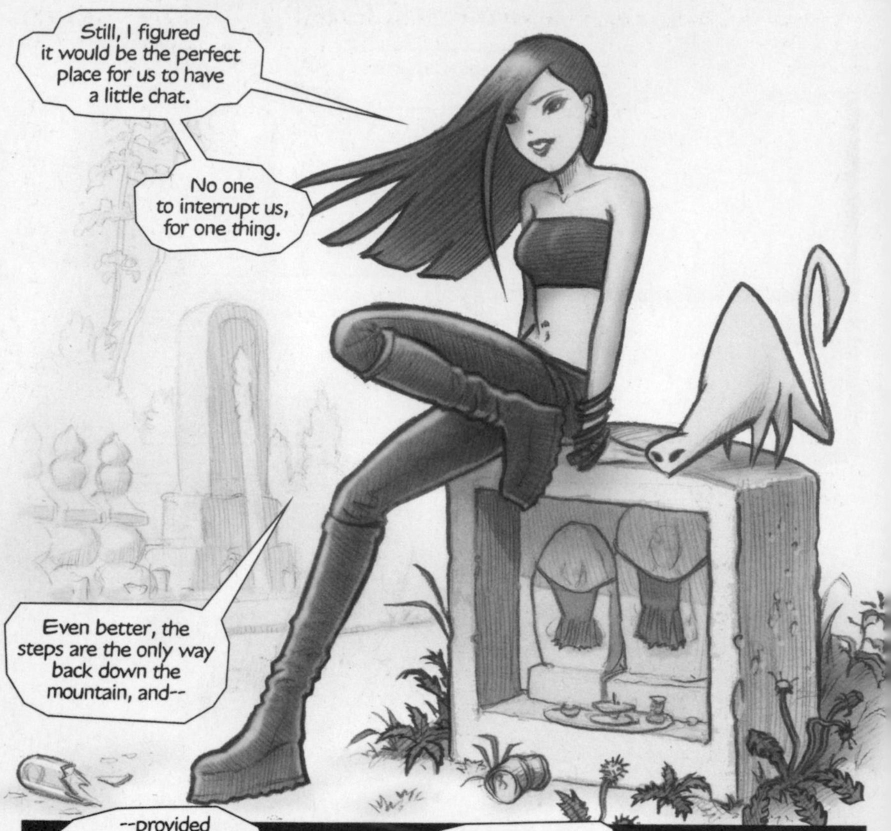
Still, I figured it would be the perfect place for us to have a little chat.
No one to interrupt us, for one thing.
Even better, the steps are the only way back down the mountain, and--

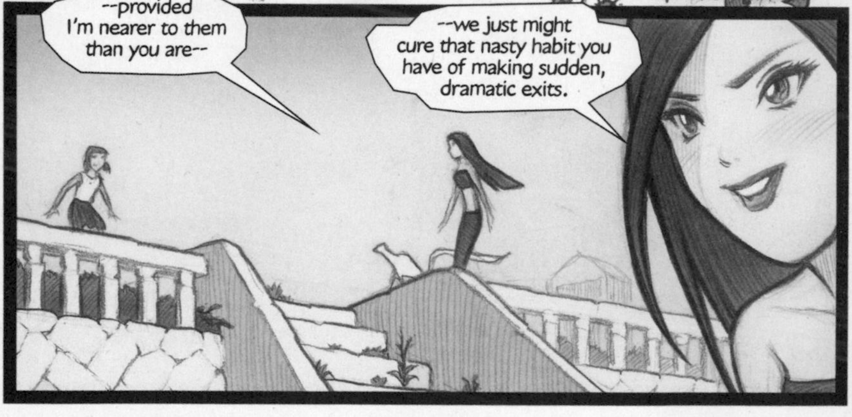
--provided I'm nearer to them than you are--
--we just might cure that nasty habit you have of making sudden, dramatic exits.

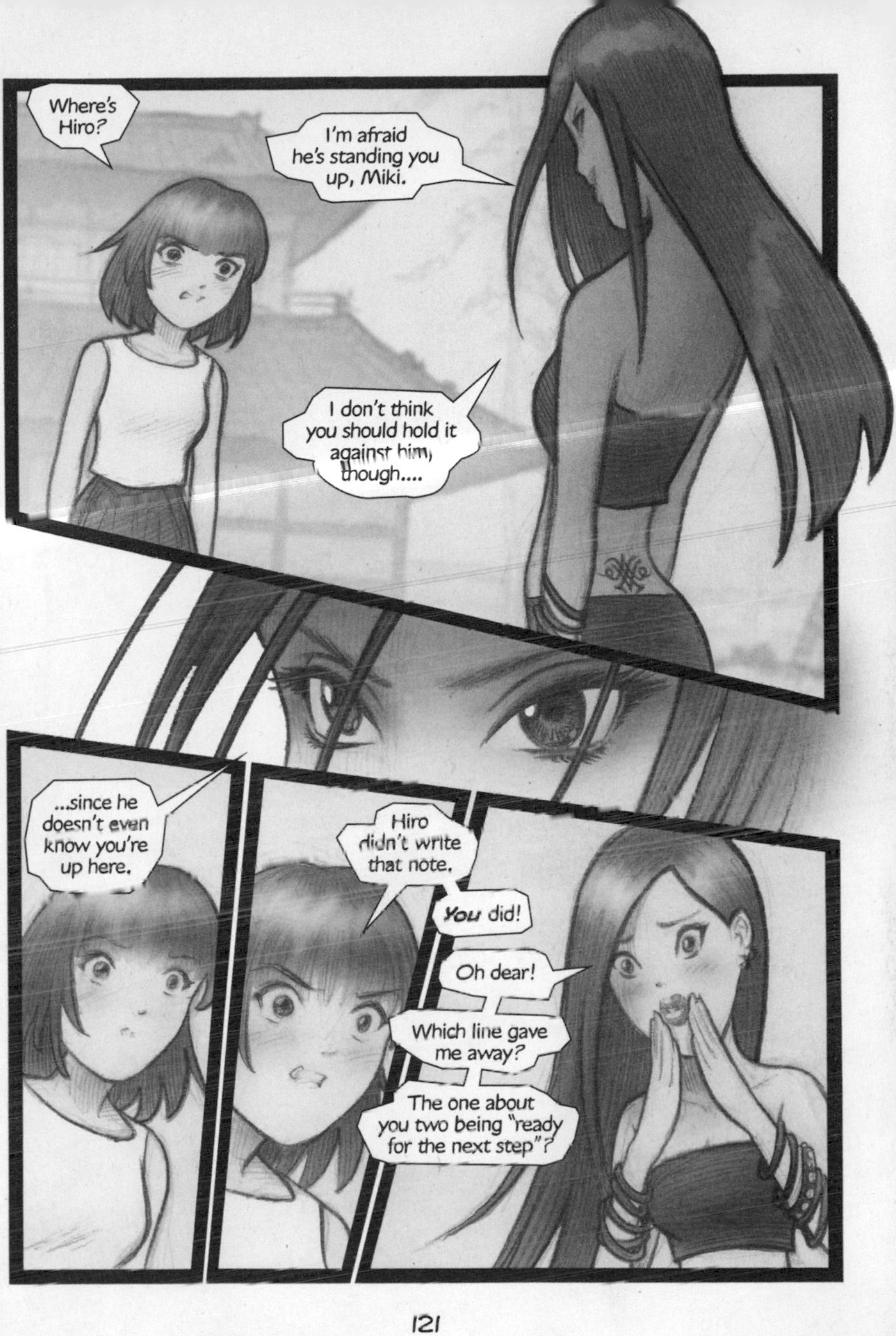
Where's Hiro?
I'm afraid he's standing you up, Miki.
I don't think you should hold it against him, though....
...since he doesn't even know you're up here.
Hiro didn't write that note.
You did!
Oh dear!
Which line gave me away?
The one about you two being "ready for the next step"?

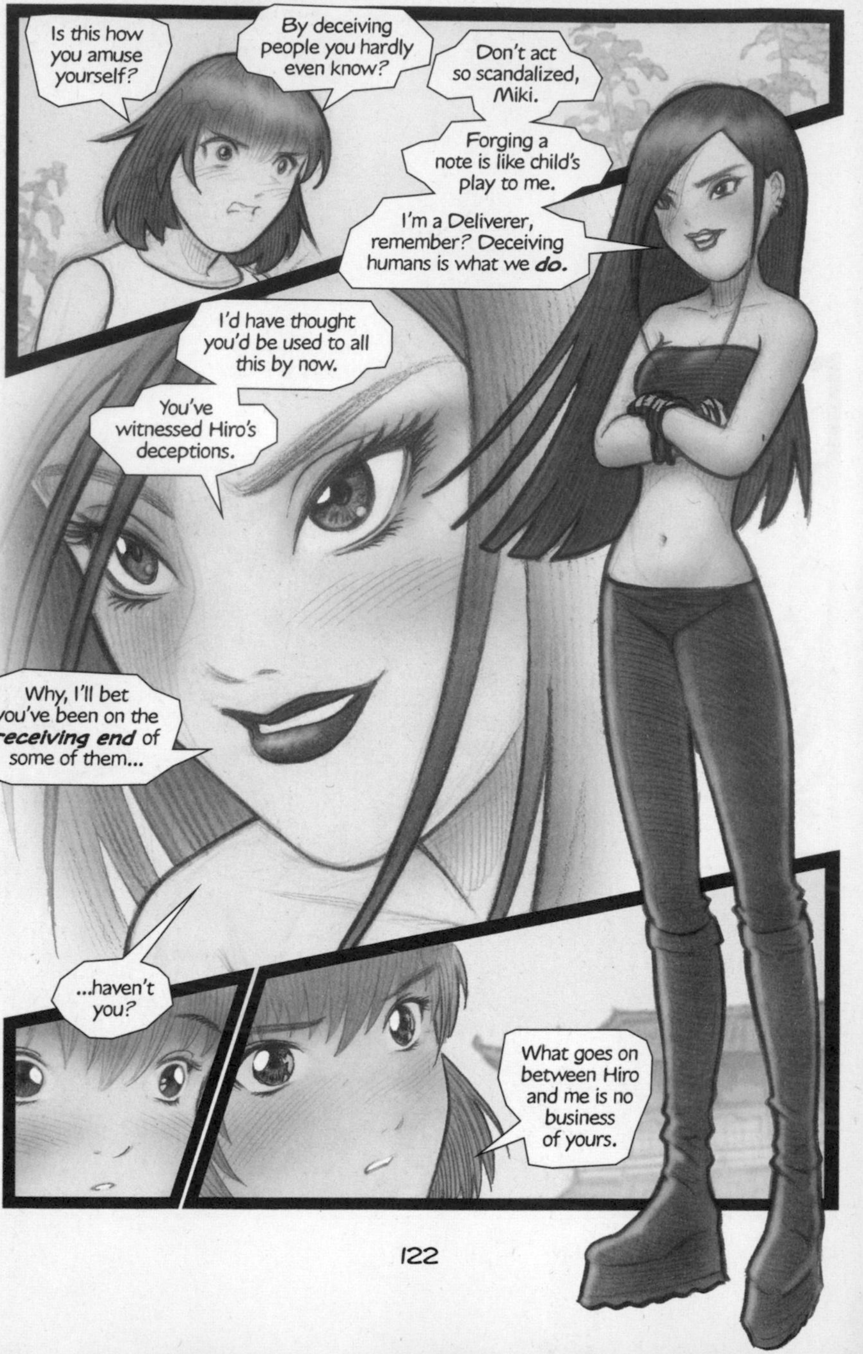
Is this how you amuse yourself?
By deceiving people you hardly even know?
Don't act so scandalized, Miki.
Forging a note is like child's play to me.
I'm a Deliverer, remember? Deceiving humans is what we ***do.***
I'd have thought you'd be used to all this by now.
You've witnessed Hiro's deceptions.
Why, I'll bet you've been on the ***receiving end*** of some of them...
...haven't you?
What goes on between Hiro and me is no business of yours.

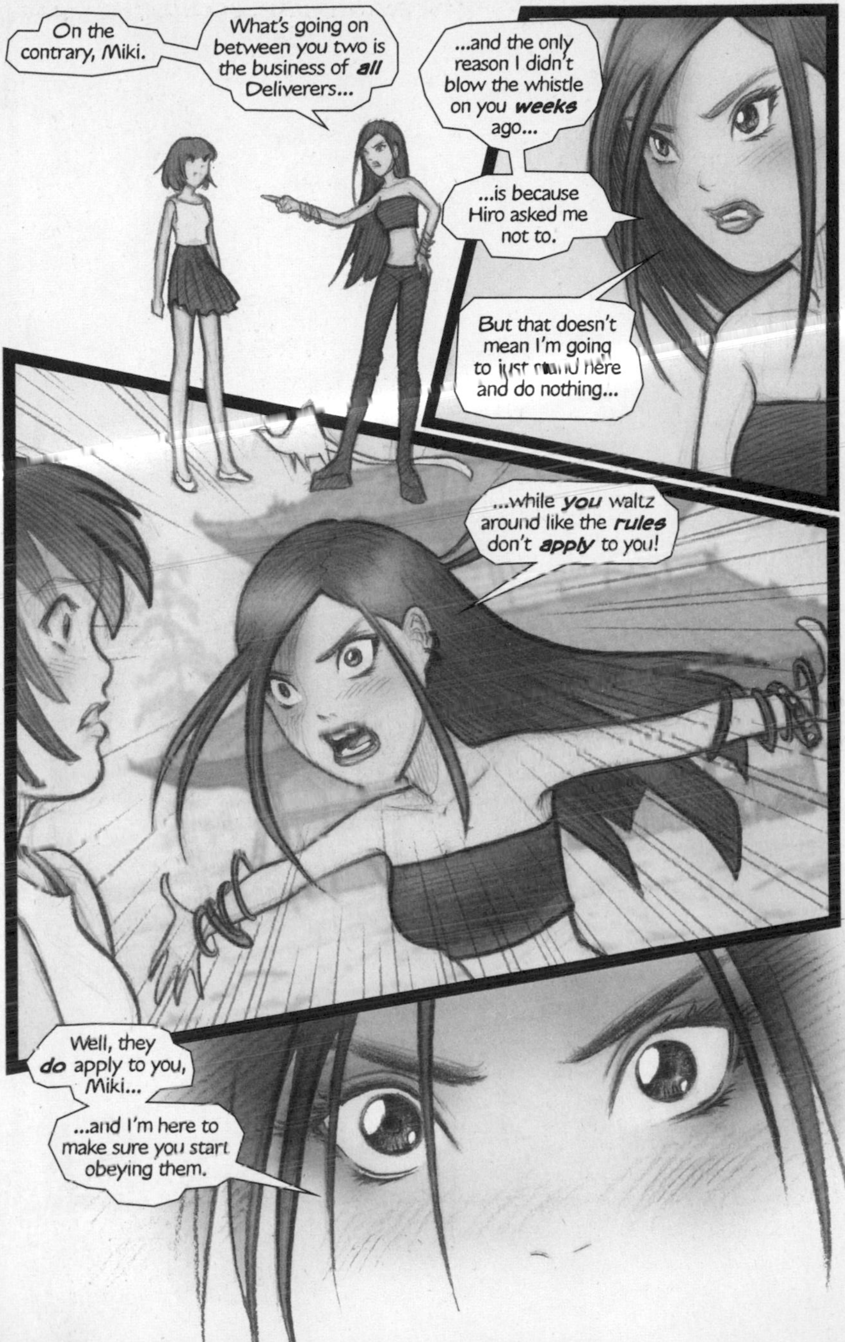
On the contrary, Miki.
What's going on between you two is the business of *all* Deliverers...
...and the only reason I didn't blow the whistle on you *weeks* ago...
...is because Hiro asked me not to.
But that doesn't mean I'm going to just stand here and do nothing...
...while *you* waltz around like the *rules* don't *apply* to you!
Well, they *do* apply to you, Miki...
...and I'm here to make sure you start obeying them.

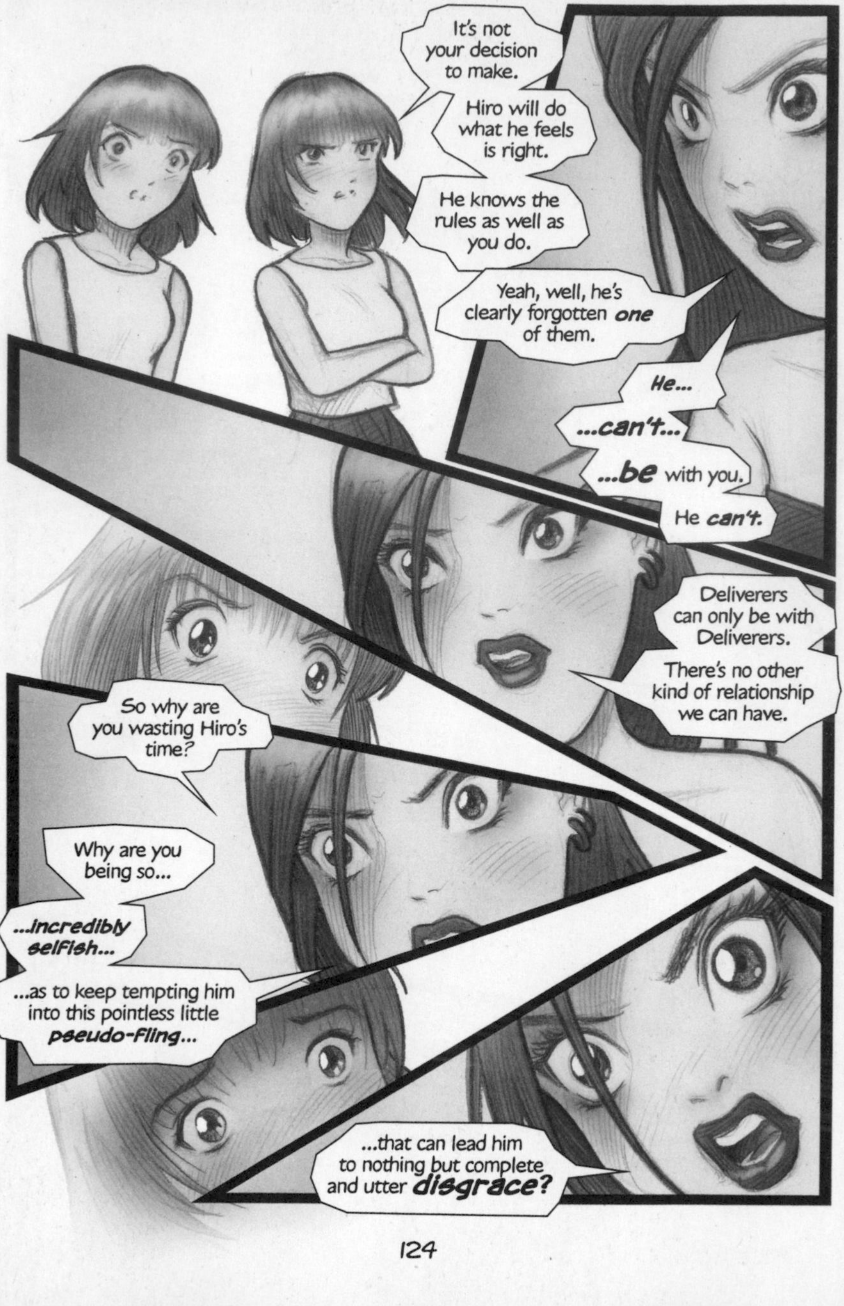
It's not your decision to make.
Hiro will do what he feels is right.
He knows the rules as well as you do.
Yeah, well, he's clearly forgotten ***one*** of them.
He...
...can't...
...be with you.
He ***can't.***
Deliverers can only be with Deliverers.
There's no other kind of relationship we can have.
So why are you wasting Hiro's time?
Why are you being so...
...incredibly selfish...
...as to keep tempting him into this pointless little ***pseudo-fling...***
...that can lead him to nothing but complete and utter ***disgrace?***

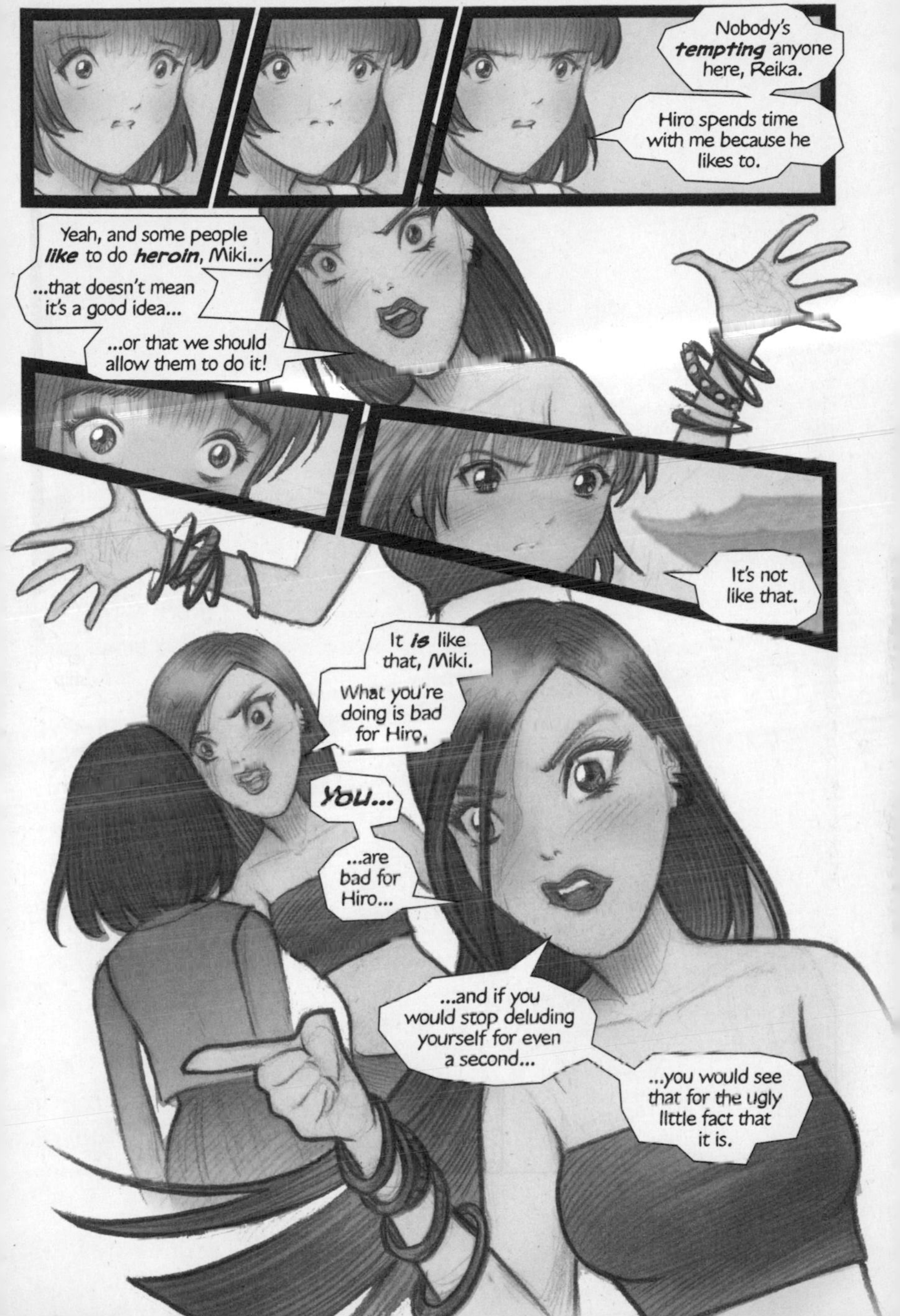
Nobody's **tempting** anyone here, Reika.
Hiro spends time with me because he likes to.
Yeah, and some people **like** to do **heroin**, Miki...
...that doesn't mean it's a good idea...
...or that we should allow them to do it!
It's not like that.
It **is** like that, Miki.
What you're doing is bad for Hiro.
YOU...
...are bad for Hiro...
...and if you would stop deluding yourself for even a second...
...you would see that for the ugly little fact that it is.

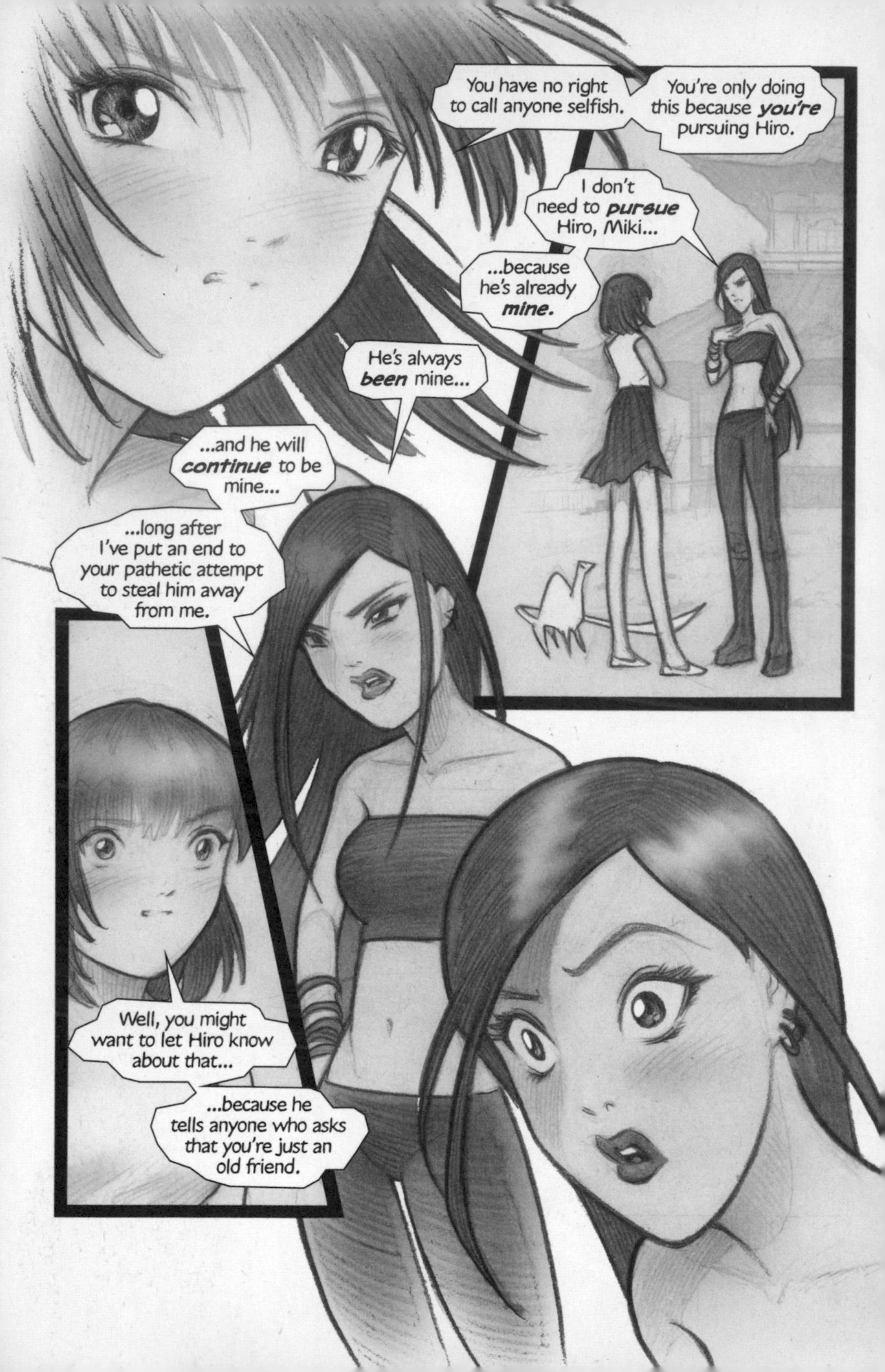
You have no right to call anyone selfish.
You're only doing this because *you're* pursuing Hiro.
I don't need to *pursue* Hiro, Miki...
...because he's already *mine.*
He's always *been* mine...
...and he will *continue* to be mine...
...long after I've put an end to your pathetic attempt to steal him away from me.
Well, you might want to let Hiro know about that...
...because he tells anyone who asks that you're just an old friend.

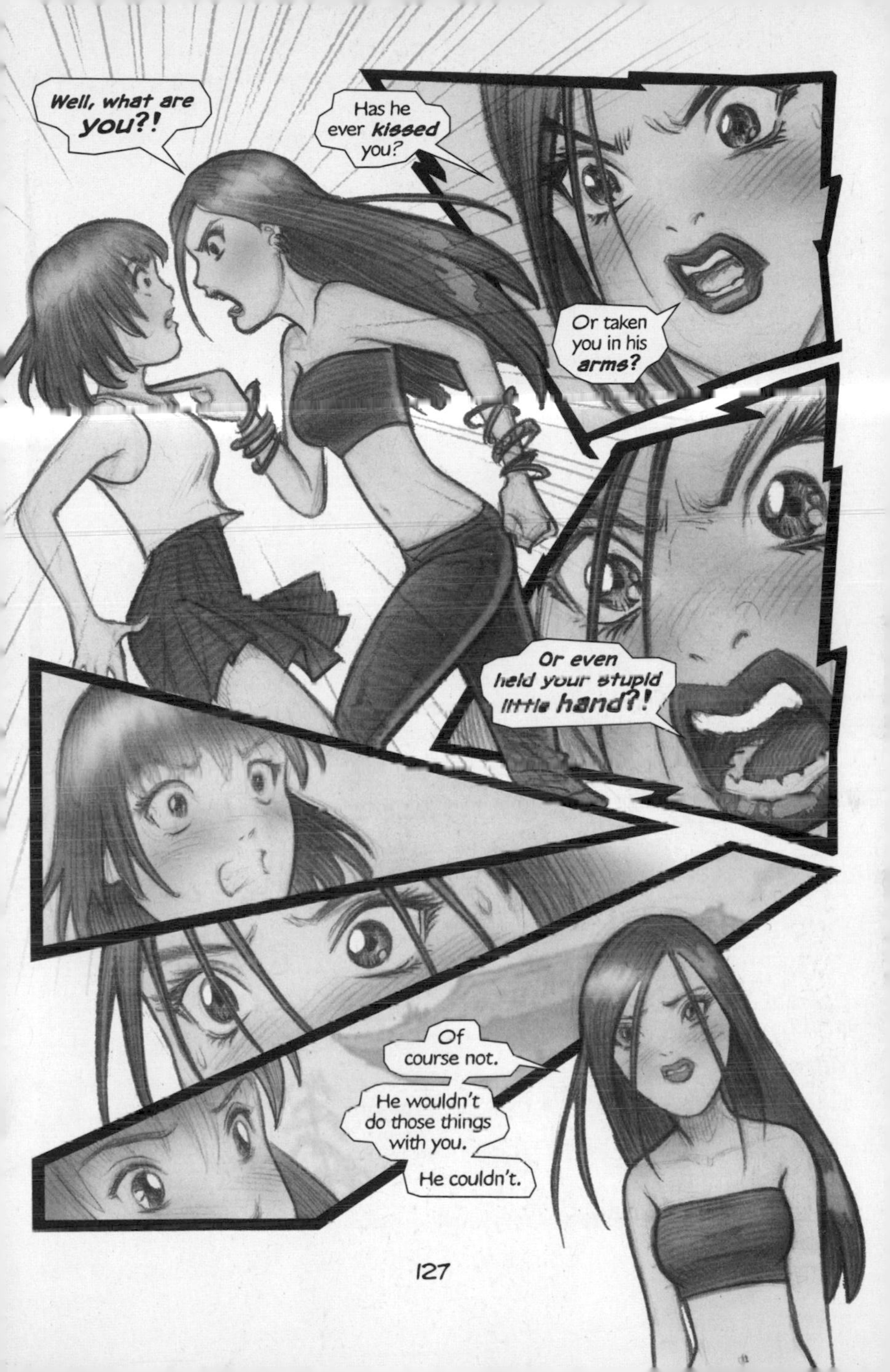

Well, what are you?!
Has he ever kissed you?
Or taken you in his arms?
Or even held your stupid little hand?!
Of course not.
He wouldn't do those things with you.
He couldn't.

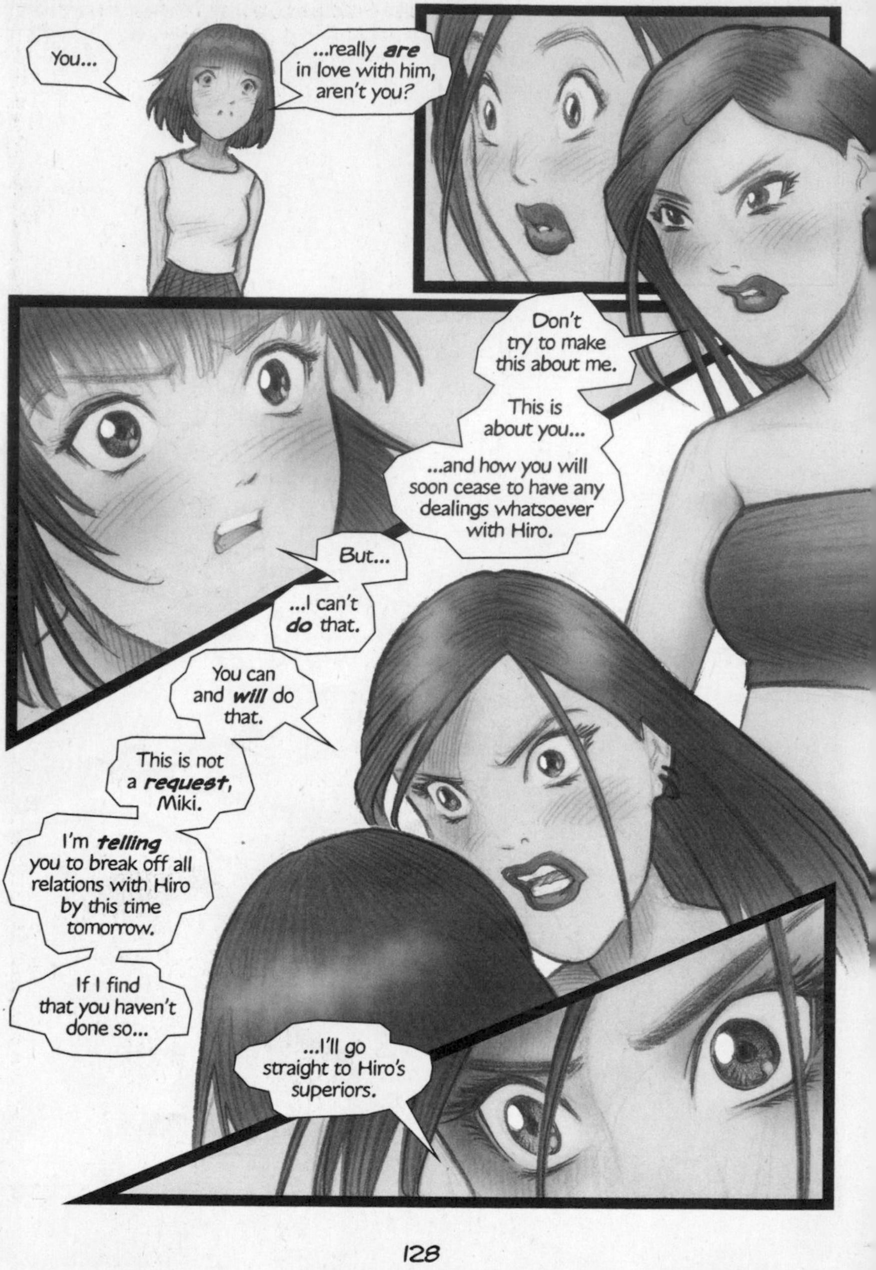

You...
...really **are** in love with him, aren't you?
Don't try to make this about me.
This is about you...
...and how you will soon cease to have any dealings whatsoever with Hiro.
But...
...I can't **do** that.
You can and **will** do that.
This is not a **request**, Miki.
I'm **telling** you to break off all relations with Hiro by this time tomorrow.
If I find that you haven't done so...
...I'll go straight to Hiro's superiors.

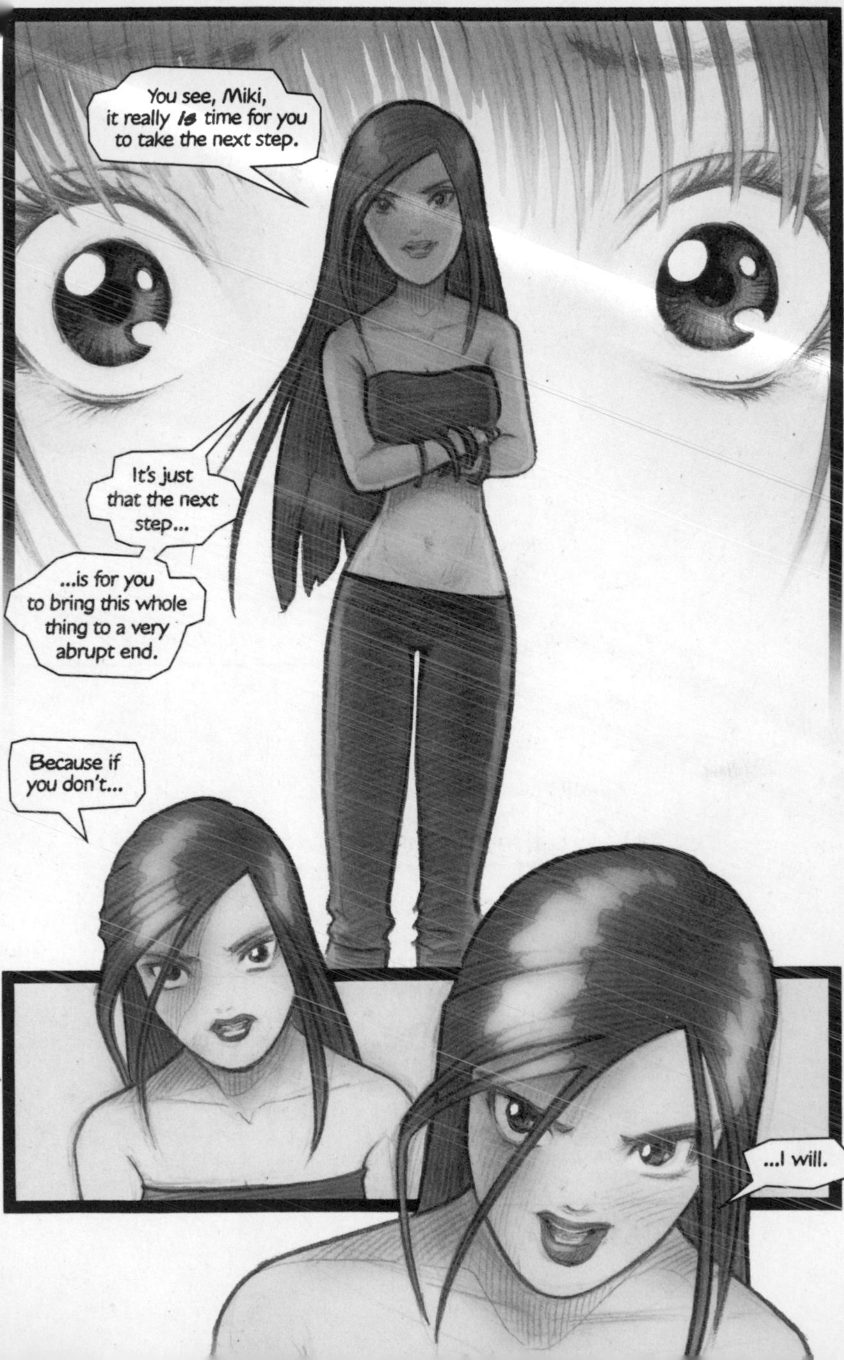
You see, Miki, it really *is* time for you to take the next step.
It's just that the next step...
...is for you to bring this whole thing to a very abrupt end.
Because if you don't...
...I will.

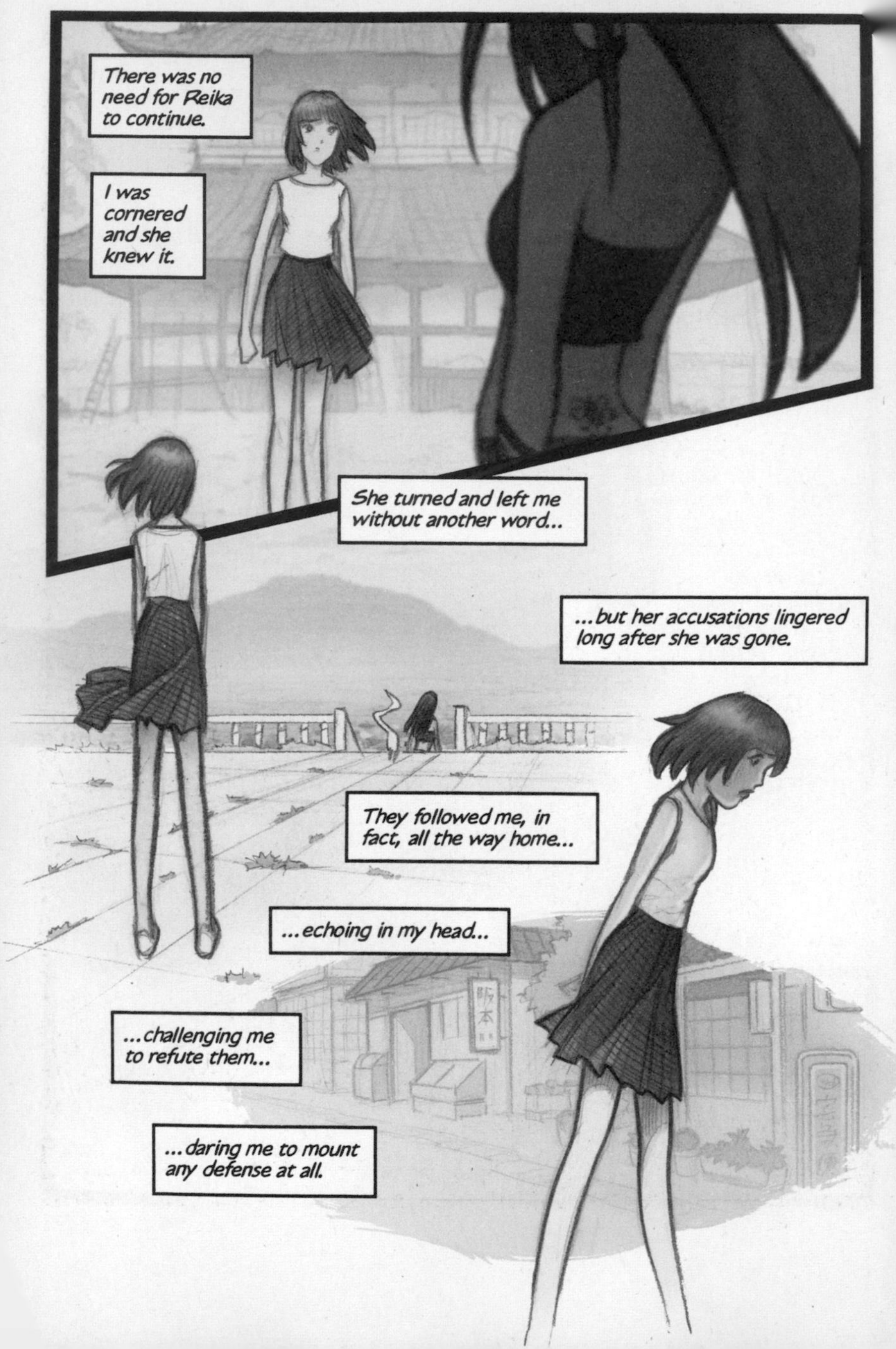
There was no need for Reika to continue.
I was cornered and she knew it.
She turned and left me without another word...
...but her accusations lingered long after she was gone.
They followed me, in fact, all the way home...
...echoing in my head...
...challenging me to refute them...
...daring me to mount any defense at all.

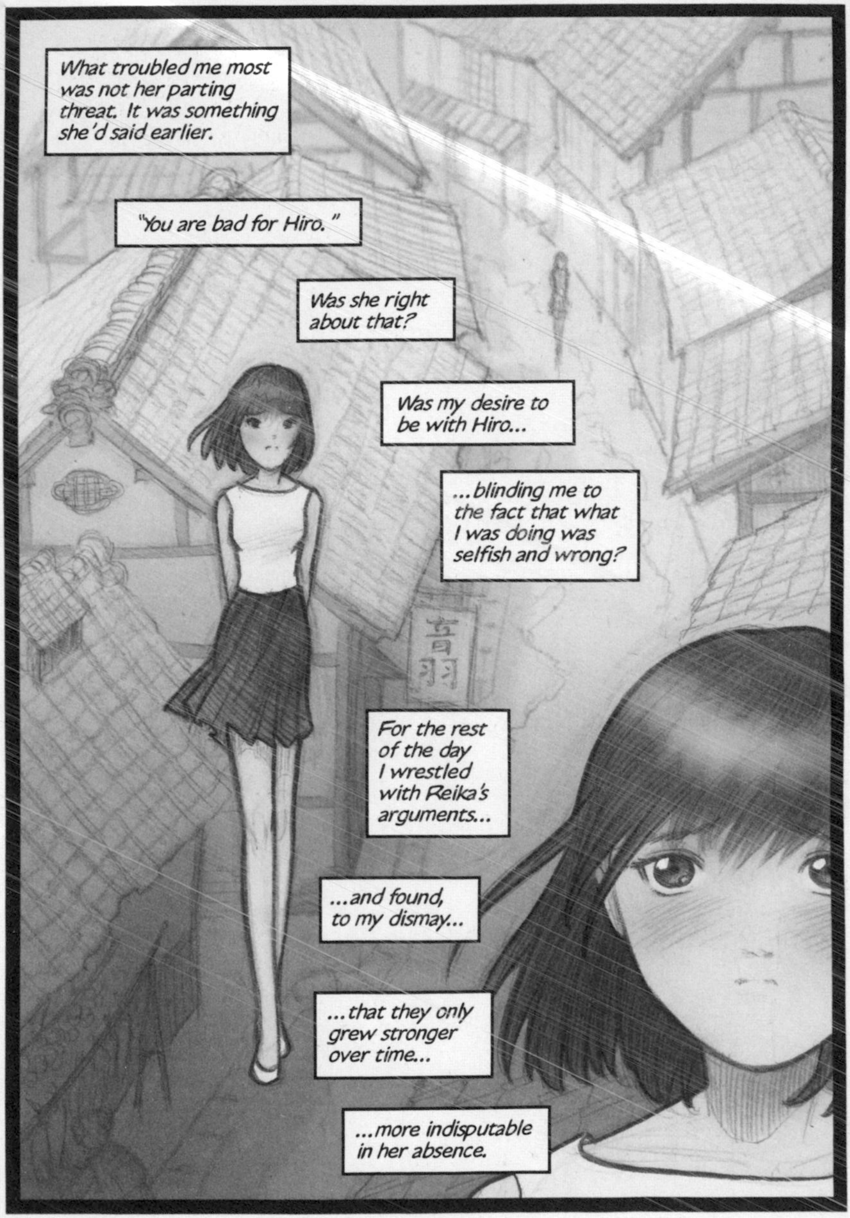
What troubled me most was not her parting threat. It was something she'd said earlier.
"You are bad for Hiro."
Was she right about that?
Was my desire to be with Hiro...
...blinding me to the fact that what I was doing was selfish and wrong?
For the rest of the day I wrestled with Reika's arguments...
...and found, to my dismay...
...that they only grew stronger over time...
...more indisputable in her absence.

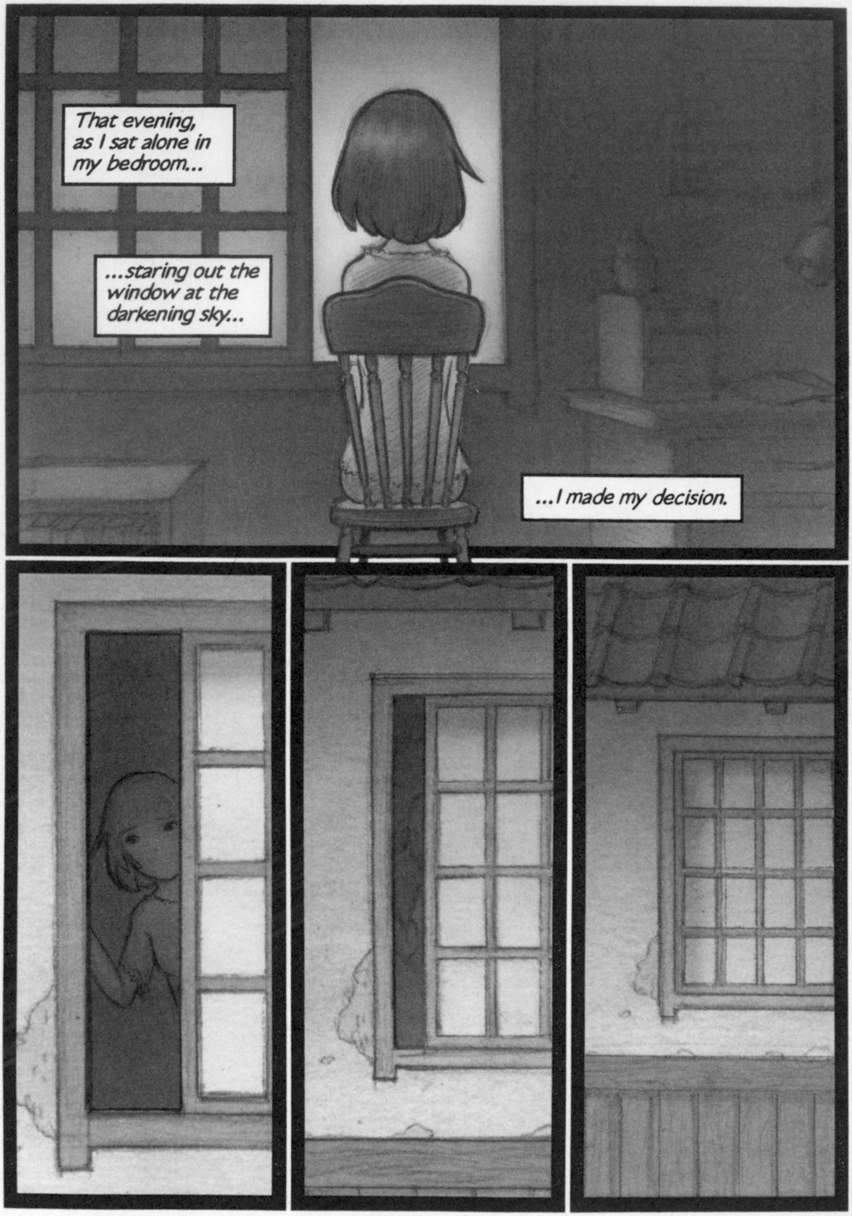
That evening, as I sat alone in my bedroom...
...staring out the window at the darkening sky...
...I made my decision.

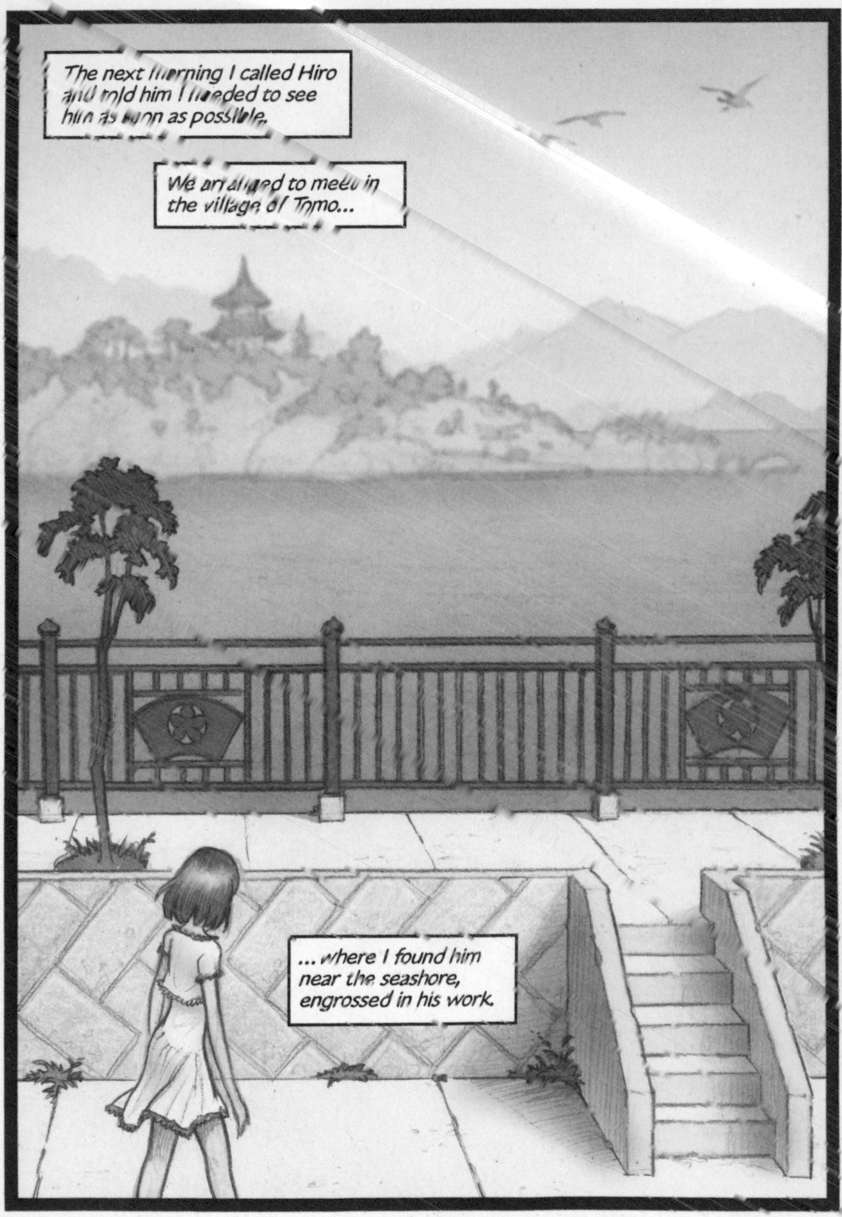
The next morning I called Hiro and told him I needed to see him as soon as possible.
We arranged to meet in the village of Tomo...
...where I found him near the seashore, engrossed in his work.

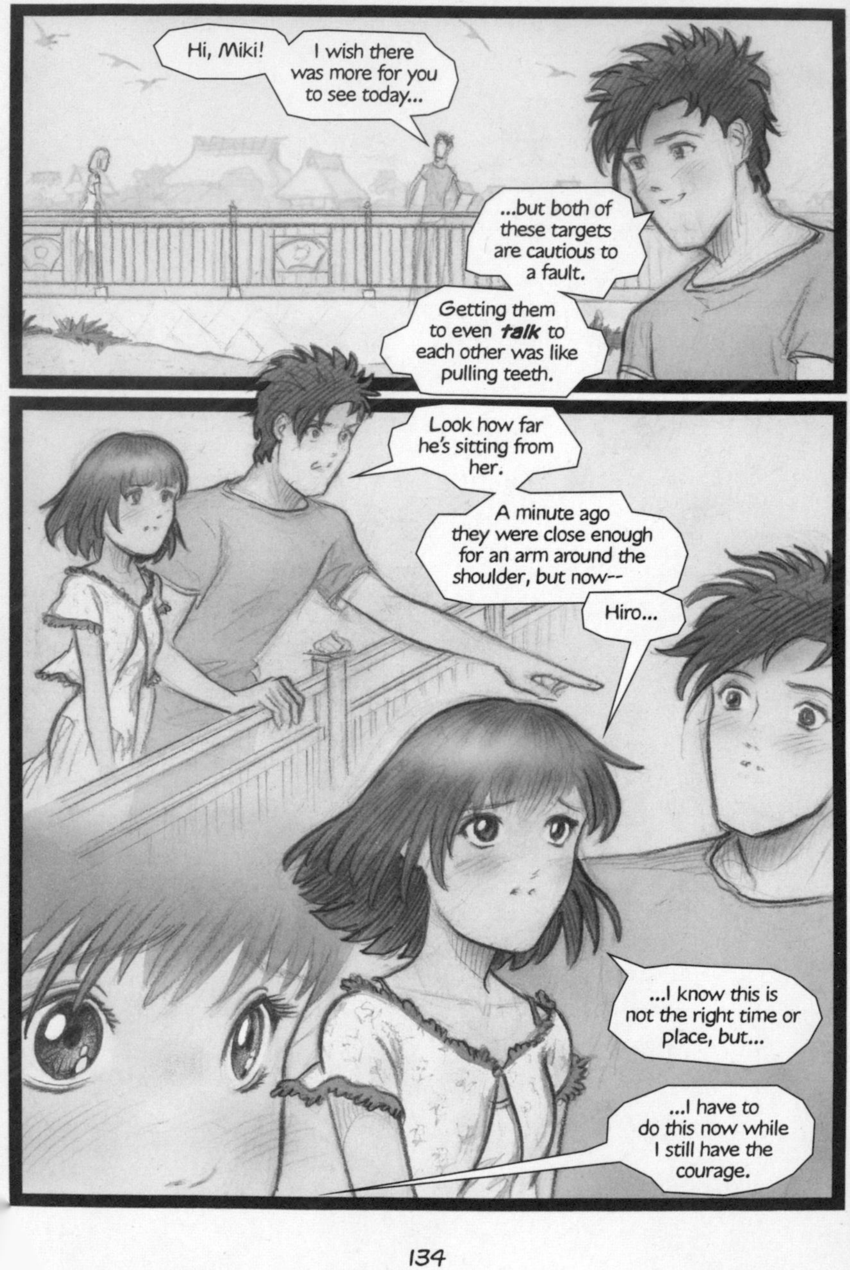
Hi, Miki!
I wish there was more for you to see today...
...but both of these targets are cautious to a fault.
Getting them to even ***talk*** to each other was like pulling teeth.
Look how far he's sitting from her.
A minute ago they were close enough for an arm around the shoulder, but now--
Hiro...
...I know this is not the right time or place, but...
...I have to do this now while I still have the courage.

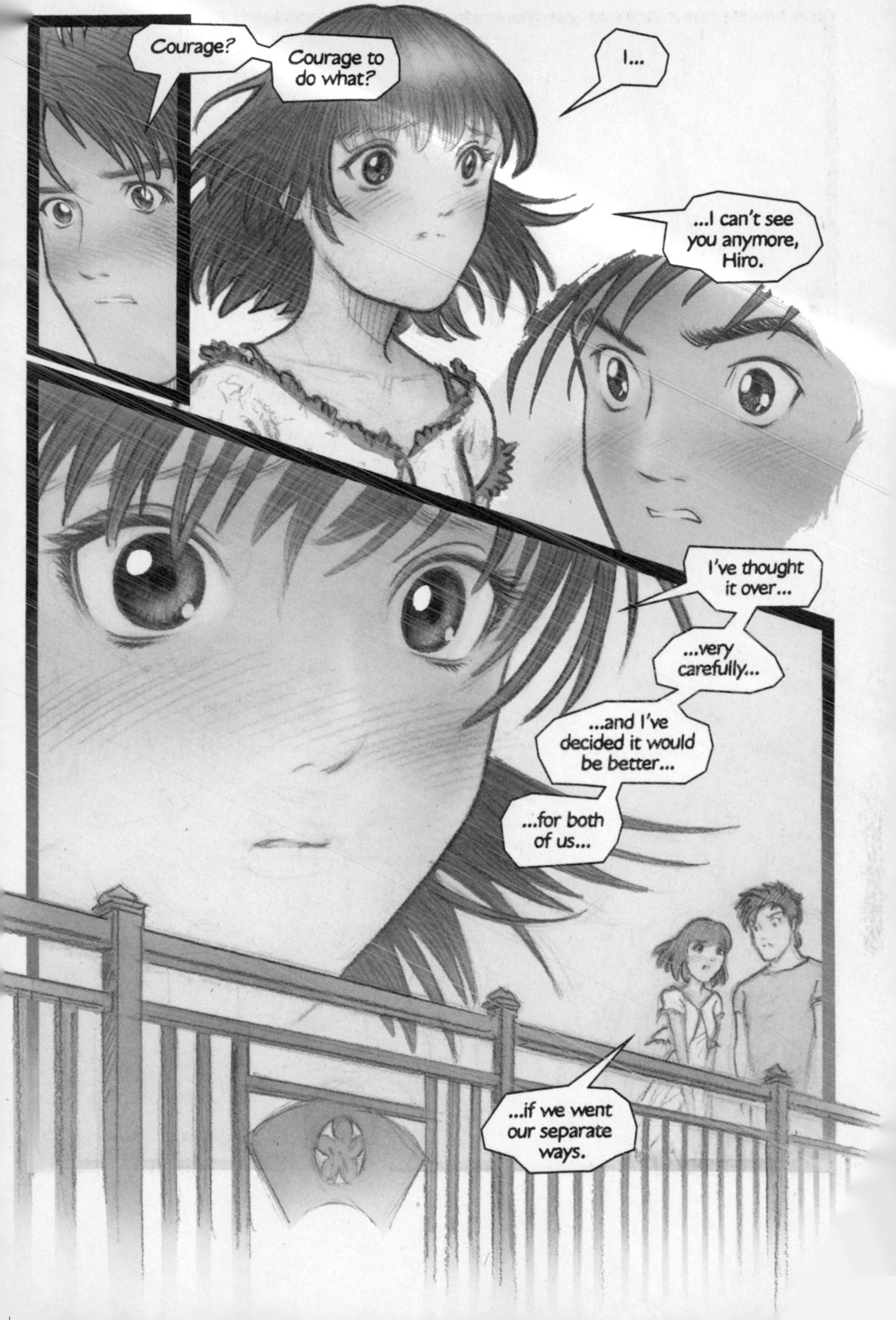
Courage?
Courage to do what?
I...
...I can't see you anymore, Hiro.
I've thought it over...
...very carefully...
...and I've decided it would be better...
...for both of us...
...if we went our separate ways.

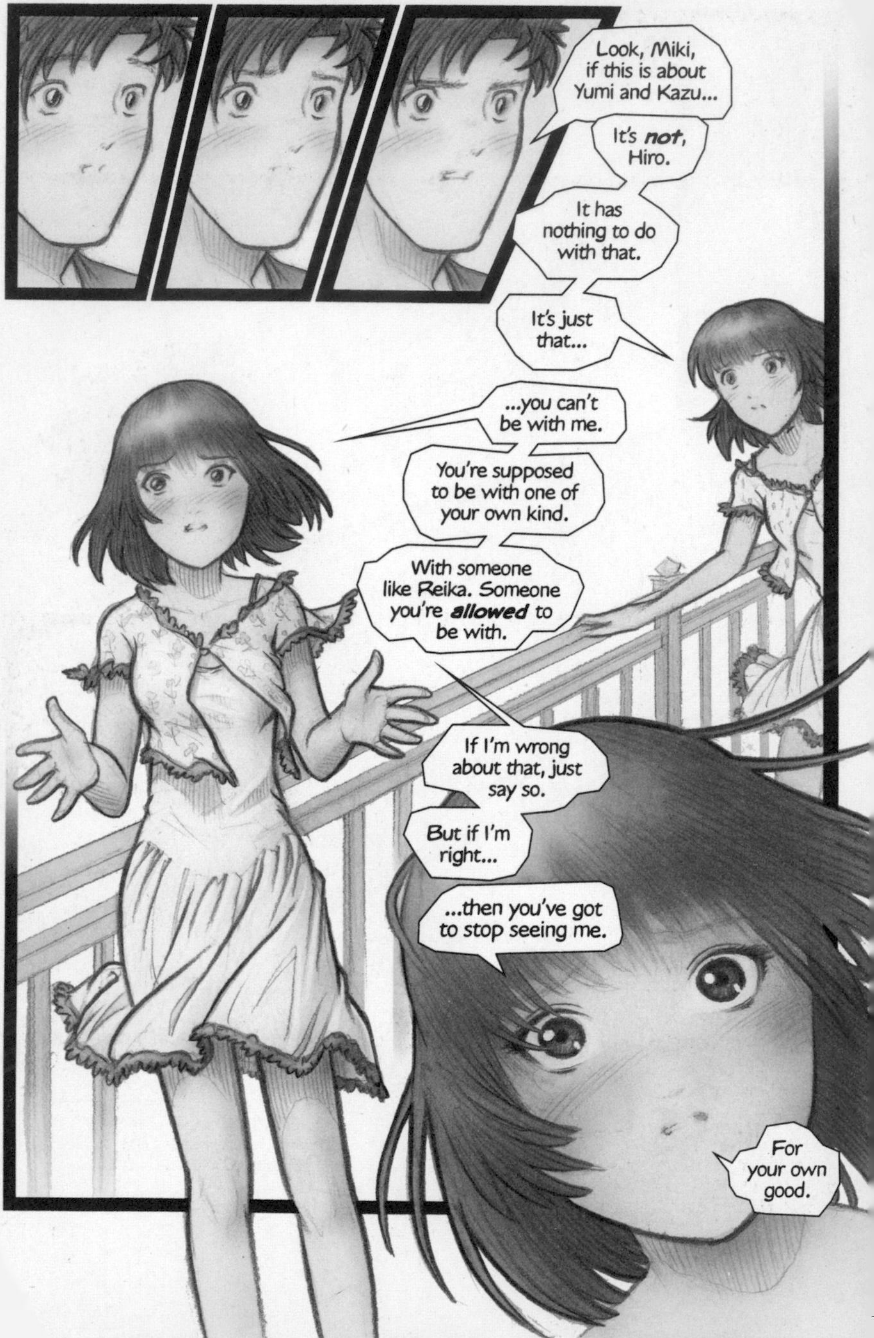

Look, Miki, if this is about Yumi and Kazu...
It's **not**, Hiro.
It has nothing to do with that.
It's just that...
...you can't be with me.
You're supposed to be with one of your own kind.
With someone like Reika. Someone you're **allowed** to be with.
If I'm wrong about that, just say so.
But if I'm right...
...then you've got to stop seeing me.
For your own good.

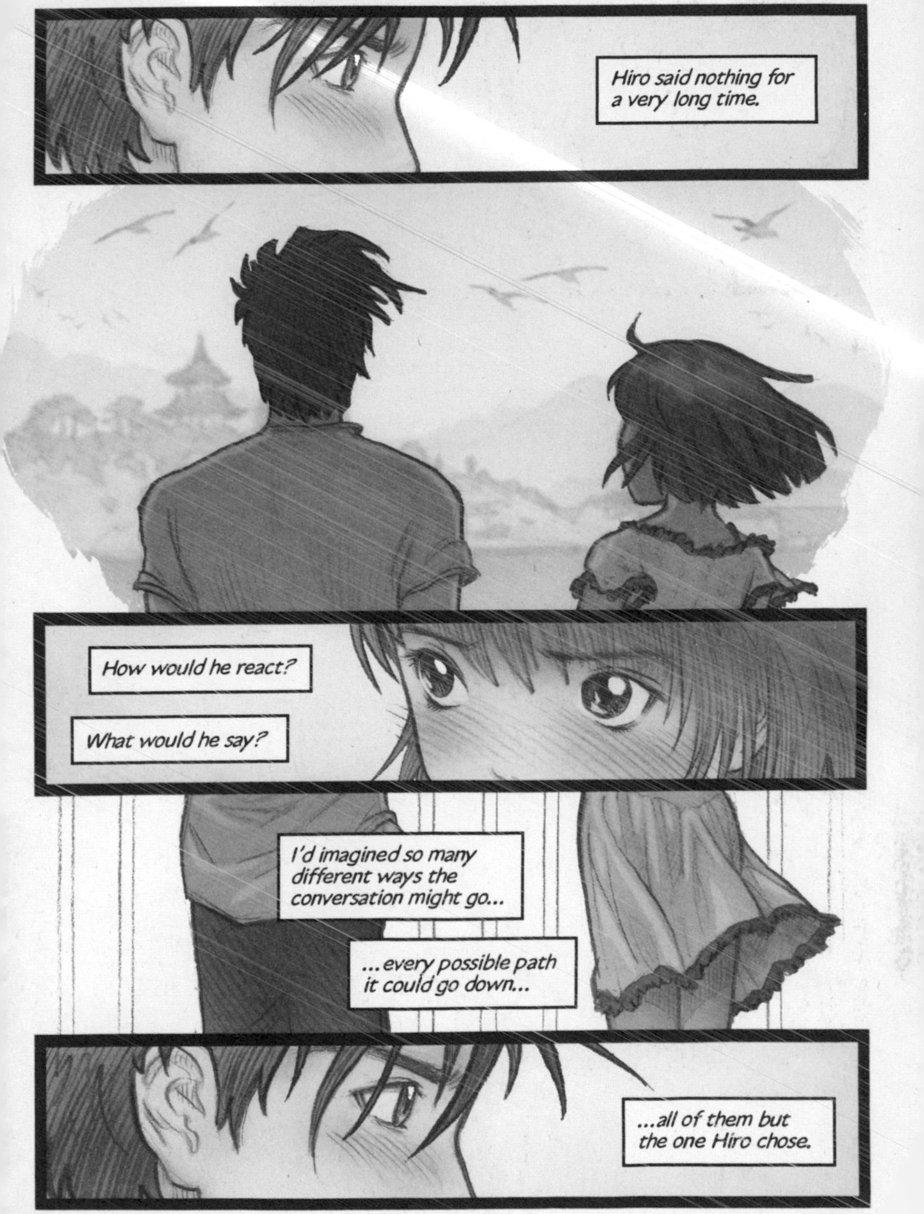
Hiro said nothing for a very long time.
How would he react?
What would he say?
I'd imagined so many different ways the conversation might go...
...every possible path it could go down...
...all of them but the one Hiro chose.

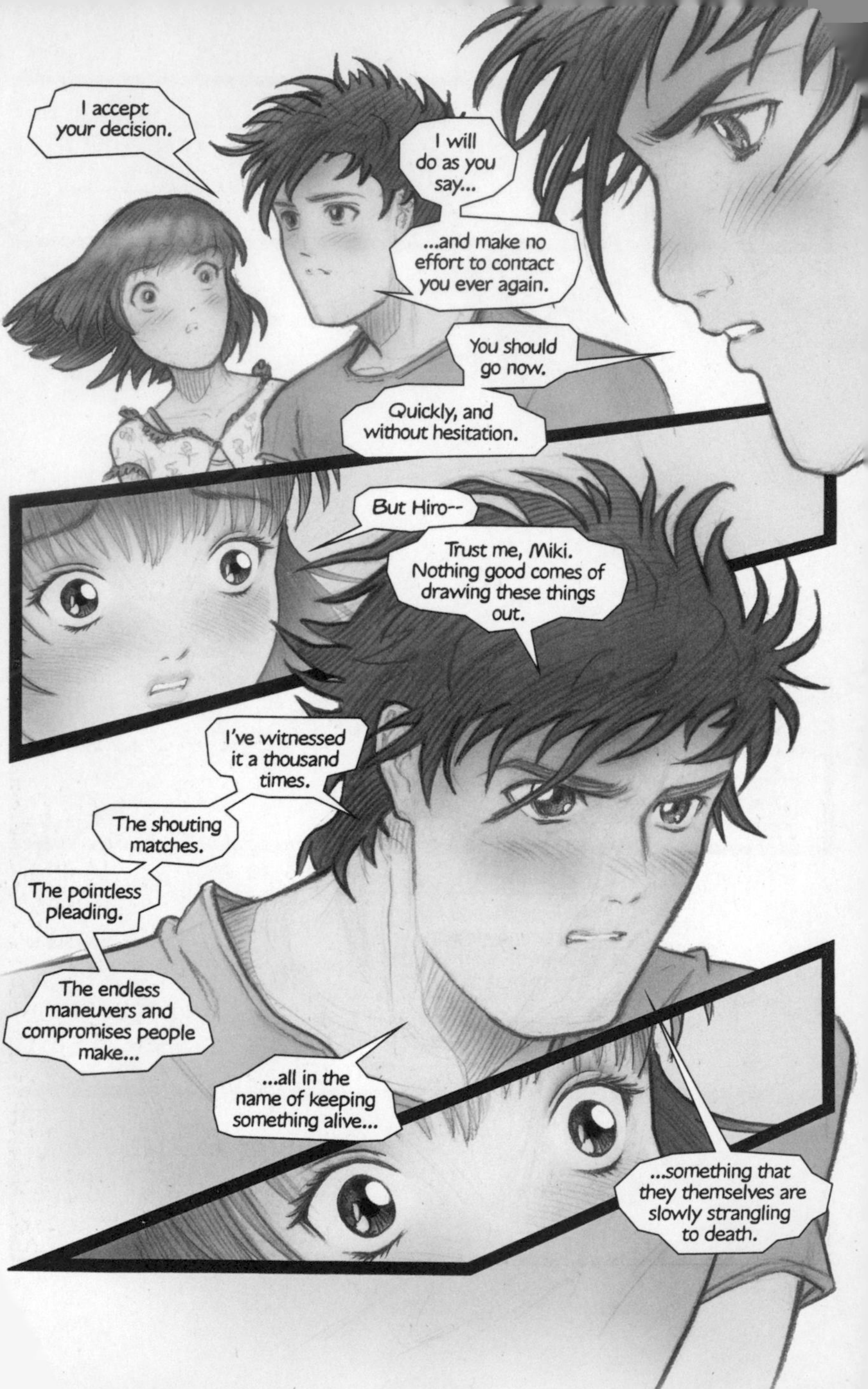
I accept your decision.
I will do as you say...
...and make no effort to contact you ever again.
You should go now.
Quickly, and without hesitation.
But Hiro--
Trust me, Miki. Nothing good comes of drawing these things out.
I've witnessed it a thousand times.
The shouting matches.
The pointless pleading.
The endless maneuvers and compromises people make...
...all in the name of keeping something alive...
...something that they themselves are slowly strangling to death.

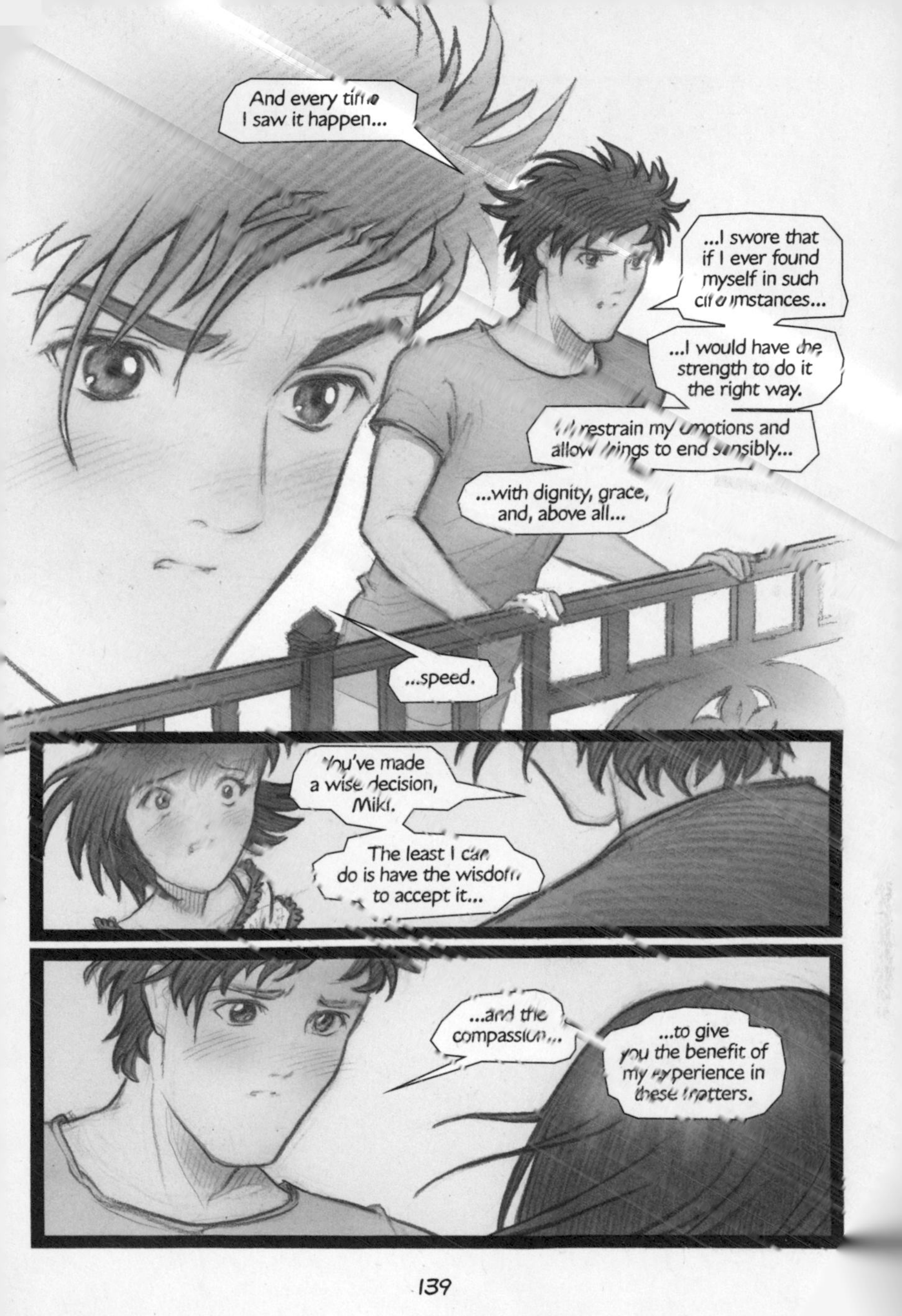
And every time I saw it happen...
...I swore that if I ever found myself in such circumstances...
...I would have the strength to do it the right way.
...I restrain my emotions and allow things to end sensibly...
...with dignity, grace, and, above all...
...speed.
You've made a wise decision, Miki.
The least I can do is have the wisdom to accept it...
...and the compassion...
...to give you the benefit of my experience in these matters.

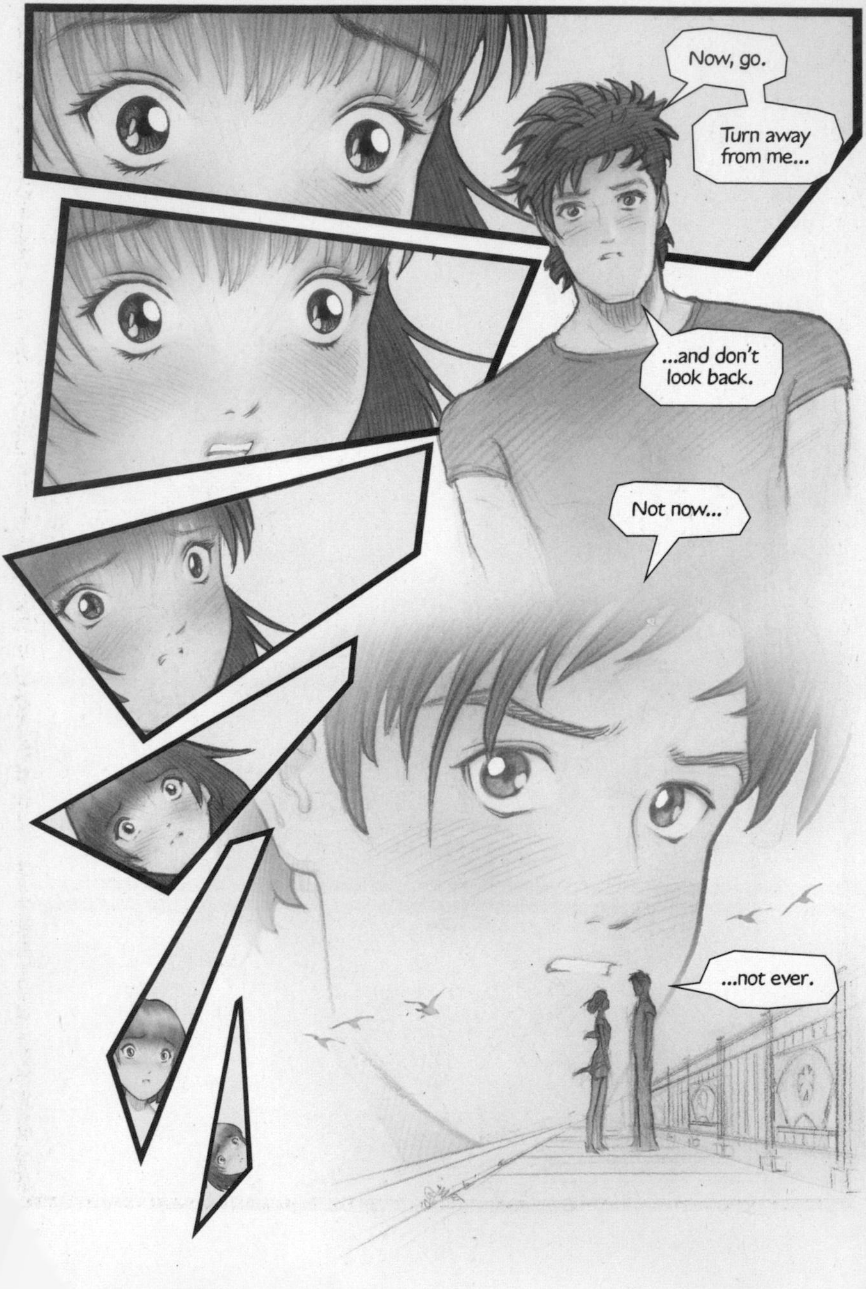
Now, go.
Turn away from me...
...and don't look back.
Not now...
...not ever.

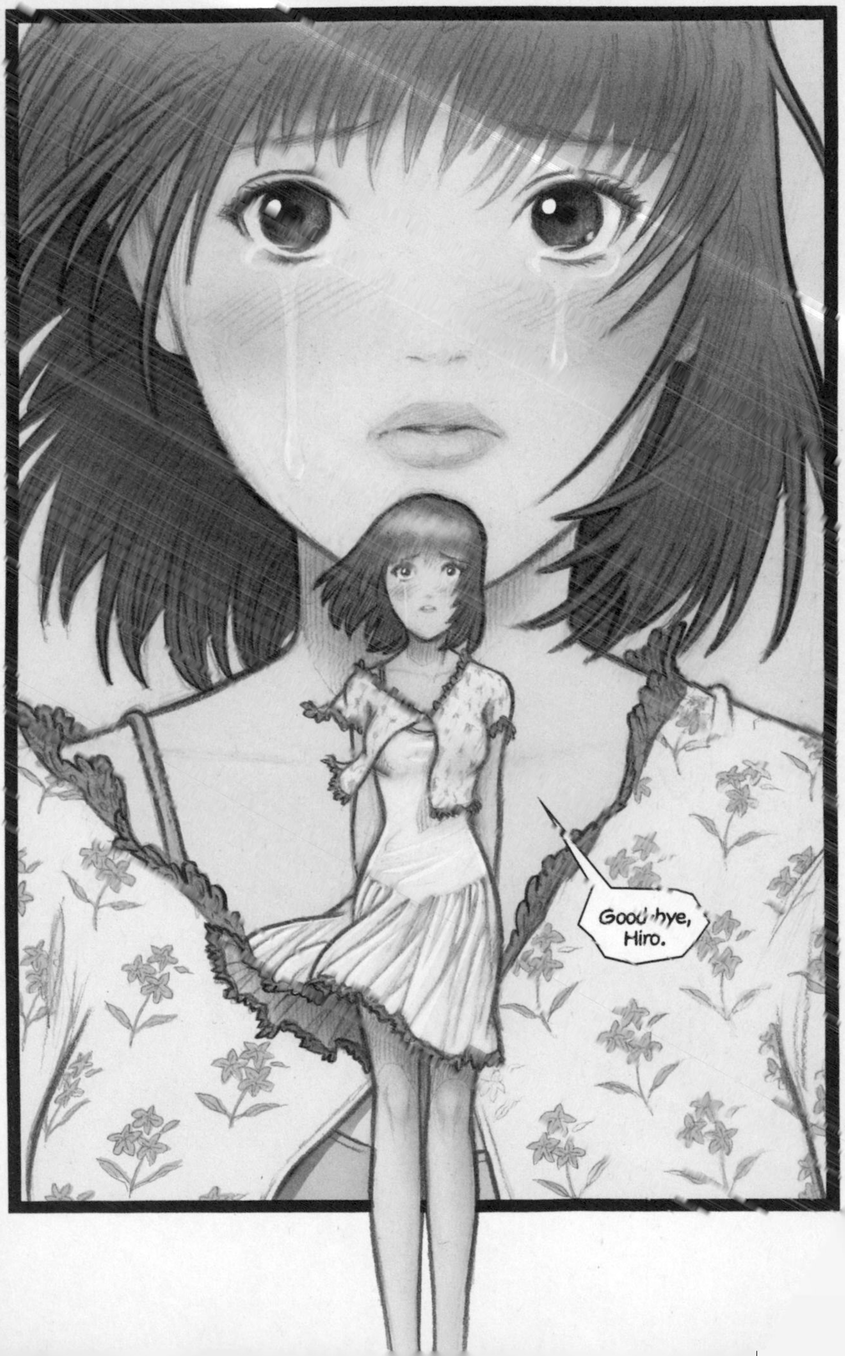
Good-bye,
Hiro.

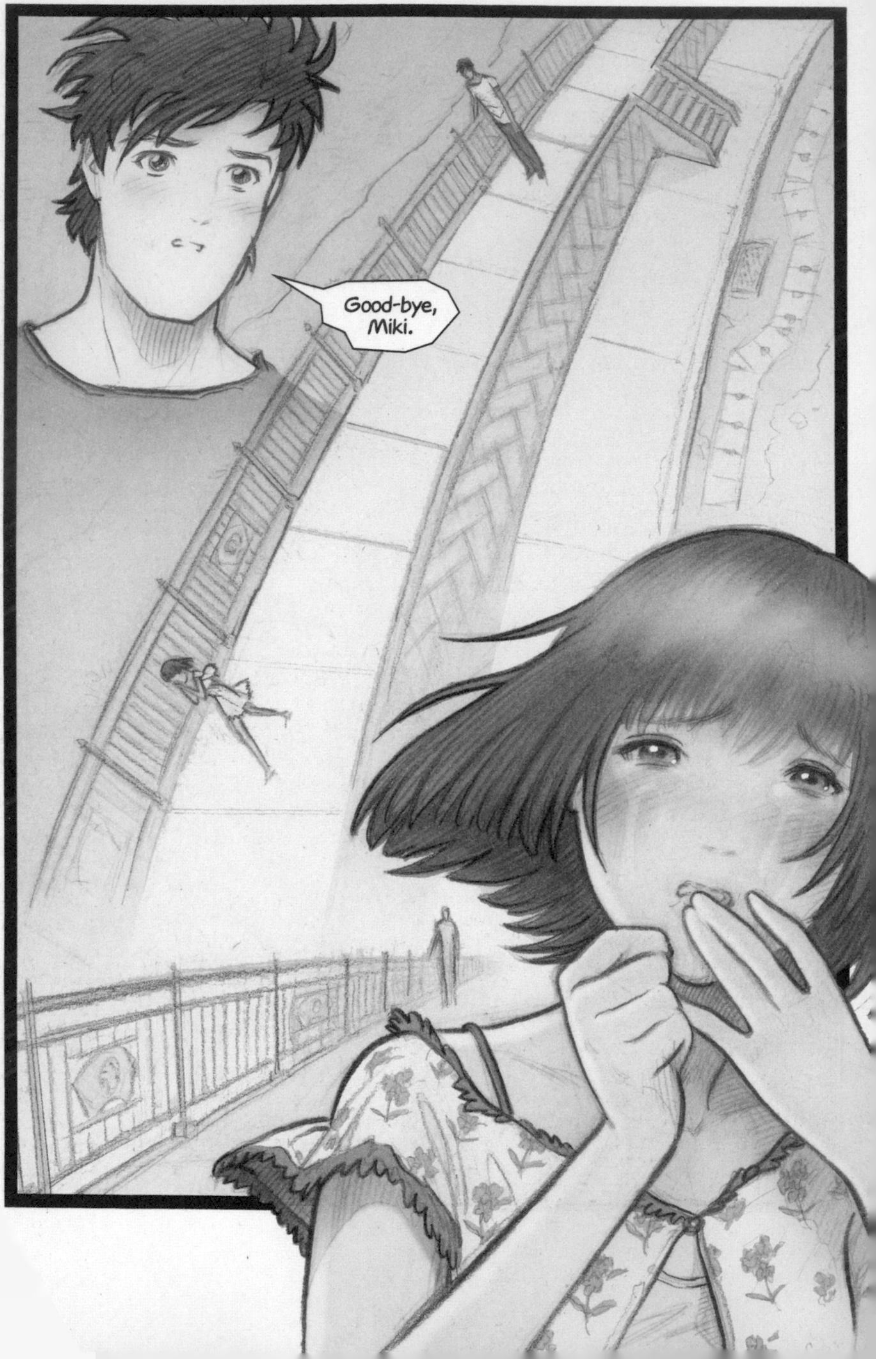
Good-bye, Miki.

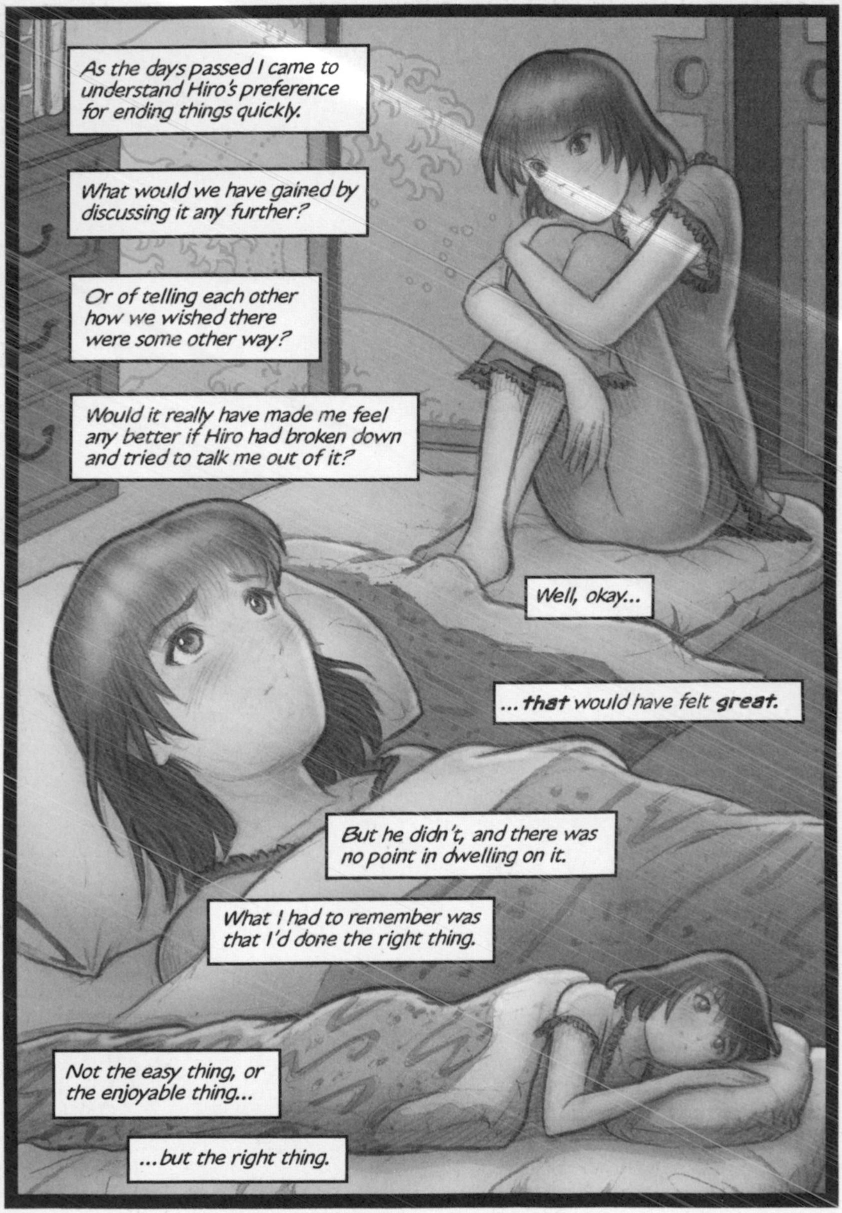
As the days passed I came to understand Hiro's preference for ending things quickly.
What would we have gained by discussing it any further?
Or of telling each other how we wished there were some other way?
Would it really have made me feel any better if Hiro had broken down and tried to talk me out of it?
Well, okay...
...that would have felt great.
But he didn't, and there was no point in dwelling on it.
What I had to remember was that I'd done the right thing.
Not the easy thing, or the enjoyable thing...
...but the right thing.

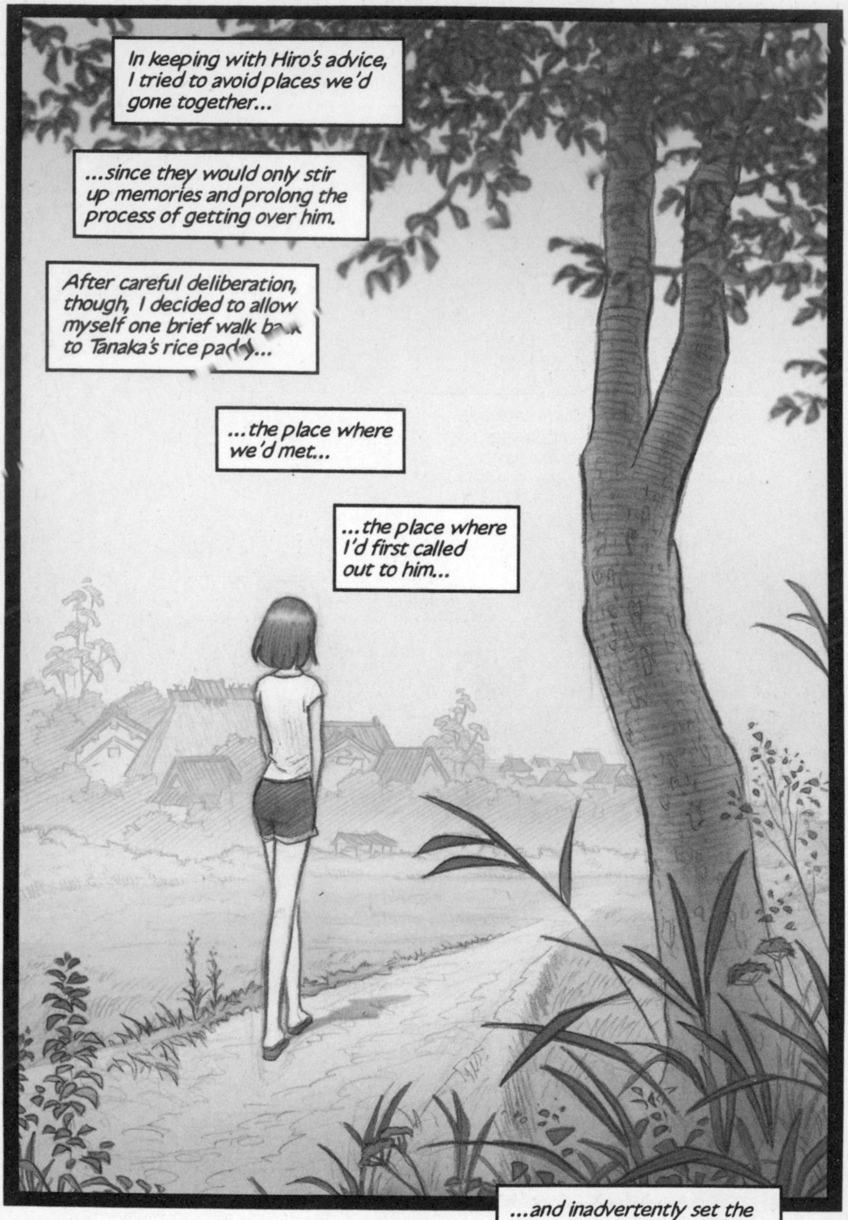
In keeping with Hiro's advice, I tried to avoid places we'd gone together...
...since they would only stir up memories and prolong the process of getting over him.
After careful deliberation, though, I decided to allow myself one brief walk back to Tanaka's rice paddy...
...the place where we'd met...
...the place where I'd first called out to him...
...and inadvertently set the whole crazy thing in motion.

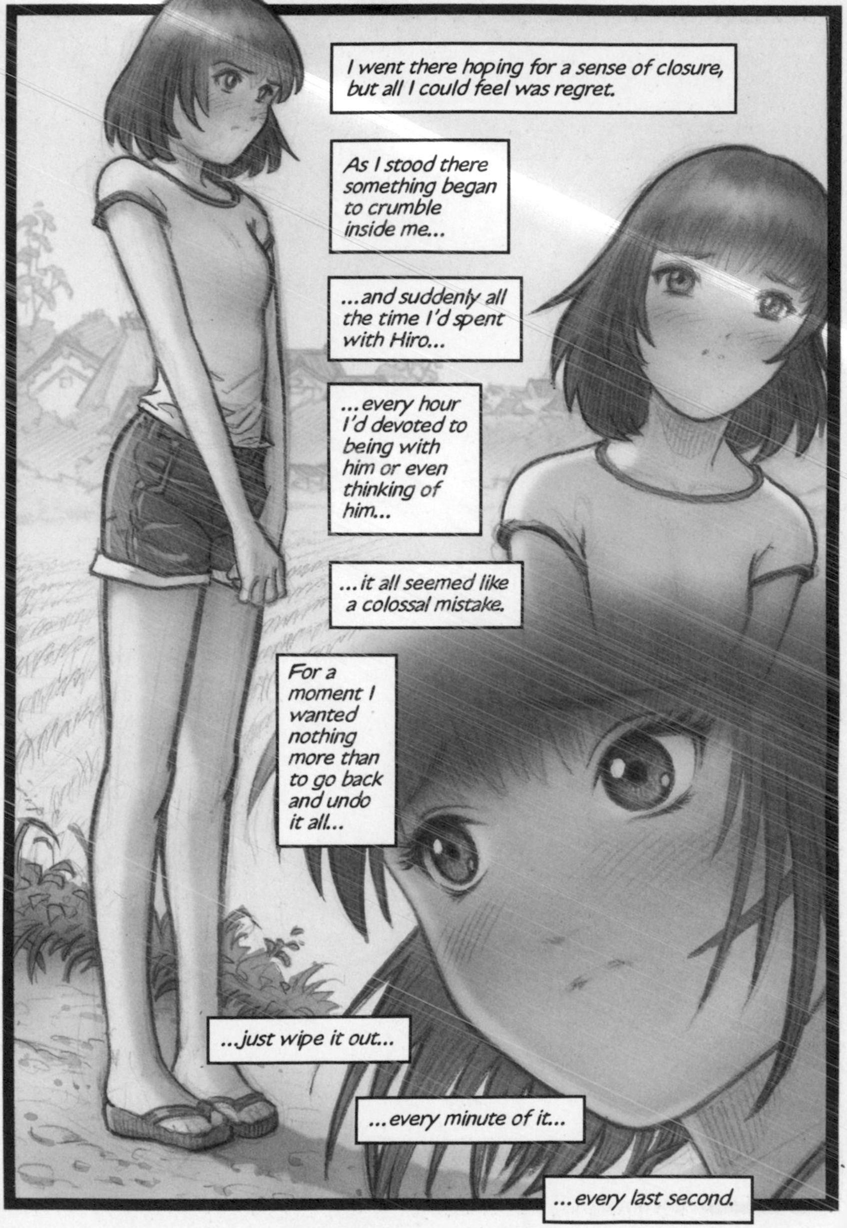
I went there hoping for a sense of closure, but all I could feel was regret.
As I stood there something began to crumble inside me...
...and suddenly all the time I'd spent with Hiro...
...every hour I'd devoted to being with him or even thinking of him...
...it all seemed like a colossal mistake.
For a moment I wanted nothing more than to go back and undo it all...
...just wipe it out...
...every minute of it...
...every last second.

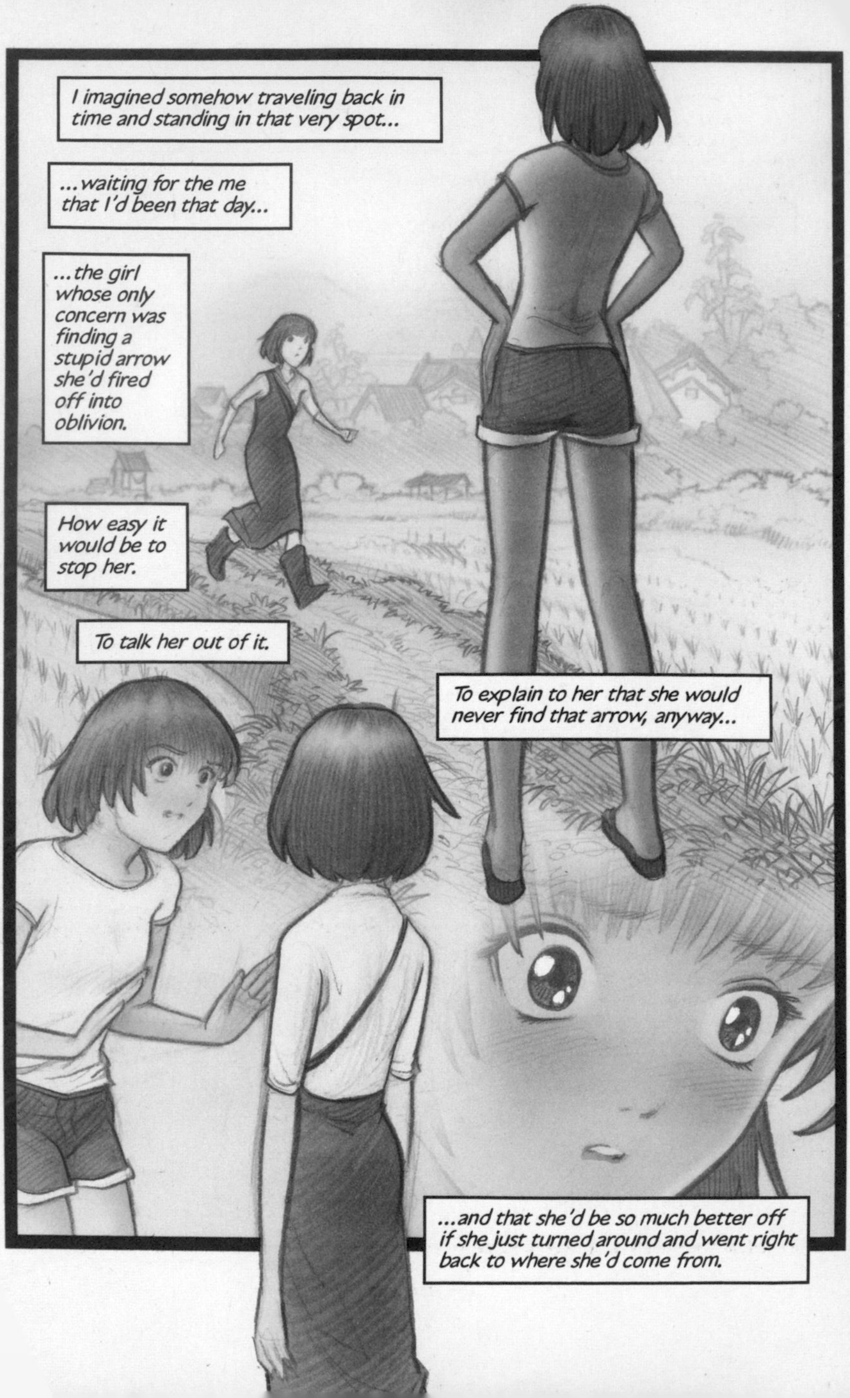
I imagined somehow traveling back in time and standing in that very spot...
...waiting for the me that I'd been that day...
...the girl whose only concern was finding a stupid arrow she'd fired off into oblivion.
How easy it would be to stop her.
To talk her out of it.
To explain to her that she would never find that arrow, anyway...
...and that she'd be so much better off if she just turned around and went right back to where she'd come from.

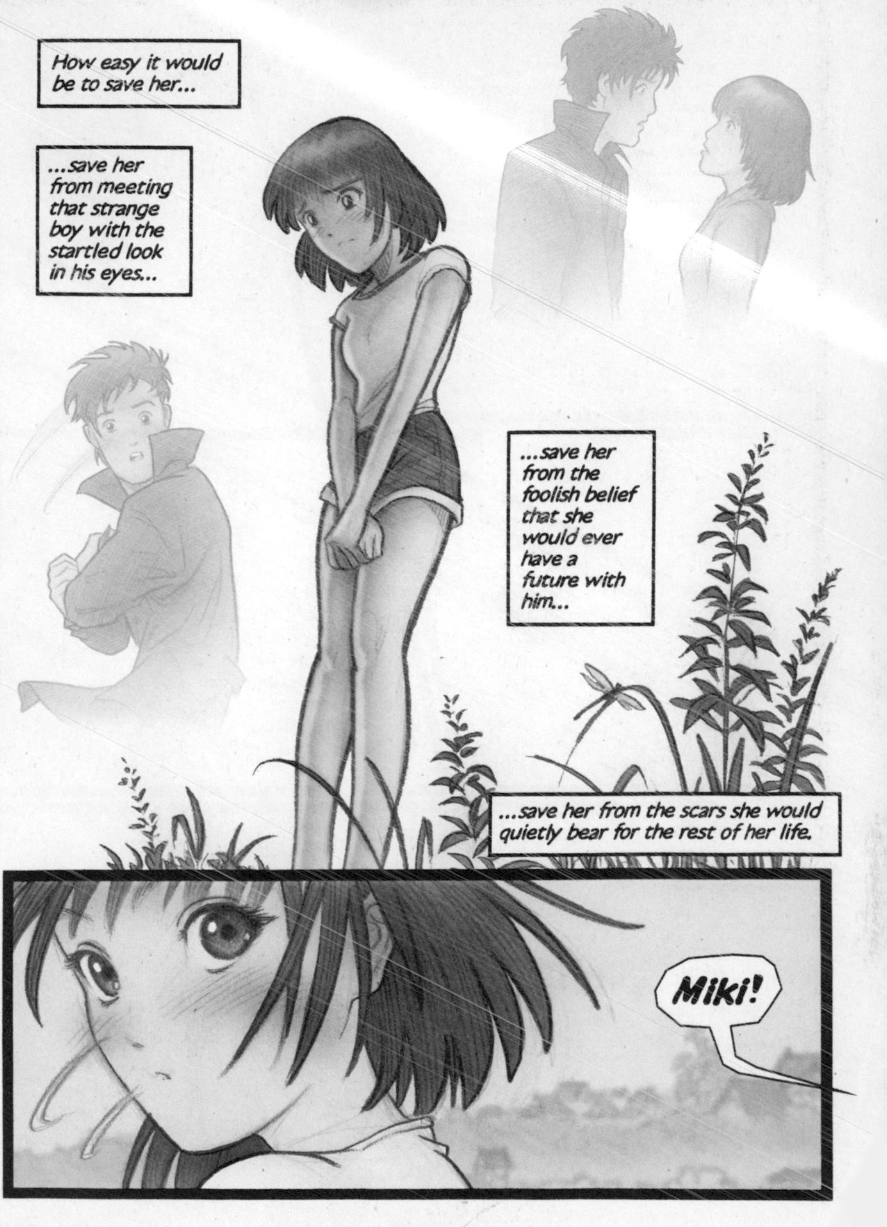
How easy it would be to save her...
...save her from meeting that strange boy with the startled look in his eyes...
...save her from the foolish belief that she would ever have a future with him...
...save her from the scars she would quietly bear for the rest of her life.
Miki!

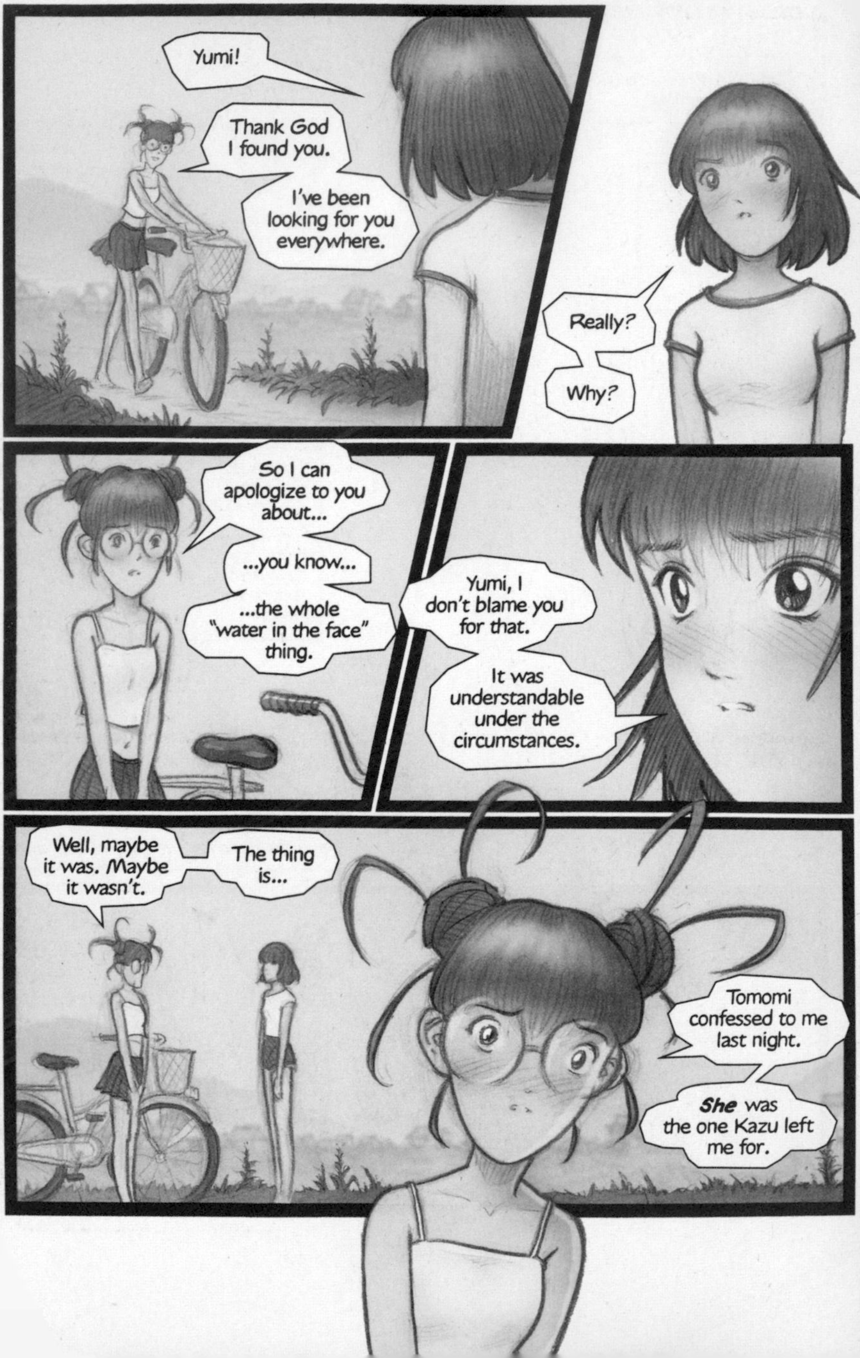
Yumi!
Thank God I found you.
I've been looking for you everywhere.
Really?
Why?
So I can apologize to you about...
...you know...
...the whole "water in the face" thing.
Yumi, I don't blame you for that.
It was understandable under the circumstances.
Well, maybe it was. Maybe it wasn't.
The thing is...
Tomomi confessed to me last night.
She was the one Kazu left me for.

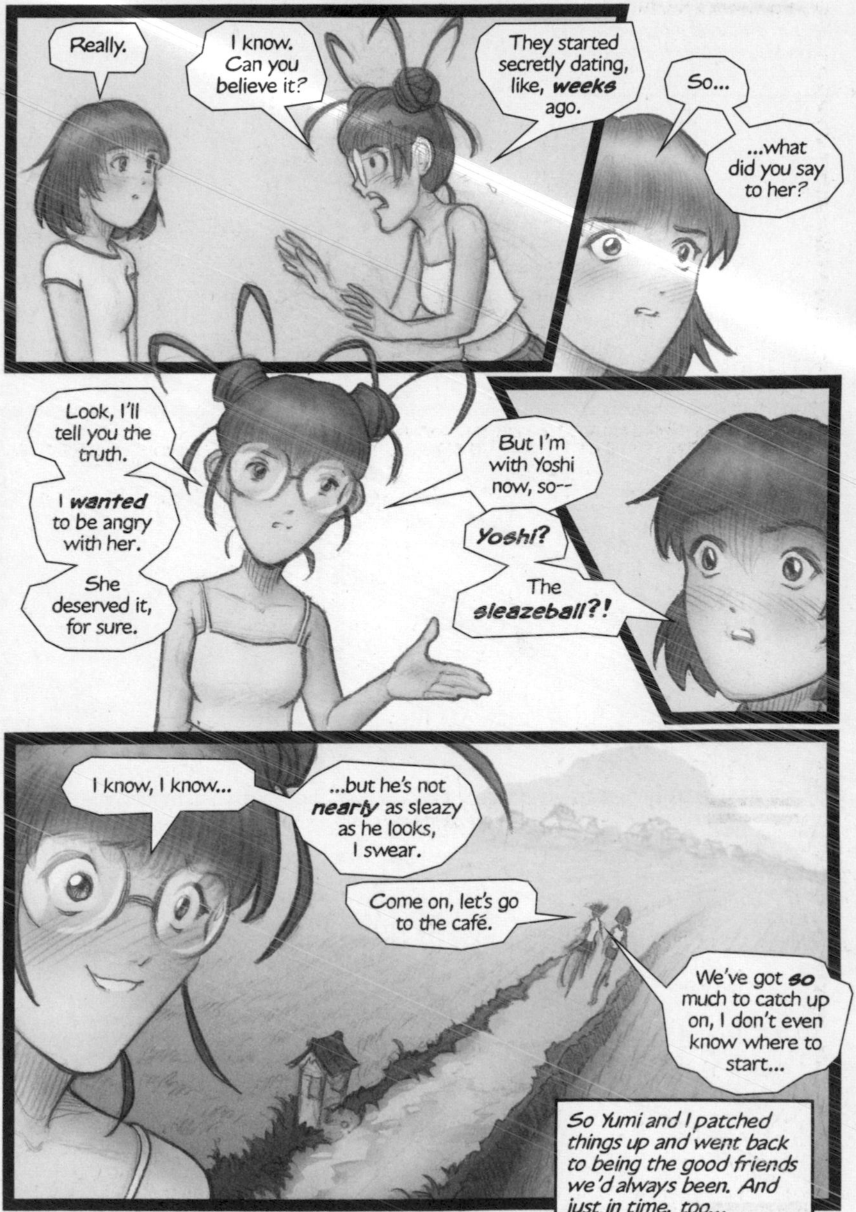
Really.
I know. Can you believe it?
They started secretly dating, like, *weeks* ago.
So...
...what did you say to her?
Look, I'll tell you the truth.
I *wanted* to be angry with her.
She deserved it, for sure.
But I'm with Yoshi now, so--
Yoshi?
The *sleazeball?!*
I know, I know...
...but he's not *nearly* as sleazy as he looks, I swear.
Come on, let's go to the café.
We've got *so* much to catch up on, I don't even know where to start...
So Yumi and I patched things up and went back to being the good friends we'd always been. And just in time, too...

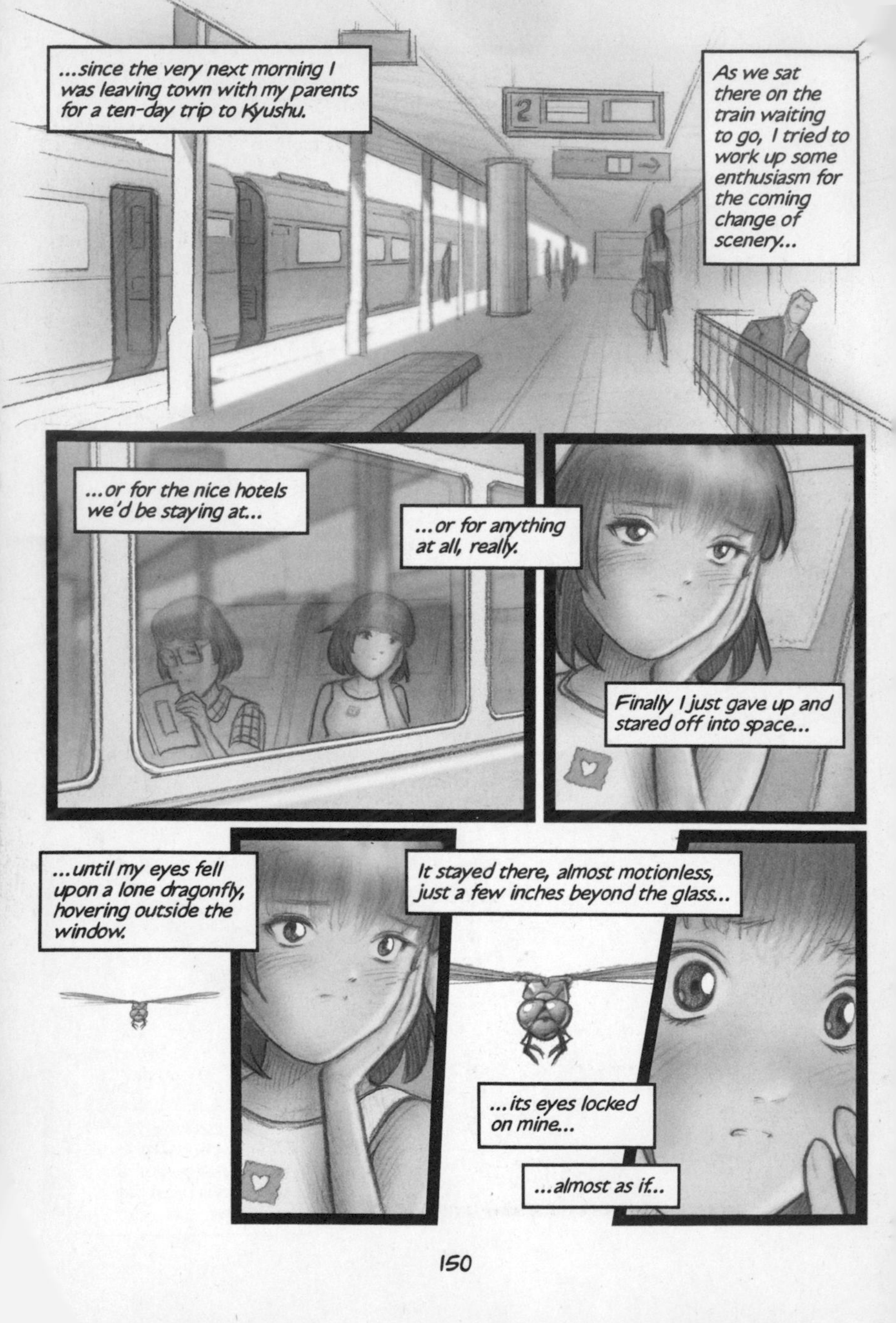

...since the very next morning I was leaving town with my parents for a ten-day trip to Kyushu.
As we sat there on the train waiting to go, I tried to work up some enthusiasm for the coming change of scenery...
...or for the nice hotels we'd be staying at...
...or for anything at all, really.
Finally I just gave up and stared off into space...
...until my eyes fell upon a lone dragonfly, hovering outside the window.
It stayed there, almost motionless, just a few inches beyond the glass...
...its eyes locked on mine...
...almost as if...

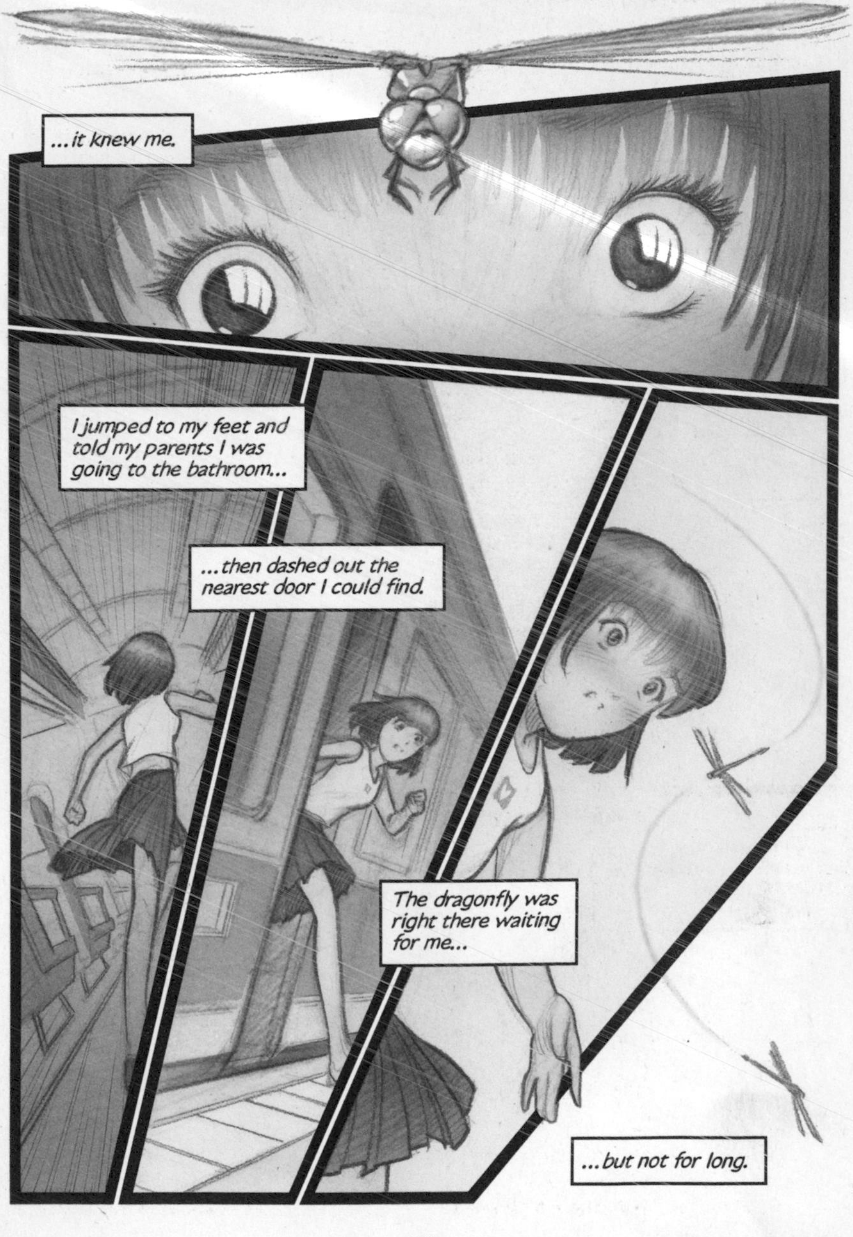
...it knew me.
I jumped to my feet and told my parents I was going to the bathroom...
...then dashed out the nearest door I could find.
The dragonfly was right there waiting for me...
...but not for long.

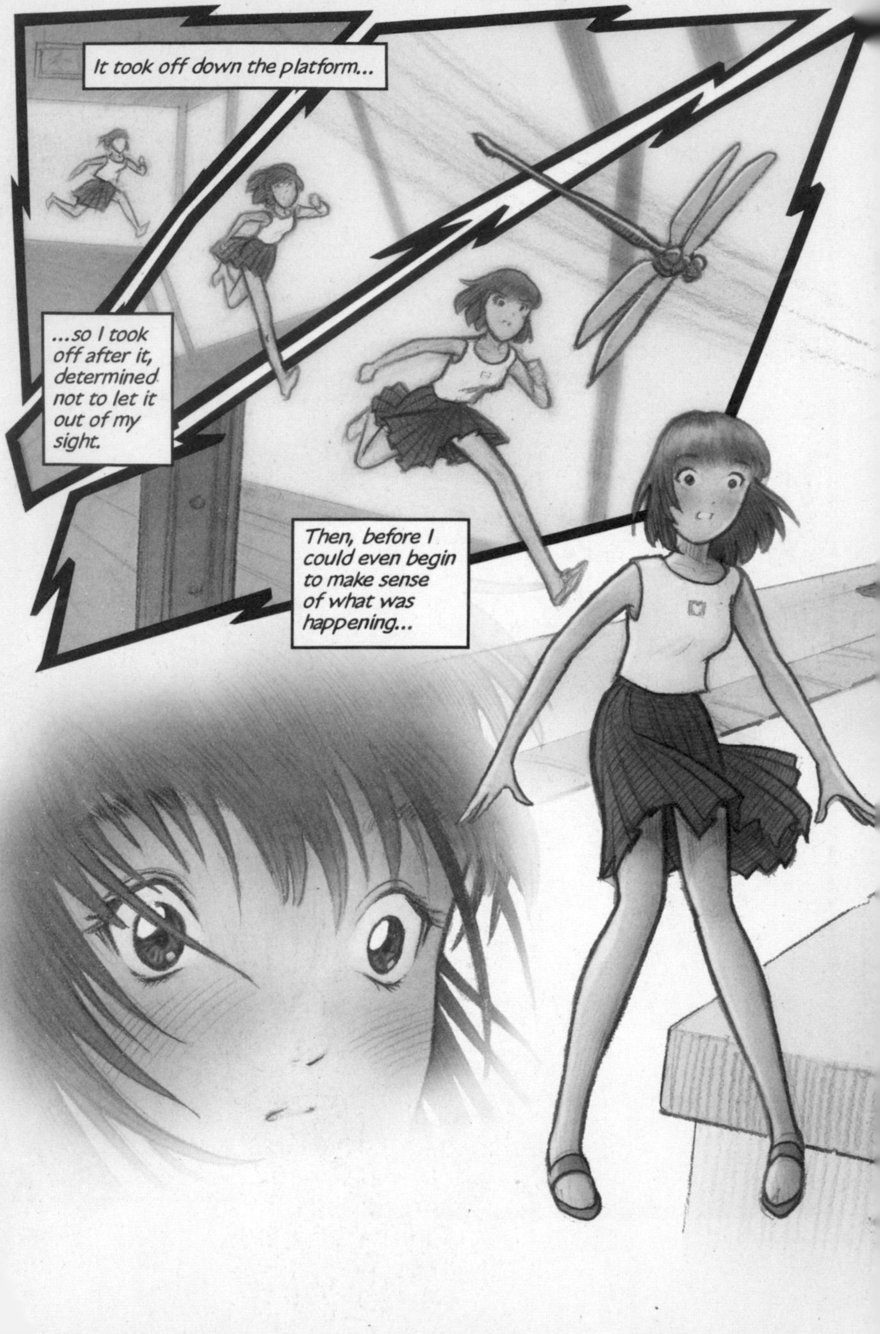
It took off down the platform...
...so I took off after it, determined not to let it out of my sight.
Then, before I could even begin to make sense of what was happening...

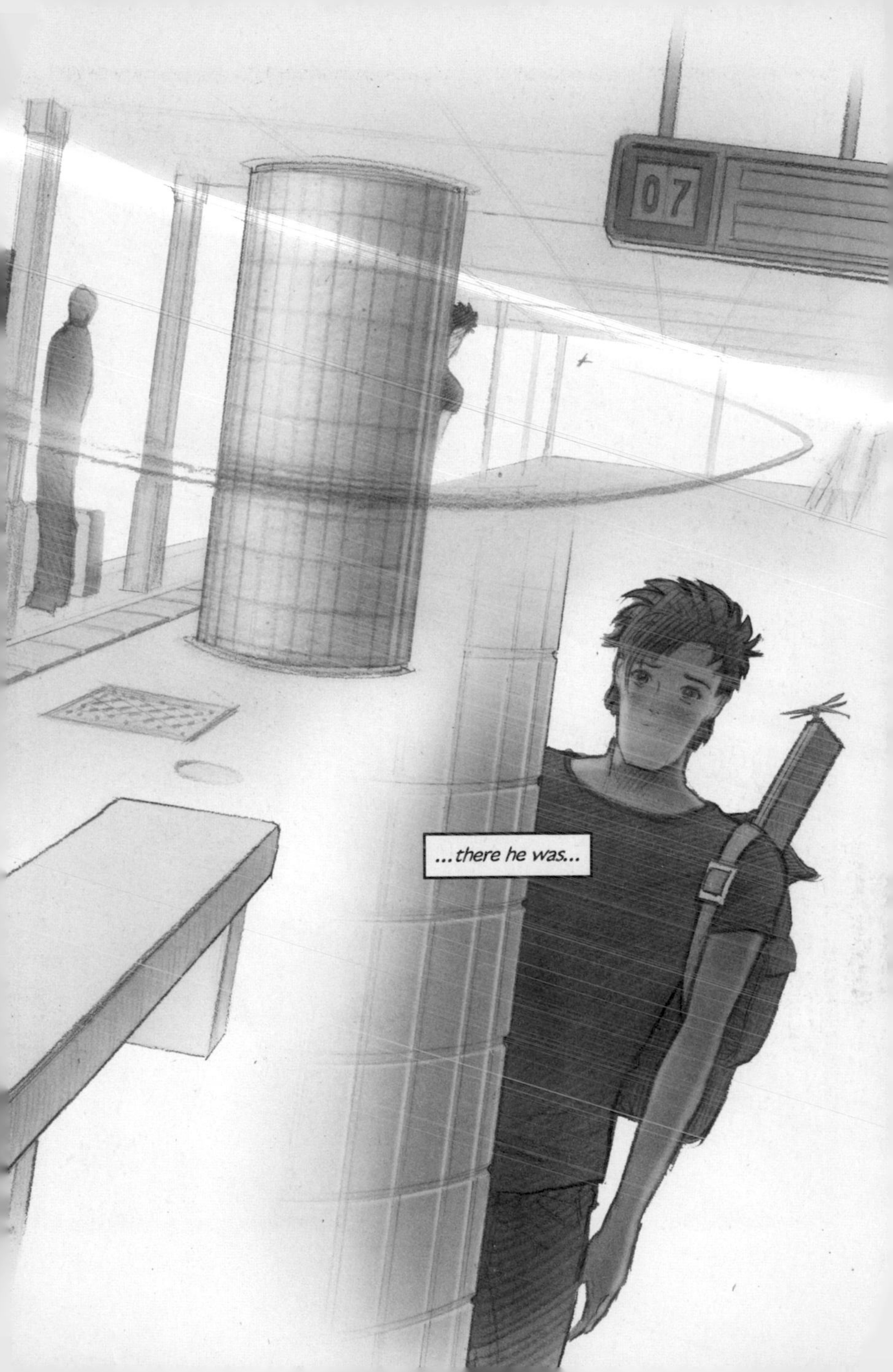
07
...there he was...

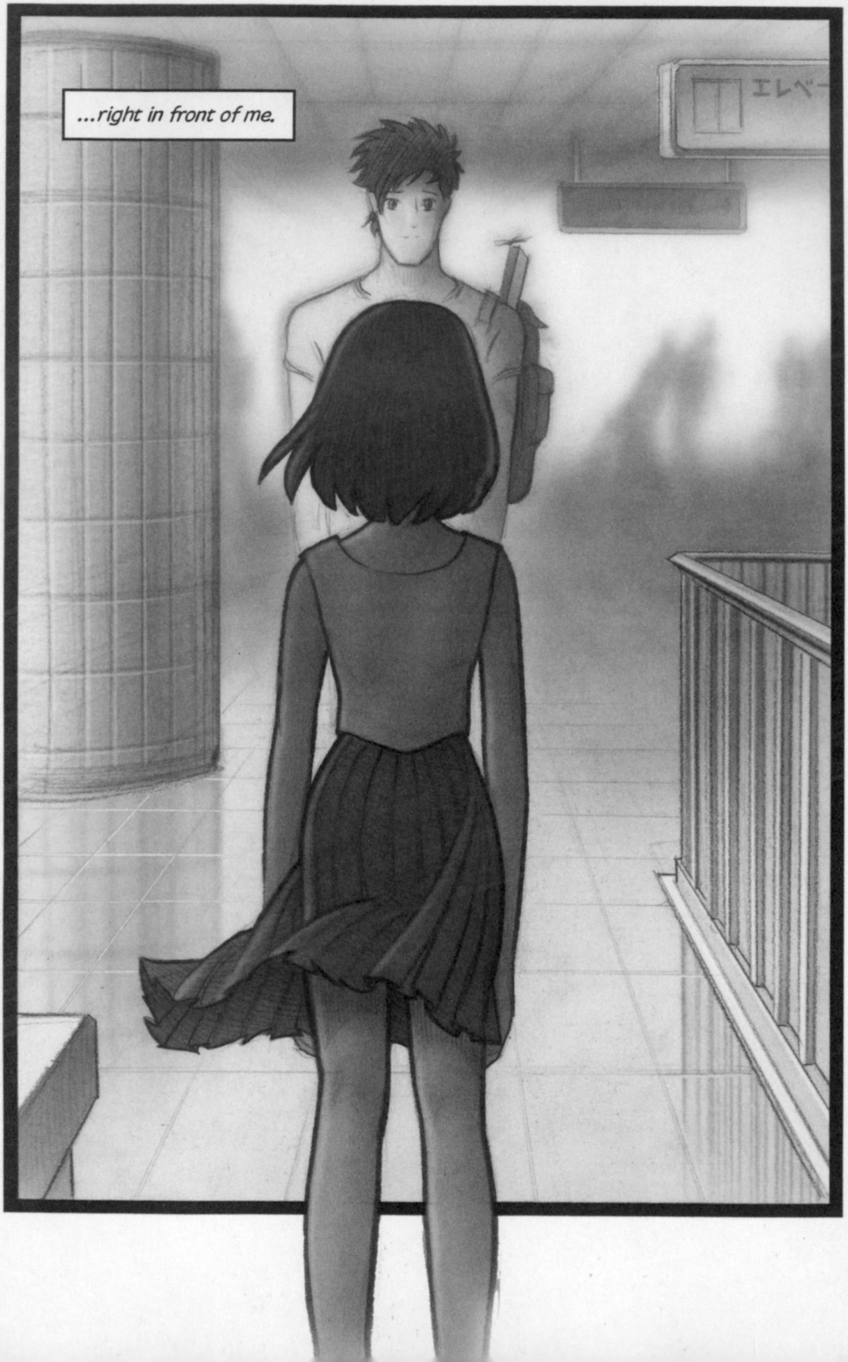
...right in front of me.
エレベー

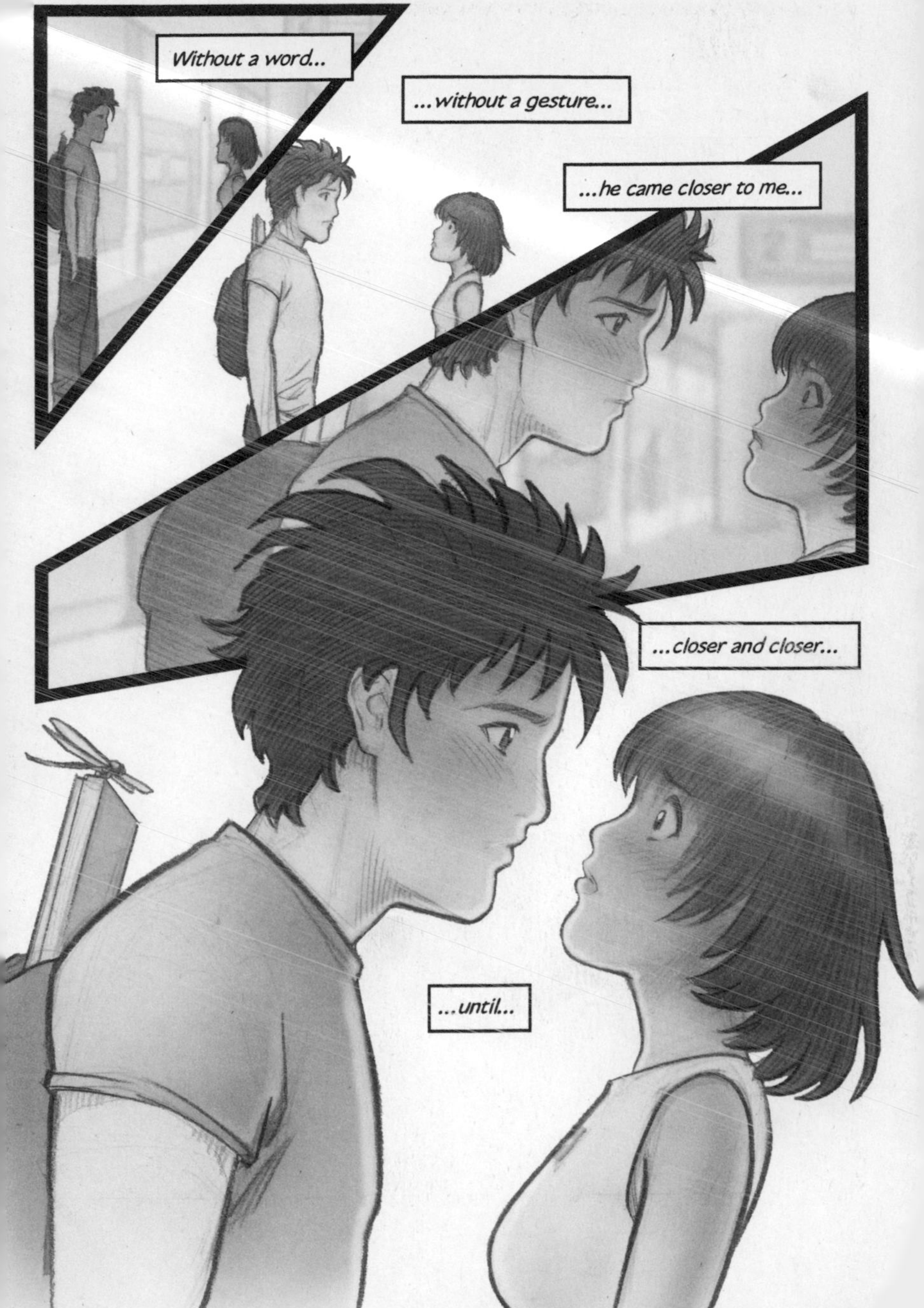
Without a word...
...without a gesture...
...he came closer to me...
...closer and closer...
...until...

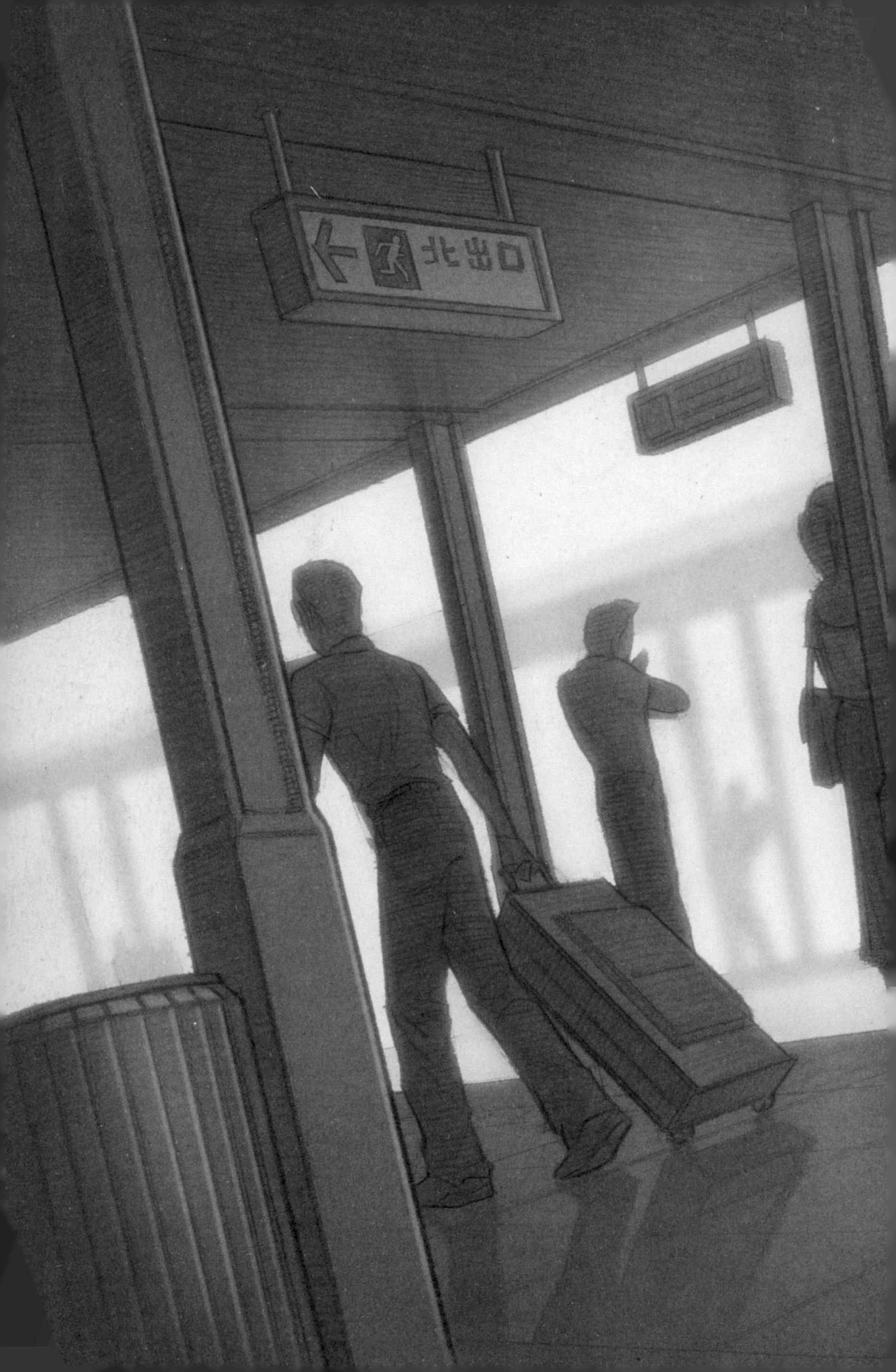
北出口

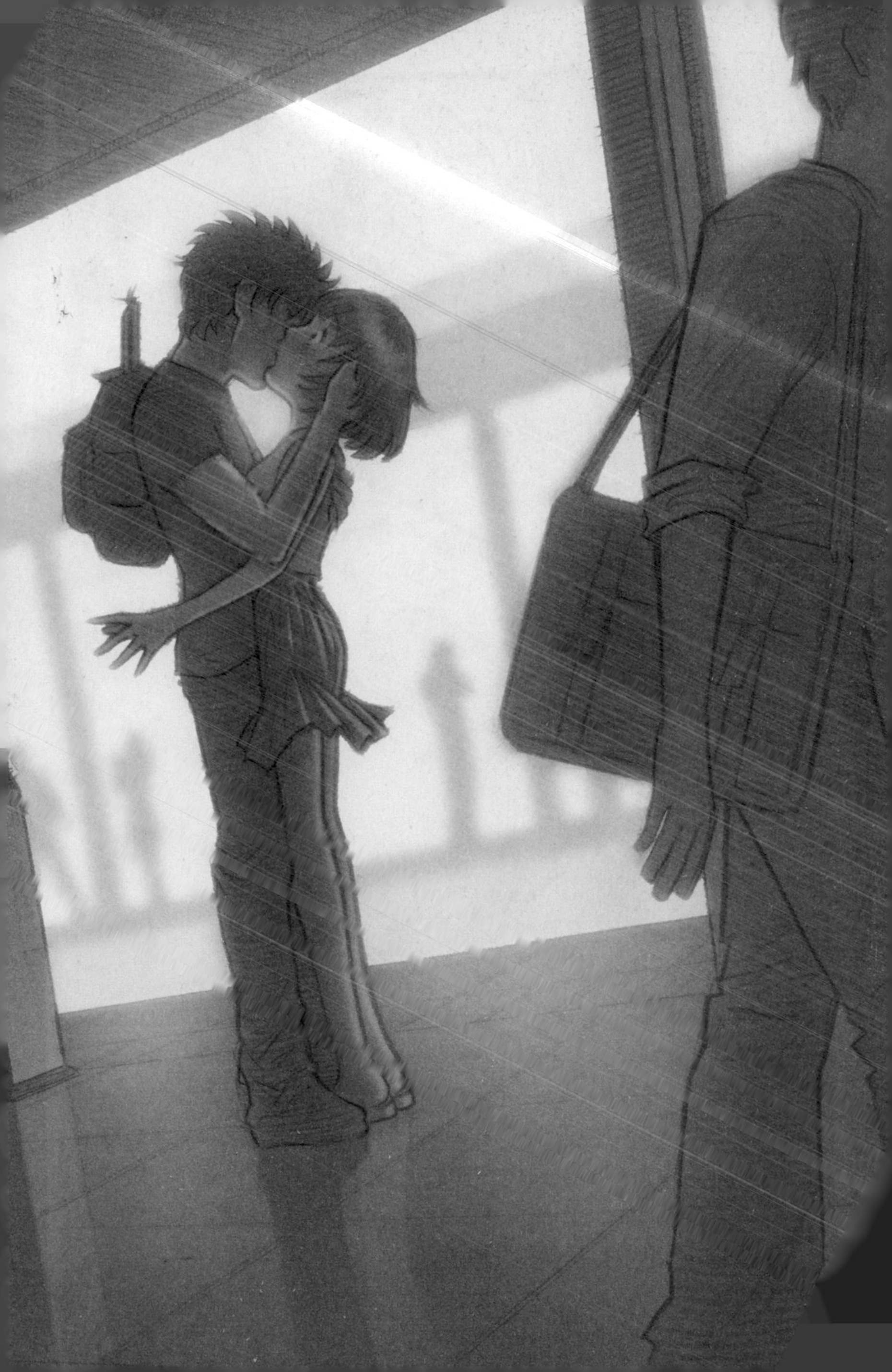

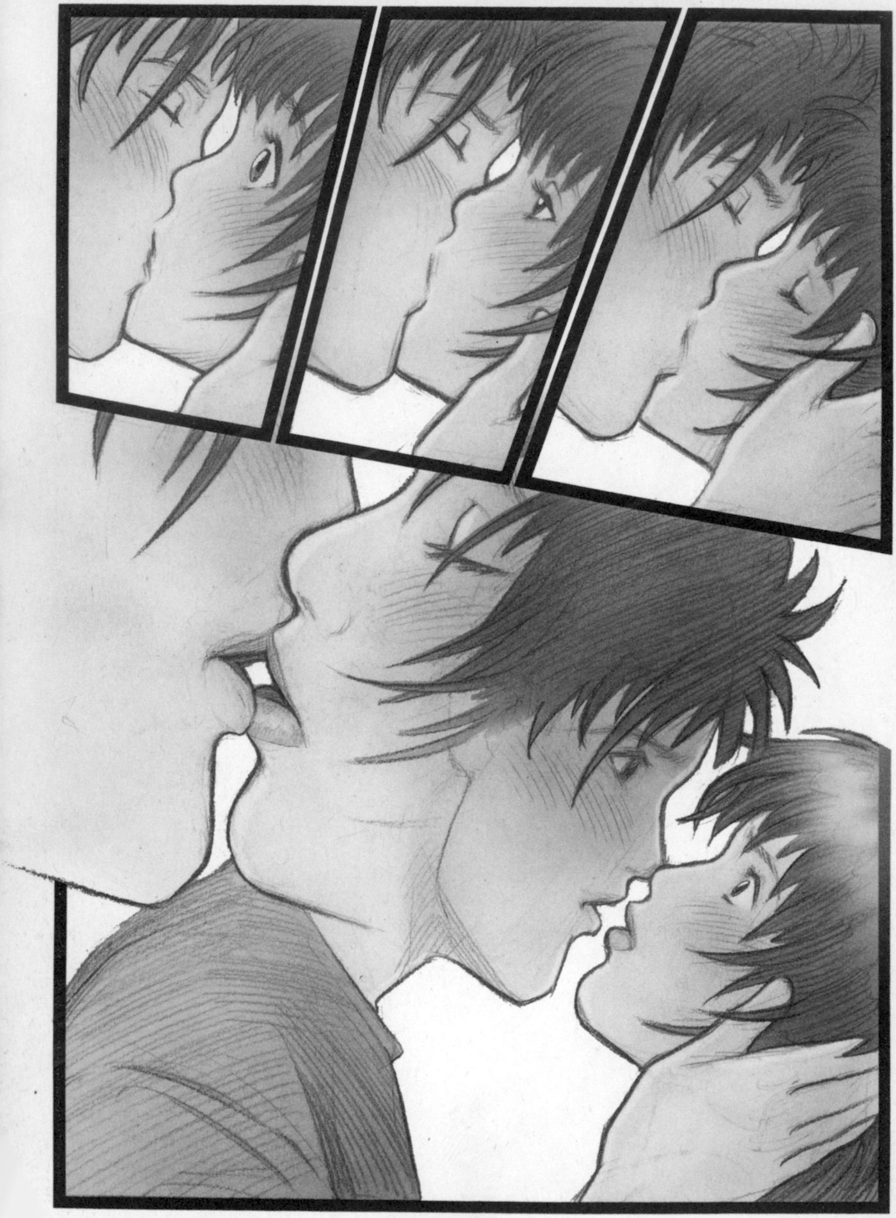

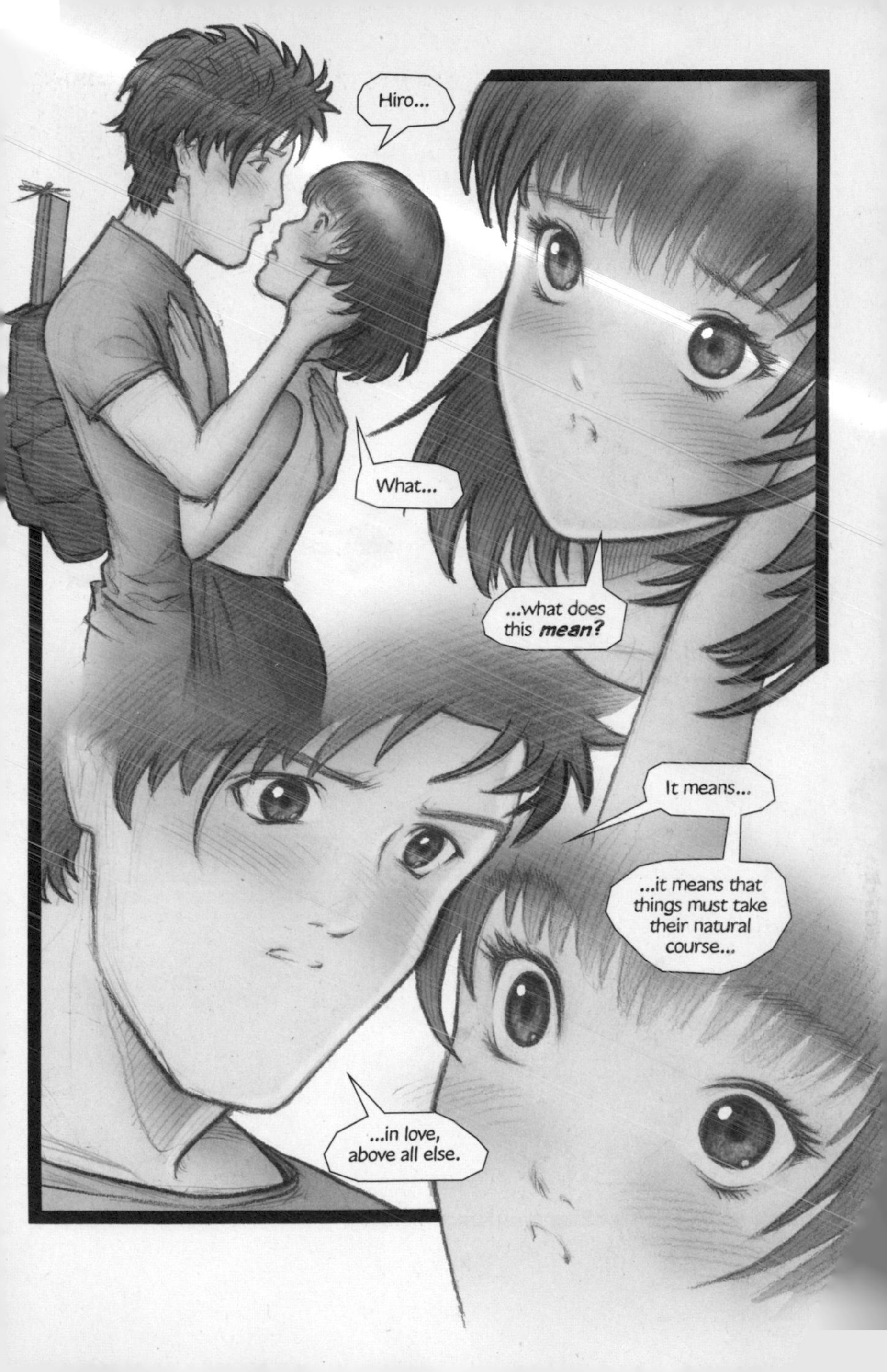
Hiro...
What...
...what does this ***mean?***
It means...
...it means that things must take their natural course...
...in love, above all else.

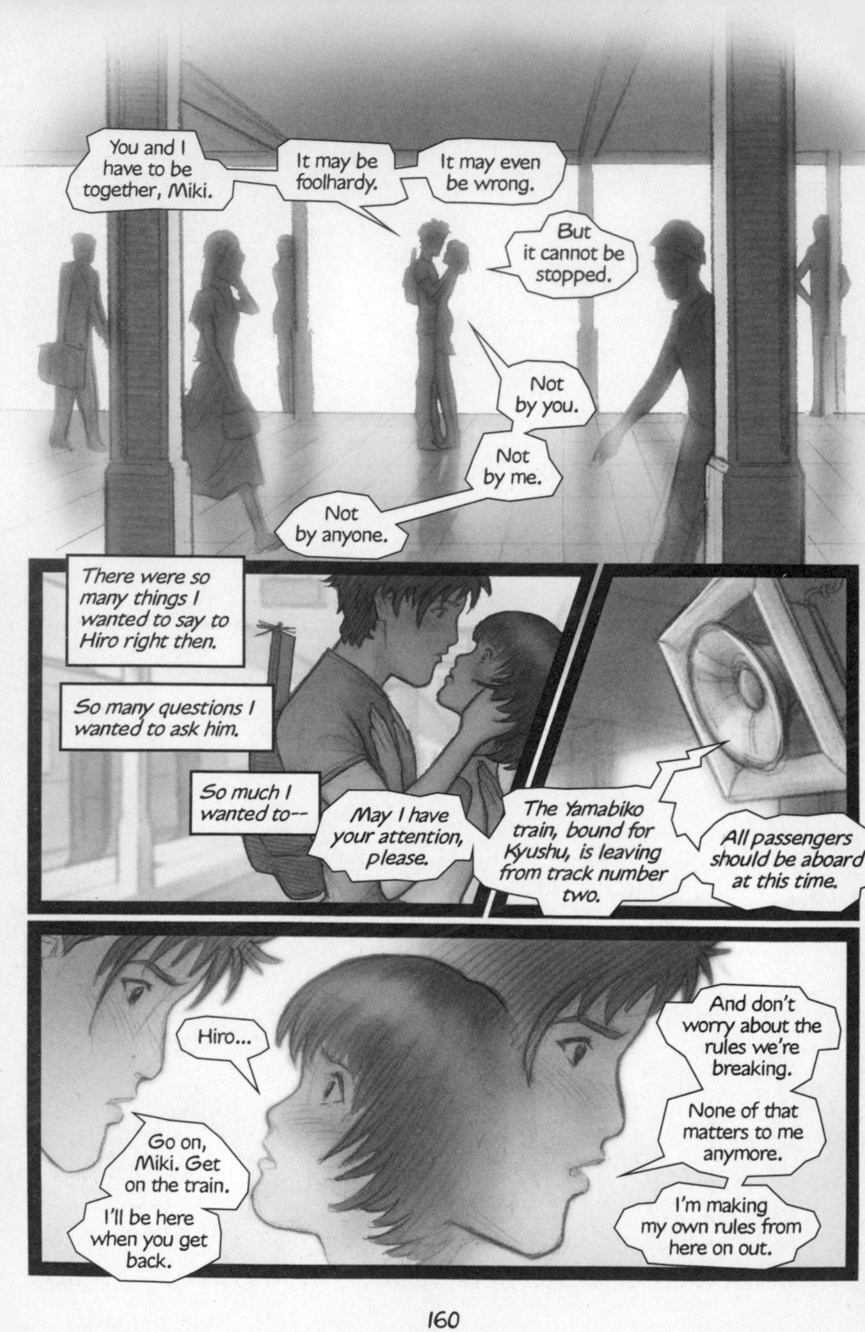

You and I have to be together, Miki.
It may be foolhardy.
It may even be wrong.
But it cannot be stopped.
Not by you.
Not by me.
Not by anyone.
There were so many things I wanted to say to Hiro right then.
So many questions I wanted to ask him.
So much I wanted to--
May I have your attention, please.
The Yamabiko train, bound for Kyushu, is leaving from track number two.
All passengers should be aboard at this time.
Hiro...
Go on, Miki. Get on the train.
I'll be here when you get back.
And don't worry about the rules we're breaking.
None of that matters to me anymore.
I'm making my own rules from here on out.

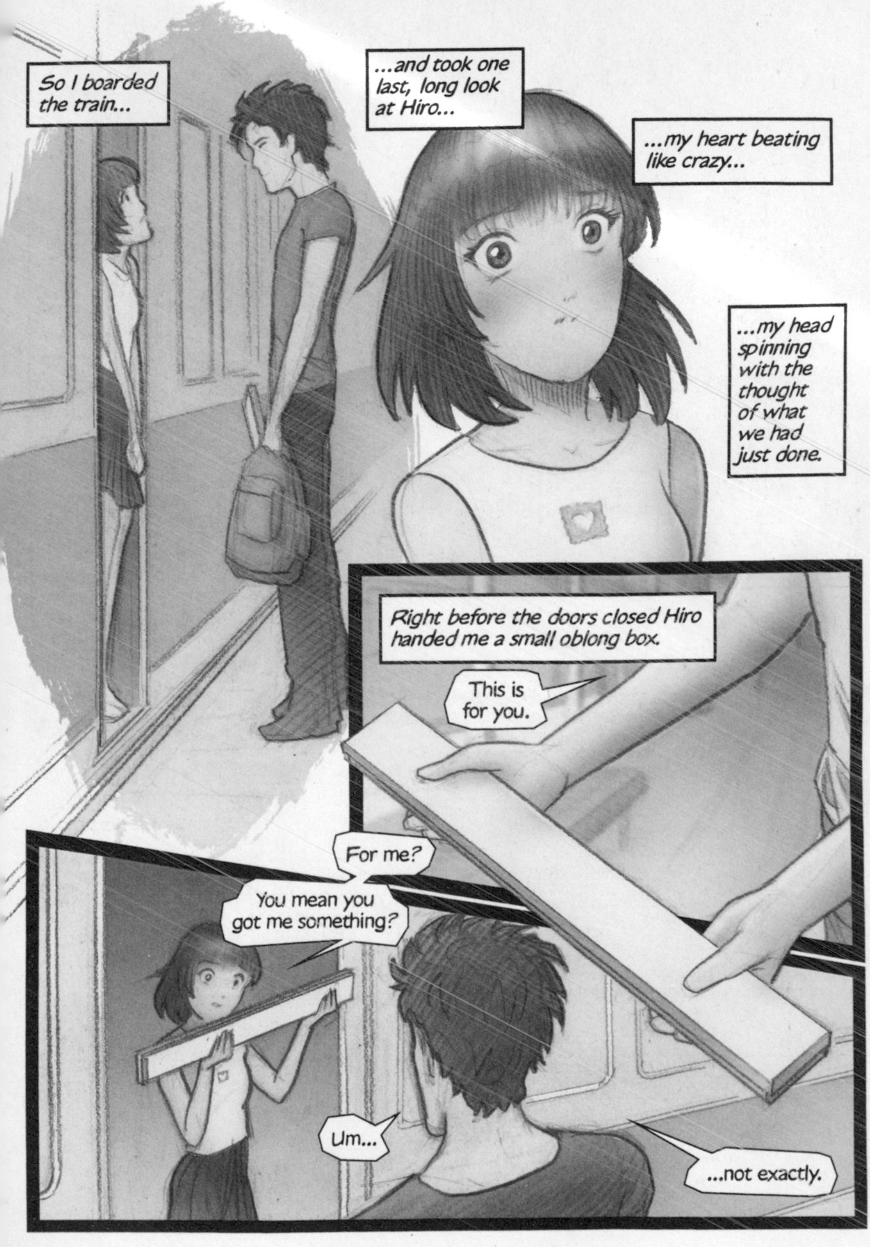

So I boarded the train...
...and took one last, long look at Hiro...
...my heart beating like crazy...
...my head spinning with the thought of what we had just done.
Right before the doors closed Hiro handed me a small oblong box.
This is for you.
For me?
You mean you got me something?
Um...
...not exactly.

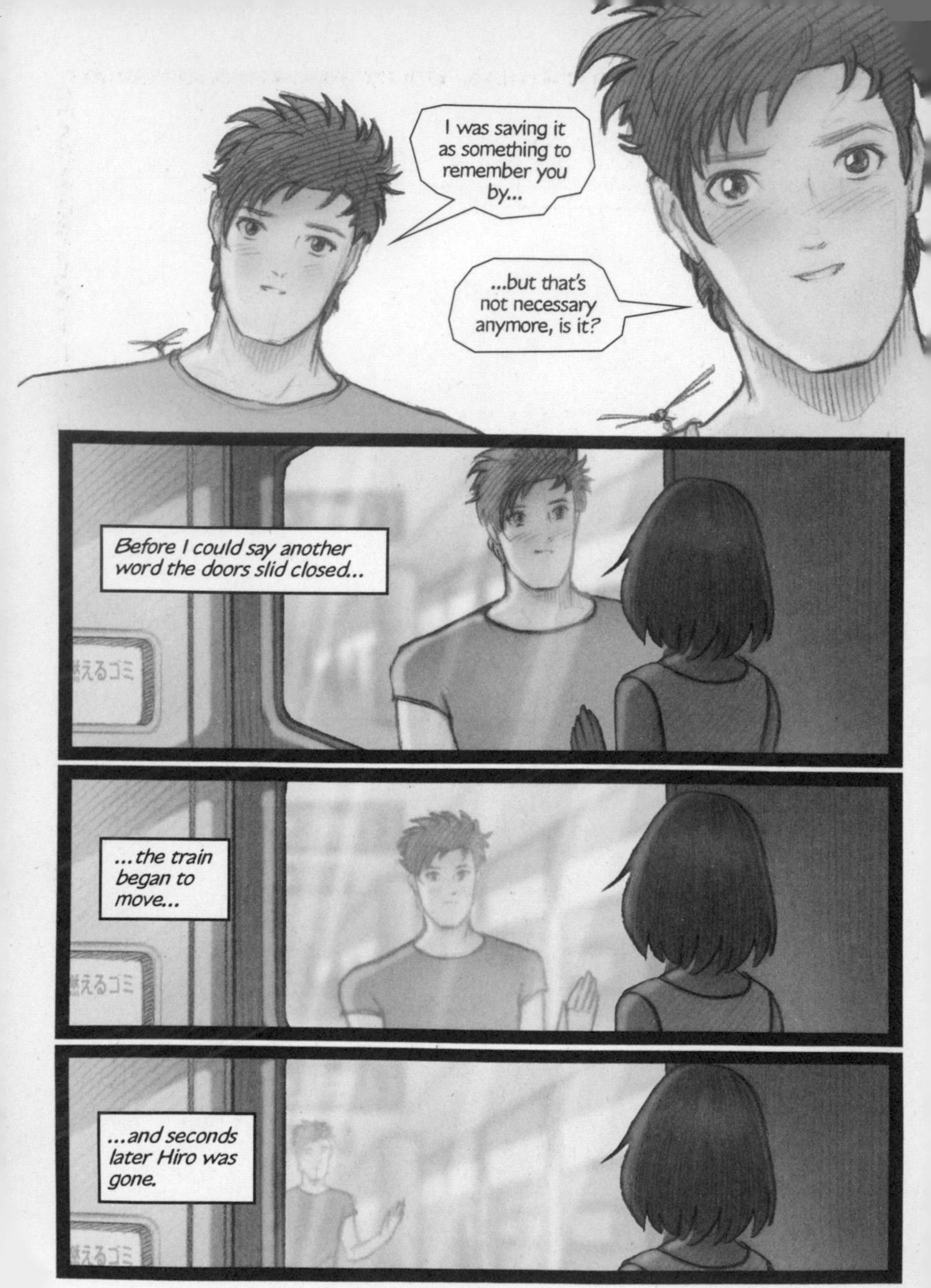
I was saving it as something to remember you by...
...but that's not necessary anymore, is it?
Before I could say another word the doors slid closed...
燃えるゴミ
...the train began to move...
燃えるゴミ
...and seconds later Hiro was gone.
燃えるゴミ

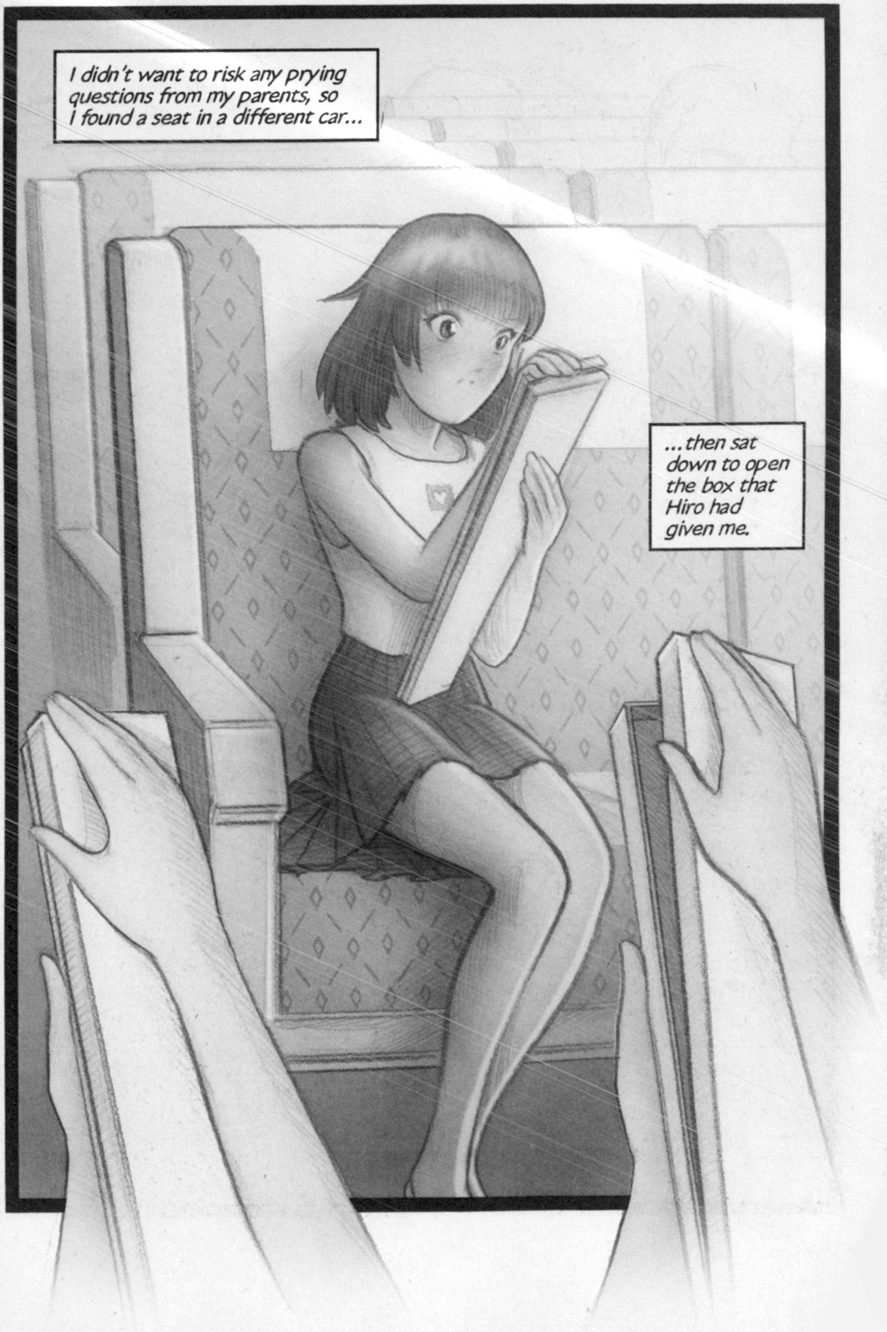
I didn't want to risk any prying questions from my parents, so I found a seat in a different car...
...then sat down to open the box that Hiro had given me.

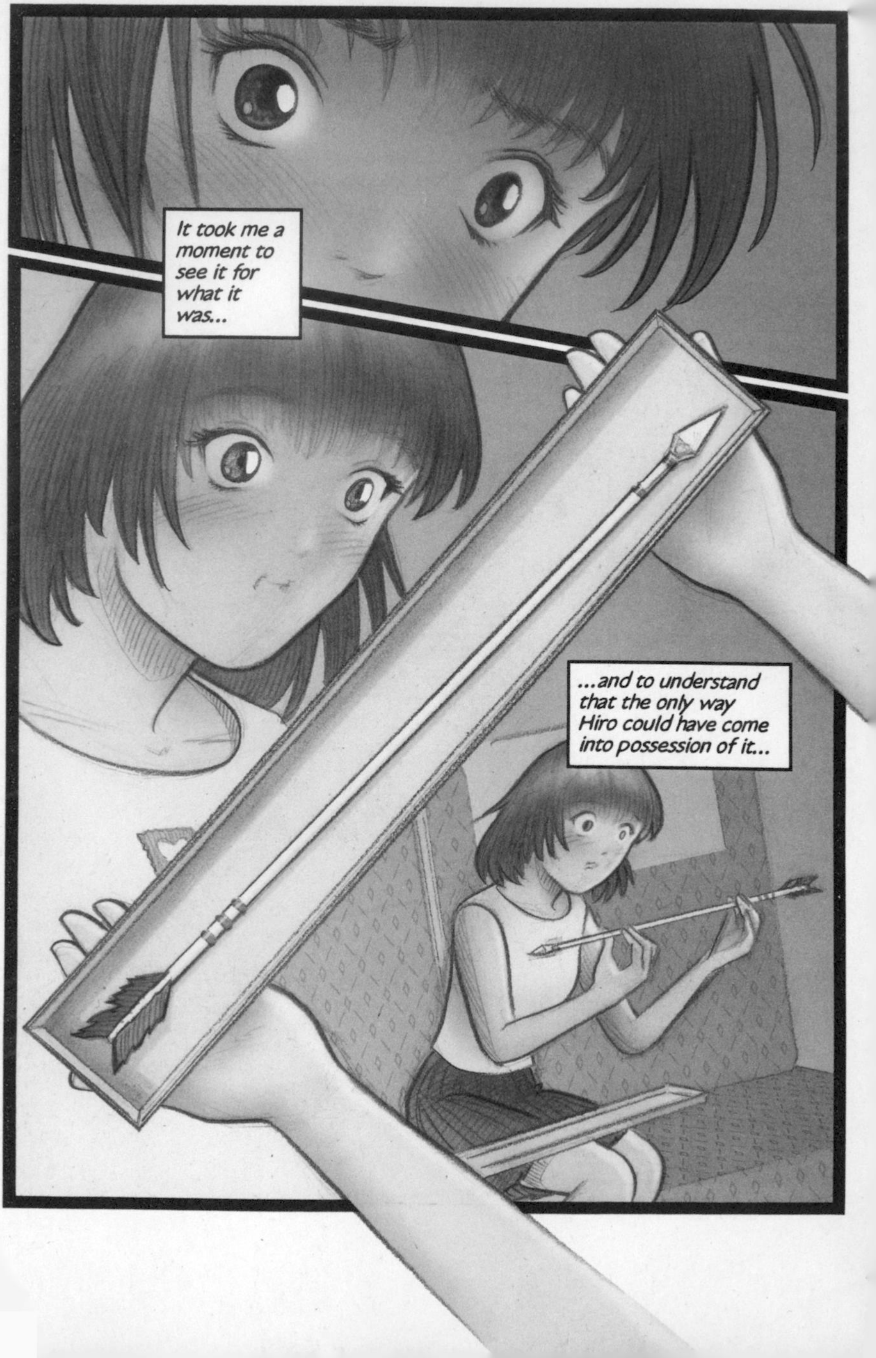
It took me a moment to see it for what it was...
...and to understand that the only way Hiro could have come into possession of it...

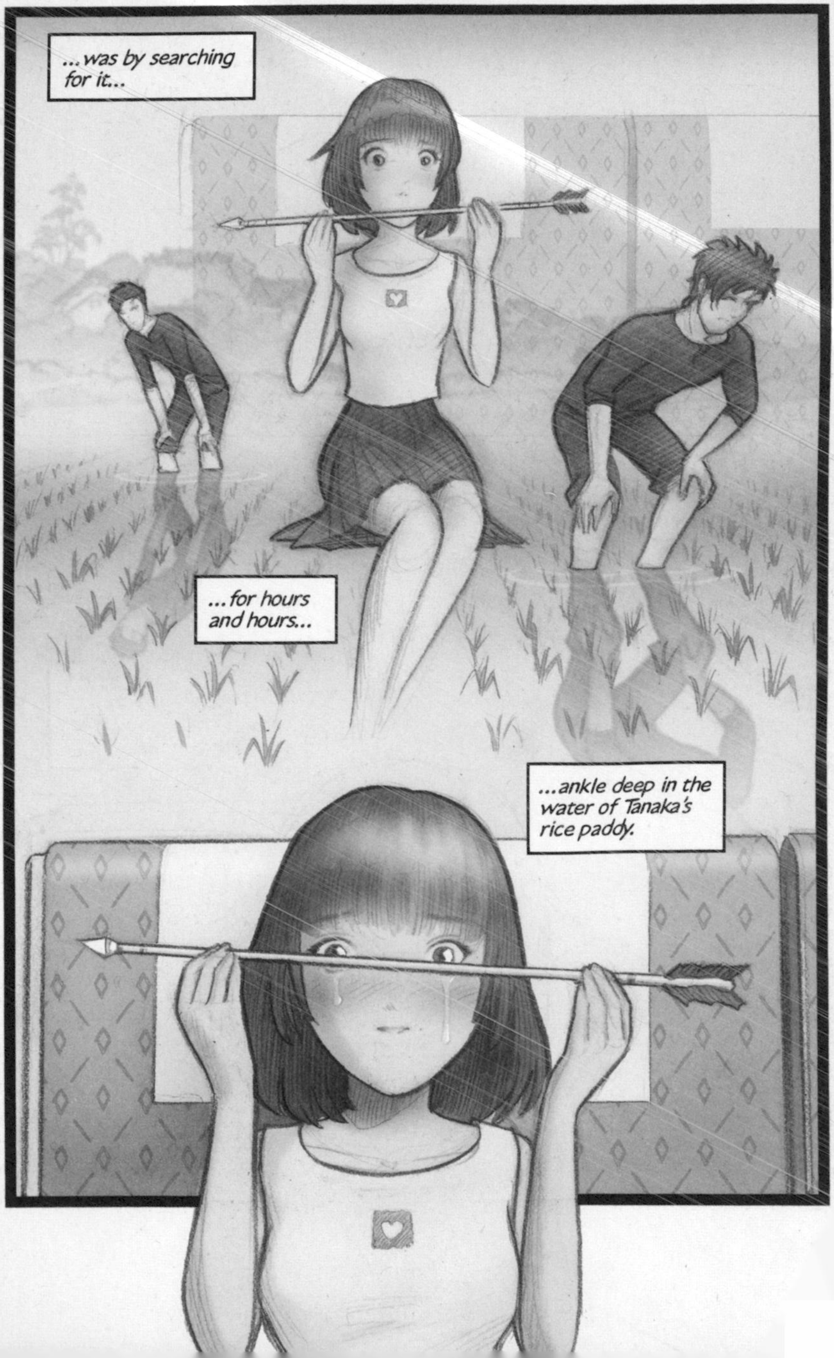
...was by searching for it...
...for hours and hours...
...ankle deep in the water of Tanaka's rice paddy.

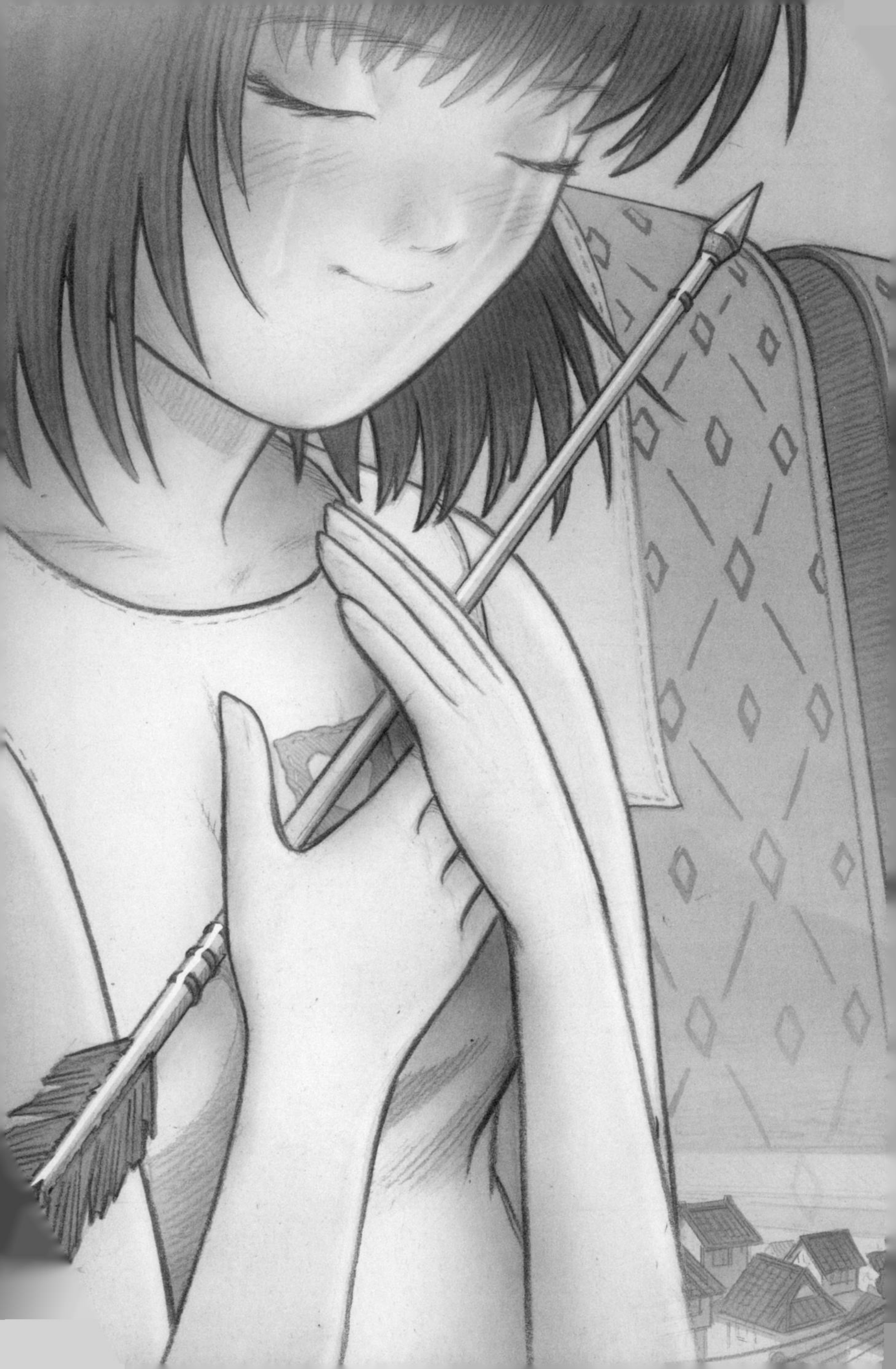

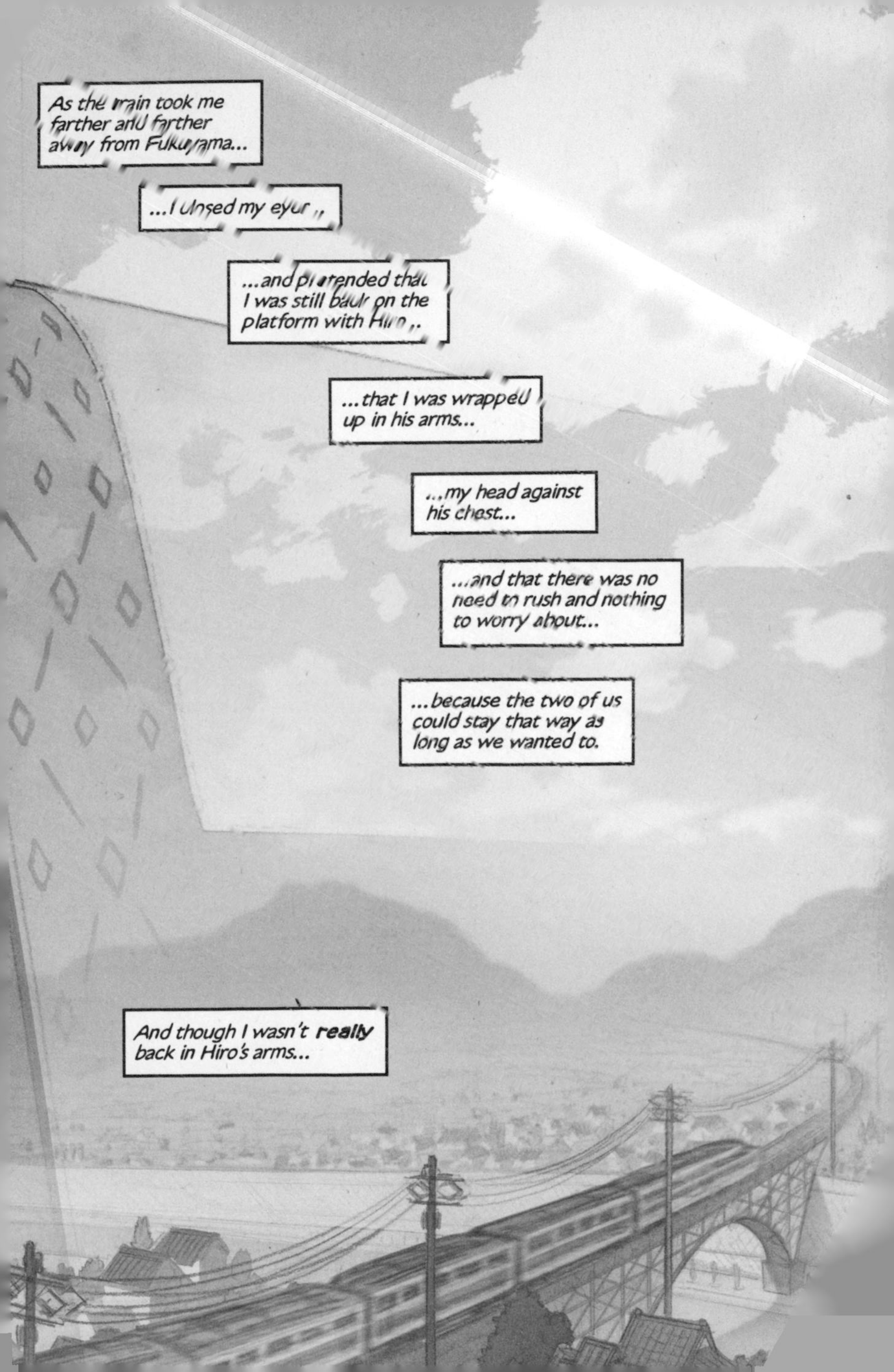
As the train took me farther and farther away from Fukuyama...
...I closed my eyes...
...and pretended that I was still back on the platform with Hiro...
...that I was wrapped up in his arms...
...my head against his chest...
...and that there was no need to rush and nothing to worry about...
...because the two of us could stay that way as long as we wanted to.
And though I wasn't **really** back in Hiro's arms...

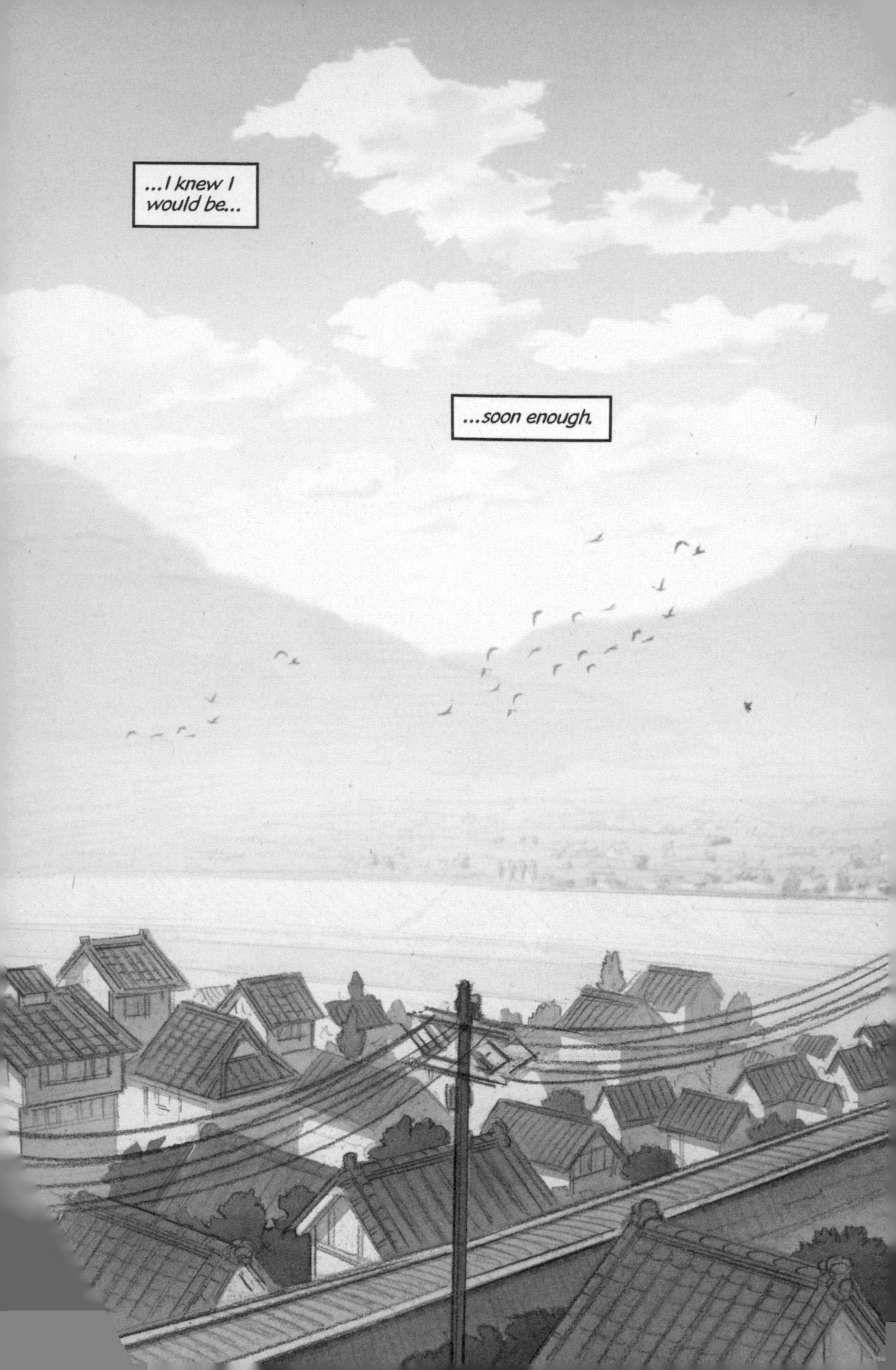
...I knew I would be...
...soon enough.

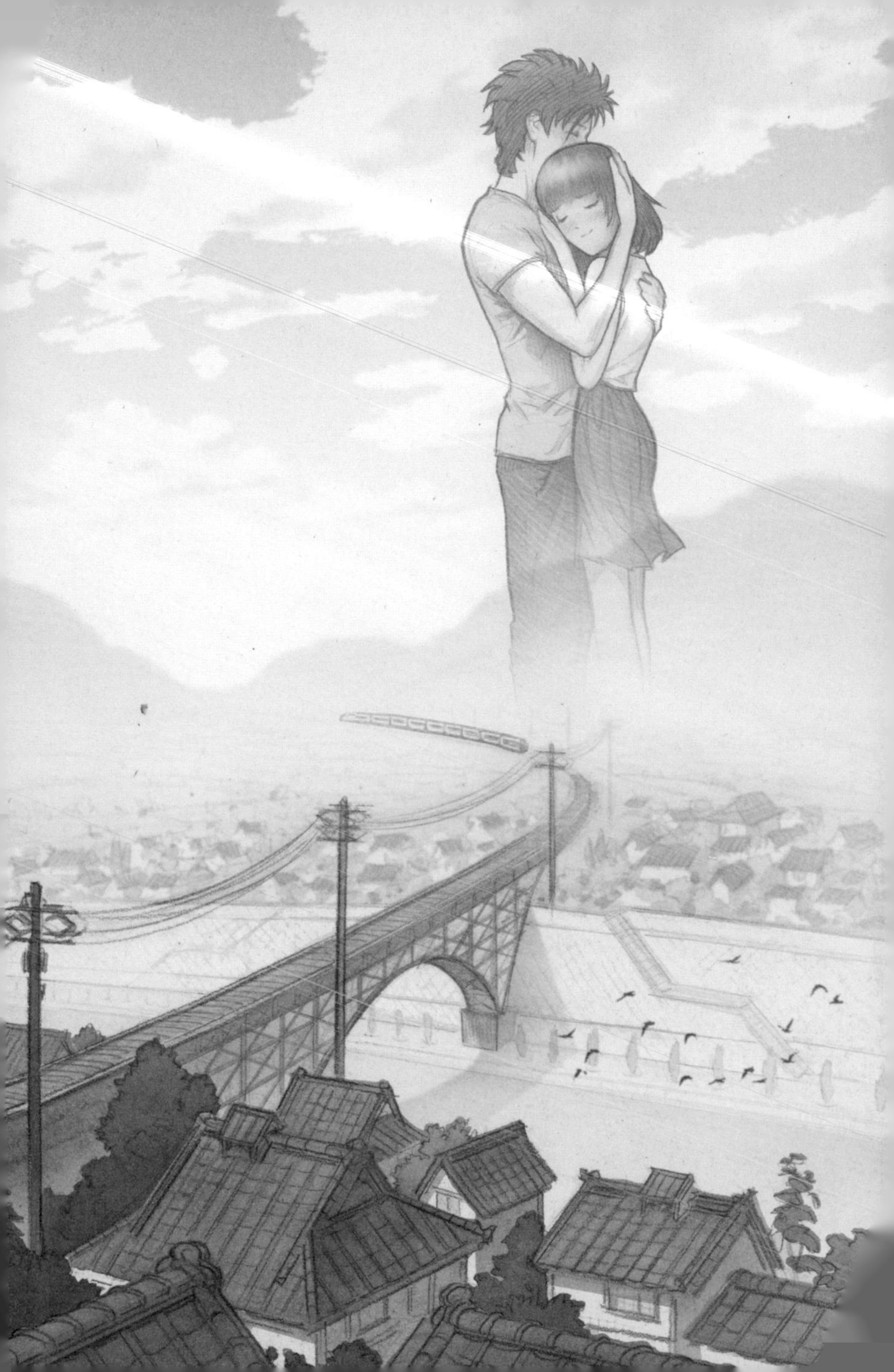

For my daughter, Mio

HarperTeen is an imprint of HarperCollins Publishers.

Miki Falls: Summer
Copyright © 2007 by Mark Crilley
All rights reserved. Printed in the United States of America.
No part of this book may be used or reproduced in any manner whatsoever
without written permission except in the case of brief
quotations embodied in critical articles and reviews.
For information address HarperCollins Children's Books,
a division of HarperCollins Publishers,
1350 Avenue of the Americas,
New York, NY 10019.
www.harperteen.com
Library of Congress Cataloging-in-Publication Data is available.
ISBN-10: 0-06-084617-8 — ISBN-13: 978-0-06-084617-6
❖
First Edition

Will Miki's love life end before it begins?
Keep reading to find out more!

Turn the page for a preview of

MiKi
FALLS
· BOOK THREE ·
AUTUMN

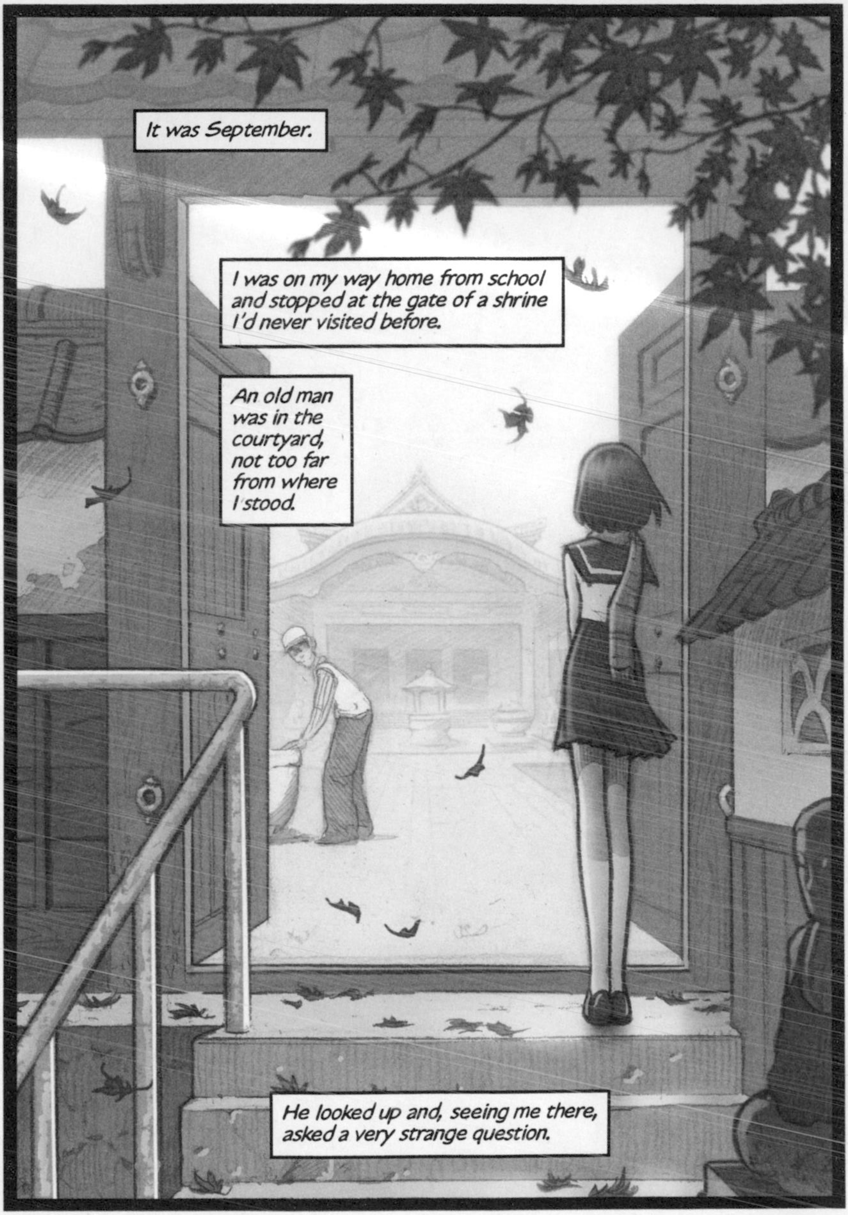
It was September.
I was on my way home from school and stopped at the gate of a shrine I'd never visited before.
An old man was in the courtyard, not too far from where I stood.
He looked up and, seeing me there, asked a very strange question.

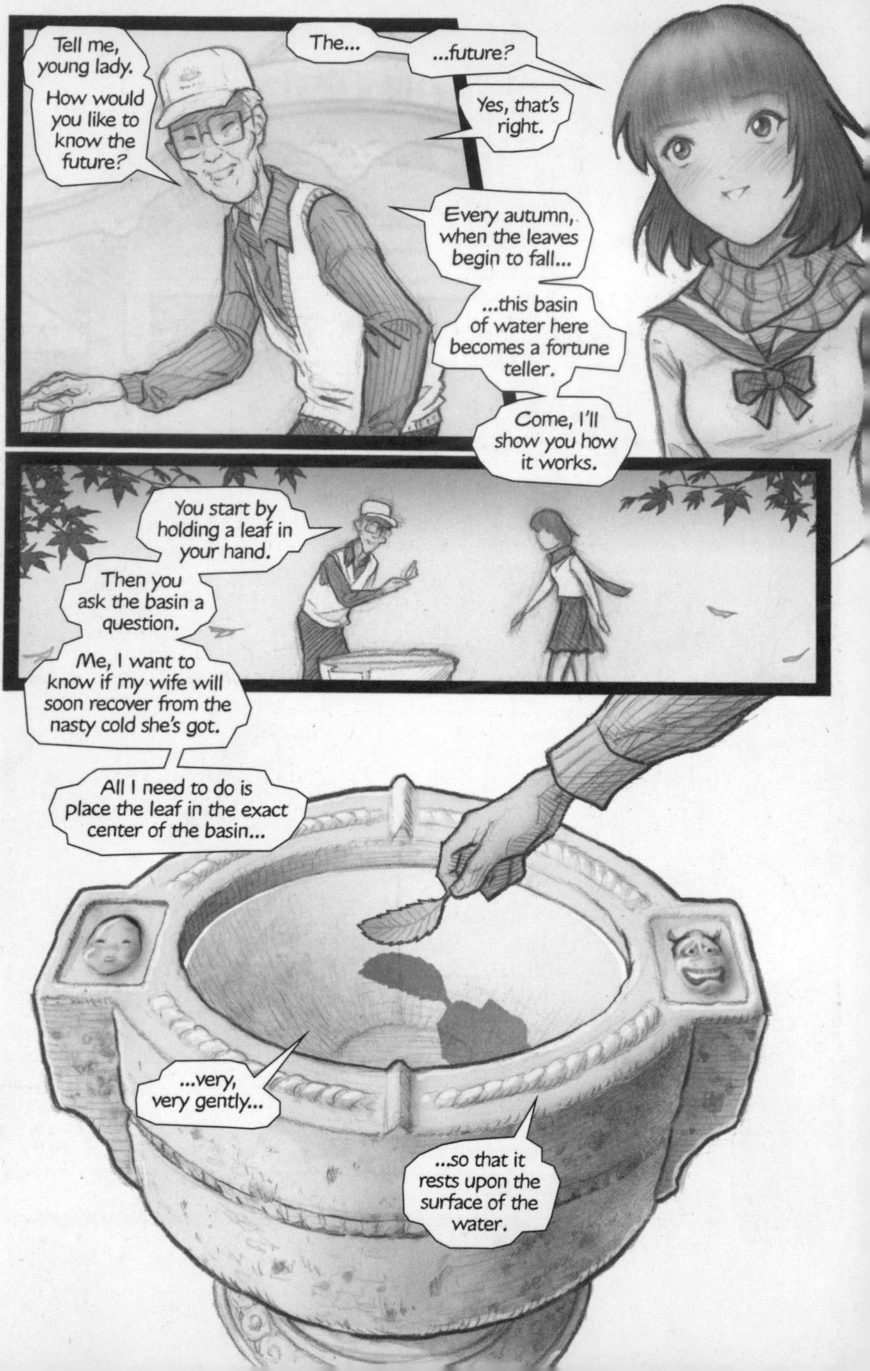
Tell me, young lady.
How would you like to know the future?
The...
...future?
Yes, that's right.
Every autumn, when the leaves begin to fall...
...this basin of water here becomes a fortune teller.
Come, I'll show you how it works.
You start by holding a leaf in your hand.
Then you ask the basin a question.
Me, I want to know if my wife will soon recover from the nasty cold she's got.
All I need to do is place the leaf in the exact center of the basin...
...very, very gently...
...so that it rests upon the surface of the water.

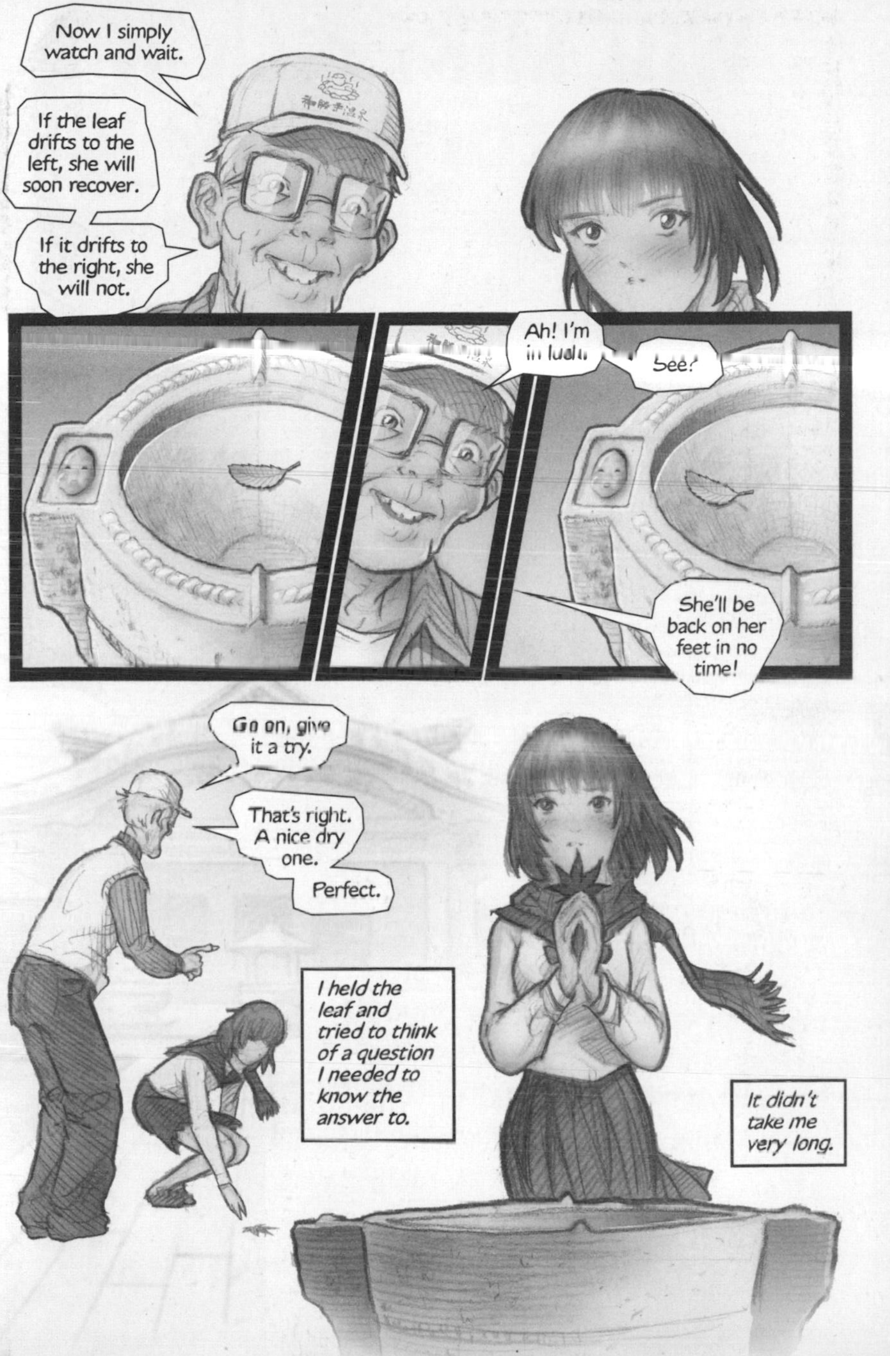
Now I simply watch and wait.
If the leaf drifts to the left, she will soon recover.
If it drifts to the right, she will not.
Ah! I'm in luck.
See?
She'll be back on her feet in no time!
Go on, give it a try.
That's right. A nice dry one.
Perfect.
I held the leaf and tried to think of a question I needed to know the answer to.
It didn't take me very long.